Praise for the works of

I Dare You to

A breezy writing style keeps the story going forward through an amazing number of funny scenes. There are a good number of characters, including the four legged variety, and all of them are well drawn, central to the plot and romance, and often hilarious. I don't remember ever being so supportive of characters taking forever to get together, but the author made me happy to wait because it provided more laugh out loud moments.

-The Lesbian Review

This enemies to friends to lovers romantic comedy by Lori G. Matthews was simply spectacular. The writing flowed effortlessly along with laugh out loud comedy, flirting, and bickering between the two women.

-Michele R., *NetGalley*

This super cute enemies-to-lovers romcom by Lori G. Matthews is funny, cute, and full of LGBT love. This book is beautiful. Highly recommend it.

-Jessica R., *NetGalley*

#CassiNova

Lori G. Matthews had me laughing in public—exactly what I needed in these stressful times. She completely sucked me in! The characters were almost familiar, like friends I already have. The romance felt real, and I never doubted the motives behind Sam and Alex's actions. I spent many years so hungry for representation that I'd read anything you threw at me, but I'm happy to say this book set the bar so much higher for me. A flirty, fun romp through Hollywood.

- MJ's Reviews, *Bookshop Santa Cruz*

#CassiNova is such a fun read. I pictured this title making its way into my beach bag for a fun, upbeat read in the sunshine. The language is trendy and at times edgy, giving the book a youthful, modern Hollywood vibe. The slow burn romance is tempered with humor that keeps the pace until the romance peaks. Keeping with great timing, there are also well written genuine and sincere moments. *#CassiNova* is a cute, funny, light read. I'd recommend it for any of my friends looking for a sweet, easygoing RomCom.

-*The Lesbian Review*

Delightfully funny. I read this with a grin and outright laughter. I will look for future books from the author.

-Kaye C., *NetGalley*

OUTLAW
HEARTS

Lori G. Matthews

Other Bella Books by Lori G. Matthews

#CassiNova
I Dare You to Love Me

About the Author

Lori G. Matthews lives outside of Philadelphia with her wife and three cats. Her first brush with literary fame came at the age of thirteen when her composition, an amusing tale told from the perspective of a soccer ball, was the only one read aloud by her teacher. To this day, she still loves to write lighthearted comedies because laughter truly is the best medicine. When she's not writing, Lori plays ice hockey, hikes, bikes, and bird-watches. But her favorite place to be is on the golf course, where she's proudly earned the nickname Long and Wrong.

OUTLAW
HEARTS

Lori G. Matthews

2024

Bella Books, Inc.
P.O. Box 10543
Tallahassee, FL 32302

First Edition - 2024

Editor: Heather Flournoy
Cover Designer: Heather Honeywell

ISBN: 978-1-64247-604-0

PUBLISHER'S NOTE

Dedication

This story is dedicated to *Chip the Cave-Child*. What she lacked in vocabularity, she more than made up for with her haunting lute play.

Acknowledgements

The origin of this story is kind of cool, at least I think it was cool. When I was in the GCLS Writing Academy in 2021, one of our assignments was to write a short scene in a different genre. My genre had been romantic comedies, so to me a historical romance was definitely "different." I wrote a scene that took place in the Wild West of the 1870s, because who doesn't like women in cowboy hats, riding horses? It starred a hot outlaw and a beautiful suffragette from Boston. The scene and characters sat in the back of my mind for quite a while, and then one day I said, "Let's write their story."

This was more of a solitary adventure for me than my last two books. I did have beta readers go over the first few chapters to make sure the story was interesting and the characters compelling. So a big thank-you to Lisa M. and Ana W., Lynne Carlson, fellow authors Cade Haddock Strong, Nan Campbell, Susan Meagher, and Rita Potter, Floss at the drive-thru window at Dunkin' Donuts, and the drunk guy at the VFW. (I wrote those last two to see if you were paying attention.) After those first six chapters, I was on my own to complete my vision. Well, the wife was there—thank you, my love. She also came up with the cover concept. Who knew she had such talent?

Of course, there are others that I need to acknowledge:

My publisher, Bella Books, for their wonderful ongoing support.

Lee Winter (you may have heard of her, she wrote a couple of books) helped with the jacket blurb. Evidently, Lee digs taking a whole story and compressing it down to a couple of paragraphs. I dig golf and chocolate, so there's that.

My editor, Heather Flournoy, who plays along with my habit of treating the comments during editing as comedy central. She also has the patience of a saint. You see, in my first novel, I had issues with pluperfect tense. Basically, I never used it. In my second novel, I had issues with adding "s" to all my forward, backward, and toward. Did I learn my lesson? Nah. Not only did I not learn my lesson and continued to make the same mistakes, I added two new ones to this book. I had a mental block with further/farther and was heavy-handed with exclamation points. To offset my punctuation obsession, Heather added a few adverbs. I said, "Aren't adverbs bad?" But she explained that, in this case, it was a good way to eliminate Mr. Exclamation Point.

Lastly, I would be remiss if I did not mention Chip the Cave-Child, to whom this book is dedicated. Who is Chip? you ask. Chip is a fictional character in a dime novel published in the 1860s. I needed a book title for a scene and this one made me laugh, so I used it, and it became a running joke during the editing process. Suddenly everything was about Chip. "What would Chip do?" "You're no Chip." By the end of editing, Heather and I had Chip being the first to advocate for heavy usage of adverbs and exclamation points in writing. She (yes, Chip was a she) also came up with the revolutionary idea of combining further and farther, creating a new word, faurther, to help alleviate confusion. She was ahead of her time, but alas… rumor has it that Chip met a tragic end when she tripped and fell on a stalagmite.

After actually reading *Chip the Cave-Child*, Heather and I feel that she is alive and well and living the dream in some dusty little cave in the Poconos.

So, dear readers and writers, use adverbs unsparingly, and use exclamation points!!! Can't decide between further and farther? Use faurther! Use it frequently, profusely, and handsomely (why not?)! In other words:

#bemorelikechip

Author's Note

This is a work of fiction set in New Mexico, 1878. I tried my best to use authentic language and terminology that would not typically be used today. I mention baseball, which I believe was spelled base ball back then, but I thought it was easier on the eyes to leave it spelled as baseball. I'm sure some other modernisms crept in because, well, I'm human and screw up sometimes. This story also contains gun violence and threats of violence. After all, it was called the Wild West. I hope you enjoy the story.

PROLOGUE

1862 Mora County, New Mexico Territory

Elle's fingers rested on the butt of the revolver sitting on her hip.

"Go," her daddy said.

She whipped out the Colt 1860 Army and shot the tin cup off the rock in front of her.

Her daddy gave a hearty belly laugh. "Damn. You're gettin' real quick, little girl."

She frowned. "I'm not little anymore. I'm ten."

"You'll always be little to me."

Elle gave him a goofy face as she replaced the gun in her holster, and not just any holster—a brand-new one he brought home for her the other day. She ran up and placed the tin cup back on the rock. "I like it here, Daddy. Do you think we can stay for a while?" They'd moved into the tiny cabin in the canyon a few months back. Elle loved the surrounding mountains, the grassy meadow nestled in between the tall peaks, and the creek that shimmered nearby. In the past, they'd never stayed in one place for long, so they'd never had a chance to put roots down. *Maybe this will be the place.*

"We'll see," her daddy said. "Came into some money last week, so maybe we can."

That was an almost promise and was good enough. Elle took her stance. "I'm ready."

"All right. Go."

Again, she whipped out the pistol and again the cup popped off the rock.

"Woo doggy! You're a damn natural."

Elle twirled the gun before jamming it back into place.

"Well, now you're just gettin' fancy," her daddy said with a smile. "You keep practicing, you'll be the fastest draw in New Mexico. You know why you gotta be quick, right?"

Elle nodded. "Gotta be able to protect myself."

"That's right. It's a dangerous world out there, and I got enemies."

Elle scoffed. "Everybody loves you, Daddy. Momma says you can charm the rattle off a snake."

"Your momma's a bit partial. Lord knows she loves me, and that makes me the luckiest man alive. But in my line of work, you can't help but make enemies. And they may come after you to get to me. So you gotta be able to protect yourself. And your momma, if need be."

Her daddy ran from the law a lot. Elle had overheard many conversations between her parents during the late-night hours, her momma pleading with him to go straight and him giving her an empty promise to do so, but Elle thought his escapades sounded exciting.

"Husband, what are you doing with our daughter?" Elle's momma ambled over.

"I'm teaching her to be the quickest draw in the territory."

"She's covered in dirt. Have you been rolling around in the mud?" she asked Elle with a twinkle in her eyes.

"No, ma'am. Just riding and shooting."

"Our girl shoots and rides better than most cowboys I know," her daddy crowed.

"Is that what daughters are supposed to do?" her momma asked. "Elinor, get down to the creek and wash up. Dinner's almost ready, and you have your lessons after that."

"But I gotta practice."

Her daddy extended his hand. "Give me your gun belt and listen to your momma."

Elle unbuckled her new prized possession and shuffled off to the creek, which was a few minutes' walk away. When she arrived at the water's edge, she took off her clothes and waded in. The shallow creek reached a depth of only two feet and measured about twenty feet across, the perfect size for a swim. She held her breath and sank below the surface, then popped up. The chilly water made her teeth chatter. *Will it get warmer in the summer?* With a sigh, she extended her arms and floated on her back. The lazy current barely carried her along. She dawdled, as her momma loved to say. The table was probably already set and the food getting cold. *But floating in the water is fun.*

A shot rang out, and she jumped to her feet. Nobody would shoot a gun unless trouble was afoot. *I gotta get back.* Her legs churned toward the water's edge. When she hit dry land, she dressed as fast as she could, which proved challenging while soaking wet. Once her boots were on, she raced toward the house. Loud voices carried on the wind. *That's not Daddy's voice.* More shots echoed around the valley, and a deep fear took root in her chest.

The barn came into view. *Approach danger with caution*, her daddy always said, so she ducked under the wagon and hid behind the wheel.

The scene terrified her. About ten men, some on horseback, some on foot, had gathered in front of the porch. Bandanas hid their faces. Her daddy, bloodstain on his shirt, kneeled in the dirt under the cottonwood tree next to the house. His hands were tied behind his back, and a large noose encircled his neck. The other end of the rope was looped around the lowest branch of the tree—a branch Elle had climbed yesterday.

Her momma lay belly-down on the ground. She cried while a scruffy man held a fistful of her hair and pointed a gun at her temple. His knee in her back prevented her from getting up.

Elle cowered in the shadows as sweat trickled down her back. If she had her gun maybe she could shoot them all, but ten against one were lousy odds even if she did have a weapon. Frustrated and fearful tears leaked from her eyes. *What do I do? What do I do?*

Her daddy spit blood from his mouth before asking, "Who are you?"

One of the masked men chuckled. He had the air of someone in charge. "You Robert Barstow?"

Her father nodded.

"Looks like you stole the wrong shipment of guns a few weeks ago."

"Where's your proof? You got no proof. And you got no badge. Who the hell are you?"

"I'm your judge and jury, and I don't need no proof." He lifted his chin toward the tree, and two men yanked her daddy onto the back of his own horse. "Robert Barstow, I do declare you guilty of theft. And you, sir, are sentenced to hang until death for your crimes." He locked eyes with the man standing behind her father's horse and nodded.

A silent scream erupted in Elle's heart. *No!*

Her mother's scream wasn't silent. It was bloodcurdling, and Elle swore it reached the mountaintops.

The man slapped at the horse's rump, and the animal shot out from under her father. He dangled from the end of the rope as his legs twitched and his body jerked.

Elle jammed a fist into her mouth to quiet the rising sobs. Her heart pounded and her stomach twisted. She swallowed the bile that rose into her throat, and seethed with rage.

With bored expressions, the men stared like they were watching a sunset instead of seeing the life seep from the man in front of them.

After a few moments, her daddy's body stilled and his eyes bulged from his no longer handsome face. He was dead.

"What about her?" the man hovering over her mother asked.

"We don't need no witnesses. Take care of it. Then burn the place down." The man in charge rode off and the rest followed, except for the one holding her mother.

His bandana slipped down, affording Elle a long look at his face. It was a face she swore to never forget. He flipped her momma over onto her back, and she kicked at him.

Fear paralyzed Elle while her mother, fighting for her life, lay helpless on the ground. *I gotta help her.* Her legs refused to work until anger and hatred freed her limbs. But before she could stand and run to her mother's aid, the man pulled the trigger.

In a stupor, Elle collapsed back onto the ground. She retched, and the meager contents of her stomach splattered into the dirt.

The man twisted around and spotted her. He raised his gun and fired. Elle wiped an arm across her mouth and bolted toward the creek. Bullets ripped the bark from the trees surrounding her as she pounded past them. Now in self-preservation mode, she ran and ran and ran until her legs gave out. An outcropping of boulders afforded her some cover, and she hunkered behind them. With eyes squeezed shut, she murmured, "This is a nightmare. I'll wake up and Momma will be cooking breakfast and Daddy will take me out back to shoot guns."

A plume of angry smoke billowed into the sky, and her heart sank.

There'd be no waking from this nightmare. No breakfast on the stove, no target shooting with her daddy.

They were gone, and she was alone.

CHAPTER ONE

Northern New Mexico Territory, 1878

Elinor Barstow gave Blaze plenty of rein as he picked his way over the uneven, rocky ground. Patches of melting snow made things slippery, so extra caution was in order. This location was a perfect spot, providing plenty of hiding space for four people and their horses.

She turned and gave an impatient wave to her gang lagging behind. After dismounting, she tied her reins loosely to a large piñon pine tree that would offer them shade from the morning sun. If her calculations were correct, the stagecoach should pass by soon. Hopefully, things would go smoother than the Richland job. The man on the back end of the coach had had a derringer hidden up his sleeve. He'd managed to fire at Elle before she shot the gun from his hand. The bullet had only grazed her hip, but still. She'd replayed the scene in her head all week since, vowing to not be caught off guard like that again.

The others arrived and slid from their saddles, and she tucked the memory away.

"How long before the coach comes, boss?" Shorty took his cap off and scratched at his threadbare patch of red hair.

"Less than an hour."

He nodded and slumped to the ground against a tree with his canteen.

Raven sat cross-legged in another small patch of shade. She removed her John Bull hat and wiped the dust from her face before reaching into her pocket to pull out a black feather. With a satisfied nod, she tucked the feather into the sash on her hat.

Willy took up residence on a boulder, keeping an eye on the trail below.

Elle joined Shorty under the tree. She stretched out on her back and pulled the brim of her low-crowned Stetson over her eyes. Some downtime before a robbery was always welcome. She rubbed at the sore spot on her hip. The bullet had nicked more than her skin and muscle—it'd nicked her pride. *How did I not react sooner? Have I slowed down?*

"This looks nothing like me," Raven said.

Thankful for a distraction from her incessant self-criticism of the Richland job, Elle tipped her brim up to take a peek at what Raven waved in the air. It was a copy of the *National Police Gazette* that they'd gotten while passing through the town of Trinidad yesterday.

Rough individual sketches of four, clearly male faces occupied the top half of the front page. On the bottom half, the four "men" stood in a group drawing, armed with pistols and rifles. The artist had no clue what any of them looked like. One bandit stood a full two heads taller than the rest, and one was so short he appeared to be a child. All had the same-shaped face with varying degrees of facial hair.

"How do you know which one is supposed to be you?" Elle asked.

Raven gave her an incredulous look. "I'm the tall, attractive one."

"You're off your nut." Shorty spit tobacco juice into the ground. "You ain't the tall one. That's me. I'm taller than all y'all." He wiped at his scraggly beard.

"That ain't you. You're the ugly one." And in case he didn't know which one, Raven tapped the most unattractive bandit in the picture, the one with rotted teeth, bulging eyes, and a fringed waistcoat. The waistcoat was the only thing the poster got right.

He scowled. "That ain't me."

"You might wanna get a new coat. And while you're at it, why don't you get a new hat? You lost the war, you know. A loooong time ago."

Shorty adjusted his faded gray slouch hat that had been standard issue for the 1st Georgia Sharpshooter Battalion of the former Confederate States Army infantry. "Quit your yammerin'. Ain't nothin' wrong with my hat. It fits good. And I know it pisses you off, so I'm gonna keep wearing it."

Elle chuckled beneath the shadow of her Stetson. Raven Blackfeather and Shorty Sullivan never got along. Their acrimonious relationship was sometimes tense and, most times amusing, depending on the amount of whisky consumed, and as long as it didn't jeopardize their plans, she let them bicker to their hearts' content.

"They think Elle has a beard," Raven said.

Elle snuck another peek at the magazine. The top sketch showed a man with full whiskers and heavy brows. Above his picture, in bold letters, were the words, *The Outlaw L and his Gang. Notorious bandits from Texas.*

She did have thick eyebrows, which were visible above her bandana. Other than that, the resemblance was laughable.

"Why do they think we're from Texas?" Willy asked.

"I don't know," Raven replied. "It says we held up a bank in Oklahoma City last month. We weren't even in Oklahoma last month."

"I think they make most of that up to sell the magazine," Elle said. "You know the people back East love to read about outlaws in the West." She inhaled the scent of pine and sighed. She loved the mountains, with their cool refreshing air and stunning vistas. When spring arrived, the landscape would explode with color, from the blues and whites of columbine and bluebell to the scarlet red of penstemon.

After taking a quick pull from her canteen, she stood and brushed the dust from her trousers. The morning sun inched up into a cloudless sky. The weather was warm for February, and soon the shade from their stand of pine trees would desert them.

Willy shot to his feet and pointed at a rising dust cloud. "Stagecoach comin'."

Elle grabbed her spyglass and scrambled up on the boulder next to him. "Four horses, two men up top. One's got a rifle, both have revolvers. And no army escort." Good. Everything was going according to plan. The large expanse of sparse grasslands in the lower foothills enabled stagecoaches to reach top speed on this stretch of the trail, and the coach below was flying. But up ahead, the trail narrowed, and the terrain grew rockier. Drivers always stopped to navigate the turn into the pass that led through the Sangre de Cristo Mountains toward the town of Albuquerque. This is where the gang would make a stand and relieve them of their finery and coin.

Elle slid to the ground. "Everybody good with the plan?"

They answered with wordless nods and hiked up their bandanas to cover the lower part of their faces.

"Okay. Let's ride."

Elle rechecked the chamber of both Colt .45 revolvers that hung low on her hips and tightened the tie-downs. "You ready, Blaze?" Her horse nickered in response, and she stroked the white streak on his nose. He loved the underside of his chin scratched, and Elle obliged every chance she got. He flipped his head and flapped his lips. Leaning close to him, she whispered, "Of course you're ready. Good boy." With a grunt, she hauled herself into the saddle. He pranced in a circle and tossed his head in excitement. She patted his neck, already sweaty from the building heat. A subtle press of her heels sent him off, and the others followed.

When they arrived at the break in the trail, Elle wordlessly pointed to everyone's spot. Shorty would lay on a rocky ledge ten feet above while Elle and Raven stayed on horseback and approached from the sides. Willy would position himself in the middle of the trail with his rifle pointing at the men driving the coach.

Fifteen minutes later, the stagecoach skidded to a stop to navigate the bend in the trail.

The driver of the coach clicked and whistled, slapping the reins onto the horses' haunches, but they refused to move forward. The lead two snorted and stomped because of the obstacle before them. Willy, his lips set in a grim line, stood in the middle of the trail, rifle at the ready.

A lone jay flew into a nearby willow and scolded from its perch when Elle and Raven, still in the saddle, emerged from the gully next to the trail. In the monsoon wet season, the gully became a raging creek, but this time of year, the snowmelt had barely begun so the water level didn't even reach the horses' hooves. With guns drawn, they approached the coach from either side.

One man up top made a fruitless play for his Winchester, and a shot rang out from above. Shorty's bullet nicked the man's arm and he tumbled to the ground, landing with a thud.

At the same time, the second man reached for his revolver, and Elle shot the bowler off his head. "I wouldn't if I were you."

The color drained from his face, and his shaky hands reached for the heavens. Willy pulled him to the ground. "On your knees with your hands up."

Raven threw open the stagecoach door and in a deep voice, yelled, "If you wanna live, come out with your hands up."

Four men stumbled out with hands held high. The cut of their suits told Elle they were more businessmen than cowboys. With a smile, she jumped to the ground. It would be a good haul today. She already had her eye on the gold watch dangling from one of their pockets.

By now, Shorty had descended from his perch and joined them. He poked the man he shot with the toe of his boot as the man writhed in agony while clutching at the small red stain growing on his sleeve. The man's pained moans prompted a chuckle from Shorty. "You ain't that hurt. Quit bawling."

"Cut the horses loose," Elle said.

Shorty pulled a bowie knife from his boot and cut through the traces holding the horses to the coach. With a wave of his hat and a boisterous *hoo-haa*, he chased the horses down the trail.

Raven circled the coach occupants. "Get on your knees." When they didn't move quickly enough, she shoved them down.

One man peered at Elle and stuttered, "We…we don't want no trouble, sir."

Raven cackled. "You hear that? These boys don't want no trouble. Sir."

They stared wide-eyed at Elle, bodies visibly shaking, and she nodded her approval. She still had it. Richland had been an outlier. With a gruff voice, she said, "Tie 'em up."

Shorty and Willy grabbed rope from their saddlebags and trussed the men up like calves at a rodeo, hands bound to feet. Shorty finished first and punched his fist in the air. "I beat your ass."

Willy ducked his head and kicked a toe in the dirt. "I ain't never been good at calf ropin'."

Raven dragged the trunks from the coach and dumped the contents on the ground while Shorty frisked the men and removed all their valuables.

After filling their burlap sacks with whatever could fetch a good price, they mounted back up.

Elle grabbed her reins. By the time their victims escaped from their bonds and rounded up the horses, they'd be long gone. After galloping away from the coach, she turned in her saddle. "Sun'll be setting in a couple of hours, so let's ride for a bit and then find a place to camp."

Raven nodded. "We can probably make it to that spot next to Cimarron Creek."

Elle squeezed her knees into Blaze's sides. "Let's go."

After riding hard for an hour, they pulled into a secluded clearing surrounded by cottonwood trees and buffeted by a small rocky hill. Cimarron Creek gurgled nearby, offering fresh water to refill canteens and quench thirsty horses.

Each had their tasks: Shorty scouted the area for trouble, Raven gathered wood and started a fire, and Willy oversaw dinner, which tonight consisted of some jerky, bread, and cheese.

Elle emptied the sacks of contraband and separated them into four piles. Hers was the largest, and nobody questioned it.

An hour later, they lazed around the small fire with full bellies. The last bit of sun on the horizon cast a hazy orange glow across the landscape before dipping down below the mountains and disappearing. Nighttime insects began to hum, and a screech owl whinnied nearby.

Dinner was never a rowdy affair. Having been together for a few years now, there wasn't much new to talk about. Raven absently poked a stick into the fire, and Willy whittled away at a piece of wood. He liked to make tiny figures for his daughter to play with.

Elle lay supine on the ground with her legs stretched out, ankles crossed. This was the most peaceful time of her day, and she relished the quiet. Mostly, she'd spend the time lost in her own thoughts, dreaming about a ranch of her own and maybe a different life.

Shorty poked through his take and bit a gold coin to test it. "We did pretty good today."

Raven agreed. "Damn sight better than that coach in Richland."

Elle stiffened at the reminder and again rubbed the spot on her hip.

"What's next, boss?" Raven asked.

Elle shrugged. "Guess we head home. Unless somebody has a better idea."

"I'm ready to head home," Willy said. "Miss my little girl."

"Okay. Home it is." Elle pulled her Stetson over her eyes and took a deep breath. Time to catch some shut-eye. "Shorty, first watch?"

"Yup."

* * *

Elle and the gang galloped into the town of Loma Parda, each flush with their share of the haul from the last six weeks of thieving.

To the outsider, Loma Parda, nestled on the banks of the lazy Mora River, was a lawless town filled with miners, thieves, gamblers, and drunks. To Elle, it was home. A perfect hideout, safe from the prying eyes of US Marshals and bounty hunters, neither of whom dared to show their faces in the aptly nicknamed Sodom on the Mora in the New Mexico Territory.

They slowed to a trot to avoid the passing wagons, stagecoaches, and cowboys hurrying along the street. Women, some in skirts and some in pants, walked with sacks of supplies from Wilson's Dry Goods. A few children ran between the buildings, shrieking with laughter.

"How you gonna spend your money, boss?" Raven asked.

Elle squinted and pulled her bandana over her mouth to keep from choking from the dirt billowing around the street that snaked through the main part of town. "Like I usually do. On a nice bath and a willing woman."

Raven laughed. "So we're goin' to Big Rose's?"

"Yep." After weeks on the trail sleeping under the stars, Elle looked forward to losing a few coins for a nice tumble in a soft bed. She wiped at the perspiration rolling down her neck. It was another hot afternoon, but the unusual heat did nothing to quell the unruly activity that permeated the town. Random gunshots rang out, and fistfights spilled from the clapboard buildings that lined the main street.

Raven turned to Shorty. "How about you and I find a poker game? I'm feeling lucky."

Shorty shook his head. "Last time we played you fleeced me."

"Ain't my fault you can't play cards. What about you, Willy? You game for a game?"

He shook his head. "I ain't no match for you or anybody else when it comes to cards. Besides, I gotta get home to my wife and baby."

"You're a good man, Willy," Elle said. "Tell Perlie we said hello."

They dismounted in front of the McIntosh Livery Stable and Boardinghouse.

Elle handed the reins to the stable boy who greeted them. "Thanks, Tom." She gave an affectionate pat on Blaze's rump.

"Wet him down and give him a good brushing." She flipped a half-bit in Tom's direction and headed uptown to Big Rose's with Raven hot on her heels.

When they hopped onto the porch at the saloon, they had to quickly step aside while Tiny Tim, one of Rose's sons, tossed a drunken soldier out the door and onto the street. He must've done something to draw Rose's ire. The soldier wobbled to his feet and clenched his fists.

Tim crossed his arms. "You best leave now if you wanna make it back to Fort Union in one piece."

The soldier tottered a bit before turning on his heel.

After brushing his hands together, Tim tipped his hat. "Afternoon, ladies."

"Howdy, Tim. See you got your hands full as usual," Elle said. Poor Tim. Always tasked with keeping order and tossing patrons. That's what happened when you were well over six feet tall and strong as an ox.

"First one today, so that's a plus." He smiled broadly. It wasn't a toothy grin—he was missing quite a few teeth, either from decay or fisticuffs—but it was a friendly one, and the warmth always reached his eyes.

"What'd he do?" Raven asked.

"Drew his gun."

Elle chuckled. He'd broken the only rule at the popular saloon. "Rose around today?"

"She's in the kitchen. One of the ladies is sick so she's filling in. I'll tell her you're here." He hitched up his trousers and headed back inside.

Elle and Raven pushed their way through the rowdy crowd. It didn't matter that the sun hung high in the sky, Big Rose's was the place to be. Men arguing over cards occupied every table. A few managed to play their poker hand with a pretty gal on their knee. Most were familiar faces, and they shouted out greetings.

"Elle! Good to have you back," Clyde Harrell bellowed. His rosy cheeks meant he'd been drinking most of the day.

"Good to be back, Clyde. How's the wife?"

"Still putting up with me."

"She's a saint. You're lucky to have her."

Arthur, another of Rose's burly sons, pounded on the ivory keys of the piano and sang an off-key, up-tempo rendition of "Home on the Range." Men twirled their ladies around the dance floor, kicking up swirls of dust that floated around their ankles. Most of the "ladies" were Rose's girls. Some of the less agile folk surrounded the dancers, clapping and singing along with Arthur.

Rob Roy, son number three and the most handsome of the bunch, greeted Elle and Raven when they sidled up to the wide wooden plank bar. "You're back. And in one piece I see." All his teeth were intact, as patron-tossing was not his job. He immediately poured two shots of whisky.

Elle removed her hat and threw hers down with one gulp before pushing the glass back for a refill. "Back in one piece and ready to celebrate."

Rob dipped his head, and a lock of blond hair fell across his eyes. He gave Raven a swoon-worthy look. "Howdy, Raven."

"Hey. Any good card games happening?"

"Fred's got some faro going on. I'm sure he'll let you in."

She turned to Elle. "Have fun. I'm gonna lighten a few purses." She wiggled her eyebrows and grabbed her glass.

As she walked away, Rob's eyes followed her across the room. When Elle cleared her throat, his eyes darted downward and his cheeks reddened. She smirked. "Someday, Rob."

He took a rag and wiped at an imaginary spot on the bar top in front of him. "Don't know what you're talking about."

"Sure you don't. How about I chase that whisky with a beer?"

"Where's my Ellie girl?"

Elle smiled broadly before turning around. She allowed only one person to call her Ellie.

There in all her glory stood Big Rose, the most powerful woman—hell, the most powerful person—in Loma Parda, with her flaming red hair piled high atop her head and her hefty frame dressed in an unusually understated gray frock. Subdued for Rose, who liked to prance around her saloon in colorful dresses, the kind that would make a Parisian debutante jealous. But despite whatever finery she chose, her Colt .45s were always strapped to her hips.

Rose extended her arms. "Give me a hug."

Elle soon found herself wrapped up in Rose's plump arms, pressed tight to her ample bosom. "You're gonna suffocate me."

"Nonsense. I raised you to be tougher than that." She held Elle at arm's length. "Where's my other daughter?"

Elle gestured across the room. "She just sat down across from Fred."

Rose narrowed her eyes. "He's gotta pay his bill. I hope she doesn't take too much from him."

"Want me to get her?"

"No, no. It's fine." She brushed some dust from Elle's shoulders. "You were due back days ago. I was worried to death."

"We got waylaid in Richland. Job went off the rails a bit, and we had to lay low for a day or two. You don't usually show so much concern. Are you okay?"

Rose tucked Elle's hair behind her ear. "It was a bad few weeks here. We lost twenty-five souls."

Elle whistled. Twenty-five? That was steep even for Loma Parda. "How many were you responsible for?"

"Only six. Some fellows had a shootout in here over one of my gals, and I had to maintain some order. Closed me down for two hours 'cause we had to clean up the mess."

"What happened to the other nineteen?"

"Oh, those damn McFadden boys rode in and took on the Tustins. Joe McFadden holed up in the hotel and decided to make his last stand. It was a hellacious afternoon. But you're back, and that makes me happy. You got a little something for me?"

"Yes, ma'am." Elle discreetly slid a leather pouch full of bills and gold pieces into Rose's hand.

Rose hefted the bag and her eyes lit up. "You take good care of me. Which is more than I can say for my own flesh and blood." Her eyes landed on Rob Roy, and he laughed.

"Things will be different next year," Elle said. "Railroad will be coming through Santa Fe. Stagecoaches will be scarce."

Rose waved a hand. "Railroads mean bigger towns. Bigger towns mean banks. Banks mean bigger money."

Elle was not keen on robbing a bank, but she kept her thoughts to herself. Robbing a stage was simple—it was just you and the coach. But a bank in the middle of town had lots of witnesses and lawmen milling around. "What's for dinner tonight?"

"Beef and potatoes. You wanna plate now?"

"I was hoping for a bath and some relaxation first."

"Say no more," she said, nodding, then shouted across the room, "Miriam, you're needed over here!"

Elle laughed at Rose's boisterousness. Miriam was Elle's favorite.

Miriam hustled across the room and threw herself into Elle's arms. "You're back!"

Rose nodded toward the stairs. "Go on up. Miriam, get one of the boys to take water up for a bath."

Miriam placed a hand on her chest. "Harry paid for a few dances already."

Rose shooed her away. "I'll take care of Harry."

* * *

When the tub was filled and the door to the room was shut, Miriam undressed Elle. After some quick scrubbing and soaping up, they tumbled into bed and enjoyed each other's bodies for the next hour before devouring the smoked beef and potatoes that Rose sent up. Good sex always made Elle ravenous.

Now sated, they lulled in the newly refilled bath water with half-open eyes, sleepy from the sex and the rising steam.

"New curtains?" Elle asked.

"Mm-hmm. Rose wanted to add some color to the rooms."

"They certainly are colorful." The white curtains strung across the double windows had a bold green-and-orange floral pattern. A bit loud for Elle's taste, but they did brighten the place.

With a sigh, she closed her eyes, thankful to be home, which was becoming the norm this past year. Usually, she itched to get out on the trail and cause some mayhem, but lately something had changed. For the past eight years, she'd laughed at danger.

Now she was more fearful. And tired. Tired of looking over her shoulder. Tired of being watchful every minute of the day when she was away from Loma Parda. It was a worrying development. And the close call in Richland had shaken her.

"You're frowning. What are you thinking about?"

Miriam's quiet voice startled her back to the present, and Elle snapped her eyes open. *Stop. You're fine.* "Nothing."

Miriam chuckled. "Liar. I see that new wound on your hip."

Elle smiled. "How are you?"

"Almost have enough money saved to get the hell out of here. Maybe move to California and leave this life behind. Turn myself into a respectable woman, find a husband."

None of Rose's girls ever made it out, but maybe Miriam would be the exception. "I hope that happens for you."

"What about you? Aren't you tired of this life?"

Elle refused to share her earlier misgivings, so she played it cool and harrumphed. "'Once an outlaw, always an outlaw,' as Rose likes to say."

"She says that so you'll never leave her, 'cause you're the only person she trusts. She needs to keep you around."

"She took me in when I was ten and raised me. The least I could do is stick around."

"Don't you think you've repaid that debt by now?"

"Can you ever repay a debt like that?" Elle asked. This wasn't the first time Miriam made comments about Rose, and it made Elle uncomfortable.

Disapproval flashed across Miriam's face. "I think she takes too much from you. Expects too much from you."

Not up for an argument, Elle focused on Miriam's generous breasts as they bobbed on the water. Her large nipples played peekaboo with the surface, and right now they begged for more attention. "How about we talk about something else?"

She kissed Miriam, slipping her hand between the young woman's legs. "Or maybe we don't need to talk at all."

Miriam groaned and her hips bucked into Elle's hand.

The discussion ended, and to Elle, it was a fitting conclusion to six weeks on the trail.

CHAPTER TWO

Boston, Massachusetts

Isabella Collins's head lolled back with every stroke of the hairbrush. She half expected to be bald after all the brushing.

Her mother finally placed the brush on the side table and began the tedious work of pinning her hair up. When she was done, she stood back to critique her handiwork. "You're beautiful. Now which dress? I think the green one. Green always looks good with your blond hair." She removed the dress from the wardrobe and spread it out on the bed next to the undergarments and stockings. The bodice was a similar green, with black piping around the square-cut neck and wrists.

Izzy offered no resistance and began dressing. Green was a fine color for her. Her mother yanked the corset strings tighter and tighter. *I hate corsets!* She cursed the devil who invented them and took a deep breath while her mother finished cinching it up. There was no letting the breath out, either. It would remain stuck in her lungs for hours.

She sighed. Another dinner, another beau paraded in front of her. Another evening spent under the watchful eyes of her parents, who would analyze each move she made, every word coming from her lips, with eyes filled with hope that she would fawn and swoon over their choice du jour.

"Now, Izzy, Jonathan Beyer is a fine young man," her mother said. "His father is a distant cousin of James Fields."

"James T. Fields? The editor of *The Atlantic*?"

"I guess so. Yes."

"Why haven't I heard of him? How distant is he?" Izzy devoured every issue of *The Atlantic Monthly*. Hmm. Maybe this Jonathan deserved a chance. Perhaps he'd be an intellectual, a forward-thinker, since it ran in the family.

"I guess you can ask him," her mother said.

Downstairs, the heavy brass ring rapped against the front door, signaling company.

"Finish up. I need to greet our guest."

Her mother hurried from the room, leaving Izzy to stare at her reflection in the mirror. The emerald dress made her hazel eyes take on a greenish hue. She tugged at the bodice and adjusted the small bustle in the back. *Ugh. Show time.*

When Izzy arrived downstairs, beau number ten, or one hundred—frankly she lost count months ago—stood and bowed at her entrance. Height was not a strong suit since he was shorter than her. Izzy feared she could pack more of a punch than the slight Mr. Beyer, and he looked more like a boy than a man. There was not a hint of whiskers on his face. Wait, maybe that was a mustache. She squinted. No. It was a shadow cast by his beak-like nose. His mousy dark hair was trimmed above his ears, and sparse sideburns almost reached the bottom of his jawline. Rosy, red patches stained his cheeks like he was in a perpetual state of embarrassment.

Her father cleared his throat. "Isabella, this is Jonathan Beyer."

Jonathan grasped her hand and placed a kiss on the back of it. "Miss Collins. I am honored to make your acquaintance."

His grip was moist. She casually wiped her hand on her dress. "I am honored as well, Mr. Beyer. May I call you Jonathan?"

"My friends and family call me Jon. May I call you Isabella?"

"Of course, Jonathan." The minor insult sailed over his head, and it didn't have to sail high.

"Excellent." With a blink of his dullish brown eyes, he slid her chair out and, with an overly grand gesture, waved his arm.

Well, where else would I sit? Isabella pretended to be impressed with his courtesy. After taking her seat, he sat down next to her.

Izzy placed the napkin in her lap. "Jonathan, I hear you are the cousin of Mr. James Fields, the wonderful editor at *The Atlantic Monthly*."

The red patches brightened. "Oh. I'm sorry, no. My cousin is James R. Fields. He owns a livery stable in Worcester."

Izzy glanced at her mother. "My mother was under the impression you were related to James T. Fields."

"I'm sorry to disappoint. I don't think I've ever even read *The Atlantic*." He gave an awkward chuckle.

She blew out a breath. So much for an intellectual match.

"No matter," her father said. "Your father owns the bank on State Street. Banking is a fine career."

He smiled. "Yes, sir. Both my brother and I work there."

Margaret, their housemaid, floated around the table and filled up the wineglasses.

"Does your mother work at the bank also?" Izzy asked.

Jonathan chortled. "No. She runs the house. It *is* a woman's job, after all."

Izzy glared, and he quickly added, "And a full-time job it is!"

Her father's jaw clenched.

Izzy sipped her wine before saying, "So you don't believe a woman should work? That she shouldn't be allowed to have a career?"

Jonathan's eyes flitted around the table. "Well, I think raising a family is a fine career for a woman." He smiled and looked to her father for approval, who, of course, was happy to give it.

"You are correct, Jonathan," her father said. "It is a fine career. Taking care of a family is the most important thing a woman can do. Mrs. Collins has done a fine job with our family." He raised his wine goblet in the direction of Isabella's mother.

Now buoyed with confidence from the paternal support, Jonathan puffed out his chest. "I'm not saying a woman shouldn't have some hobbies to keep her busy—"

"Oh, how big of you," Izzy mumbled.

"Like knitting. Or afghan-making. I hear that's a thing now. Do you have some hobbies, Isabella?"

She knew the perfect turnoff. "Well, I'm a suffragette."

Jonathan's brows knitted. "Sorry, what?"

"A suffragette."

Confusion clouded his features. "I don't know what that is." He sought out the aforementioned paternal support, but her father's face was pinched, and he refused to meet his eyes.

"I'm involved in the women's suffrage movement."

He brightened. "Bravo. Is that some sort of charitable endeavor?"

Izzy wanted to smack her palm against her forehead. *How could he not know about the suffrage movement? Is he an illiterate buffoon?* "It's a movement dedicated to giving women the right to vote."

"Vote…politically speaking?"

"Yes."

"Is that such a good idea?"

Her father groaned.

Izzy kept her attention squarely on Jonathan. "Of course. Why wouldn't it be?"

"Well, politics can be tricky. A woman has enough on her mind running her household. She doesn't have time to be caught up in political intrigue."

"Are you saying a woman's mind is not sharp enough to handle family *and* politics?"

The rosy hue in his cheeks deepened. "N-no…no. I just—"

"Are we to sit around all day having babies and afghaning? Waiting for our husbands to come home so we can feed them and pamper them the rest of the evening?"

"Well, I'm…I'm not sure about the pampering part—"

"I'm a firm believer in higher education for women. I plan on studying law. And I assure you, my mind is plenty sharp enough to handle a career and a marriage."

Jonathan grabbed his wineglass.

"Perhaps I won't get married at all," Izzy said. "Isabella Collins, spinster. It has a nice ring to it, don't you think, Jonathan?"

Jonathan mumbled something incoherent and sought solace in his wine. His cheeks were aflame. They looked hot enough to cook a biscuit on.

"Or perhaps I'll run for president someday."

The comment caught Jonathan midsip, and he spit out his wine.

"Don't be ridiculous," her father stated. "You'll get married."

Izzy straightened her shoulders. "Maybe I won't."

"Why can't you be more like your sisters?" her father growled. "They both were married with two children by the time they were twenty-one."

Izzy gritted her teeth at the mention of Celia and Anne, the perfect daughters. "Because I'm my own person."

"Nonsense. You'll get married, and you'll have children. End of discussion." He swallowed the last of his wine and picked up his spoon.

A wide-eyed Jonathan glanced around the table. His Adam's apple bobbed. After a moment of silence, he said, "Yes. Well. This beef stew is delicious."

Dinner was over in an hour.

Afterward, Izzy sat on the couch in the living room while her mother paced with hands on her hips. "Is Father joining us?"

"He's in the library, having a drink. You've driven him to drink! He's almost at his wit's end with you." She rubbed her forehead.

"Why?"

"You've refused every suitor he's brought to the house. A young man comes to call, expecting a lovely evening with a lovely young woman, and ends up practically running out the door before the dishes are even cleared away. Poor Jonathan didn't even wait for dessert."

"He said he didn't feel well. He did look a bit gray," Izzy said.

"Gray because of you! And your wild ideas. Every time we invite an eligible man over, you inevitably say something outrageous to sabotage the entire evening." She pointed an accusing finger in Izzy's direction. "Your father had high hopes for this one tonight. He's been in discussion with Jonathan's father regarding a loan for the store."

Izzy gaped. "So he's dangling his own daughter as some sort of prize, a sort of collateral?"

Her mother frowned. "Stop it. That's not what I meant. I'm sure in their initial discussions, you both came up as unattached, so he saw no harm in arranging a meeting."

"Is the store in trouble?" The Collins General Store had been a staple on High Street for years. Her father hadn't mentioned any issues, but of course, why would he? Women, according to him, couldn't wrap their pretty little heads around the business of running a business.

"Not that I'm aware."

"Why does he need a loan?"

"I'm not sure. Now, listen to me. You're nineteen. Soon you'll be an old maid, and no one will want to marry you."

"Aunt Bea never married."

"Don't you mention Bea in front of your father."

"Aunt Bea was always kind to me. She took me on walks and taught me about trees and flowers, and I loved her. Why did she leave? I never understood."

"Please stop."

"She is your only sister."

Her mother raised a hand. "Isabella, enough. You need to get married. Do you plan on living here for the rest of your life?"

Her mother's tone suggested that Izzy would not be welcome to live out her days in the arms of her loving family. She may have misread the tone, but she raised her chin anyway. "No. I'll live on my own. Like Catherine. Just two days ago we looked at houses near her."

Her mother tsk-tsked. "You were told to stop seeing that woman. Your father forbade it."

"I'm not going to stop seeing her. She's my friend."

"She's much older than you. And there's something not right about her."

"Much older? She's twenty-eight. She's smart, and well-spoken, and passionate about her beliefs."

Her mother's voice rose in volume. "What twenty-eight-year-old woman lives alone, and wears…trousers? Trousers! It's scandalous."

Izzy shot to her feet. "She lives her own life and answers to no one. And I love that about her."

"There are rumors about her."

"What rumors?"

"Never mind." Her mother's body sagged. "I guess your father's not joining us. You've managed to send him over the brink this time." She threw one more disapproving glance in Izzy's direction. "It's late. I'm going to turn in."

Izzy soon followed. Before climbing the stairs, she hesitated. *Should I apologize to Father? No. Best to leave him to his thoughts.* He'd be better in the morning. He was always better in the morning.

* * *

Izzy strode down the hallway the following day and heard her name. She stopped and pressed an ear against the door to her father's study. Her father was speaking with someone. After a moment, she recognized Walter Jackson's voice.

"Has your Isabella found a husband yet?" Mr. Jackson asked.

"Not yet," her father answered. "We have tried to find her a suitable match, but she has yet to settle on one."

"Soon she'll be past her prime childbearing years."

Her father sighed. "I'm well aware of the situation. I'm hoping she chooses someone soon."

"You need to choose a man for her. Women are not capable of making these types of decisions. They're too emotional, especially when they're young. Their heads are filled with fairy tales of falling in love. And we know that's not how things work."

"I agree. I was giving her a chance to find someone."

"Well, maybe I can help. You remember my brother, J. Beauregard?"

"Yes. He moved out West some years back."

"He certainly did, and he has done quite well for himself. I just came back from visiting him. He owns the largest cattle ranch in the New Mexico Territory now."

"I see. And what has this to do with my Isabella?"

"His current wife recently passed away before she was able to give him children."

Izzy opened her mouth in dread, fearing what would come next.

"Tragic," her father said.

"Yes. Well, he's tasked me with finding him a new wife. Said to find someone from our good Boston stock." Mr. Jackson chuckled.

"And are you suggesting Isabella?"

"I am. My brother is willing to pay handsomely."

Izzy balled her hands into fists. How dare he? Was she some livestock to be bartered over? She pressed her ear closer, holding her breath in anticipation of her father's response. Surely, he wouldn't sell his daughter to some cowboy.

"Isabella is a headstrong girl, very lively. Fancies herself as independent. I can't imagine he'd want that in a wife."

"Don't be so sure. It's hard living out West. His last wife was a frail thing. Caught the fever and died in a week. A good strong woman is exactly what's needed out there."

"Mrs. Collins wouldn't want her baby daughter to move clear across the country. She's quite attached now that the other children are out of the house."

"Understood. But take some time to think it over. My brother is willing to negotiate a fair price. I know you've talked about expanding your business but needed an infusion of cash to do so. Perhaps this is the perfect solution."

"Thank you, sir. I will keep it in mind."

Izzy sensed the conversation was over and hustled toward the front door and out into the crisp morning air. She stomped down the sidewalk. Her blood boiled. She felt like a prized broodmare put up for sale to the highest bidder. *Men!* This made her work at the suffrage office even more important now. *Women need rights. It's high time men stop telling us what to do.*

By the time she made it to the suffrage's small office on Beacon Street, she was in a tizzy. Her body temperature was sky-high. She wanted to rip off her clothes and jump into the Charles River.

When she tried the door to the office, it was locked. Cupping her hands around her eyes, she peered into the window. Movement confirmed someone was there, and relief flooded through her. Catherine hurried over and unlocked the door.

"You're early. Nobody is supposed to be here for half an hour." Her reddish-brown hair hung loose down her back. She kept it shorter than most women did. And, of course, she wore pants with a men's style button-down white shirt.

"I'm sorry. I was supposed to go to the bakery for my mother, but I lost track of where I was and ended up here." She collapsed into a chair and covered her face with a hand.

"What's wrong?"

When Izzy took her hand away, she found a concerned look on Catherine's face.

Catherine grabbed Isabella's hand and held it. "Are you hurt?"

Izzy stared at their clasped hands. The familiar warmth of Catherine's touch caused the usual sensation of a pleasant tingling inside her chest. She adored Catherine. Adored the way they laughed and had spirited discussions on the goings-on in the city. Izzy tried to imagine not seeing her friend, and the more she thought about it, the more her heart hurt, and the more determined she was to ignore her father's decree. *I won't get married. I won't.* Tears welled in her eyes and she tried to hold them at bay, but once one leaked out, others followed.

"Oh, my." Catherine wrapped her arms around Izzy and held her. "Tell me what's wrong."

Through choked sobs, Izzy recounted the conversation she'd overheard. When she was finished, she made no move to leave Catherine's arms. They felt comforting and strong. If only she could remain here all day.

Catherine stroked her hair. "It's okay. I'm sure your father would never banish you to New Mexico."

Izzy finally pulled back but stayed in the circle of Catherine's arms. She dabbed at her eyes with a handkerchief. "I don't want to get betrothed. I try to imagine myself married, and I can't. I feel like I don't belong here or anywhere. Why can't I have a career? I told my father I wanted to study law, and he laughed." She shook her head. "What is wrong with me?"

Catherine caressed her cheek. "My poor Izzy. Nothing's wrong with you. You're just…different. And studying law is a fine idea."

"I think so too. If I know the law, I can help change the law."

"Perhaps you can enroll at Wellesley. It would be a start. And then perhaps a law school."

Izzy nodded. "Perhaps." Of course, her father would forbid it. When Wellesley opened two years prior, he had scoffed at the idea of an all-female college, calling it a waste of time and money and good real estate. "Some days I want to jump on a horse and ride away to someplace where I can be myself. Of course, I have no money of my own to buy this horse." She managed a small smile.

Catherine chuckled and rested her forehead against Izzy's. "You are one of a kind, Isabella Collins."

They remained that way for a few seconds until Catherine inched back and stared into Izzy's eyes.

Izzy's pulse quickened, and the room turned hot and stuffy. Catherine's eyes shifted down to her lips, and Izzy's mind went blank. It was unclear who kissed who, but the press of Catherine's lips against her own made her heart beat even faster. An unfamiliar hunger throbbed deep inside, and a soft moan escaped her lips. She didn't want to stop. It was wonderful and exciting and daring. And…right.

The bell above the front door jangled, and they jolted away from each other. Two older women, with looks of horror on their faces, stared.

Izzy's heart, which had beat with such pleasure a moment ago, stopped. Mrs. Heacock and Mrs. Pennington, two notorious gossips. Her stomach twisted in fear.

"What is going on here?" Mrs. Heacock asked.

Izzy stammered something incoherent. She'd lost the ability to speak.

Catherine tried to rescue them from a potentially disastrous situation. "Miss Collins was upset."

Izzy found her voice. "Miss Fretz was merely offering me comfort." A shoddy defense if ever there was one.

Mrs. Heacock sneered. "Come, Mrs. Pennington. I will not be privy to such wickedness."

With a swish of petticoats, they marched out the door.

Catherine held a hand to her chest and, with wide eyes, said, "I'm sorry. I don't know what came over me."

"Don't apologize. It wasn't anybody's fault." Izzy had wanted that kiss, was thrilled by that kiss, but now there would be consequences. Overwhelmed by fear and guilt for having such feelings, she grabbed her purse. She had trouble meeting Catherine's eyes. "I should go." She hustled toward the door.

"Izzy, wait," Catherine called, but Izzy ran out to the sidewalk. When she was a block away, she leaned against the side of the drug store at the corner of Washington Street and tried to calm herself. Deep, shuddering breaths wracked her body. *Do I go home now and try to get ahead of the situation? Or do I run and hide?*

Her survival instincts took over and she walked. And walked. For hours.

* * *

When she finally arrived home, she slipped inside and listened. The eerie silence was deafening. She placed a foot on the stairs, filled with hope that she'd worried for nothing. But alas, it was not to be.

Her mother appeared. "Your father is in the study."

Izzy walked down the hallway like she was walking to the gallows. Slow and measured. One foot in front of the other. She entered the study with her mother close behind. Her father stood facing the fireplace. When he turned, his face was a blank slate.

Izzy wasn't sure if she should speak, so she stared at the floral pattern on the oriental rug.

"I told you to stay away from that woman," her father finally said. "You defied me."

Izzy lifted her chin. "She's my friend."

"She's immoral. And now it seems she's infected you with her depravity."

"She didn't infect me."

"I had to plead with Mrs. Heacock to be discreet. I had to practically pay for her silence." His voice rose in volume. "You've embarrassed me and this family for the last time. Pack your bags! You leave for New Mexico in a week." He faced her mother and pointed. "This perversity comes from your side of the family. First your sister, and now your daughter." With that, he stormed from the room.

Izzy froze. Was this happening? Was she just banished to a desolate Western outpost? She begged her mother for sympathy. "Mother, please. He's not serious, is he?"

"He is. You're to be married to Mr. J. Beauregard Jackson."

Izzy stomped her foot. "I won't go."

Her mother's face flushed. "You will not disobey your father."

"I'll run away!"

"Don't be ridiculous." With a shake of her head, she left the room, leaving Izzy alone.

"Watch me." It was an empty threat. Without money, she was a hostage in her own house, and her father knew everyone in Boston, so no one would come to her rescue. She collapsed into the nearest chair as her heart pounded in her ears. *This isn't happening. It's a nightmare, and I'll wake up tomorrow and everything will be normal.*

But deep down, she knew the nightmare was real. In a week, she'd travel across the country to marry a man she'd never met, and her dream of having a career and living an independent life was over.

She'd never see Catherine again. Catherine, with her kind blue eyes and auburn-streaked hair, with her soft touches and her newly discovered soft lips, with her easy laugh and funny stories. Over the past few months, Izzy had daydreamed about sharing a house, waking up each morning and reading the paper together over a cup of coffee, taking long walks in the afternoon. *How naive was I? How childish.* There would be no life together.

Tears swam in her eyes, and a sharp pain in her chest made her gasp and clutch at her lace chemisette.

Is this what a broken heart feels like?

CHAPTER THREE

Pueblo, Colorado

Blaze trotted along the trail, and a shot rang out over the ridge. Elle yanked the reins back and cocked an ear in the direction of the sound. Loud voices carried on the wind.

"Must be trouble," Raven said.

Shorty dismounted and hustled to a small overlook. "We got a holdup," he whispered to the gang. He peered back at the scene below. "Looks like the Watkins gang got themselves a fancy coach."

Elle gritted her teeth. The Watkins gang was a nasty bit of business. Their leader, Jed Watkins, was meaner than a cornered rattlesnake and answered to no one, taking what he wanted when he wanted. He managed to get himself run out of Helena, one of the most lawless towns in Texas. Rumor was he shot the local smithy for having the audacity of telling Jed to wait his turn. Elle had run-ins with Jed in Loma Parda, mostly over cards, but he didn't dare cause trouble there because Rose would put a bullet between his eyes if he so much as cursed at Elle.

They quietly slid to the ground and joined Shorty at his perch. They were close enough to get a good view of the action.

The scene below was familiar, and one they'd often been a part of. Five desperados surrounded a coach and the four horses in front. The coach was sleek and large. It looked new and had to have cost a pretty penny. Elle had a pang of regret at not being the one who pilfered its occupants.

Jed Watkins, unmistakable with his wispy whiskers and scraggly black hair that hung below his collar, surveyed the scene. Even from far away, the hatred and ugliness packed into his wiry frame was palpable. His signature bowler hat sat askew atop his head. He didn't bother to cover his face.

The driver of the coach had his hands in the air while a bandit aimed a rifle at his heart. One man, with blood seeping from his chest, already lay on the ground, unmoving.

"Damn. They killed someone. Bastards," Raven said.

One of the bandits opened the coach door and pointed his revolver at the occupants. "Git out!"

After a second, a man poked his head out and the bandit grabbed him by his lapel and threw him to the ground. As others slowly followed, the bandit yelled, "Git your hands up or I'll shoot you."

Two men and an older woman with gray hair stumbled out. Two of the outlaws frisked them, grabbing revolvers and anything that could be used as a weapon. After their search, they pushed the prisoners to their knees.

"Hands on your head or you're dead," one man said. He chuckled. "Hey, that's like a poem."

Jed glowered at him. "Shut up, Bobby." He pointed to the front of the stagecoach. "Get them horses outta here."

Bobby lifted his lip in a huff and mumbled, "You shut up."

Jed pointed his gun at him. "What'd you say?"

Bobby's shoulders sank low, and his chin touched his chest. "Nothin'." He shuffled to the horses and set them free, giving each a whack on their rumps.

"Better say nothin'."

"We got one more in here," the outlaw at the coach door said. "Out. Now!"

A woman with blond tresses piled below her feathered hat stepped down and stood with her head held high. Her light-blue dress flowed around her, and a rose-colored belt cinched the dress around her tiny waist.

Elle felt mildly intrigued.

Jed dismounted and rambled over. "Well, well, well. Looky here, fellas. We got ourselves a proper lady." With a leer, he lifted a curl that hung next to her cheek and rubbed it between his grimy fingers.

What happened next was a blur. The woman lifted her reticule and whacked an unsuspecting Jed in the noggin, knocking his bowler off. He rubbed at the newly formed probable lump and cursed. She didn't stop the assault. She hit him again across the face and stamped on his foot with the heel of her shoe. "Don't you touch me, you filthy man!"

Elle and the gang snickered, but their voices remained hushed.

"Damn," Raven said. "She hit 'em in the face with that bag. Hit 'em again, girl."

"Jed ain't used to a woman hittin' back," Shorty said.

Elle managed a wry smile at the woman's feisty spirit, but it would not bode well for her once Jed stopped hopping around in pain. In fact, it would become downright dangerous.

Jed growled in anger. "Tie that bitch up."

Bobby and one of the other men approached the woman, and she swung the reticule around. Bobby made a grab for her arm, and she connected with his nose. With a howl he fell to the ground, and blood seeped between his fingertips.

"Sweet Jesus, what's she got in that purse?" Willy asked, with wide eyes.

"Maybe a brick or something," Raven answered.

The woman stood her ground and the other man backed off.

One of the prisoners, a man dressed in a fine, dark-blue suit, cleared his throat, and in a heavy Southern accent, drawled, "Sir, I would seriously reconsider your actions."

Jed wiped a spot of blood from his mouth with the back of his hand and approached the gentleman. "Now why's that?"

The man looked him dead in the eye. "Because this coach belongs to J. Beauregard Jackson." He let the words sink in.

Elle and her gang tensed. Things just became a whole lot more interesting. J.B. was a powerful man.

Raven sucked in a breath. "Damn, Jackson's gonna be pissed."

"Maybe Jed finally met his match," mumbled Shorty.

An unimpressed Jed snorted with contempt. He grabbed the man's hair and yanked his head back. "I ain't afraid of J.B. Jackson," he snarled and let him go.

"Sir, this is his bride-to-be, and if a hair on her head is harmed, he will hunt you down and kill you."

Elle gave the suited man his due. Faced with possible death, he continued to antagonize Jed. She pursed her lips. It was only a matter of time now.

Sure enough, Jed smashed the butt of his revolver into the man's head and he slumped to the ground, blood seeping from his temple. "If this is his bride," Jed said, "then I bet he'd pay a pretty penny to get her back. Course, he may not want her back after I get done with her." He guffawed at his own joke and glanced at his men, who quickly laughed along with him. He waved at Bobby. "Give me your rope."

Bobby tossed it to him.

Jed waved it in a circle around his head and threw it at the woman, pulling back hard when it settled around her chest. She landed with a thump in the dirt. "Now tie her up."

With her hands now trapped to her sides, she was unable to defend herself, and they made quick work of it. Jed yanked her to her feet and leaned close to her ear. "I gotta feeling you and me are gonna get to know each other real good."

When he pulled back, she spit into his face.

Elle sucked in her breath and waited for the retaliation from Jed, but he surprised her by laughing.

"Oh, we gonna have fun, you and me." He pushed her to the ground and wiped the spittle from his face with his sleeve before addressing his gang. "All right, boys, let's clean up."

They spent the next few minutes stealing anything of value from the coach occupants. Next, they dumped the travel trunks all over the ground and took what they wanted.

Shorty nudged Elle's shoulder. "We need to skedaddle."

"Yeah, boss. Let's go," Raven said.

Elle's blood boiled at the mistreatment of an innocent woman. "What about her?"

"Nothing we can do," Raven said. "I don't wanna get into a fight with that lot."

Shorty nodded. "She's right. It's their take."

Elle tried to tamp down her anger, to no avail. Her nerve endings craved action. And violence. This woman was innocent and didn't deserve what Jed would do to her.

"Let's go." Raven slid down and walked off.

Elle stood, her mind made up. She would not allow the woman to be harmed. If the gang gave her pushback, she'd go it alone. When they got back to the horses, she said, "We'll follow them."

"What?" Shorty asked.

"We're gonna follow them. Make sure they don't hurt that woman."

"C'mon. It's none of our business," Raven pleaded.

"It's my business now. If you don't like it, ride on. I'll catch up."

They looked amongst themselves and shuffled their feet. They'd never split up on the trail, so this was something new, and confusion clouded their features.

Raven quoted from their favorite book. "What happened to one for all and all for one?"

"I could ask you the same thing," Elle said.

After a few seconds of neck-rubbing and dirt-toeing, they made their decision.

"Nobody goes it alone," Shorty said.

Raven nodded and mounted up. "We stay together."

Elle exhaled. She was more than willing to do this by herself, but it would be safer with everyone. She gave them a grateful smile. "All for one, one for all."

A shriek from behind them pierced the air.

* * *

Izzy had never experienced this kind of fear before in her sheltered life. Her heart pounded and her throat constricted, making each breath a fight. One of the men had thrown her over his shoulder and walked away while the others stayed with the coach—except for the awful man in charge, who followed with a wicked grin. Was this the end? Would she meet her maker in a few moments? Or was something more sinister going to happen first? *I will not go quietly.* She pounded the man in the back with her bound fists and screamed in his ear.

"Ow, damn it. Shut up."

After putting a good bit of distance between them and the coach, he dumped her on the ground.

The awful man nodded and the other left them alone. The evil in his eyes sent ripples of terror along her spine. She stood and tried to run, but he laughed, a cruel sound, and tugged on the rope that was still around her waist. She fell and tried to crawl away, but he only laughed harder and tugged her toward him. She turned on her back and gaped in horror as he came closer. He undid his gun holster and tossed it aside. "Won't be needing that, will I? I think you'll be a good girl." When he stood over her, his hands fumbled with his belt.

As his pants fell around his ankles, a husky voice called out, "Now, Jed. Is that any way to treat a lady?"

His head whipped around.

A tall cowboy with dark hair down to his shoulders stood a ways off. He was clad all in black with a hat pulled low over his eyes. Revolvers rested on both of his slim hips. The cowboy sauntered over with no urgency. He strolled, like one would walk down a promenade. He took his time, and Izzy took umbrage. Obviously, he didn't realize the severity of the situation. She made sure to let him know. "Help me!"

The awful man, Jed, pointed at her. "You shut up." He seemed less of a threat with his trousers twisted around his ankles and his pale skinny legs on display. Something else was on display as well, and Izzy turned away in disgust.

Her possible savior came closer. When he was a few feet away, he hitched his hat up with his thumb.

Izzy sucked in her breath. *It's a woman!* Before she could properly process this startling revelation, one of the bandits came rushing at the woman cowboy with his gun drawn. "Look out!" Izzy shouted.

But the woman didn't need Izzy's warning, she had already spun and shot the man. Izzy's mouth dropped open after the attacker slumped to the ground.

Jed made a grab for his pants, but the woman shot at the dirt in front of him. "Don't move."

He straightened and his face twisted in rage. "What are you doing here, Elle?"

She kept her gun leveled at Jed. "I heard a scream. Thought I'd check it out."

Her casualness would've been amusing if Izzy didn't fear for her life. Was she going to help or not? Izzy rose to her feet and moved away from her attacker.

"This is our take," Jed said. "You leave now, and my boys won't follow and kill you."

Elle tilted her head to the side. "Your boys are indisposed at the moment."

Another woman appeared next to Elle. They were similar, yet different. Both dressed the same, both had dark hair to their shoulders, but where Elle's was wavy, this new woman's was straight. She also had a darker complexion than Elle and stood a couple of inches shorter.

The new woman chuckled. "Yeah, Jed. Your boys ran off. Sans pants." She smiled. "That's French for 'no pants,' in case you didn't know."

Elle cocked a brow. "You took their pants?"

"Sure did."

Elle gave an appreciative nod.

Jed's eyes shot back in the direction of the stagecoach then searched the ground wildly for his gun, which lay a few feet away. He made a desperate move toward it and another shot rang out. A bullet nicked his boot, and he howled in pain. "Goddamn it."

"Aw, c'mon Jed. I barely got you," Elle said. "If you want, I could really make you scream."

He gnashed his teeth. "What do you want? We lifted some silver. I could spare a few pieces."

She frowned. "In exchange for what, exactly?"

"You go on your way and leave me to my woman."

Elle glanced at Izzy. "She certainly is not acting like your woman."

"Please help me," Izzy begged.

"She doesn't sound like your woman either." Elle took a seat on a large rock a few feet away and stretched her legs out. "How about this? You run off and find your boys and leave the woman with me."

"What?"

"I'll let you keep your take. But she stays."

"And if I don't agree to this deal of yours?"

She casually brushed a spot of dirt from her pants. "Then I'll shoot that thing off that's hanging between your legs."

The color drained from his face.

The woman next to Elle grinned. "You think you're that good a shot? That thing's pretty small."

"I'd like to think I am. Might take a few tries though." She opened her revolver and checked the chamber. "I have a few more bullets left."

"I'll hold him down for you. Might be easier."

Jed covered his privates with a hand and cowered, all bravado disappearing when faced with the loss of his beloved manhood.

Elle stood, pulled the hammer back on her gun, and pointed. "Nah. I like a challenge. Jed, might wanna move your hand, unless you wanna lose that too."

Izzy wished she wasn't the prize in this little game of wits, otherwise she'd be enjoying it immensely.

Jed raised one hand in surrender. "All right. I give up. You take her."

Elle uncocked her gun and, with a twirl, slipped it back into place. "I'm glad we came to an agreement. Now step out of the pants."

He hopped around and tugged the trousers over his boots. After a few curses, the pants dropped to the ground and the other woman snatched them away, along with his holster and gun.

Elle waved him off. "Go. Before I change my mind."

"You ain't seen the last of me." He turned to Izzy. "You neither." He mumbled ugly threats as he wandered off.

Izzy expelled her breath. "What a horrible, horrible man."

"You should meet his father," the woman next to Elle said. "Makes Jed look like the angel Gabriel."

Izzy couldn't imagine anyone worse than the beady-eyed animal who almost violated her. She shuddered. "I don't know how to thank you."

Elle undid the rope twisted around Izzy's hands. Her brownish eyes flashed with warmth, and when she smiled, her teeth shone brightly against her tanned face. "You just did."

"Are you marshals?" Izzy asked.

A wry smile touched her lips. "No, ma'am."

Jed's familiarity with these women made Izzy pause. *Oh no. Have I traded one bad situation for another?* "Are you…outlaws?"

After a slight hesitation, Elle said, "Yes, ma'am."

Izzy had trouble finding her voice. When the words came out, they came in a whisper. "Am I safe with you?"

"Yes, ma'am."

Should I believe her?

They held each other's gaze for a few seconds. Elle was attractive, and her masculine attire accentuated her good looks. Izzy's gaze wandered over her face. High cheekbones, full lips, thick lashes surrounding her eyes. Back in Boston, the men would fall all over her. Heat rushed into Izzy's cheeks. *Stop. Staring.* To distract herself, she rubbed at the reddish scrapes around her wrists. "Well, thank you again," she mumbled.

"You should be safe now. We ran them off, so you can go back to your coach." Elle tipped her hat and walked away.

A sudden vision of her upcoming nuptials to an old man she'd never met flashed in Izzy's mind. Without thinking, she shouted, "Take me with you!"

* * *

Elle froze.

Raven shook her head. "We can't take you. Go on back to the coach."

"No! Please, don't leave me here."

Raven narrowed her eyes at Elle, code for, *Don't you dare.* Elle agreed. "Uh, I'm sorry, I don't know your name."

"Isabella Collins. Or just Izzy is fine."

"Or, soon to be Mrs. J.B. Jackson," Raven chimed in.

"Nice to meet you, Miss Collins. I'm Elle Barstow, this is Raven Blackfeather." Elle paused before continuing, "We can't take you with us."

"Why not?"

Elle, not used to being questioned, widened her eyes. "Because."

"Because why?"

"Because we don't have time to mollycoddle you," Raven said.

"You won't have to. Please take me with you."

"We can't," Elle said. "We've got a long ride home. You'll slow us down."

"I won't. I promise I won't. I can help."

Raven's lip curled. "Help? How are *you* gonna help *us*?"

"I can…I can do chores."

"Chores?" Raven scoffed. "We ain't a farm. We're outlaws, and we gotta couple more things to do before we head home."

Elle reached for Izzy's hand and turned it over. She ran a finger over the smooth palm. "These hands have never seen a hard day's work in their life."

Izzy snatched her hand back. "I can learn to work hard. I can wash your clothes, I can cook."

"What exactly can you cook?" Raven asked.

"I…I can bake cakes."

The way Izzy's eyes flashed from green to blue fascinated Elle. *What color are they trying to be?* "I'm sure you're a wonderful baker, Miss Collins, but I'm afraid we're fresh out of flour at the moment."

"I can play the piano and sing."

Raven threw her arms wide. "Well, damn, boss. Maybe that's what we've been missing. A piano player. I bet we could load one in a buckboard, and Miss Collins here can drive along behind us. Every time we stop, she could play us a tune."

Annoyance flashed in Izzy's eyes. "You're making fun of me."

"How astute of you," Raven said.

Elle tried to hide a smile, not wanting to cause any undue embarrassment to Izzy. But the image of this young woman driving a wagon loaded with a grand piano made her chuckle. She coughed to cover up her amusement. "Ma'am—"

"Izzy."

"Yes. Izzy. You'll have to forgive Raven. She can be a bit... sassy. But we can't take you."

Raven glared. "Sassy? Take that back."

"I'm not taking it back. I like it."

They ambled away.

"Please." Izzy's voice wobbled. "I don't want to marry that man. Please help me."

The fear and despair in Izzy's plea were evident. Elle had met J.B. once a few years ago, and he had to be in his sixties, so she couldn't blame Izzy for not wanting him. Izzy was young and beautiful. How awful to be tied to someone so much older. *Wait. Older and rich. Hmm.* Jed may have been on to something. She slowed her stride and considered Izzy's cry for help.

Raven sensed her hesitation. "Uh, boss? A word." She nodded her head and walked far enough away so that Izzy couldn't hear. With arms crossed, she kept her back to Izzy. Elle joined her. "I know what you're thinking."

Elle crossed her arms also. "What am I thinking?"

"You're thinking you wanna help her."

Elle nodded. "Yep. That's what I'm thinking."

Raven stomped her foot. "No. If that woman comes with us, J.B. will have every US Marshal in New Mexico on our tail."

"They'll be chasing after Watkins. Nobody at the stagecoach saw us."

"Watkins will sic them on us. It's not worth the trouble. Let's just finish what we set out to do and go back home to rest up."

Elle leaned closer. "Hear me out."

Raven huffed. "Fine."

"J.B. is a wealthy man who bought himself a mail-order bride. What do you think he'll do when his bride goes missing?"

"Get angry as a badger."

"That, and…he'll post a reward for her. I hate to give Jed his due, but he's right. J.B. might pay handsomely for her return."

This gave Raven pause. Money always made the gang pause. "I didn't think of that."

The thought of Izzy having to submit to an older J.B. made Elle's stomach churn, but a nice, fat reward would certainly go a long way toward looking past that. "Now you get it?"

Raven nodded.

"All right good. Let's keep this between you and me for now. We'll cut the boys in when we collect the reward. I don't need Shorty getting swizzled at the saloon and blabbing."

They walked back toward Izzy, but before Elle spoke, Izzy blurted out, "I can pay you!"

Never one to turn down an easy buck, Elle hooked her thumbs into her gun belt and asked, "How much?"

"I can pay you four hundred dollars."

Four hundred dollars was nothing to sneeze at. Add that to the sizable reward from J.B., and the day was getting better by the minute.

"Where you gettin' four hundred dollars?" Raven asked.

"Here." Izzy reached under her dress and pulled out a wad of greenbacks. She waved it around. "Just take me to your town. Or wherever you live."

Loma Parda was no place for a genteel woman like Isabella Collins. But that wasn't Elle's problem.

Raven nudged her shoulder. "Uh…boss? Another word?"

They once again walked away from Izzy.

"We can double-dip," Raven whispered. "She can pay us, and J.B. can pay us."

"You read my mind," Elle whispered back.

When they turned around, they were all smiles. Elle cleared her throat. "So, all we have to do is take you with us, and you'll pay us four hundred dollars?"

Izzy held up a finger. "And one more thing."

"What?"

"You have to teach me how to be a cowboy."

"I'm sorry?"

"Teach me how to be a cowboy. Or a cowgirl, I don't know. Teach me how to survive out here."

Elle exchanged a look with Raven, who had gone bug-eyed. She suppressed a laugh. "Okay. We can do that." She grabbed the wad of cash from Izzy's hand to inspect it. "This isn't four hundred."

"It's one hundred. I have more sewn into my petticoat."

Elle tucked the cash into her vest pocket.

Izzy tried to grab it back. "Hey!"

"This is a down payment. For the job. You can give me the rest when we get to Loma Parda." She turned on her heel. "Let's get out of here."

Shorty and Willy arrived with their horses.

"We're short a horse," Raven said. "Want me to go round up one of the stage horses?"

"No," Elle said. "I don't want to risk anyone from the coach seeing us. She'll ride with me until we find one."

"Of course she will."

Elle did not appreciate the smirk on Raven's face.

"Oh. I don't know how to ride like that," Izzy said.

"You don't know how to ride like what?" Elle asked.

"Um, I've only ridden sidesaddle, and not that often. I wasn't very good at it."

"Where you from?" Raven asked.

"Boston."

Elle hopped into the saddle and reached a hand down. "I guess that'll be the first part of your education."

A flicker of fear flashed in Izzy's eyes, but only for a moment. She grasped Elle's hand and allowed herself to be pulled into the saddle.

When she was situated, Elle wrapped her arms around Izzy and dug her heels into Blaze's sides.

CHAPTER FOUR

Izzy shifted in the saddle and softly moaned. Her backside was killing her, and her muscles ached. The saddle horn pressing between her legs hurt like the dickens also.

"You okay?" Elle asked.

Her breath tickled Izzy's ear. "I'm a little sore. But I'm fine." They'd been riding for hours. At first, Izzy tried to hold herself away from Elle's body, but eventually exhaustion took hold and she sagged against her. Elle's arms had been around her the entire time to hold her in place, and she had to confess, it wasn't unpleasant. It was comforting.

At one point early in their journey, Izzy had felt relaxed and happy. And excited. Excited to be on this adventure. But soon the pain kicked in. Her thighs were rubbed raw. Pain shot through her lower back. She yearned to get out of the saddle and rest her sore body, but she didn't want to slow them down because they might abandon her. The idea of being left alone in this wild land made her shiver. *I'd never make it.*

"Are you cold?"

Izzy shook her head.

"We'll be stopping soon at a shelter. Can you hang in there a while longer?"

"Of course." She could stick it out. She had no choice. The time might pass quicker with some stimulating conversation, but the group had been quiet most of the time. Shorty would grunt a question in her direction on occasion, asking about life in Boston. He spoke with a Southern drawl and had crow's feet around his eyes. Izzy assumed he was the oldest in the gang. Willy also had a Southern lilt, although not as thick as Shorty's. He had a pleasant face to match a pleasant demeanor and took pride in pointing out natural landmarks. His lack of facial hair gave him a youthful appearance. Izzy had been surprised to learn that he was married with a new baby. Raven rode far ahead to scout, so at least Izzy was spared from her biting wit. And Elle was Elle. Quiet, stoic. The group was an odd mix of personalities.

The landscape changed from grassland to mountain as they climbed into the hills.

About an hour later, they veered off the dirt path and headed deeper into the tree line. Soon, a small wooden structure appeared. It had a porch with two rickety chairs and a door that clung to the doorjamb with the help of one rusty hinge. On a normal day, Izzy would probably turn her nose up at the accommodations, but this tiny shack looked like the best thing she'd ever seen in her life.

Elle dismounted first and reached for Izzy, who tried to be graceful, but because of the pain wracking her body, grace was a long shot. She slipped from the horse and fell into Elle's arms.

Elle steadied her. "Whoa."

"Sorry." Izzy made a valiant attempt to stand, but her shaky legs offered no support. Thank God for Elle's strong arms. She led her over to the porch and deposited her into one of the chairs. One of the most beautiful chairs she'd ever encountered. She loved this chair. She was not leaving this chair. Slumping down, she rested her elbows on her knees. Her head dipped low, and she said a silent prayer of thanks for de-horsing or dismounting, or whatever it was called.

Elle addressed the others. "We'll spend the night here."

"She okay?" Raven asked.

Without lifting her head, Izzy said, "I'm good."

"Until we get a piano, why don't you help us get some wood for a fire?" Raven said. "Consider it a chore."

"Of course." Izzy gritted her teeth. With a quiet moan, she heaved herself up and shuffled off the porch. She nearly stumbled down the steps but righted herself.

Elle, her face filled with concern, was by her side in an instant. "Are you sure you're okay?"

Izzy waved her away. "I can help."

* * *

Elle had to give Izzy her due. She did indeed help, bringing armfuls of wood and kindling and taking the verbal needling that Raven dished out. She could only imagine what kind of pain Izzy was in after hours in the saddle. And the pain would only be worse tomorrow.

As the sun set over the mountains, the group huddled around the fire. Willy stirred a small pot filled with his famous rabbit stew. Shorty had a few potatoes and carrots in his saddlebag and added them to the broth.

Elle gave a low whistle. "Smells great."

Everyone filled their tin bowl and sat on the ground, leaning against their saddles. Everyone except Izzy, who had no bowl and no saddle.

When Elle finished, she refilled the tin and handed it to Izzy, along with her spoon.

Izzy smiled. "Thank you." She shoved a healthy spoonful into her mouth and grimaced.

"You don't like Willy's stew?" Raven asked.

Izzy forced the stew down her throat. "It's delicious."

Elle hid a smile while an ember of admiration ignited in her chest. How Izzy could still look so beautiful after six torturous hours in a saddle was a wonder. The ride had also been torturous for Elle. Holding Izzy and feeling her body pressed against her had sparked all sorts of feelings. Probably because it'd been a while since she'd seen Miriam. She cleared her throat. "All right. Let's talk about what we're gonna do with Izzy."

Izzy sputtered. "What you're going to *do* with me? What does that mean?"

Elle raised a hand. "Don't panic. We're not throwing you to the wolves."

"Yet," Raven added.

Elle scowled at Raven. Poor Izzy had been through enough today. "I mean, you're kind of a fugitive right now. At some point someone's gonna come looking for you." *And I need to protect my investment.*

"What should I do?"

Elle stroked her chin. "Well. We can try and keep you out of sight as much as possible."

"I can change my name."

"That's a good first step," Elle said.

"I can take my mother's name. MacPherson." Izzy's brow knitted. "How about Belle MacPherson?"

Elle bobbed her head. "Okay, good. You should probably ditch that dress. Nobody out here wears anything like that."

"I don't have anything else."

"We'll have to get you something in the next town," Elle said.

The horses in the small corral next to the shack whinnied softly.

Shorty's head shot up. "Somebody's comin'."

They all drew their guns. Raven and the boys jumped behind cover while Elle pulled Izzy to her feet and unceremoniously shoved her into the shack. "Stay here."

This ramshackle house was a known hideout for anyone running from the law, but it was always first come, first serve. On rare occasions things would get testy, and Elle hoped this wasn't one of them.

Four horsemen rode into the clearing, and one man dismounted. He held his hands up. "Don't want no trouble, just seeing if there's room for four more."

Elle recognized Jesse James. His gang usually stayed in Missouri or Texas, and she was surprised to see them this far west. She stepped out of the shadows and made a show of putting her revolver into the holster. "Jesse. What brings you all the way out here?"

"Elle, that you?"

"Yep."

"We got some business in Wellington. Was hoping we could hole up here for the night."

The rest of Elle's gang came and stood by her side.

"Ain't no room," Shorty said. "There's five of us here already."

Jesse took a moment before answering. "I only count four."

Raven nodded her head toward the trees. "Johnnie's out in the woods taking a piss."

Jesse's eyes narrowed briefly before he relaxed. "Fair enough. We'll move on." He tipped his hat before climbing back into the saddle. "Night."

They headed back into the darkness.

After a few moments, the gang gave a group exhale.

"Phew." Elle patted Raven on the back. "Way to think on your feet."

"Well, somebody's gotta have a brain." She whacked Shorty on the arm. "Why'd you say five?"

"Izzy makes five."

"You damn lunkhead. Didn't Elle just tell us we gotta keep her hidden?"

He scratched at the stubble on his chin. "Tarnation. Sorry, boss, don't know where my head's at. Can't even blame it on the firewater 'cause I ain't had none."

"It's okay," Elle called toward the house. "You can come out, Iz."

Izzy peeked around the barely useful door. "Is it clear?"

"Yeah."

They settled back around the fire and split a loaf of bread. Tension filled the air. Shorty kept cocking his head to listen, and Raven's eyes constantly swept the surrounding area.

"See?" Elle said. "We have to be careful." She didn't need to lose her big payday. "We'll take turns on watch tonight."

They all nodded in agreement.

* * *

Izzy huddled numbly by the fire. At least her stomach was full. One less pain to worry about. The moon hung high in the sky, and she wanted to go to sleep.

Elle kicked dirt onto the flames. "Willy, you wanna take first watch?"

"Sure." He checked the chamber on his gun and slung a rifle over his shoulder before disappearing into the woods.

Izzy tried to stand but had no strength left in her limbs. With a groan she collapsed in a heap. Quite an inauspicious beginning to her new life as a cowboy. She tried again. Muscles she didn't even know she had screamed in defiance. A helping hand appeared in front of her face. Elle to the rescue again. With a tired smile, Izzy grabbed Elle's hand and allowed herself to be pulled into an upright position. "Thank you."

"There's a small stream behind the cabin if you want to freshen up before turning in," Elle said.

The thought of rinsing the six hours of dust from her face made her positively giddy. Sleep could wait. "That would be wonderful."

"Follow me."

With a herculean effort, Izzy put one foot in front of the other and made it to the stream without falling flat on her face. A small victory.

Elle removed her hat and splashed water on her face before unbuttoning her vest and shirt. Next came the pants. When completely naked, she waded into the stream and splashed water all over her body.

Izzy sucked in a quick breath and hid her face in embarrassment. It wasn't that she'd never viewed another woman's body before—she had two sisters and a mother—it was that she'd never seen a body like *this* before. Most women that Izzy knew, herself included, were soft and round and full of curves. But Elle was lean, her arms sinewy and legs muscular, her breasts small and tight against her chest. Unable to help herself, she snuck another peek. Would her skin feel soft? Would it be rough? Heat settled in her cheeks. *What in God's name are you thinking?*

Properly self-chastised, she tore her eyes away from Elle and knelt at the water's edge. Some cold water ought to snap her out of it. She dipped her hands into the depth of the creek and splashed at her face.

"It gets deeper over here, if you wanna come in," Elle said.

The idea of fully immersing herself in the creek tempted Izzy. Her legs were sore, not just her muscles but her skin, and she suspected she may have developed blisters from rubbing against the saddle all day. Stockings did not offer much in the way of protection. More than once today she had envied the leather leggings on her companions. But stripping down in front of Elle would prove too embarrassing. "Oh. That's okay. I'm fine here."

"You don't get many chances to bathe on the trail. You should do it while you can."

"I'm good, thanks."

"I have soap. You can wash your face." Elle waded over, and when she hit the shallow water, her naked body was once again on full display. Rivulets of water rolled down the length of her, and the bright moonlight illuminated every detail. "Here."

Izzy grabbed the soap and mumbled, "Thanks." She was struck by the oddly intimate moment of a naked woman handing her a bar of soap.

"I'll take that when you're done."

Izzy jumped with fright and a gurgled sound tore from her throat. The soap slipped to the ground. "Oh my God. You scared me."

"You sure are jumpy." Raven bent over and scooped it up. Soon she was also naked and splashing around.

While they discussed the plan for tomorrow, Izzy took off her shoes and rolled down her stockings. A pained puff of breath fell from her lips. She did have blisters on both of her inner thighs, angry blood-tinged welts. The rawness of the skin made her stomach tighten. *How am I going to get back in the saddle tomorrow?*

"You have saddle sores?"

Izzy jumped for the second time in five minutes.

Elle stood quietly in front of her.

Izzy nodded. "I guess."

"I have some ointment in my saddlebag. You should put some on."

Raven joined them. "Let me see."

More heat rushed into her cheeks. "I'm fine." Izzy pulled the dress down to cover her legs.

"You don't have to be embarrassed," Raven said. "We're all women. You ain't got nothing we don't got."

Elle dropped to her knees. "C'mon, Iz. Let's see."

If anyone had told her that she would one day find herself surrounded by two naked women in the moonlight insisting she hike up her dress, she would've laughed in disbelief. But here she was. With a deep breath, she inched up the dusty fabric.

"Ouch," Raven said. "You better put something on them."

A thoughtful expression settled on Elle's face. "You can't ride in that dress. You need clothes."

"And a horse," Raven said.

"Okay. Here's what we'll do. Willy and I will ride into Jesper City tomorrow and get you clothes and some gear."

"And a horse," Raven added.

Elle nodded. "And a horse."

"How much will that cost?" Izzy asked.

"Don't worry, I'll use some of the money you gave me."

"Don't go to Dugan's Dry Goods," Raven said. "Bill Crawford runs that trading post outside of town. He's got horses and saddles for a decent buck."

"Good idea," Elle said. "You and Shorty will stay with Izzy."

"She needs pants. And chaps," Raven said.

"Oh, pants would be great," Izzy said as she peeled off her dress. *Modesty be damned, might as well try and wash off some of this dirt.* She waded into the creek in just her undergarments. Getting a day off from the saddle would be even greater than pants, but she didn't verbalize that. No need to give them an excuse to leave her behind because she couldn't tough it out.

Right now, they were her only hope for freedom from a loveless marriage.

CHAPTER FIVE

The next morning, Izzy opened her eyes and tried to turn over. Alas, her body did not cooperate. With a pained groan, she pushed herself up to a sitting position. An eerie silence permeated the cabin. *Where is everybody?*

When they'd returned from the creek last night, a fire roared in the hearth, courtesy of Shorty. Raven had cards and tried to teach Izzy poker, but she kept nodding off. Soon the others were yawning, and the decision had been made to call it a night.

The small cabin had two tiny areas separated from the main room by makeshift curtains, and each one contained a few straw beds. Shorty had claimed the room on the right, and Raven, Elle, and Izzy had taken the other. Willy was out in the woods on first watch.

Elle had been kind enough to let Izzy borrow her blanket, and as soon as Izzy had covered herself, she'd fallen instantly asleep.

Now, her body protested any movement, however slight. Sunlight seeped in from the cracks in the roof. *How long did I sleep?* With much whimpering and moaning, she managed to stand erect. She hiked up her dress and checked her sores. They looked better, not nearly as inflamed as last night. Must've been the balm that Elle gave her.

The smell of coffee wafted in the air, and she inhaled deeply. Her stomach gurgled in anticipation, and she pushed aside the threadbare curtain.

Raven straddled a chair at the rickety table and sipped from a tin mug. "Mornin'."

"Morning," Izzy replied. "Do I smell coffee?"

"Yeah. There's some Arbuckles' in the pot by the hearth, along with bread."

"What's Arbuckles'?"

"Coffee. Grab some before Shorty gets back."

"Where is he?"

"Watering the horses."

"Where's Elle?"

"She and Willy left a while ago. They rode into town to get you some supplies."

Izzy stretched her arms above her head and moaned. "What time is it?"

Raven pulled out a pocket watch. "Ten."

"Oh." Izzy bit her lip. "I usually get up much earlier."

"No worries. You had a long day yesterday. How's the legs?"

"Much better. I'll have to thank Elle for that ointment." Izzy hobbled over to the hearth. She feared she'd be hobbling all day because of her sore muscles.

"Elle left you her cup."

Another kindness. "I'll have to thank her for that also." She poured some coffee and cut a slice of bread from the loaf. When she settled down across from Raven, she sighed. "I have a lot to thank her for."

Raven grunted an approval of sorts.

An awkward silence followed, and Izzy fidgeted. "So, how long have you known Elle?"

"We're sisters."

Izzy squinted. Dark hair was the only feature they shared. And didn't they have different last names? Maybe one of them was married.

"Not by blood," Raven clarified. "Well, sorta by blood."

"Oh, okay."

"We were both orphaned around the same time. Ended up at the San Miguel Mission outside of Santa Fe."

"I'm sorry you lost your parents."

"Nothing to be sorry about. My father dropped me off when my mother died. She was Apache, and my father was white. My mother's tribe didn't want me." She shrugged. "Met Elle there. Been like sisters ever since." She held up her hand and pointed to a long scar that ran the length of her palm. "Blood sisters."

Izzy drew her brows together.

"When we were in the orphanage, we became blood sisters. Cut ourselves and shared our blood."

"Ouch. That must've hurt."

Raven chuckled. "Naw. We were tough."

"So you consider yourself sisters, doesn't that make you equals? She seems to be the one in charge."

Raven poured more coffee into her mug. "She is in charge. Number one, she's older than me by a couple years. Number two, she's smarter than me. Always has been. And number three, I tend to be a little hot-blooded, make decisions based on my emotions at that particular moment, but Elle...Elle is always level-headed." She lifted a shoulder. "So it's fine."

Izzy wanted to ask how they both ended up as outlaws but didn't want to pry. "I have two sisters." She rolled her eyes. "They're both perfect, according to my parents."

"What makes them perfect?"

"They both married wealthy men and have two children."

Raven made a comical face. "Good for them."

Izzy giggled. "So, I guess today is my first day as Belle MacPherson." The cabin was stuffy, and she lifted her hair off the back of her neck. When not tressed up, it fell well down her back, and debutante hair had no place on the trail. An idea came to her. "Would you help me with something?"

* * *

Elle and Willy arrived back at the cabin a few hours later.

Elle tied up Blaze and gently tugged on the lead of the old gray gelding she'd purchased for twenty-five dollars. She pulled a couple of burlap sacks from the horse's back.

Raven threw open the front door, and it fell off the hinge with a thud.

Shorty, who lounged nearby cleaning his gun, grunted. "Great. You broke the damn door."

"Now you got something to do besides sitting around on your ass all day. Fix the door," Raven said. "Now. If I can please have everyone's attention."

"What the devil for?" Shorty asked.

Raven cleared her throat. "I'd like to introduce to you, the one and only...Belle MacPherson. Or Mac, for short." She swept her arm toward the door.

A barefoot Izzy, with Raven's hat propped on her head, walked onto the porch. The Boston socialite had disappeared and was replaced by the most fetching cowboy Elle had ever seen. Her blond hair was much shorter, and it fell in waves to the top of her shoulders.

Gone was the fashionable blue dress, tressed-up curls, and fancy shoes. They'd been replaced by ill-fitting trousers, suspenders, and a baggy shirt and vest. Gone was the reticle, and in its place was an empty gun belt.

"Is that my shirt?" Shorty asked.

"Yes." Izzy gave him a toothy grin. "We borrowed it."

Raven pointed to the swayback gray horse. "What in the dog-durned hell is that?"

"It's a horse for Izzy," Elle said.

"Is it dead?" Raven asked.

"Looks like buzzard bait to me," Shorty added.

"That's all he had. Jesse and his boys paid Bill a visit the night before and took off with all the good horse stock." Elle patted the horse's hindquarters. "He'll do."

Izzy approached the horse. "It's a he?"

"Yeah."

"What's his name?"

Elle smiled. *Damn, she looks good in that hat.* The sunshine from the day before had kissed her cheeks and a few freckles had popped out. "Whatever you wanna call him."

"How about Jack?"

"Jack it is. Here. Got you some clothes. They'll fit you better." Elle pulled out a hat and a pair of tan pants, along with a white shirt and black jacket. She removed the contents of the other sack and laid them on the ground.

"I get my own gun?"

"You're an outlaw now, girl," Raven said. "Of course you get a gun."

Izzy picked up the leather belt. The bullet loops were filled with ammo, and a six-shooter rested in the holster. The whole thing felt heavy. "I don't know how to shoot."

"I'll teach you," Elle said. "How are your legs today?"

"Better. But still sore."

"I got you chaps, that should help. We'll take a little ride today so you can get used to them, but we'll wait til tomorrow before heading out. Give 'em time to heal."

"We gotta get going, boss," Raven said.

"Another day won't hurt."

* * *

Dressed in her new getup, Izzy fidgeted. Wearing pants with chaps was…interesting. The chaps were stiff, but they provided a welcome protective barrier for lesson number one: riding astride Jack. She gave herself a passing grade. A part of her wanted to continue to ride with Elle because she felt protected with Elle's arms around her, but that wasn't the cowboy way. And it was more a damsel-in-distress sort of thing. She needed to stand on her own two feet if she was going to survive out here. Or sit on her own horse, as it were. *This is the new me. Time to leave Boston behind.*

The jury was still out on the rest of her outfit. The gun sitting on her hip annoyed her and the high boots pinched her calves, but she liked her new hat. It was similar to Elle's, and Izzy was thankful for the protection from the scorching sun.

Elle and Raven set up some rocks on a ledge about ten feet away. Willy and Shorty idled nearby. Such a big audience made Izzy nervous. She wiped her palms on her trousers.

When the target range was finished, Elle stood by her side. "First things first. This gun will kill someone. Don't point it at anyone you don't wanna kill."

Izzy bit her lip and nodded.

"Yeah. Never point the gun at someone you don't wanna kill," Shorty repeated.

"Especially at us," Raven said. "We're the good guys...sorta."

"Got it," Izzy said.

Elle held the revolver up. "Here's how we load it. Open this gate and pull the hammer back halfway, or two clicks. Now the chamber can spin." She spun it. "No bullets are in there, so we'll slide them in like this." Elle loaded the chamber with six bullets and snapped it shut. "Now it's ready to shoot."

Shorty stepped closer. "Hold it like this." He pulled his gun out, and with one hand lifted it to eye level. His thumb cocked the hammer back. "Then pull the trigger. Easy. Like lickin' butter off a knife."

"I like to hold my gun like this." Willy drew his, held it hip level, and pretended to pull the trigger. "Bang, bang."

Raven scoffed. "That ain't no way to aim a gun."

Izzy whipped her head around to Raven, who drew both of her pistols to shoulder height and yelled, "Bang, bang, bang!"

"You ain't hitting nothin' shootin' like that," Shorty chimed in. "She needs to do it like this."

Izzy got dizzy from all the instructions. Elle rescued her.

"Okay, everybody. Let's put our guns away. Iz, for your first time, maybe hold the butt of the gun in two hands, like this." She cupped the handle with two hands and aimed it toward the targets.

Raven nodded. "Yeah. That's probably best."

Shorty spit his tobacco into the dust. "Yeah. You gonna get kicked back, girl. So two hands to start is better."

Izzy's confidence waned, and she sought out Elle for support.

A tiny smile tugged at Elle's lips, and her eyes offered encouragement. "Ready to try?"

Am I ready? She swallowed and dipped her head. After grasping the gun in both hands, she raised it.

Elle moved behind her and wrapped her arms around Izzy, sending an odd sensation of prickly heat throughout her body. It wasn't unpleasant. It was similar to the heat she'd experienced with Catherine all those weeks ago. But it couldn't be the same, could it? She barely knew Elle, and she adored Catherine.

"Spread your legs apart more." With her foot, Elle nudged Izzy's boot out a few inches. "There. Now look down the barrel and point it at one of the rocks. When you're ready, use your thumb to cock the hammer back and squeeze the trigger, slowly." She stepped away, and Izzy felt a twinge of disappointment. *Stop it. You need to focus.*

"Nice and slow now," Willy said.

"Don't jerk it."

"Hold it steady."

Izzy had no idea who said what anymore while she tried to concentrate on the task at hand. She took a deep breath and squeezed. The loud bang hurt her ears. The gun jerked back, and the vibration shot up her arm. She lowered the revolver. "What did I hit?"

Elle stood with a hand under her chin. "Hmm."

"Nothing," Raven volunteered.

"You might've nicked that tree back there," Willy said.

Izzy's body sagged. The tree was nowhere near the targets. "Darn it."

"It was your first time. Try again," Elle said. "This time, keep your eyes open."

The others snickered.

Izzy glared. "It's hard enough with an audience without you all laughing."

Properly chastised, the gang mumbled their apologies.

"All right, girl," Shorty said. "Remember, you got five beans in the wheel."

"I don't know what that means," Izzy said.

Elle chuckled. "You got five bullets left. Always good to know how many you've got left in the chamber. Now go on."

Izzy repeated her stance and motion and pulled the trigger. This time she was ready for the recoil. A minor victory.

"Gettin' closer, girl," Raven said.

"What'd I hit?"

"That boulder over there." Raven pointed left. Waaay left.

Izzy groaned. "I'm horrible at this."

Shorty scratched at his beard and said, "I reckon you should leave the shootin' to us."

Izzy stomped her foot. "No. I need to learn to do this." She waved the gun around for emphasis, and they all ducked.

"Whoa," Elle said. "Gun pointed down."

She grimaced. "Sorry."

"Why don't you guys find something for dinner?" Elle said. "Give Izzy some space."

The gang shuffled off to the cabin.

Izzy relaxed now that she was alone with Elle. "This is harder than I thought. Is it even possible to hit those targets?"

"Sure."

"Can you?"

Without looking, Elle drew her gun and pulled the trigger. The large rock in the middle exploded. "Big one in the middle?"

Izzy widened her eyes and gaped. "How did you do that?"

"I've had a lot of practice."

They spent the next ten minutes firing away, with limited success.

"Ugh. I'll never get this." Izzy hung her head.

Elle handed her a canteen. "Take a break."

She swigged a mouthful of water and handed the canteen back. "How did you learn to shoot so well?"

"My daddy taught me when I was six."

"Six years old?"

"Yep. After my momma had me, she couldn't have any more children. So, my daddy treated me like the son he always wanted. I was riding bareback at seven, I think."

"I was learning to read and write at that age."

"Out here, your survival depends on protecting yourself and your family. Shooting a gun is the first thing you learn, riding second."

"Things are so different from Boston. People aren't trying to kill you when you walk down the street."

Elle cocked a brow and tilted her head. "They don't call it the Wild West for nothing."

"I better learn to defend myself." Izzy took her stance, stared down the barrel of her Colt revolver, and pulled the trigger. The bullet bounced off the bottom part of the ledge, and she squealed. "I hit something!" She reholstered the gun and did what felt natural—she jumped into Elle's arms. "Woo-hoo!"

Elle caught Izzy because she'd left her no choice. She set her down, and a strained smile played on her lips.

I've embarrassed her. Why did I jump into her arms? "I'm sorry. I'm acting like a dullard."

Elle flicked a finger at the brim on Izzy's hat. She brought her face inches from Izzy's. "You're not a dullard. Good job, cowboy."

Izzy's gaze flitted to Elle's lips. The odd prickly heat she'd experienced earlier came back with a vengeance. Was it excitement from finally hitting something?

"I don't know about you, but I'm hungry," Elle said. "Let's go see what the gang rustled up for dinner."

Yes. It's just excitement. As she followed Elle, Izzy's chest swelled with pride. *I did it. I rode a horse astride, and I shot a gun.*

When they arrived back at the cabin, they found Willy and Raven fussing over dinner at the fire.

"That smells great," Izzy said. "What is it?"

"We got some beans and tamales," Shorty said.

"I thought we all deserved a treat," Elle said. "Bought them at the trading post this morning."

Willy held up a bottle of beer. "They had this too."

Raven held out a cup. "Pour me some of that, Will."

Willy filled each person's cup with a shot of beer.

Shorty filled his plate with a big pile of beans and a few tamales.

"Save some for us," Raven groused.

"Shut your pan. I'm hungry tonight."

One by one, they took their turn at the pot and settled in for some good chow.

Izzy took a bite from the doughy roll. She widened her eyes. "This is good. My compliments to our chefs." She took her new tin cup and toasted Willy and Raven.

"Thank you, Miss Mac." Willy smiled.

Raven drove her shoulder into his. "It's just Mac. Miss Mac don't sound like someone who runs with outlaws."

"True. Sorry. Thanks, Mac."

"You're welcome." Izzy held up the rolled dough. "What's this called again?"

"It's a damn tamale," Raven said in a lighthearted manner.

"We don't have these back in Boston."

Raven feigned disbelief. "What? Shame you ain't got no culture back there. We're loaded with culture here. Our culinary delights are second to none. Besides tamales, we got rabbit stew, we got snake stew, we got lizard stew. Why I bet Willy here could make a stew outta rocks from a creek bed. Ain't that right, Willy?"

Willy grinned. "Sure can."

Izzy laughed.

They fell silent as they ate. Appreciative humming rolled around the campfire.

Elle patted her belly. "That was great. Thanks for cooking."

"Who's cleaning up?" Raven asked.

Izzy, eager to contribute, raised a hand. "Me." When everyone finished, she gathered up the plates and walked down to the creek. She relived her day while she washed the dishes. It had been a good one. She wasn't fond of the gun, but maybe there wouldn't be a need to use it. The pants and chaps were comfortable, and her new hat kept the sun off her face.

When she arrived back at the campfire, Elle was stretched out with her legs crossed and hat brim pulled over her eyes. Raven poked at the fire, and Willy whittled away with his knife. Shorty stared into the flames. Izzy plopped down and glanced around expectantly. Coffee and lively conversation usually followed dinner in Boston. Mostly it was she and her father butting heads over some trivial matter, while her mother clucked her tongue and said, "Oh, Izzy."

This group was quiet. Too quiet. "You know, this isn't the first time I've worn pants."

Willy put his knife down and smiled.

"I feel a story coming on," Raven said.

"When I was younger—"

"How young?" Shorty asked.

"About seven or eight, I guess. Anyway. We would go out to the country—"

"You mean, like Missouri or Kentucky?" Raven asked.

Raven was being her sassy self, and Izzy was fine with it. "No. I mean, go outside of Boston to visit my father's cousins. They had a pond in the back of their house filled with frogs and salamanders. I used to sneak into my brother's room and steal a pair of pants. I would roll them up and wade into that pond to catch frogs."

"Why didn't you just wear your dress?" Raven asked.

"Where's the fun in that?"

Raven dipped her head. "Less work. You can hike up your skirt, instead of rolling up two pant legs."

"No. If I wore my dress it would've gotten wet and dirty. Instead, my brother's pants got wet and dirty."

"Was that fair to your brother, to ruin his pants?" Raven asked.

"I was eight. I didn't care."

"If I had a sister who did that, I'd throw her into the pond," Shorty said.

"I didn't have a sister," Willy chimed in. "But if I did and she got my pants dirty, I'd toss her too."

After they shared a laugh, Izzy asked, "Shorty, how did you meet Elle?"

He loosened the bandana around his neck and revealed an ugly scar on his throat. "She saved me from a hanging."

"Oh my God. What happened?"

He gave her a sheepish grin. "Back in the day I spent most of my time loaded for bear."

Izzy puckered her forehead. "What's loaded for bear?"

"You know, roostered."

"What does that mean?"

"Pickled, fuddled—"

"Drunk. Jesus," Raven grumbled. "Just say drunk like the rest of us."

Shorty nodded. "Drunk. Happy? Where in Sam Hill was I?"

"You spent your days loaded for bear." Izzy enjoyed Shorty's colorful lingo.

"Right. Back in the day I tended to drink a bit too much. And gambled a bit too much. Owed money to some bad jackaroos. These fellas tracked me down, strung me up. Elle came along and scared 'em off. Cut me down, and the rest is history, so they say."

Izzy nudged Elle's boot with her own. "You're a hero. You saved his life."

Elle remained motionless.

"Are you asleep?"

Elle lifted the brim of her hat. "How can I sleep with all the talking going on?"

"You're a hero," Izzy said.

"I'm no hero. I just don't like hangings." And with that, she pulled the brim back down.

Izzy huffed. Elle was no fun. At least not at the moment. "What about you, Willy? Where are you from? How did you become a part of the gang?"

"My family were slaves on a cotton farm south of Richmond, Virginia. When I was eleven, some Union soldiers robbed the plantation and told us all to git, so we up and left. Headed west to find a better life. Daddy got killed in Kansas by a couple of bushwhackers two months later."

"What's a bushwhacker?" Izzy asked.

"You mean *who* are bushwhackers," Shorty said. He held up a pouch. "Who wants a quirly?"

"Roll me one," Willy said.

Shorty poured the contents of the pouch into a piece of corn husk. When finished, he handed one to Willy, who stuck a stick in the fire and used it to light the newly rolled smoke. Raven stuck her hand out, and he rolled her one too.

Izzy hugged her knees to her chest. "So, who are bushwhackers?"

Raven took a puff from the homemade cigarette and handed it to Izzy. *Why not?* She inhaled and promptly choked. *Ew. Dreadful.* With a screwed-up face, she handed it back to Raven.

Shorty continued, "Bushwhackers were a bunch of lawless cutthroats pretending to be law-abiding citizens. Did most of their damage in Missouri and Kansas during the war. Feller by the name of William Quantrill once led a raid in Lawrence, Kansas in 1863. Almost two hundred men ended up in the boot yard."

"Boot yard?" Izzy asked.

Shorty nodded. "Bushwhackers were as savage as a meat axe."

"A boot yard is a cemetery," Elle said. "Shorty's got a language all his own sometimes."

A shiver ran through Izzy, accompanied by a pang of homesickness. Boston was heaven compared to this place. "They sound horrible."

Willy nodded. "Yes, ma'am."

Izzy hoped she'd never run into a bushwhacker. "What happened after your father died?"

"It was me and Momma for quite a while, then she met someone and got married again. I headed out on my own 'cause I didn't get along with the man she married. Ended up in Loma a few years back, and Elle took me under her wing."

The fireside chat continued for another half hour. Finally, Elle declared it bedtime and gave first watch to Shorty.

Izzy spread her new bedroll on the ground and climbed under the blanket. Tomorrow would be a new day, her first as a real cowboy. The horror stories from the earlier conversations gave her pause about her situation.

Can I survive out here? Will I make it?

She gazed up at the multitude of stars twinkling in the sky. *Of course I will. This is the new me.*

CHAPTER SIX

Elle brought her spyglass up and scouted the area. No movement. No dust clouds. She held out hope for one last heist before heading home. This trip hadn't been as profitable as expected, and it affected her mood. She hated to disappoint Rose, although the trip wasn't a total bust because she still held one chip: Izzy. But that might take a while. A pang of uncertainty shot through her brain at the thought of handing Izzy over to J.B. *Stop. She's a payday and nothing else.*

Somebody lay down next to her. "What do we got, boss?"

Elle jerked her head around, half expecting to see Raven, but instead found Izzy chomping on a long piece of straw grass and staring over the horizon.

With an animated expression and sparkling eyes, Izzy asked, "Is there a coach coming?"

"Not yet." Elle brought the glass back to her eye. "You know, you're staying here if a coach comes by."

"What? No. I'm ready."

"Izzy. You are not ready."

"Izzy may not be ready, but Mac is."

"Who's Mac?" Elle asked.

"Me. I'm Mac. Remember? Belle MacPherson?"

Elle smirked. "I know. I'm teasing you."

Izzy gave her a playful punch in the arm. "Mac sounds better than Belle. Raven and I made a whole backstory for her. Or me."

"Oh?" She arched a brow. "Do tell."

"I'm a bank robber from Chicago. Things got too hot for me there, so I have to lay low for a while. Met you on the trail and joined up."

Elle shook her head and returned to scouting. "You'll stay here and guard the camp."

"Why? I can ride. I can shoot. I can help."

Elle dipped her chin. "You can shoot?"

"I hit that wall."

"Once. When you tripped."

"So? I can help. Don't mollycuddle me!"

"It's mollycoddle. And my orders. You stay put."

In a huff, Izzy rose to her feet and stomped off.

Elle stared after her. She gave Izzy her due. She'd adapted quite well to life on the trail these past two weeks. Would Elle want Izzy at her side during a shootout? Hell, no. She still couldn't hit the side of a barn. But, she was an agreeable companion, and her personality changed the dynamics of the group. Dinners around the fire used to be boring affairs, mostly small talk or silence. Now? Why, dinner was downright lively. Izzy always shared a funny story from her life back in Boston, and most times she even managed to pull a chortle from Shorty. No small feat.

But Izzy would stay at camp today. She was worth too much to risk losing. Elle had plans for that money. She hoped to buy a parcel of land outside of Loma Parda and build her own ranch someday.

A far-off rumble caught her attention. The telltale cloud of dust rising on the horizon lifted her mood. "We got company," she yelled back to the gang.

* * *

The gang had headed down to the trail about fifteen minutes before, leaving Izzy behind.

She grabbed Elle's spyglass. At least she could relieve her boredom by watching the action below.

Nearby, Jack grazed on a patch of long grass, slowly chomping back and forth.

"I should be with them. I'm a damn cowboy now, right, Jack?"

He turned his big gray rump toward her and searched for more food.

Crunching noises from the other direction startled her, and she shot to her feet.

A man with a drawn gun stood in the middle of camp. He was tall and thick, with a greasy dark mustache and stubble on his chin. His beady eyes locked on her. "Howdy."

Her gut twisted in fear. "What do you want?"

He slid the gun into his holster and raised both hands. He gave her a mirthless smile. "Was hungry. Just wonderin' if you have any food to spare."

She shot a glance in the direction of the others. How long did it take to rob a coach? She placed a hand on the butt of her gun and tried to act tough. "We don't. So leave."

His took note of where her hand rested. "I don't want no trouble. Surely a good woman like yourself would find it in her heart to be a little…charitable."

"You need to leave."

"I'm gonna poke around. Maybe you got some here and you forgot." He bent over and fished through Shorty's bag. With a whistle, he pulled out a wad of cash. "Not food. But just as good." He shoved the money in his pocket.

Izzy's heart pounded in her chest. This was bad. This was very bad. She slowly pulled her gun out and with a shaky hand aimed it in his direction. "Put that back. Now." She silently cursed because her voice shook. Maybe he didn't hear it.

He slowly stood. "You ain't gonna shoot me."

She nodded. "I will. I will shoot you if you don't put that back and get the hell out of here."

He chuckled and walked closer. "I don't think you're gonna shoot me."

He kept coming closer, and Izzy took a step back.

"You're scared, girly. And you ain't got the guts to shoot me. I can see it in your eyes."

Izzy's arms shook and sweat dribbled down her back. *Do it. Shoot him.* But her trigger finger didn't cooperate.

He was close now. So close, the muzzle of the gun pressed against his chest. His sour, putrid odor made her lip curl.

"Go ahead. Pull that trigger, girl." When she didn't, he laughed and slapped the gun out of her hand. "Just like I said. No guts." He began rummaging through Elle's belongings.

I have to stop him. Without thinking it through, she jumped onto his back. He stood while she locked her arms around his neck and squeezed. He tossed her to the side like an empty sack and she landed with a thud. With a groan, she pushed herself back up and attacked him again, only this time the end came quickly. He punched her in the jaw, and everything went dark.

* * *

Back down on the trail, the gang had the coach pull to a stop. Elle sidled up to the front with her gun drawn.

The driver wiped the sweat from his brow. "Hey, Elle."

Elle slouched in the saddle and slid her gun back into the holster. "Andy." There'd be no take today. Andy ran liquor for Rose.

"Andy!" Shorty shouted.

They all chatted for a few minutes before passing a bottle around.

Elle glanced in the direction of camp. An uneasy feeling settled in her gut. "Hey, I'm gonna go check on Iz. You guys can stay and talk for a bit if you want."

When she got back to camp, Elle dismounted and dropped the reins. "Izzy?" The skin on the back of her neck prickled. *Something's wrong.* Before she drew her gun, that *something* hit her in the temple. Bright lights flashed behind her eyes as she fell to her hands and knees. She shook her head and scooted away from her attacker, but she wasn't quick enough. A burly man charged and knocked her down. When he hovered over her, she swept a leg out and sent him to the ground. He landed on his ass and grunted, then grabbed her ankle and pulled her close. She kicked out with the free leg and booted him in the nose.

Blood spewed forth and he yelped. "Bitch!" He rose and pointed his gun at her heart.

From her position, it was impossible to draw and shoot. She was trapped. *Is this how it ends?*

The hammer clicked back, and Elle waited for the explosion of pain. And there was an explosion. Followed by another and another. But it didn't come from his gun. A red stain spread across his shirt, and he pitched forward into the dirt.

Behind him stood Izzy, with wild eyes and a stunned expression on her face. Her arm sagged and the gun dropped from her hand before she collapsed onto the ground.

Elle drew a thankful breath for still being alive before getting up and rushing over to her. She placed a hand on Izzy's shoulder. "You okay?"

Izzy rocked back and forth on her knees. Her wide eyes stared at the unmoving body in the grass. "I just killed someone, I just killed someone."

"It's okay. You had no choice."

The rest of the gang thundered into the clearing.

"We heard gunshots," Raven said as she jumped from the saddle. When she saw the body, she froze. "Shit. What happened?"

"Izzy saved my life," Elle said. She gently tugged Izzy to her feet and led her away from the bloody scene.

* * *

A few hours later, the gang cozied up to the fire and feasted on a nice potato and onion stew, courtesy of Andy. The whisky was long gone and the mood light because they'd be home soon.

Raven elbowed Elle and nodded in Izzy's direction. Izzy had been morose all evening, and now she just stared into the fire. "Talk to her," Raven whispered.

Elle covered her mouth with her hand. "What am I supposed to say?"

"I don't know."

Shorty pulled Raven into their conversation while Izzy stood and slipped away.

Everyone quieted, and they stared after her.

"Go talk to her," Raven said.

"Jesus. Okay."

Elle found Izzy huddled against a large rock and sank down close to her. "You okay?"

Izzy shrugged.

Elle gently turned Izzy's chin. An ugly bruise glowed in the fading sunlight. "How's your jaw?"

"It hurts. How's your head?"

Elle fingered the spot on her temple. The bleeding had stopped, and a hard scab covered the area. "It hurts." She tried to lighten things up. "We look like we were in a bar fight."

Izzy shrugged again.

Well, that didn't work. Izzy had led a sheltered life, and now she found herself in a lawless, harsh land. Some sympathy was in order. Elle cleared her throat. "It's never easy taking a life. But you had no choice."

"What if he had a family? What if he had children?"

"We don't know if he did or didn't. But what we do know is that he was gonna kill me. And you." Elle paused. "You saved my life, and yours."

Izzy tugged her knees in tight and buried her face in her arms.

Elle had managed to make it this far in life by remaining detached, by keeping emotions in check, and now because of that, she felt ill-equipped to handle Izzy. She didn't know what to do or say to make her feel better.

In an effort to provide some form of comfort, she gently nudged Izzy with her shoulder. "Listen. It's hard living out here. It's dangerous. People die. From bullets, from fever, from starvation—" Suddenly Izzy was in her arms, with silent tears running down her face. Elle froze and her chest constricted. *What do I do with this?* Her arms had a mind of their own, or perhaps it was instinct, and they wrapped around Izzy's body.

After a few minutes, Izzy pulled away and wiped at her face. "I'm sorry. That wasn't very cowboy-like."

Elle's equilibrium returning coincided with getting her personal space back. Offering comfort was awkward. And strange. And why should she care about offering comfort anyway? Izzy was money in her pocket. Nothing more.

"I can't believe I killed someone. I took his life." The unshed tears in Izzy's eyes made them bluer than normal.

"That man had murder in his heart. I'm not saying he had it coming, but he was no saint. And he would have killed all of us if he had the chance."

"Still. It doesn't seem right." Izzy stewed in silence for a few moments. "Have you killed anyone?"

"Sure."

"How many?"

She raised one shoulder and let it drop. "I don't know. Never counted."

"That many?"

"No. I mean, I don't know." Elle shifted her position. "I don't like killing anyone. I try not to. But if it's me or someone else, I'm damn sure defending myself."

"I guess I have to toughen up. I won't survive otherwise."

"First one is never easy. Took me a while to get over mine."

"How old were you?"

Elle furrowed her brow. "Uh, sixteen I think."

"Sixteen? That's so young."

"Yeah. He deserved it. At least that's what I told myself. But it didn't matter if he deserved it or not. I still felt horrible." It had been a while since Elle thought about Frank Businsky, the man who killed her mother. The memory had faded due to time and other battles, but not before torturing her with many sleepless nights and internal discussions about revenge and justice. With a sigh, she reached into her vest pocket and pulled out a flask. "Here." She winked. "Load your bear."

Without missing a beat, Izzy threw down a sizable gulp. She immediately spit it out and sputtered. "That's awful."

A smile tickled Elle's lips. "Don't tell Shorty that, it's his home-brewed hooch."

"Home brew? Where did he brew it, in his dirty socks?"

Elle gave a hearty laugh, and soon Izzy joined her.

A series of short howls and yips carried on the wind.

Izzy jumped and grabbed Elle's arm. "What is that?"

"Coyotes."

"Are we safe?" Her death grip tightened.

"They're a ways off. We're okay." She gently pried Izzy's fingers loose. "You can—"

"Sorry." Izzy let go. "I definitely need to toughen up." Taking a deep breath, she tried another swig. She managed to keep this one down, but her face twisted. "That's some bad hooch."

Elle laughed again. "Atta girl. You're brave. But you don't have to drink it."

"Mac would drink it."

"Mac would certainly drink it."

"I gotta be more like Mac."

Elle took the flask from Izzy and raised it. "To Mac." She gulped down a mouthful and grimaced before handing the hooch back to Izzy.

"To Mac." Izzy guzzled. And guzzled. And guzzled.

"Whoa, girl. Take it easy. I ain't carrying you back to camp."

Izzy wiped her sleeve across her mouth. "Mac doesn't need to be carried. She needs to load the damn bear."

A half an hour later, Elle dragged a sozzled Izzy back to camp. Raven and Shorty snored away in their bedrolls.

Willy sat nearby with a rifle in his lap. With wide eyes, he asked, "She okay?"

"She'll be fine," Elle said. "She guzzled Shorty's hooch. Drank the whole flask."

He whistled. "That'll do it."

Elle lowered Izzy down onto the ground. She tucked a rolled-up shirt under her head and tugged a blanket over her body. Izzy's eyelashes fluttered against her cheek, and she mumbled something incoherent. Elle brushed a strand of hair from her face, a face no longer pale but tanned a golden brown. She resisted the urge to run a finger down her cheek. *Stop it.* "I need to see Miriam," she muttered.

"What was that?" Willy asked.

"Nothing." After spreading out her bedroll, she lay down. She was acutely aware of Izzy lying next to her. And no amount of flopping around banished the young Bostonian from her mind. *I really need to see Miriam.*

CHAPTER SEVEN

Izzy awoke to birdsong and back pain. *Will I ever get used to sleeping on the hard ground?*

It'd been a couple of days since the shooting, and the painful memory had started to fade. *I hope I won't have to use my gun again.* However, if she or one of her new friends faced a life-or-death situation, she'd have to pull the trigger. A distressing thought, but a necessary evil—according to Elle.

Shorty had a small fire going, and the smell of coffee and biscuits filled the air. Izzy inhaled and her belly rumbled.

The rest of the gang stirred, and Elle, who'd been on last watch, strode into camp. Shorty handed her a cup and she nodded her thanks. "I have to go into Preston this morning and take care of some stuff for Rose."

Willy stretched and yawned. "Need company?"

"No. You all hang back. I shouldn't be long."

"Bring back some bacon," Shorty said. "Getting tired of biscuits and cheese."

"I can do that. Anything else we need?"

Izzy sat cross-legged and rested her chin in her hand. She daydreamed about the big breakfasts back home. The table would be laden with eggs and fruit and bacon and all sorts of breads. Her father would sit at the head of the table reading the newspaper, and when he finished with a section, she'd snatch it, along with a second helping of fried potatoes, and read and eat until her belly was full.

"Iz?"

Elle's voice pulled her back into the present. "Huh?"

"Do you need anything?"

"I would love some eggs." A girl could dream, right?

Elle gave a slight nod. "I'll see what I can do. When I get back, we'll head out and try and get a few miles in before sundown."

Izzy perked up. Eggs for breakfast would make her day. Thinking about breakfasts at home brought back other memories. "I wonder how my Red Stockings are doing," she mused.

"What's a red stocking? Is that some kinda sock?" Raven asked.

Izzy gave them her best I-can't-believe-it face. "It's a baseball team. From Boston."

Raven gave her a blank stare.

"Haven't you heard of baseball?"

"I've heard of it. Don't know much about it. Isn't it a game for you fancy city people back East?"

"No. It's not just for fancy city people." Izzy puffed out her chest. "It's considered America's favorite pastime."

"Out here our favorite pastime is not getting shot," Raven said.

Willy snickered and Izzy made a face. "Shorty, you know baseball, right?"

"Yeah. Saw a few boys play during the war. They'd mess around and make up their own rules. I never partook."

Izzy turned her eyes to Elle.

"Don't look at me. I don't know much about it either."

Izzy raised her brows. How could they be so ignorant when it came to America's favorite pastime? A pang of homesickness engulfed her. There'd be no more family picnics at South End Grounds, the home field of her beloved Red Stockings. *Will I ever see them play again?* "Last year we attended almost every game." Izzy snapped her fingers. "Wait." She hopped up and searched through her saddlebag. "Aha!" When she found her reticule, she held it aloft. "Guess what's in here?"

"I remember that bag," Willy said. "You gotta rock in there or something?"

"Not a rock." Izzy pulled out a ball. "This is an official Spalding ball. It's what they use in a baseball game."

"How did you come by it?" Shorty asked.

"We were sitting in the grandstands, and a player hit a ball right at my father. He caught it and gave it to me."

"Why they hitting balls into the grandstand?" Willy asked. "That sounds dangerous."

"It was a foul ball, like out of bounds. They don't mean to. It just happens sometimes."

"Give it here," Raven said. Izzy handed her the ball and Raven tossed it gently up and down. "Not as heavy as I thought. But I guess it's heavy enough to break Bobby's nose." She guffawed.

Willy chortled. "It sure did break his nose."

It was time to educate this group about the joys of baseball. "Who wants a baseball lesson?" Izzy asked. Nobody answered. *No matter. Their interest is simply not piqued yet.* "There are six teams in the league. Boston, Hartford, Cincinnati, Chicago, St. Louis, and Louisville."

The bored expressions continued, but Izzy refused to be discouraged.

She continued, "When you play baseball, you have a bat, and someone throws the ball at you, and you try and hit it."

"That sounds dumb," Raven said.

Izzy made a face. "It's not dumb. When you hit the ball, you start running the bases. If you touch all four bases, you've scored a run."

Raven pointed. "That's a lot of running in this heat. Which is dumb."

Izzy held back a sharp retort. "The players on the field have to catch the ball in the air or throw it to a base before a runner gets there to get an out. After three outs, they get to come in and bat."

"That's dumb too." Raven was being purposefully churlish.

"Stop saying dumb," Izzy snapped.

Elle stood and pulled on her hat. "All right. I'm gonna head out. Try not to dumb each other to death."

A half an hour later, and after a quick overview of the rules, Shorty stood next to a makeshift home base made from a burlap bag folded in a square. One edge pointed forward and its opposite edge pointed back toward a horse blanket that hung over a pile of rocks. The blanket would act as a backstop, since no one wanted to stand behind a batter wielding a bat that Willy had quick-whittled from a fallen piñon pine branch. The bat was built to Izzy's specifications, of course. It wasn't smooth like the ones used back home, but it would serve its purpose. A strip of burlap was wrapped around the handle to make it easier to hold.

Shorty gripped the bat in both hands and swung.

"Your swing needs to be more level," Izzy said. "Let me show you." She grabbed the bat and swung it back and forth.

"All right. Gimme it. I can do it." He snatched the bat back.

Raven stood about forty-five feet away, tossing the ball up and down. Small twigs outlined her pitcher's box. "You ready?"

Shorty nodded. "Go ahead. Toss me the ball."

"Wait," Izzy said. "Shorty, you get to tell Raven where to pitch. Like high or low. Low is from your knees to your belt. And high is from your belt to your shoulder. Got it?"

"Well, that's dumb," Raven said. "I should be able to pitch where I want to."

Izzy pointed at her stubborn pitcher. "It's the rule," she said with tone before jogging to the field beyond the pitcher's box.

Shorty took another practice swing before saying, "Okay. I'll take a low one."

Raven wound up and threw an overhand pitch with blistering speed. Right at his head.

He collapsed to the ground and grumbled. After dusting himself off, he threw the ball back. "That was not low. That was at my head. Can't you see my damn head?"

"It's the only thing I see. It's overly large. Probably why I threw at it."

Izzy cupped her hands around her mouth. "Raven. You can't throw overhand. That's not legal. You have to throw underhanded."

"Says who?"

"Says the National League of Professional Baseball, that's who. It's the rule."

"Another rule? Ppfft. I'm making my own rules." She gestured at Shorty. "You ready?"

"Go."

She threw another fastball, this time over home base, and Shorty swung so late the ball had time to hit the backstop and dribble past his feet before he completed his rotation.

"I can barely see the damn ball," Shorty said.

Izzy hustled in from the outfield. "Let me pitch."

"Yeah, let Izzy pitch," Shorty said. "'Cause you ain't pitching right."

"I'm pitching fine." Raven handed the ball to Izzy. "Not my fault you ain't coordinated," she said over her shoulder on her way to left field.

Izzy stood in the pitcher's box, hiked up her trousers, and pulled her hat low across her brows. She'd seen Tommy Bond do the same thing before throwing a perfect strike. Wrapping her fingers around the ball, she closed her eyes and watched Tommy's pitching motion in her head.

"Jesus. What are you doing? Throw it," Raven yelled.

She scowled back. "I'm picturing Tommy Bond in my head."

"Who the hell is that?"

"The pitcher for the Red Stockings. He's my favorite player. He had forty wins last year."

"Blah blah blah. Throw the damn ball."

She spread her arms out wide. "Why are you so impatient?"

Raven grumbled something too soft to hear.

Izzy turned back to Shorty. "Okay. Ready?" Izzy tossed the ball underhanded, and Shorty squared up the bat. The ball scooted along the dirt past second baseman Willy, who made a valiant attempt to field it but ended up kicking the ball farther away. Izzy pointed toward the flat rock that acted as first base. "Run, Shorty!"

"Oh, right." Shorty began a slow jog up the baseline, bat in hand.

"You have to drop the bat."

He dropped the bat and continued along the base path, picking up a hitch in his giddyup before reaching the rock.

Izzy beamed. "You hit a single."

He lifted his chin. "Damn right I did." He rubbed at his thigh. "Think I hurt my leg running so fast."

Willy cackled. "Fast? I've seen turtles move quicker."

And so it went on for the next hour, everyone taking their turn at pitching and hitting and fielding and running. A fair amount of good-natured ribbing filled the air, along with hoots of laughter.

During a water break, Elle galloped into camp.

"You missed all the fun," Izzy said.

After dismounting, Elle stood with her mouth agape and hands on her hips.

Izzy glanced at her teammates. Willy had a bloody bandana wrapped around his elbow, Shorty had a piece of rawhide tied around his thigh, and Raven sported a bloody lip.

After Elle assessed the damage, she asked, "What the hell happened? We get ambushed?"

"Nope," Shorty replied. "We've been playing baseball."

"We'd probably be less bloodied if we *were* ambushed," Raven said.

The situation begged for a further explanation, so Izzy broke it down for Elle. "Well, Shorty strained his leg running to first base—"

"Calling that running is a bit generous," Raven said.

"—and Willy dove after a ground ball and scraped his elbow."

Willy nodded. "And missed. Darn thing scooted right past me."

"And Raven fouled a ball off into her own face."

Raven pointed at Shorty. "He threw a peculiar pitch. Felt a little retaliatory if you ask me."

"Nobody's asking," Shorty groused. "And that was my curveball."

Elle gave Izzy a questioning look. "You seem unharmed."

She smiled. "I guess I play baseball better than they do."

"Elle, pick up the bat," Willy said. "Give it a try."

"Yes. Give it a try." Izzy handed her the bat.

"I don't know. It seems a bit…violent."

"No, it's not. Hold it like this." She arranged Elle's fingers on the bat. "And you swing at the ball. I'll pitch to you."

"Let me pitch." Raven grabbed the ball and headed to the pitcher's box. "Boss, by the by, I'm gonna give up outlawing and join the Chicago White Stockings. 'Cause nobody can hit my pitches!" She set up and waved her arm. "Get outta the way, Iz."

Izzy groaned. "Don't hurt her."

"I won't hurt her. She ain't even gonna see the ball. Ready, boss?"

Elle took a deep breath. "I guess."

Izzy raised a hand. "Hold on." She helped Elle set up in the batter's box. The role reversal finally made her feel competent at something. "You stand like this." She positioned Elle's slim hips just right. "Hold the bat up like so." She lifted Elle's hands.

"C'mon, Tommy Bond. Set her loose already," Raven said.

"Yeah. Let her go," Shorty said.

Izzy huffed.

"Who's Tommy Bond?" Elle asked.

"Never mind." She patted Elle on the back. "Good luck."

Elle frowned. "I need luck?"

"You might need some luck." Izzy jogged onto the field along with Willy and Shorty.

"Here it comes." Raven cocked her arm back and delivered the ball to the plate.

Elle swung the bat and made perfect contact. The ball sailed high in the air and way over everyone's head.

They all gaped and stared at the disappearing baseball.

"How in tarnation did you hit it that far?" Shorty asked.

Elle drew her shoulders up. "Luck?"

Izzy clapped, feeling ridiculously proud of her pupil. "Wonderful."

Raven shoulders sagged. "Guess I'll stick to outlawing."

Later, Izzy lay on her back, wide awake. After a few hours in the saddle, they'd made camp under a stand of pine trees. Raven had first watch, and Shorty and Willy slept on the other side of the dying embers of the fire.

Elle lay next to her, and with a soft groan turned toward Izzy.

"Are you awake?" Izzy whispered.

Elle's eyes slowly opened. "I am now."

In the dark, Elle's eyes still held some light. The small flecks of gold around her pupils glittered. Izzy thought them beautiful. "Sorry. I can't sleep."

Elle raised herself up on her elbow. "Something bothering you?"

"No. It's just that today was so much fun. I keep thinking about it because it reminded me of home. My cousins and I used to play baseball, until my father would yell at me to come inside because"—she lowered her voice—"'young women shouldn't be outside playing sports. It's unseemly.' And, 'nobody wants to marry a woman whose face is browned by the sun.'"

"Good thing he can't see you now," Elle said.

"Why?"

"Because your face is tan. And you have a few freckles."

Izzy inhaled and her hand flew to her face. She had no idea. Mirrors didn't exist on the trail. "I have freckles?"

Elle nodded. "A few. Not a lot. But a few."

"Oh, God. Do I look awful?"

"No. Not at all."

Something flashed in Elle's eyes, some look Izzy couldn't decipher. It wasn't disgust, like the look her father would give her. It was something else. Something that made her feel warm. And nervous. Not a bad nervous. More like a good nervous, if such a thing existed. Maybe a change of subject was in order. "I can't believe you hit the ball that far today."

"I think I got lucky."

"Oh, I don't know." Izzy lowered her brows. "You had a good teacher."

Elle chuckled and the warmth inside Izzy grew. She didn't quite understand the warmth. *I like making her laugh, that's all. She doesn't laugh enough.* There. A simple explanation.

"You should try and get some sleep," Elle said. "We have a long day tomorrow." She turned over and pulled the blanket over her shoulders.

Izzy did the same, but now instead of baseball, her thoughts centered around warm, brown eyes with gold flecks.

CHAPTER EIGHT

Izzy rode behind Elle because she liked to watch her. Elle exuded confidence, with her strong posture and grace in the saddle. She was truly one with Blaze, and Izzy found it hard to tear her eyes away.

Elle turned and smiled, pointing to the right. "That's our view."

Izzy turned and took it in. Majestic snow-capped mountains shimmered in the distance. The afternoon sun cast purplish shadows down the sides, and the peaks reached into the clouds. "You mean our view every day?"

"Yep. The Sangre De Cristo mountains."

Everything out West was so big. So vast. So unspoiled and wild compared to Boston. The air smelled crisper, the sky appeared bluer, the clouds whiter.

On the train to Colorado, Izzy had marveled at the miles upon miles of open plains. And now she marveled at a different landscape, one more varied, with mountains, hills, creeks, and cliffs. No multistory brick buildings jutted above the ground, no smokestacks belched black grit into the sky.

With the mountains on one side and the lazy Mora River on the other, Izzy was in a visual paradise. Excitement pulsed through her body. She couldn't wait to see Loma Parda, her new home for the foreseeable future. She envisioned herself walking to the general store every day, getting the newspaper, maybe *The Atlantic Monthly* or something similar. Probably something similar, it was too far to get *The Atlantic* here. Maybe they had a playhouse, and she could take in a performance. She used to love to go to the Boston Music Hall on a Saturday night. "Does Loma have a playhouse?"

"A what?" Shorty asked.

"A playhouse. A theater. For shows."

"Where in Sam Hill do you think you are, girl?" Shorty asked.

"Now, Shorty," Raven said. "We do have shows. Just not Boston kinda shows."

All right. Now we're getting somewhere. "What kind of shows do you have?" Izzy asked.

"Once every few months a preacher comes down from Amarillo and reads the newspaper," Raven said.

"That's a show?"

"Around here, it is. He packs 'em in."

Impossible. How could anyone consider reading a newspaper a show? Raven had to be pulling her leg. Izzy paid her no mind and asked Elle, "Are we almost there?"

Elle pulled Blaze to a stop. "About another half hour."

The gang reined in alongside her.

"Let's go over how we're gonna handle Izzy," Elle said.

Izzy huffed. "Don't talk about me like I'm not here."

"I'm sorry, you're right. We're gonna have to try and keep you out of sight as much as possible."

"I don't want to stay hidden."

"It's just for a little while. We don't know if anybody knows what happened to you. You'll stay with me."

Raven smirked. "Of course, she will."

Elle glared back at her. "You have a better idea?"

With a dip of her head, Raven said, "No. Guess not."

"We have to remember to use her new name if we're around other people. Belle MacPherson, right? Or I guess, Mac." She glanced around and everyone nodded.

With a squeeze of her knees, Elle urged Blaze forward, setting a meandering pace for the group.

"What about Rose? Are you gonna tell her who she is?" Raven asked.

Elle gazed off into the distance and took a moment before answering. "I prefer not to. We should keep Izzy's real name between us."

"She's gonna suss it out," Shorty said. "Nothin' gets by that woman."

"Who's Rose?" Izzy asked.

"She owns the saloon in town," Willy said.

"Hell, she owns the town," Shorty added.

Raven slapped her thigh and guffawed. "Saloon. That's a nice word for it."

"Nothing happens without Rose's say-so," Willy said.

"Quick to shoot, slow to talk." Shorty grinned.

"Shoot first, ask questions later."

"What we're saying is, you don't wanna get on her bad side," Raven said.

They didn't paint a pretty picture, and Izzy made a mental note to stay away from this Rose. "How old is she?"

Elle pursed her lips. "I'd say about fifty?"

"Does she have a husband?"

With a snort, Shorty replied, "She's fresh out of husbands right now. Went through four of them."

"Four?" Izzy asked. "How'd she managed to have four?"

"They were all killed," Raven said. "Her first one was kidnapped. The Hudson gang in Missouri thought they could get Rose to do their bidding. Let's just say she cut her losses. The second one was dragged behind a horse from one end of town to the other. To prove a point. I don't recollect what the point was. I forget how the third one died. The fourth one was hung by US Marshals."

"She lost a son too," Willy said.

Now Izzy didn't know whether to fear Rose or pity her. "That's sad."

"When you live the kind of life we do, your family and loved ones become a target," Elle said. "A way to get to you. That's why it's best to not get attached."

"So outlaws are supposed to be alone their whole lives?"

Elle nodded. "Then the only person they can hurt is you."

"Don't you all consider yourself family? You're together all the time."

"True. We spend a lot of time together. But we all know the deal. We're all living this life with our eyes wide open."

Izzy wasn't buying it. How could such a lonely life be appealing to anyone? "What if you fall in love?"

Elle stared straight ahead. "You don't."

"Or you do," Raven said, "and accept that you might lose them."

"Or…you don't," Elle said.

Izzy felt a pang of sadness for Elle. *Is that how she's going to live her life? Alone?* "Wait. Willy has a wife. Don't you?"

"I do. A wife and a baby."

"See? It's possible."

"That don't count," Raven said. "That was a shotgun wedding."

"What's a shotgun wedding?"

"His wife's daddy shoved a shotgun into his face and said, 'You will marry my pregnant daughter. Or else.'"

They all laughed, and a sheepish Willy nodded. "That's about how it went down."

* * *

As they galloped into Loma Parda, Izzy's first impression was…disappointment. Her second impression was…more disappointment. It looked nothing like what she'd pictured. There was no vibrancy, no color, no air. Just dust, and block after block of nondescript brownish-gray clapboard buildings. There was a lot of fighting, however, and gunshots, and shouting, and more dust. And in case there wasn't enough dust, it got dustier toward the town center. Horses pulling buckboards clogged the street. Some cowboys rode on the porches to avoid the congestion. *Are all Western towns like this? Dingy and dull and brown?* Her earlier open-country-feel-goods evaporated, and now Izzy missed Boston's cobblestone streets and longed for the colorful signs that adorned the plate-glass windows of the stores that lined Cambridge Street.

A huge brawl spilled out in front of them, and they pulled to a stop. The rowdy group, some wearing blue army garb, wrestled and punched their way across the street. A woman sweeping the porch of the bakery beat them with the broom handle when they got too close.

"Where's the sheriff?" Izzy asked.

Shorty pointed at the melee. "Right there. One in the black vest."

Izzy hung her mouth open. What kind of sheriff engaged in fisticuffs with the townsfolk? "I think you need a better sheriff."

"Ain't no better sheriff gonna step foot in this town," Raven said. "Many have tried."

Shorty nodded. "Fella by the name of Earp came riding through a few years ago thinking he was going to restore order."

"What happened?" Izzy asked.

Elle chuckled. "Rose suggested he move on."

"Rose and the fifty Winchester rifles that were pointed at ol' Wyatt's head," Raven added.

"True," Elle said. "He decided he liked his head. Turned tail and made for Dodge City instead."

"So nobody goes to jail?" Izzy asked. "You can fight and shoot at people, and nothing happens to you?"

Raven smiled. "Yup. Beautiful, ain't it? No Wanted posters hanging up, no lawmen, no jail. Welcome to Loma Parda." She cackled.

"What about these soldiers? Don't they keep the peace?"

Shorty hooted. "Keep the peace? Hell, they're the ones causing the most trouble."

"Fort Union is about eight miles away," Elle said. "The soldiers come here to blow off some steam."

Elle stopped in front of a livery stable, and four of the five dismounted, handing their reins over to a young boy with red hair poking out from his hat, and a generous sprinkle of freckles on his cheeks.

"Afternoon, Elle," he said.

"Afternoon, Tom." She slipped him a few coins.

He tipped his hat and led the horses inside the stable.

Willy said his goodbyes and rode on.

"Are we going to Rose's?" Raven asked.

"Might as well get it over with," Elle mumbled.

Raven slapped Izzy on the back. "Mac. You ready?"

Izzy wished she could have a day or two to prepare herself to meet this Rose. She swallowed a lump of apprehension. "I...I guess so."

"Remember. You robbed banks in Chicago," Raven said.

"Should that be her backstory?" Elle asked.

"I think so. They'll respect her."

"I like being a bank robber," Izzy said.

"Okay. But try and lay low," Elle said. "Don't talk to anyone unless you have to. And definitely don't talk too much to Rose."

They walked a couple of blocks to the saloon. Here was the first colorful sign. *Big Rose's Saloon and Dance Hall* was plastered in red across the front of the building. Elle stopped them before they entered. She directed her gaze at Izzy. "Remember what I said."

Izzy nodded. "Lay low."

Elle pushed open the swinging doors and they waltzed in. Izzy was shocked at the size of the crowd. Bodies were packed tightly together. A colorful sea of faces—white, black, brown—dotted the room. It was midafternoon and dancers twirled on the dance floor. Well, it really wasn't a floor. Just dirt. Certainly not like the polished oak of the Liberty Hotel in Boston. All the tables were filled with patrons, most playing cards. A few women in low-cut bodices served drinks or sat on the laps of leering men. Izzy was not so naive as to think it was harmless fun. She'd been exposed to the dark underbelly of Boston on rare occasions. These were women selling their wares. A wide staircase with a thick oak banister led to the second floor, where rows of closed doors lined the hallway. Rose's Saloon was code for brothel.

Elle pulled Izzy along. A few people nodded hello as they passed by. At least they seemed friendly. Shorty left to join a table across the room.

When they made it to the bar, a handsome young man called out, "Look who's back."

Elle nodded. "Rob Roy."

Without direction, he laid out three shot glasses and poured some amber-colored liquor in each. When he locked eyes with Izzy, his light blue eyes held a warmth and curiosity. Elle made no move to introduce her, so Izzy kept quiet. *Lay low.*

"Where's my Ellie girl?" someone shouted from behind them.

Next to her, Elle's body tensed. With rigid shoulders, she turned around with a smile.

"Hey, Rose," Elle said.

Raven leaned into Izzy's ear. "Gird your loins."

Izzy gulped and peeked behind her. A rotund woman in a scarlet-red dress walked toward them. The dress was only a tad redder than her hair. Instead of a pretty cloth or leather belt around her waist, she wore a holster with two guns—bright red to match her dress. *Interesting fashion choice.* Her cheeks were painted with rouge and her eyes lined with black. A bit garish for Izzy's taste. But she wasn't about to tell a woman who used guns as a colorful sash that she didn't like her makeup. *Lay low.*

Rose wrapped Elle in her arms and squeezed. When she pulled back, she cupped Elle's cheek. "How'd things go?" She released Elle and hugged Raven.

"Pretty well. Not quite the take we had last time." Elle slipped a small bag into Rose's hand.

Rose jiggled it. "Feels a bit light. I'm sure you'll make it up to me next time." Her eyes landed on Izzy. "Who's this?"

"Um. This is Belle MacPherson," Elle said. "We met up with her on the trail."

"We call her Mac," Raven said. "She ran into a bit of trouble back in Chicago. Told her she could hide out in Loma for a bit."

Rose studied Izzy.

Izzy stuck out a hand. "Nice to meet you, Miss Rose."

"Just Rose'll do." Rose continued to stare, and Izzy fidgeted. It felt like Rose's blue eyes bored into her soul, peering into every corner. Did she know they were lying? Izzy almost shouted, *I'm Isabella Collins and I'm supposed to marry J.B. Jackson but I ran away*, but she didn't. Rose's eyes were the same shade of blue as the barkeep's but lacked the warmth. Finally, the enigmatic proprietress turned away, and the knot in Izzy's gut eased.

"I'll get your room ready for you," Rose said to Elle.

"Oh. I thought I'd just grab some food with Raven and Mac."

"Nonsense. I know how you are after weeks on the trail. Go on up and I'll take care of everything." She pointed to an empty table by the window. "You two go sit, and I'll send over some steak and potatoes."

Raven tipped her hat. "Yes, ma'am."

Izzy followed Raven and they sat down. Before they had a chance to settle in, three men pulled up chairs and joined them. Their hair and beards were matted, and they smelled like sweat and alcohol. Izzy flared her nostrils. Bathing must not be a favorite pastime in the West.

"Raven," one said in greeting.

"Howdy, Pete."

"Who's this lovely lady?" Pete asked.

"This is Belle MacPherson. Goes by Mac. She's down from Chicago. Robbed a few banks and needs to hide out for a bit. Things gotta little hot up there."

Pete gave Izzy the once-over. "You rob banks?"

Izzy cleared her throat and tried to affect an outlaw accent. If there was such a thing. Her Boston dialect certainly wouldn't cut it here. "Sure do," she twanged. "My gang and I had to hightail it out of there." She paused, then added, "Right quick," to make it sound more outlaw-y.

"Couple of those Pinkerton boys chased them down toward St. Louis," Raven said. "But she managed to shake them. Right, Mac?"

Izzy stared at Elle, who climbed the stairs and disappeared into one of the rooms. *What's she doing?*

"Mac."

"Huh? Oh. Right."

"Where's your gang now?" Pete asked.

"Dead," Izzy blurted out.

The men's eyes grew as big as dinner plates.

"What happened to them?" one man asked.

"I shot them." Better to be thought of as too dangerous than sort-of dangerous.

Raven choked on her whisky, and some dribbled from her lips. She wiped her mouth and murmured, "'Scuse me."

A still wide-eyed Pete asked, "Why'd you shoot 'em?"

Izzy gaped as she saw another woman enter Elle's room upstairs. She was attractive, with soft curves and long auburn hair. She went in empty-handed. Maybe they were friends and wanted to catch up.

Raven kicked her shin.

"Ouch." Izzy rubbed the new bruise and scowled.

"Pete asked why you shot them." Raven smirked. "I'd like to know too."

"Oh." *Think.* She raised her glass and took a swig before saying, "They were snoring. Kept me up all night." She smacked her glass down on the table for emphasis.

The men pushed away and looked amongst themselves. Was that fear in their eyes? Izzy raised her chin. She liked being Mac.

* * *

Elle dressed quickly. She hadn't intended to see Miriam, but Rose was right. Her body had craved release.

"You leaving already?" Miriam cooed from the bed.

"I have to get back downstairs." She gave Miriam a long kiss goodbye. "I'll see you soon."

"You know where to find me."

Elle hustled from the room.

Hopefully Raven and Izzy were having an uneventful meal. As she rushed down the steps, a woman's voice rang out from below, singing "Oh! Susanna" in time to the piano. *Did Rose find a new singer?* The voice was strong and clear and in key, a far cry from Arthur. When she reached the bottom of the staircase, she craned her neck to see who possessed such a beautiful voice. When she saw the siren, she cursed. Izzy pounded away on the ivory keys, and the lyrics to the song echoed around the room.

A man standing next to Elle said to his friend, "That's Mac. Heard tell she's down from Chicago. Robbed the mayor at gunpoint."

The man nodded. "I heard she killed her husband-to-be on their wedding day."

His friend's mouth dropped open. "Good Lord, why?"

Another man turned around and said, "She didn't like the cut of his jib."

Elle fumed. So much for laying low. She pushed her way through the throng of bodies to get to the piano. An animated Izzy smiled and laughed while she sang and played. When the song ended, cheers erupted from the crowd. Elle barreled past Izzy's admirers and grabbed her upper arm.

Izzy's eyes widened. "Ow."

Elle tugged her away toward a less crowded area of the saloon.

Izzy pried Elle's fingers from her arm. "Ouch. That hurt."

Elle narrowed her eyes. "What are you doing?"

Still using her new cowboy accent, Izzy said, "I was playin' the piano."

"What part of laying low didn't you understand?" Elle said through clenched teeth. "And why are you talking like that?"

"I'm trying to fit in."

"Well, stop. It doesn't suit you." Elle raised her eyes to the heavens and took a breath. "I was gone for one hour. And in that time, you've become the headliner at Rose's."

"What were *you* doing for an hour?"

She pointed a finger in Izzy's face. "None of your business."

Izzy swatted the finger away. "I saw you go into that room upstairs."

Raven poked her head between them. "What's happening?"

"I told you to keep her out of trouble," Elle said.

A sloshed Raven giggled. "I can't help it if they wanted Mac to play a tune. Or three."

Elle covered her face with her hands and groaned. "The whole town knows her now."

"Nah. They're all roostered," Raven said.

Elle waved an arm back at the crowd. "They think she's a killer."

"Good." Raven raised a glass of whisky. "Better they're afraid of her."

"Let's go." Elle made a grab for Izzy's arm, but Izzy moved away.

"Don't grab me again. And apologize."

"For what?"

"For hurting my arm."

Elle closed her eyes and counted to ten. "I'm sorry. I'm sorry I hurt you. Can we go now?"

When they made it out to the street, Elle heaved a sigh of relief. "I can't believe you did that."

"It wasn't a big deal. I sang a few songs."

"Everybody knows you now."

"Don't be ridiculous," Izzy said. "Nobody knows me."

A man in a suit and bow tie tipped his stovepipe hat. "Evening, Mac."

Soon after, another greeted them. "Mac, have a good night."

Elle gritted her teeth.

"Mac!" someone behind them shouted, and they turned.

Joe Gibson trotted up to them. "I need some advice. Oh. Hello, Elle. I need to talk to Mac."

She looked sideways and flicked her hand at Izzy. "Go ahead."

"So, Mac. Tom Hellerton stole my boots. Insists he didn't. But I see the dang things on his feet. What'll I do?"

Without missing a beat, Izzy said, "Shoot him."

Elle squeezed her eyes shut and groaned.

Joe's head bobbed. "Right." He turned tail back to his wayward boots.

Elle glared.

"What?" Izzy asked. "He won't listen to me—"

A gunshot rang out behind them. They both froze. With a small voice, Izzy asked, "What did he do?"

Elle peeked over her shoulder. "He shot him."

"No! Did he kill him?"

Elle tossed another glance behind them. Poor Tom Hellerton hopped on one leg, howling. "No. Shot him in the foot."

Izzy's hand flew to her chest. "Oh, thank God." After a pause, she cocked her head. "Why would he shoot him in the foot if he's wearing his boots? Now the boot has a hole in it."

"Probably didn't think it through. Like you didn't with your 'shoot him' comment." Elle jerked her thumb up the street. "C'mon."

* * *

Izzy hustled to keep pace with Elle's long strides.

A few more "hellos" and "good evening, Macs" were thrown her way, and with each one, Elle's face grew darker.

Izzy felt bad. She'd have to try and stay out of sight from now on. No sense angering the one person who had been kind enough to help her.

They passed by Wilson's Dry Goods, and Izzy stopped short. "Do you have paper for writing letters at your house?"

Elle spun around. "No. I have no use for letter writing."

"Can we go in here and get some?"

Elle rolled her eyes and huffed. "Sure."

Izzy directed a grateful smile in Elle's direction. "Thanks." She wanted to write to her aunt in San Francisco. Of course, she had no idea if the address on the outside of the letter she stole from her mother's desk was still valid, since it was from two years ago, but she'd send it anyway. In the letter, she'd beg for help. She loved her Aunt Bea. They'd spent so much time together when Izzy was younger, exploring the fields and forests together. Her sudden departure nine years ago left a gaping hole in Izzy's heart.

They entered the busy store. It was bigger than expected, with multiple aisles filled with all sorts of goods. People ambled with bags of beans and flour and other sundries tossed over their shoulders. Some clogged up the works chatting, and Izzy had to politely push her way through. She scanned the shelves for paper. She'd need an envelope too. And God knows if there was a post office in Loma. When Elle was in a better mood, she'd speak to her about it.

A young man with a lithe frame and blond hair sticking out from his bowler cap approached her. He wasn't much taller than Izzy and had a pleasing face with boyish features. "Excuse me, ma'am." He removed his hat. "I believe you're Mac?" He gave her a warm smile that reached his eyes.

How in the heck did a few songs in a saloon make her the most popular person in Loma Parda? "Ah, yes. I'm Mac."

"My name is William H. Bonney, and I was wonderin' if I might have a word?" He nodded toward Elle. "Evening, Elle."

"Billy. What brings you up from Lincoln?"

"Let's call it a visit and leave it at that."

Izzy had no clue what he wanted to talk about, but Elle would not be pleased that another stranger acknowledged her. "What can I help you with?"

"If you need some work while you're in the area, my boss, Doc Scurlock, is always looking for help. He likes someone who knows how to take care of themselves. Pays decent, and you'd get three squares a day."

"Now, Billy," Elle said. "You know Rose doesn't like it when Scurlock recruits up here."

His eyes roamed around the room. "I know. I figured, with Mac being new in town, perhaps Rose hasn't employed her yet."

Izzy took note of Elle's posture, which had stiffened on Billy's approach. *Lay low.* "That's a kind offer, Mr. Bonney, but I'm gonna lay low for a while here in Loma."

A tinge of disappointment creased around his eyes. "I understand." He placed his hat back on his head. "Perhaps we could meet for dinner later."

"Dinner?"

He dipped his chin. "I can't imagine a more pleasing way to pass the time than with a lovely woman such as yourself."

Izzy glanced at Elle, whose eyes flashed with...anger? Or some other unreadable emotion.

"We have some things we need to take care of," Elle snapped, "so she'll have to decline your offer."

Billy's lips set in a thin line. He and Elle had a bit of a stare-down.

Izzy intervened. "Thank you, Mr. Bonney, but Elle's right. We have some business to…ah…do. Tonight."

His smile returned, although it lacked the warmth from earlier. "Very well. Mac, if you change your mind about working for Mr. Scurlock, you can find me down in Lincoln. Ladies, have a good evening." And with that, he left the store.

Izzy stared after him. "My goodness, he looked fourteen."

"That's why they call him Billy the Kid. He is young, but I assure you, he's no child. Stay away from him."

"Why?"

"Just do it."

"He was handsome."

Elle grunted.

"What?"

"Nothing." Elle stalked away and Izzy hurried after her.

"He seemed sweet."

Elle stopped so fast Izzy banged into her. "He is not sweet. Okay?"

Izzy snickered.

"What's so funny?"

"Are you jealous?"

"No, I'm not jealous."

"A handsome man asks me to dinner, and you're suddenly ill-tempered."

"I'm not ill-tempered. You see a handsome man, and I see a cold-blooded killer."

Izzy gasped. "Killer?"

"Yes. A killer."

Izzy bit her lip. Looks were certainly deceiving. He appeared so wholesome.

"Still wanna have dinner with him?"

Izzy shook her head.

"Good. Let's go."

The rest of the walk to the stables was uneventful. Young Tom brought their horses out and they mounted up. Elle set a brisk pace down the main street. They passed Rose's again and continued along for a bit, taking a left turn at the sheriff's office and then a right on the next dusty road. They passed the post office, and Izzy made a mental note.

Elle tipped her hat to a few passersby. Perhaps her earlier mood had lightened.

At this end of town, there was less bustle, and the clapboard buildings that had stretched on and on gave way to sporadic grayish wooden houses. None were large, although some were two stories.

Elle pulled Blaze to a stop at one of the smaller ones. "Here we are."

Izzy dismounted and tied her reins to the post in front of the house. It was no grand townhome like in Boston. Two wooden chairs sat on the front porch. A rickety roof perched overhead. *Guess this is home for now.* She followed Elle into the house.

Elle stood in the middle of the main room. "This is it. I have a small barn out back. When I get you settled, I'll put the horses away."

"Okay." There wasn't much to look at. No curtains on the windows, no rug on the slatted floor. Four chairs and a table sat near the fireplace. Izzy ran a finger over the table, and it left a dust trail.

She must've made a face, because Elle quickly said, "I've been away for weeks, so…it may be a bit dirty."

A red velvet couch with ornate wooden trim was against one of the walls, an odd piece compared to the rest of the room. Izzy directed a questioning glance toward Elle.

"Oh. That used to be at Rose's."

Izzy curled her lip up. What in God's name took place on that couch?

"It was in Rose's office, not…in a room." Her cheeks pinkened.

A tall shelf filled with books stood next to a desk. Izzy wandered over and ran a finger over the spines. The titles ran the gamut from novels and history, to physiology, anatomy, and more. "You read?"

"Are you asking *can* I read? Or, *do* I read?"

"I know you can read, silly. I'm surprised you have a bookshelf full of novels and textbooks."

"Are we outlaws not supposed to read for enjoyment?" she asked with a bemused smile.

"No, that's not what I meant."

Izzy pulled a tattered copy of *The Three Musketeers* from the shelf and thumbed through it. "This has been read a million times."

"Raven and I loved that book as kids. We'd read it every night. We fancied ourselves Musketeers. Used tree branches as swords and dueled to the death. Or the poke to the heart, which meant death."

Izzy laughed. "Which one were you?"

Elle bowed. "D'Artagnan, of course."

Izzy pictured a cocky young Elle dashing around and thrusting her pretend sword. "Of course you were. Brave and reckless. Where did you get all the books?"

"Some from Rose, most from stagecoaches."

"So, you stole them."

Elle tilted her head to the side. "I guess you could say that, yes. Or maybe…permanently borrowed is a better choice of words."

Izzy imitated the head tilt, but in the opposite direction. "I think we should stick with stolen, don't you?" Elle's lip twitched with an almost smile, and Izzy was pleased with herself. Elle didn't smile enough, in her opinion. She replaced the book and checked out the rest of the room.

A cast-iron stove took center stage along the back wall. Small wooden tables stood on each side. One had pots and pans on it, and the other had a ceramic blue pitcher and bowl. A bit rudimentary. Certainly not like their kitchen back in Boston. Izzy would be hard-pressed to bake a cake here.

"This is the bedroom." Elle gestured to an open doorway.

Izzy peeked in. A wooden tub against the wall caught her attention. *Good.* An occasional soak in warm water would be welcomed. The rest of the room contained the basics, a chest of drawers, a table with a wash basin, and a nightstand. An oval mirror hung on the wall.

The bed consisted of two stacked mattresses on a wooden bed frame. The rounded legs of the frame looked like short, stout tree trunks. A few colorful quilts covered the top mattress. "One bed? Are we supposed to share?"

"It's plenty big enough. Or I could sleep on the couch."

It *was* a large bed, and Izzy would feel bad kicking Elle out of her room. And in no way did Izzy want to sleep on the red couch. Who knows what salacious activities took place in that office? "I guess we could share."

"Good. The privy is out back. C'mon, I'll show you."

Izzy followed Elle out the back door. A small structure was about twenty yards from the house.

"Probably not what you're used to, but it's all we've got," Elle said. "If you come out after dark, bring a lamp. Sometimes snakes get in there because it's warm."

"Snakes?" *Good God. Boston, where art thou?*

Elle pointed to a round stone structure. "That's the well. The pump sometimes works, but the well is always full. Just lower the bucket." She showed Izzy how everything worked. "Worst case, we got the river right there." The Mora gurgled nearby. Down this end of town, it was more stream than river. "Why don't you go inside, and I'll get some water for the wash basin. You can clean up first."

"Okay, thank you." Izzy wandered back into the house. She took a deep breath and gazed around. It wasn't so bad. It was almost cozy. And after spending weeks on the trail sleeping on the hard ground, the bed would feel heavenly.

Yes. Things were looking up.

* * *

When it was time to turn in, Elle returned to the bedroom and found Izzy all tucked in. Having washed up out back by the pump, she extinguished the hurricane lamp next to the dresser. Moonlight streamed into the windows, and a soft breeze fluttered around the room. The bed dipped under her weight as she climbed in. She'd never had someone next to her all night long. The longest she'd stayed with Miriam was a couple of hours. *Will I be able to sleep?*

As if reading her mind, Izzy said, "Don't worry. I don't move around much when I sleep. And once my eyes close, I don't wake up until morning."

Of course, Elle already knew this from the weeks on the trail. She had marveled every night how quickly Izzy drifted off. "I'm the exact opposite. Kind of a light sleeper. I guess I'm always on guard."

"But this is your house."

"Still."

Izzy sighed. "I hope you get some sleep." She smiled. "Good night."

"Good night."

Elle fussed around and got comfortable, ending up on her right side, facing the wall. Izzy's breathing became shallow. Now that her bed partner slept, Elle's body relaxed and her eyes became heavy. *Good, maybe I'll fall right to sleep.*

Alas, her peaceful slumber didn't happen. What did happen was that Izzy turned over with a grunt and tossed an arm over Elle. Then she scooched closer and snuggled against Elle's back. Elle waited. Surely Izzy would move away soon, but remarkably, she managed to get even closer. *Maybe if I move, she'll turn back over.* In slow motion, Elle turned onto her back. Another soft grunt escaped from Izzy's lips, but instead of moving away, she somehow ended up laying on Elle's chest. *What fresh hell is this?* Elle shifted again, but Izzy was like a prickly cholla cactus burr stuck to a pant leg. There was no shaking her.

The other side of the bed was vacant, so Elle slipped out from under Izzy, walked around, and climbed in. *Now I can sleep.* Before she had a chance to enjoy being home and sleeping in her own bed, Izzy grunted and rolled all the way over and ended up next to her again.

Good Lord, this woman. So much for, *I don't move around much when I sleep.* Elle raised the white flag. She lay still, and Izzy settled in on her chest again. A lock of hair tickled her nose, and she puffed it away.

It was going to be a long night.

CHAPTER NINE

The next morning, Izzy awoke to an empty bed. Sunlight streamed in from the window and danced along the floorboards, showing a healthy gathering of dust. A good cleaning was in order. *I'll handle that. It's the least I can do.* She stretched her arms above her head and pointed her toes. She felt well rested. The bed was more comfortable than expected.

Voices out back made her pause. *Is someone else here?*

She hopped from bed and dressed in the same clothes she'd been wearing. Maybe Elle would take her to the store today. A plate filled with pastries sat on the kitchen table. Starving, Izzy took a massive bite of a cinnamon cake.

Through the window, movement caught her eye. Elle, in shorter pants and a sleeveless undershirt, and with sweat sparkling on her skin, sparred with another woman. The woman was shorter than Elle, with straight jet-black hair that was pulled away from her face. She was thin and wiry. Both wielded a long staff and jabbed and parried the other's blows. It was fascinating to behold. They displayed a gracefulness and power that Izzy found oddly attractive. She pushed open the back door.

The distraction caused Elle to let her guard down, and she was deposited on her bum with a leg sweep from her fellow combatant. The woman reached out a hand and tugged Elle to her feet.

Elle brushed the dirt from her pants. "I thought you'd never get up," she said to Izzy.

"I'm sorry. I guess I was tired."

They walked over, and Elle made the introductions. "Izzy, this is Matsu. Matsu, Isabella Collins, or Izzy."

She must trust this woman if she used my real name.

Matsu placed her hands on her thighs and bowed but didn't speak.

Izzy bowed back, since that seemed like the right response. "Nice to meet you."

Matsu smiled, and her brown eyes crinkled at the corners. Her skin was flawless, except for a long scar that started above her left eye and continued into her hairline.

Elle bowed to Matsu. "Thanks. See you tomorrow."

She bowed to both and left.

"Not a big talker," Izzy said.

"She can't talk."

"Why?"

Elle took a seat on the back step. "From what I can gather, it was a head injury that caused her to lose her speech. She didn't offer up anything more than that."

Izzy joined her. "That explains the scar. So how did you two meet?"

"I was riding through—"

"Wait." Izzy raised her hand. "I think we need cakes and coffee for this story." She hurried inside and returned, balancing the plate full of pastries and two cups of coffee. "Okay."

Elle bit into a cake and her eyes lit up. "I love these."

"Me too. So, you were riding where?"

"We were in Denver for supplies a few years ago. It was dark out, and we stumbled upon this fight in the middle of the street. Three cowboys against one, and the one man more than held his own. He used his legs and arms in a way I'd never seen before. It was impressive. He walked away and left them all bloodied and probably embarrassed, since there was quite a crowd watching and betting on it."

"Fighting seems to be a thing out here."

"Mm-hmm. So we stayed over in Denver that night and left the next morning. Outside of town, we run into the same three men who got their asses whupped the night before. But *with* them, tied up and beaten up, was the guy who beat *them* up the night before—"

"And that was Matsu."

"Can I tell the story please?"

"Sorry."

"Yes, it was Matsu. She had short hair and was dressed like a man."

"You dress like a man. And I guess I dress like a man now."

"True. But it's different. I think she was trying to pass as a man. You'd be surprised how many women do that out here."

"Interesting." Izzy patted Elle's arm. "Keep going."

"Where was I?"

"They had Matsu tied up."

"Right. They were fixing to hang him...her. She was on a horse with a rope around her neck."

"Let me guess. You saved her."

"Correct."

"'Cause you don't like hangings."

"Correct."

"I don't know who does."

"You'd be surprised. Hangings draw quite a crowd out here."

Izzy made a face. "Horrible. Sorry. Continue."

"We all stormed in there, firing into the air to scare them off. But first I made sure to shoot the top of the rope, because if her horse spooked, then she would've hung."

"Good thinking on your part."

"Are you being sarcastic?"

Izzy smiled. "No. What happened next?"

"When I got close to her, I realized she was a woman. I asked what her name was, and she sort of made it clear she couldn't speak. She pulled out a paper. On the top of the page was written 'Matsu.' She pointed to that, then pointed to herself, so that's how we got her name. Her name was the only thing we could read on the paper."

"Can she write?"

"No, but she mostly understands when I talk to her."

"So you don't know anything else about her?"

Elle shook her head. "I know she's from Japan. But other than that, no. If I had to guess, she probably landed in San Francisco and somehow made it out here."

"Where does she live now?"

"She rents a room from Mrs. Stenson, a widow up town. Does odd jobs for her. Also helps the doc out too. She's pretty good at stitching people up. She's helped me out quite a few times."

"My goodness, what a story she must have to tell." Izzy snapped her fingers. "I'm gonna teach her to write so she can tell us her story."

"I guess it couldn't hurt," Elle said.

"So, what's all this you were doing." Izzy mimicked swinging the staff. "Is that how she fights? Was she teaching you?"

"Yes. I asked her to teach me. We spar when I'm home. Either with the staff or hand to hand. Keeps me in shape. Helps with my reflexes."

"Where'd she learned to fight like that? Is it something I need to know?"

"Oh. I don't think so."

"I think I do. I need to learn to fight."

Elle made a face. "You have trouble with a gun. I'm not sure you'll be able to handle this."

Izzy hated when people underestimated her. She could handle anything. She would attend the next session, no matter Elle's protestations. *I need to learn how to defend myself.*

* * *

The next morning, Elle and Matsu sparred without the staffs. At one point, Elle managed to put Matsu on the ground, which didn't happen often. Before she had a chance to gloat,

Matsu grabbed her arm, twisted it, and flipped Elle onto her back.

"Oof." She remained on the ground, exhausted.

"Good morning."

She picked her head up. Izzy waved and walked toward them. She was dressed like Elle, in short pants and a sleeveless white shirt. She must have raided Elle's chest of drawers. "What's up, Iz?"

"I'm here to learn how to fight." She bowed. "Matsu will teach me, won't you?"

Matsu looked to Elle for direction. *Why fight it?* "Sure." Dragging herself up, she hobbled over to the porch. With a groan, she settled into a chair and rubbed at her lower back.

The back door creaked open, and Raven plopped down in the other chair, a day-old cinnamon cake in her hand. "Hey."

"Morning."

Raven nodded in Izzy's direction. "What's happening?"

"Izzy wants to learn how to fight."

"She can't even shoot a gun."

"I know."

Raven nibbled on the cake. "How do you like sharing your domicile?"

"Yet to be determined."

Raven hooted. "You poor thing. But, I'm sure *you* could think of worse things than sharing a bed with a pretty woman." She shoved the last bit of cake into her mouth.

Elle glared at her, but she took Raven's good-natured ribbing in stride. Years ago, she'd confided her preferred choice of sexual partner to Raven, because if you couldn't share that with your blood sister, who could you share it with? Raven had no issue with Elle's revelation. Her only words of advice were to be careful. "What are you doing today?"

"Nothing. Thought I'd pop in and see how you two crazy cowboys are doing."

"We're fine. She's a bit of a bed hog. And she thrashes around a lot. She didn't do that on the trail. Guess she feels more comfortable in a bed."

"Maybe you need to tire her out." Raven wiggled her eyebrows before another cackle escaped her lips.

"Shut up." At this new innuendo, Elle felt heat rise in her cheeks because the jab hit a little too close to home. At one point last night, Izzy's hand had rested at the top of her thighs. Elle's body roared awake, and it took an hour to shut the desire off. And during those hours, Elle fantasized about doing all sorts of things to Izzy. All sorts of wonderful, passionate things. The first order of business this morning had been a dip in the cold river. The second order of business should probably be a visit to Miriam sometime today.

Raven leaned forward and rested her elbows on her knees. "Saw Rose yesterday. Said she wants us to start doing banks when the railroad's done."

"Ugh. I don't wanna rob banks."

"Neither do I."

"What brought that up?"

"Who knows? Maybe all the talk about this one." Raven gestured toward Izzy.

"I'm not doing a bank," Elle stated. "And you can tell her so."

"She ain't gonna wanna hear it from me. You tell her. You're the chosen one."

Elle looked askance at her. "What's that supposed to mean?"

"It means, you tell her we ain't robbin' no bank. She'll only listen to you."

Elle harrumphed. "I'm not the chosen one."

"Sure you are. Always have been."

"You're imagining things."

"She's always liked you best. You're the one she puts in charge, you're the one she trusts the most. You're the one she seeks advice from. It's always been you."

A stunned Elle asked, "Why didn't you tell me you felt like this?"

Raven's shoulder touched her ear. "'Cause it don't matter. I'm over it. Been over it for a while. When I was younger, it bothered me. I was always trying to get her attention, but she never looked past you." She waved a hand in the air. "It's fine now. I've accepted my place."

Elle thought back to their early days with Rose, and a pang of sadness struck her. *She's right. Why didn't I notice it at the time?* Maybe deep down she did. Maybe because, at ten years old, it felt good to be, as Raven put it, the chosen one. Which would make her a shitty blood sister. "I'm sorry."

"Eh. Like I said, it don't bother me anymore." Raven crossed her ankles and locked her hands behind her head.

They sat in silence for a few moments.

Not sure what to say next, Elle instead focused on the action in front of her. Of course, Izzy was completely overmatched, but Elle gave her credit for hanging in there. "She wants to teach Matsu to write."

"That's ambitious."

Izzy landed on her hip bone and yelped.

"Uh-oh. That's gonna bruise," Raven said.

"You okay?" Elle called.

Izzy teetered to her feet, and with a big smile plastered on her face, waved. "I'm fine."

Elle chuckled. "She's got some pluck, that one."

"When do you think we'll head out on the trail again?"

"I don't know. You getting restless already?"

Raven stared at the sky. "Nah. Something to be said for sleeping with a roof over your head." She sat back and stretched her legs out. "Do you ever think of what you'd be doing if we weren't outlaws?"

"Miriam asked me that a few months back." She took a moment before answering, "I think I'd like some land of my own. Have some horses, maybe a few head of cattle." She had the perfect spot in her mind picked out. *Someday.* "What about you?"

"Same, I guess. Maybe we can do it together."

"You sound ready now."

"Some days, I think I am," Raven said.

"Me too."

CHAPTER TEN

The sun was barely a hint on the horizon when Izzy opened her eyes. Elle's breath was still even and shallow. Izzy snuggled closer for warmth. At least that's what she told herself. Elle was warm. And made her feel safe. Izzy was aware that she sprawled all over Elle during the night hours. Elle never mentioned it, so she either didn't notice or didn't care. *Maybe she enjoys it as much as I do?* Maybe it was comforting to Elle also. Elle, the lonely outlaw who kept her outlaw heart locked away.

Izzy gazed at Elle's face. When sleeping, she looked younger and carefree. Her long lashes rested on her cheeks. Izzy's eyes dipped to Elle's lips. What would they feel like? Would they feel like Catherine's? Or would they feel softer? They were fuller than Catherine's, so probably yes. They'd feel softer.

This was what she did if she awoke first—stared and wondered. At first, she was confused and worried something was wrong with her, but then she chalked it up to curiosity. Just normal curiosity. And the need to snuggle? Why that was a basic human need to touch and be touched. The lip infatuation?

Debatable. But Izzy missed her mother's hugs, and Elle was a more than suitable replacement.

Elle stirred and moved onto her side away from Izzy.

Izzy wasn't about to lose her human blanket, so she sidled closer. "Are you up?"

"Barely."

"I'm up."

Elle gave a soft sigh and turned back to Izzy. Now their faces were inches apart. "It's early. Go back to sleep," she whispered.

"I'm awake now." Izzy stared at Elle's lips again. They were close. She was struck by how much she wanted to test them, compare them to Catherine's. She drew in a breath. *What is wrong with me?* When she met Elle's eyes, something was there, hidden in their brown depths. Something Izzy couldn't quite comprehend.

A small crease appeared between Elle's eyes as she frowned slightly.

Does she know what I'm thinking?

"I guess I'll get up," Elle said.

The moment passed. Or maybe Elle forced the moment to pass, Izzy wasn't sure. She wasn't even sure what the moment was about. But it definitely felt like a moment. *Stop it. I admire Elle. That's all.*

* * *

On Elle's trip to town, she thought about her new housemate. The past week had been challenging at first. Elle wasn't used to someone underfoot, but they fell into a routine.

Elle got up first and made coffee and breakfast. When Izzy joined her, they'd sit on the back porch and watch the river. Sometimes a duck floated by, and Izzy pointed it out and mused about taking a lazy float down the river and how relaxing it must be. Nights proved interesting. That first night was a precursor to how things would be every night, Izzy tucked into or onto Elle's body. Each night Elle tried to free herself, and each night Izzy found her way back, so Elle had given up. Now, she welcomed the contact. She may have even scooched back on several occasions to be closer to Izzy, whose scent now clung to both pillows and the bed linens.

As she loped up the steps to the saloon, she banished Izzy from her mind. Tim swept away the dust from the doorway. "Morning, Tim."

"Morning."

When she got inside, she headed straight to Rose's office behind the bar.

Rose lounged behind her desk, smoking a pipe. "Morning. How are you today?"

"I'm good." Elle settled into the leather chair in front of Rose's desk.

Rose blew a perfect circular puff of smoke into the air. "How's your new...friend?"

The slight hesitation between *new* and *friend* gave Elle pause. *Does she think there's something between me and Izzy?* Of course, the way Izzy looked at her this morning made *her* think something was between them. It almost felt like Izzy wanted a kiss, but that would be crazy. *She's a payday, and nothing more.* "Um, Mac's good. Settling in."

"How long she gonna be here?"

"I don't know. Probably not more than a month or so." *If everything goes to plan.*

"I heard Billy approached her the other day."

"Yeah, he offered her a job with Scurlock."

"Is Scurlock in charge now? Been hard to keep up with all the killing."

"I guess."

"I hope she didn't take him up on the offer."

"No, no. She refused. Wants to keep a low profile."

Rose nodded. "Nerve of him asking in my town. I would think if she wants a job, she'd ask me."

"Of course. I told him as much. That he was out of line asking in Loma."

Rose refilled her pipe with tobacco and struck a match. "Can't do business in Lincoln right now. Everybody's getting shot. I liked John Tunstall, and it was a damn shame he got killed, but I don't know if he's worth all the bloodshed happening down there. You know he gunned down Sheriff Brady in April? Gunned him down in cold blood."

"Who, Billy?"

"Billy and his band of merry men. That boy is bad news." Rose sucked on her pipe and the aromatic smoke curled upward. "We sure about this gal?"

The quick change in subject made Elle's insides twist. "What do you mean?"

"I mean, she doesn't seem like the bank-robbing type."

Elle didn't remember telling Rose that Izzy robbed banks, but someone must have. "I have no reason to doubt her."

Rose's shrewd eyes pinned Elle to her seat. Rose hadn't become the most powerful woman in the county by accident. She had a knack for seeing through lies, and Elle was playing a dangerous game by not being truthful.

Rose's features softened. "If you vouch for her, that's good by me."

Elle relaxed a bit. She'd gotten away with it—for now.

"All right. Now to business," Rose said. "I need you to ride out to the Hollister homestead. He's late on his rent. And while you're out there, check on Guifford. He was short last month and promised to make it up to me this month. Take Raven and Willy. A little show of might always loosens the purse strings."

Elle grabbed a small piece of paper from Rose's desk and made notes while Rose ticked off her to-do list for the day. It was good to stay busy, and Rose compensated her well. After receiving her marching orders, Elle tucked the note into the inner pocket of her vest.

"Here, got this the other day. I know you lost yours." Rose handed her a copy of *Moby Dick*.

"Thanks." Elle's book had gone missing while out on the trail last year. It was one of her favorites. "I need to read it again."

When she left Rose's, all the earlier tension eased. It was odd feeling tense around Rose, but keeping Izzy safe from her seemed paramount.

She gathered up Willy and Raven, and they headed to Fergus Guifford's place. Elle disliked him. He was a useless drunk, a lousy husband, and shitty father, and he sorely tested Elle's patience.

The Guifford farm was right outside town, so the ride didn't take long. Smoke billowed from the chimney, indicating someone was home.

They dismounted and tied up their horses. Elle rapped on the front door. Annie Guifford, Fergus's wife, opened the door a crack. "Elle?"

"Annie. We're looking for Fergus."

"He's out back. C'mon in." She patted her reddish-blond hair and smoothed down her plain cotton dress.

They filed into the house. A baby cried in a crib under the window, and two barefoot kids cowered at the table. They had smudges of dirt on their faces and grime on their clothes.

"Let me go find him for you," Annie said.

Willy stayed by the door with his thumbs hooked into his gun belt. Raven stood next to him with her arms crossed. Elle made herself at home by taking a seat and putting her feet up on the edge of the stove. She'd found over the years of collecting Rose's debts, that the more indifferent she appeared, the more fear she instilled.

Fergus shuffled into the room. He had to grab the doorframe to steady himself. He was taller than Elle, but his waistline was larger. His limp black hair hung below his jaw and his matted beard needed a good washing. "Elle. When did you get back?"

"About a week ago."

"What brings you out here?"

Elle withdrew her knife and used it to flick a spec of dirt out from under her fingernail. "Rose wants her money."

It was barely midmorning and already he stank of whisky and sweat. "Tell her I ain't got it."

She tsk-tsked. "Now, Fergus. You know I can't tell her that."

He rubbed his hands on his pants. "I ain't got any right now. Work's hard to find."

"Funny. You had enough money to get drunk at the saloon the other day."

"I said I ain't got it."

"Well." She stood and slid her knife into her boot. "You leave me no choice."

"Whachu mean?"

Elle nodded at Raven and Willy. They all left via the back door with Fergus close behind. Elle pointed to the small herd of cattle that stood nearby in the meadow. "Round them up."

"You got it, boss," Raven said.

"You can't take my cattle."

"I sure can," Elle said. "Consider them collateral until you pay what you owe."

A vein in Fergus's neck throbbed. "Why you…"

He charged forward and took a swing at Elle. She blocked it and kneed him in the stomach. He bent over, clutching at his belly. After he caught his breath, he attacked her again, taking a wild swing at her head. She ducked and kicked the legs out from under him. He landed in the dirt with a grunt. He picked himself up, clenched his fists, and snarled. "Ain't nobody takin' my cattle."

Again he charged, and again Elle stopped him in his tracks, this time with a well-placed punch to the face. He howled and fell to his knees as blood poured out his nose. She placed her boot on his backside and shoved him all the way down. "Fergus, you're drunk. Why don't you sleep it off? Come get your cattle when you have the money."

With a defeated look on his bloodied face, he rolled onto his back. "Hold on. I might have some cash."

"Now we're talking." Elle waved him toward the house. "Go on and get it. We'll wait right here." After he left, she shook her hand and flexed her fingers. *Nothing broken, good.* But the knuckles were bruised and bleeding, or maybe it was just Fergus's blood. A water pump stood nearby, so she washed her hand and reinspected. Bruised yes, a few small cuts, yes, but most of the blood wasn't hers. She frowned at Willy and Raven. "Thanks for helping."

Raven smirked. "We knew you could handle it."

* * *

Izzy had the day to herself since Elle would be gone until the evening, which was perfect, because she needed to get something done away from the prying eyes of Elle or anyone else.

She made some coffee and ate a biscuit slathered with butter. Her hunger assuaged, she hunkered down at the desk against the wall and pulled out a sheet of paper. The envelope with a San Francisco return address lay nearby. The letter inside contained mostly pleasantries and small talk, but the most important thing was the address. Was her aunt still living there? Lord knew, but it was worth a try. This had been Izzy's plan before Elle came along. But now, after seeing the hardships of the Wild West, the plan was laughable. It had consisted of an escape from the coach, losing herself in a small town along the stagecoach trail, and sending a letter to Aunt Bea, begging for an invite to join her in San Francisco. *How naive was I?*

So, she'd write the letter now and pray the address was valid. Over the next few minutes, she wrote about her "adventures," if one could call them that, although almost getting killed twice qualified as more than an adventure. When she finished with a plea for help, she sealed the letter in an envelope. *What do I use as a return address?* She could ask Elle, but she wanted to keep this private. What if her aunt had moved and never replied? Izzy didn't want to see the pity in Elle's eyes every time Izzy asked the postman if there was a letter for her. She also didn't want to appear ungrateful for Elle's help and generosity. If her aunt responded, then she would broach the subject with Elle.

Maybe the post office could tell her what return address to use. Yes. A trip to the post office was the first order of business. And maybe a quick stop at the dry goods store. If she was going to teach Matsu to write, she'd need more paper and pencils.

After dressing, her hand hovered over her gun belt. *Do I need it?* Izzy Collins didn't feel like putting it on, but Mac surely would. She belted it around her waist, then headed outside and threw a saddle on Jack. Saddling a horse had been her first cowboy lesson a few weeks ago, and she was quite good at it now.

"Jack, we're heading out for a while."

He tossed his head and she laughed. "I know. I've been bored too!"

As she ambled down the street, swaying side to side with the old gelding's gait, a sign caught her eye: *Law Office of Charles Berenson*. A wild idea took root. "Let's stop here, Jack."

A gentleman walked by and called out, "Good day, Mac."

Izzy had no recollection of ever meeting him, but she smiled and waved anyway. "Same to you!" She began to feel a bit famous.

She cupped her hands around her eyes and peered into the window. Someone slouched behind a large desk, but a newspaper hid their face. *Oh, a newspaper.* She'd give anything to read a newspaper right now. A large shelf lined with books stood behind the desk. Perfect. She pushed open the door.

The newspaper folded down to reveal a portly face with saggy jowls and a bushy salt-and-pepper mustache. His receding hair was similarly colored. The man's eyes widened, and his face turned white as milk toast. He quickly placed the paper on the desk. "May I help you?"

"Are you Charles Berenson?"

"I am."

"Good morning. I'm—"

"I know who you are." He glanced down at her gun and swallowed thickly.

Izzy approached the desk and the man inched backward. Sweat beaded on his forehead. *He's afraid of me.* She almost giggled. But Mac would never giggle. She'd take advantage of the situation and feed on someone's fear. A tall glass filled to the brim sat next to the newspaper. The whisky bottle next to the glass was almost empty. "A bit early for a drink, isn't it?"

"It's…medicinal. Helps my gout."

"I see. I was wondering if you could help me."

"Do you need representation?"

"No. I wanted to borrow a book or two."

His brows rose. "Excuse me?"

"Don't worry. I'll return them."

His mouth opened and closed. "For what purpose?"

"Why, to read, of course. The law interests me." Izzy scanned the bookcase, taking note of all the titles it contained. "So perhaps something for a beginner, like myself."

"I...I...never," he stammered and stopped.

"You never what?"

"I never had anyone of your...uh...ilk inquire about a law book."

"I think it makes perfect sense, don't you? Before one breaks the law, one should know the law."

"I guess, if you put it that way."

"So. What do you suggest?"

He stood and rubbed his chin. "Yes. Let's see." He fingered a few volumes, then pulled one out. "I suppose you could start with this."

He handed her *Blackstone's Commentaries on the Laws of England*. Izzy paged through it. "This will be perfect." Her eyes landed on the newspaper. It was dated two months ago, but any news was good news, even if it was old news. "May I borrow this when you're finished?"

"Take it." He shoved the paper in her direction, and it almost slid off the desk.

Izzy enjoyed this new power. It was heady. She certainly never felt this way in Boston. With a jaunty step, she headed out the door. Before she left, she waved. "Good luck with your gout."

She placed the book and the newspaper into her saddlebag. "Okay, Jack. Off to the post office."

The post office was a block away. As she dismounted and reached for the front door, an older woman with a child in tow spotted her and turned tail.

Izzy had seen the flash of fear in the woman's eyes, and now her earlier bravado faded. "Mac would not hurt a woman or a child," she mumbled under her breath.

The elder gentleman behind the big wooden counter was slight of build, and his rheumy eyes peered at her over his wire spectacles. A red bow tie rested at the base of his wrinkled neck. "May I help you?"

No fear in his eyes, nothing but boredom. Obviously her name and reputation did not precede her here. "I hope so, ah, Mister...?"

"Poulter."

"Mr. Poulter. I need to mail a letter, and I'm not sure what return address to use. You see, I'm staying with Elle Barstow." She stopped there and hoped he'd fill in the blanks.

"Write your name on there, in care of Elinor Barstow, Loma Parda, New Mexico Territory. That should do the trick."

Izzy nodded and wrote the address on the envelope. "Will this go out today?"

He cocked a brow. "Today? Maybe next week. Maybe the week after."

"You don't have postal service every day?"

"No, ma'am. Not out here."

Izzy bit back her annoyance. God knows when her letter would get delivered. "Okay. If that's the way it works."

The bells on the door tinkled and Izzy glanced back. When she saw who walked through the door, she quickly moved away from the counter. *Please don't see me, please don't see me.*

"Good morning, Mr. Poulter. Good morning, Mac."

Damn it. Izzy pasted a smile on her face and spun around. "Rose. Good morning." Rose's fashion choice was interesting. She had stuffed herself into a bright yellow-and-white lace gown, the kind a young Bostonian woman would wear to a high society ball. Her cleavage barely left anything to the imagination. Izzy would've gone up a dress size, but she considered herself modest. Rose was anything but. The large-brimmed fancy-feathered orange hat clashed with the dress color, but her gun holster belt complemented it perfectly. It was a deeper yellow than the dress. *Where does she get matching gun holster belts? I might have to ask.* "How are you today?"

"I'm fine, thanks for asking. How you finding Loma? Hospitable, I hope."

"Yes, everything's been fine. Elle is a wonderful hostess." *Oh my God. What kind of outlaw calls someone a hostess?* She cleared her throat and tried to sound tougher. With her shoulders thrown back, she said, "She leaves me be. Which is what I want right now. Peace and quiet."

"Guess that's why I haven't seen you much around town."

"Yep. Just laying low. Keeping to myself, mainly." Izzy hitched her thumb toward the door. "Well, I should get going."

"Now, hold on. Don't rush off. You might be in here." Rose tapped her finger on a pile of papers that Mr. Poulter had deposited on the counter. "In which case, we might have some business."

Business? "What...what...do you mean?" She craned her neck to get a gander at the papers. Across the top of the first page, in big letters, was the word WANTED. It was a stack of Wanted posters. She suppressed a smile. *Phew. I won't be in there.*

Rose picked the first page up. "Don't know this one." She moved it to the side. "Ah. Emmaus, you've been a bad boy. He still renting a room from Widow Stenson?" she asked Mr. Poulter.

"I believe so."

"Tell him to come see me."

"Are you going to turn him in?" Izzy asked.

Rose chuckled. "Lord, no. Loma is a safe harbor for all souls. I make sure of it. But safety comes with a price." She continued perusing the stack, placing some on the left and some on the right. "Well, Mac, nobody's looking for you."

If that was a good thing or a bad thing, Izzy wasn't sure. "Yet, right?" She gave a nervous laugh.

"I suppose. But we'll keep our eye out."

It was time to make a getaway, but before Izzy said goodbye, Rose asked, "Where are you from originally?"

Her pulse quickened. *Careful.* "I was born in Boston." Maybe that would suffice. She took a quick glance down at her chest to make sure her pounding heart wasn't visible through her shirt.

Rose's eyes locked on to Izzy's. "And how does a pretty thing like you end up robbing banks in Chicago?"

Oh, Lord. Stay calm. And think. "My family moved around a lot. We were dirt poor. 'Bout the only thing my daddy was good at was drinking. You know how that is."

"Not really. I don't partake. I like to keep my wits about me."

"Oh, I didn't mean to imply that you personally drank, but, other people…do. And you've probably seen it, owning a saloon and all." Izzy needed to do something with her hands, so she drummed her fingers on the counter and tried to appear casual. "My brother did some petty thievery. And I helped." She lifted a shoulder and let it fall. "We needed to put food on the table somehow." Izzy was proud of herself because her voice didn't shake and her story sounded plausible.

"I've been to Chicago a couple times. What bank did you rob?"

Izzy made sure her expression of casualness remained plastered on her face. *I have no idea what banks are in Chicago. And she does.* The jig might be up.

The door opened and a tall, fully whiskered man in uniform strolled in. "There you are, Miss Rose. I've been searching for you."

"Why, Colonel McIlheny. What brings you to Loma on such a fine day?"

"We haven't had a visit in a while. Thought I'd stop by and take you to lunch."

He offered Rose his bent elbow, and she slipped her hand through it. "That would be lovely."

He patted her hand. "I hope my boys have been behaving themselves."

Rose smiled. "I don't want them to be too behaved now, do I?"

He let out a booming belly laugh and escorted her out the door.

Izzy's upper body collapsed on the counter. That was a close call. Elle would've had her head if Rose had managed to pry the truth out of her.

Mr. Poulter gave her a puzzled look.

She straightened. "Ah, I thought he was here to arrest me." *That's thinking on your feet, girl!*

He inclined his head and went about his business.

An hour later, Izzy pulled Jack to a stop in front of Elle's house. The small wagon behind her stopped also.

Shorty lollygagged on the porch, smoking a cigarette. "Mac."

"Hi. What brings you here?"

"Thought I'd catch up with Elle."

"She's gone for the day." Izzy walked to the wagon and grabbed a package. She could only fit so much in her arms. "Well, are you gonna help or not?" she asked. "All these packages need to come inside."

He grumbled, "Hold your horses," and pried his butt off the chair.

When everything was inside, Izzy sent the driver of the wagon on his way.

"What in the Sam Hill is all this?" Shorty asked.

"I bought some things to brighten up the place."

"Does Elle know?"

"No. It'll be a surprise."

He grimaced. "That dog won't hunt."

"What?"

"She ain't too keen on surprises."

"I'm sure she'll love it. Now, I need a hammer. Does Elle have a hammer?"

"Don't know. Maybe she's got one out back in the barn." He made no move to fetch it.

Izzy lowered her brows.

He raised a hand. "All right. Don't git your back up. I'll go look."

They spent the next half an hour hanging a few pictures and curtains. Izzy learned all about Shorty's childhood in Georgia, and he got an earful about the suffrage movement in Boston. It wasn't unpleasant. She invited him to stay for lunch, but he had prior plans.

* * *

After collecting Rose's outstanding debts, Elle and Raven galloped to Elle's for dinner. Trying to be menacing yet persuasive exhausted her. Strong-arming tenants was her least favorite job. She wiggled the fingers on her hand. *And fistfights are a close second.* Thanks to her innate quickness and Matsu's tutorage, she usually held her own. Like today—a drunken Fergus had been no match, but still, here she was nursing bruises and cuts.

Her thoughts turned to Izzy, and she smiled to herself. *I missed her. What did she do all day?*

They stopped in front of her house and slid from their saddles. A splash of color caught her eye. Floral-patterned cushions were on the porch chairs. And that wasn't the only colorful thing. Curtains now hung from the two front windows, and a flower wreath made from bright yellow goldeneyes hung on the front door.

Raven let out a low whistle. "What in tarnation happened to your house?"

Elle gnashed her teeth in frustration. So Izzy didn't lay low today at all. "I think it's *who* happened to my house." *Where in God's name did she go?* Elle silently fumed. *Does this woman want to be found out? Has she no regard for her own safety?*

Raven smacked her on the back. "I think I'll take my leave and let you deal with your wife."

"Shut up. She's not my wife."

"Sure." Raven hopped back into the saddle. "Actually looks nicer now. Maybe you should keep her."

Elle glared. "Get out of here."

"Am I invited to the wedding?"

"Go!"

Raven laughed and headed out.

Elle led Blaze around to the back of the house. After tying him up, she removed his saddle and gave him a good brushing. Doing these menial tasks helped calm her down. No sense going into the house in a mood.

When finished with Blaze, she set him loose in the small corral and headed for the back door. The windows on the back of the house also had curtains. Apparently, Izzy went curtain crazy.

She walked inside.

"Stop right there." Izzy stood in front of her with a mop in hand and her hair pulled up with one of Elle's bandanas. She pointed at Elle's feet. "Take your boots off, please. I just cleaned the floor."

Elle tamped down her anger at being ordered around in her own home. However, the stern expression in Izzy's eyes cowed her, and she slipped off her boots and placed them next to the door.

Izzy brightened. "Thank you."

Elle inhaled. The place smelled clean. A new rug rested in the middle of the floor and a vase of cut flowers sat on the kitchen table, which was no longer bare. It was adorned with a lovely tablecloth. A few small tapestries and pictures hung on the walls. A quilted blanket with squares of blue and red was casually tossed over the couch, and blue pillows anchored each end. Her barren, dull home was no longer. "What the heck is all this?"

"I went shopping."

Elle feigned ignorance. "No. Really?"

Izzy smirked in response. "I told Louise at Wilson's that the place needed sprucing up. You couldn't expect me to live in this"—she waved a hand around—"dingy brown place. Now it's bright. And clean. Think of it as me bringing a little Boston to New Mexico." She punctuated it with a smile.

"How did you pay for all this?"

"They said you had an account."

Elle glowered. She needed to have a talk with Louise.

"Oh, and I bought you something." She walked over to the bookcase and handed her a copy of *Walden*. "It's one of my favorites. The author is from Massachusetts."

Elle had read it before, but she didn't want to appear ungrateful, because it was sort of sweet that Izzy bought her a book, even if it was with Elle's own money. "Thank you."

"How was your day? You must've been busy to be gone for so long."

"I had to run a few errands for Rose."

Izzy grabbed her hand. "What happened here?"

"I broke Fergus Guifford's nose. Is that my shirt?"

Izzy gently rubbed her fingers over Elle's sore knuckles. "Why did you break Fergus Guifford's nose?"

"He refused to pay his debts. Is that my shirt?" she asked again.

Izzy brushed dirt from the tan shirt. "Yes. I don't have any clothes. Maybe we can go into town, and I can get something else to wear."

"More shopping?"

"You can't expect me to have only one pair of pants and one shirt."

"Why didn't you buy some new clothes today?"

"I was busy doing other things." Izzy tapped her chin. "Maybe a simple dress would be nice. With no bustles or corsets."

"Mac wouldn't wear a dress."

Izzy slumped. "Sometimes I forget I'm living a total fabrication of a life."

A pang of sympathy echoed in Elle's heart. "We'll get a few more clothes for you. And I guess if Mac wants to wear a dress, she can wear a damn dress."

Izzy brightened. "Thank you. I don't want to wear one all the time, but maybe once in a while. Besides, Rose wears a dress. Something tells me she's not the most law-abiding citizen in New Mexico."

Elle laughed. "True, but Rose is…Rose."

"Speaking of Rose and dresses, I ran into her today."

"Did you talk to her?"

"Yes."

Elle let her head fall back. "Ugh. What did you talk about?"

"She asked where I was from. I told her Boston."

"No! Why did you say that?"

"She caught me off guard."

"What else did you say?"

"I said my family was dirt poor and my daddy was a drunk and my brother was a thief and I helped in his thievery—"

"Oh, God." Elle placed a hand on her forehead and groaned.

"It's a good story. Although she did ask me what bank I robbed, and—"

Elle interrupted her with another groan.

"Yes. It could've been a problem because I had no answer."
Izzy held up a hand. "But I didn't have to give one. Some colonel
walked in, and she left with him."

"She's gonna be suspicious."

"I think I did fine. She won't even remember talking to me."

Elle scoffed. "You think a woman like that forgets anything?"

"Don't be mad at me."

"I wish you would listen. Lay low. Lay. Low. Why did you
go into town anyway?"

Izzy hesitated before saying, "I needed paper and pencils for
Matsu's lessons. I told you I'm teaching her to read and write.
And guess what? She can already write her name. So there. Stop
being mad."

"Okay. Just stay away from Rose."

"You should've seen her dress today. It was bright yellow.
Like a canary. And her hat was orange. It didn't match at all."

"Did you tell her that?"

"No. She'd probably shoot me. She's scary."

"Good. Keep that healthy fear and stay the hell away from
her."

"Did you know she collects money from people on Wanted
posters?"

"Of course, I knew that."

"Do *you* pay her?"

"We all pay something. Freedom has a price. Around here
anyway."

CHAPTER ELEVEN

The next morning, Elle tied a blanket to Blaze's saddle.

Izzy burst through the back door. "Where are you going?"

Elle tucked her new copy of *Moby Dick* into the saddlebag. "Out for a ride."

"Can I come?"

"You stay here."

"C'mon. I'm tired of hiding out. I'm going crazy."

"You were out yesterday and almost blew your cover with Rose."

"So?"

Elle tightened the cinch on Blaze's saddle. Her rides into the canyon were sacrosanct—quiet, peaceful, and solitary. And if Izzy came, quiet would not be what she'd find. Before she voiced her displeasure, she caught the silent pleading in Izzy's eyes.

"Please. I'm so bored. Please?" Her head tilted to the side, and Elle swore she batted her lashes.

It was hard to resist any woman, let alone Izzy, when such a look was given. With a sigh, she nodded.

"Hooray!" Izzy fetched Jack and threw her saddle onto his back. "Is this a picnic? Did you bring food?"

"I brought an apple and a blanket."

"Sounds like a picnic to me. I'll go get some bread and cheese."

After Izzy stuffed her saddlebag with food, Elle set Blaze to a loping pace toward the mountains.

As they rode side by side across the foothills, Izzy asked, "Do we have to worry about Indians?"

Elle slowed their pace down to a brisk walk. "Not anymore. Not around here, anyway."

"What happened to them?"

"They were rounded up before the war. Taken down to the Bosque Redondo Reservation. Small bands of Jicarilla Apache and Ute roam around here and southern Colorado, but they mainly keep to themselves. Too many army forts around now, and after the Navajo Treaty disbanded the reservation about ten years back, would you want to be anywhere near the people who locked you up? But in the western part of the territory across the Rio Grande, it's a different story. A medicine man named Geronimo still leads raids with the Chiricahua Apache."

"It's not right. Kicking them off their own land."

"No, it isn't."

They traveled through stands of yellow-green juniper, blue-tinted piñon pine, and sagebrush. When the tree line thickened, Elle turned left, and they followed a single-file path paved with pine needles. The soft thud of the horses' hooves soothed Elle's soul. As they climbed, the air became cooler, and the juniper and piñon gave way to ponderosa pines that towered over them. Eventually the landscape changed again, and the trees opened into a meadow filled with boulders, wildflowers, and waving grasses. A creek gurgled nearby. On the far side, a huge wall of sheer rock rose from the ground. Patches of green clung to crevices, small plants and flowers holding on for dear life. A waterfall cascaded down the face of the rock.

Izzy gasped. "This is gorgeous."

Elle smiled. "I know. It's my favorite place." She reined Blaze in. "We'll stop here."

She spread a blanket on the ground, kicked off her boots, and stretched out on her back. *Moby Dick* awaited.

"Have you always liked to read?"

Elle hadn't even gotten to page one. So much for a quiet, peaceful day. But then again, spending the afternoon with a captivating woman wasn't half bad either. "I guess so. When Raven and I lived at the mission, we devoured all the dime novels we could get our hands on. When Rose took us under her wing, she introduced us to"—Elle raised her voice to imitate Rose—"proper lit-tra-ture."

"Lit-tra-ture?"

"Yes. That's how she liked to say it. No more stories about outlaws and frontier life. She introduced us to Dickins, Sir Walter Scott, George Eliot, and the like."

"And Alexandre Dumas."

Elle nodded and continued in Rose's voice, "'You two get to reading now, there's lots to learn from books.'"

Izzy giggled.

"She has a wall full of books in her office," Elle said.

"I guess that explains her sons' names. Tiny Tim and Rob Roy. Arthur."

Elle dipped her head. "Very astute of you to pick up on that. Not many folks out here would. Silas was the son who died."

"Named after Silas Marner? How did he die?"

"Cholera took him about five years ago."

Izzy's face fell, and the barrage of questions stopped. Elle opened her book. *Chapter one…*

"When did you become an outlaw?"

With a sigh, she closed the book. Chapter one would have to wait. "You're full of questions today, aren't you?"

"I'm just curious. So, when?"

Elle placed the book on the blanket and turned onto her side to face Izzy. She cradled her head in her hand. "I guess when I was ten."

Izzy mimicked her position. "You did *not* become an outlaw when you were ten."

Elle made a show of rolling her eyes. "Maybe not ten. But Raven and I were not well-behaved."

"That's so unbelievable," Izzy said with a healthy dose of sarcasm. "You both have such angelic natures now."

Elle laughed. Which was becoming a more frequent habit. She couldn't remember ever laughing and smiling as much as she had in the last few weeks. "Angels, no. Devils, maybe? We were both…I guess angry. Angry at life, at what had become of us. Raven more so. I think it really hurt when her mother's tribe rejected her."

"That's awful."

"So, what do you think two angry kids did?" Elle asked.

"Got into trouble."

"Exactly. We'd sneak away from the mission and go into Santa Fe. We'd pickpocket. Steal from the stores. One of us would create a distraction and the other would lift a loaf of bread, that sort of thing."

"You never got caught?"

"Oh, we did. Once. Raven tried to pickpocket Rose."

Izzy's mouth dropped open. "Oh no. How did that go?"

"Not too good. She grabbed us both by the ears and laid into us. Did you ever have your ear grabbed?"

"No."

"It ain't pleasant. After she, uh, expressed her displeasure, she bought us something to eat."

"That was nice of her."

"Yeah. She took a shine to us. She was an orphan too. Lived on the streets of New York and had to learn to take care of herself. I think she saw a bit of herself in us. She'd come to visit and take us on trips to Albuquerque. Taught us how to help her cheat at poker."

"How?"

"Kids are invisible. Especially dirty little urchins like we were. We'd sneak around the tables, look at everyone's cards. Had hand signals to let her know who had what. Simple stuff. Three fingers, three of a kind. Fist was a full house."

"So Rose started you down your lawbreaking path."

"She sure did."

Izzy grabbed Elle's hand and turned it over. She ran a finger down the scar on her palm. "Raven told me about this too." Her eyes sought out Elle's.

A pleasant tingle shot through Elle at Izzy's touch. Izzy's eyes were blue today, not bright blue like the sky, but more muted. Darker on the edges, lighter toward their golden centers. "Yeah. Blood sisters." Their gazes held, and the pleasant tingle spread to other areas of her body. *Another perfect time for a kiss.*

Izzy finally pulled her eyes away and rolled onto her back. "I'm sorry. I'm probably talking too much. Go ahead and read your book. I'll be quiet."

Elle was thankful for the change of subject and the physical distance. Thoughts of kisses twice in two days was a bit much. She needed to exert some mental fortitude and stop reading into things.

A thunder of hooves pounded across the valley.

Izzy stood and shielded her eyes from the sun. "Are those horses?"

"Yeah. I see them a lot when I'm here."

"They're beautiful."

The herd of about twenty stopped and began to graze.

"That big bay is the stallion," Elle said.

"Do they ever come closer?"

"No. They keep their distance. I love to watch them, and they don't seem to be bothered by me."

"Look at that one." Izzy pointed to a pearl-white horse with large black polka dots on its flanks, and smaller dots from the belly to its neck. "He's got spots."

Elle squinted. "Huh. She's new."

"Oh." Izzy smiled. "*She's* got spots. I've never seen one with that coloring."

"It's an Appaloosa."

The horse studied them and, perhaps realizing they didn't pose a threat, wandered closer.

"She's coming over." Izzy snatched Elle's apple.

"Hey!"

"Stop it." Izzy walked toward the mare.

"She's gonna run."

"Maybe she won't." Izzy crept toward the horse.

The stallion flared his nostrils and whinnied. He began pawing the ground.

Elle wasn't sure of the stallion's intentions. The big horse continued to paw at the ground and flick his head up and down. "Please be careful. He might charge you."

"He's not gonna charge me."

Damn if she wasn't right. He gave one last snort in Izzy's direction and grabbed a mouthful of grass. The mare observed Izzy's approach. She lifted her head and sniffed the air.

When Izzy got within ten feet, she stopped and held up the apple. "Hey, pretty girl. Come here. I've got something for you."

The mare ambled over.

Elle had been sitting with this herd for a long time, and never had any of them gotten within a mile of her. And here was Izzy, a greenhorn if ever there was one, coaxing a wild horse to take an apple from her hand.

The mare got to within four feet of Izzy and stopped, so Izzy stretched out her hand. The mare's lips flapped, and she mashed the apple down in her mouth. When finished, she took another step closer and nuzzled Izzy's hand.

Izzy laughed. "I think she wants more."

"That was my only apple."

"I'm sorry, pretty girl. Elle didn't bring enough food for us. Next time." Izzy touched the mare's muzzle and stroked up to the gray forelock that hung between the horse's eyes. She gave her a good scratch. "Her hind end looks like the moon. You know how the moon has those dark spots?"

Elle nodded.

"I'm gonna call her Luna."

Elle shook her head and smiled. Only Izzy would name a wild horse.

"I think she likes me, by the way."

"I think you're right. She must've been someone's horse. She's too tame."

Luna gave a snort when no more apples appeared, but she didn't leave, instead choosing to pull at some of the grass growing nearby.

Izzy plopped back down. "I had a pony once when I was younger. I think I was about nine. We happened to walk by an auction, and he was waiting in the corral. I fell in love with him immediately. He was light brown with a black mane and white socks. I told my father that I had to have him. I refused to budge until my father bid on him. I may have thrown a little tantrum."

Elle lay back on her elbows and crossed her feet. "So you were stubborn way back then too."

"I'm not stubborn. I'm strong-willed. There's a difference."

Elle raised her eyebrows. "Sure."

Izzy gave her a gentle shove. "Go back to your book."

* * *

The clouds danced across the sky and brought with them happy memories from Izzy's childhood. Memories of her and her sisters at family picnics, staring into the sky and turning clouds into images like animals or faces or flowers. Whoever found the most was rewarded with an extra piece of cake, or whatever sweet was in the basket. Izzy usually won, which wasn't surprising, according to her father, since her head was always up in the clouds.

She gazed into the distance. *Do they even miss me? Do they know I never made it to J.B.'s? Would they even care?*

Elle napped next to her. Elle, an unlikely rescuer, who saved her from a fate worse than death. At least, in Izzy's eyes, a fate worse than death. The moment earlier, when Elle had been so close, her lips so very close and Izzy wanted to kiss them, and it shocked her. Just like yesterday morning. *What is wrong with me? First Catherine and now Elle. Why am I suddenly yearning to kiss women?*

Moby Dick lay on Elle's chest, and Izzy picked it up. She folded down the corner of the page to keep Elle's place and turned to chapter one. She had every intention of immersing herself in Ishmael and Captain Ahab's world, but her thoughts kept returning to Elle.

How devastating it must've been to lose your parents at such a young age. To end up at an orphanage, alone and afraid. No wonder she was so devoted to Rose. Elle didn't have the privileged childhood that Izzy had. And her adult life seemed fraught with danger. How different would Elle's life have been if her parents hadn't died? Would she have become an outlaw?

Izzy stood to stretch her legs. Luna rested nearby, so Izzy ambled over and stroked her nose. The horse showed no fear. Izzy whispered into her ear, "Elle's right, you must be someone's horse. Are they missing you, pretty girl? Next time I'm bringing more apples. And sugar cubes. I bet you like sugar cubes."

The valley spread out before her was stunning, with the horses grazing far off in the distance and an assortment of wildflowers blooming. *I'll pick some flowers for the house.*

She wandered away from a still napping Elle, and Luna plodded behind her. She pulled a few yellow flowers and continued along. She wasn't familiar with the flora in New Mexico. She'd ask Elle what they were. After fifteen minutes, she had a nice batch of colorful blooms that smelled delightful. She turned to check in on Elle, who waved and stood. Izzy continued to wander as the trail turned rocky. Up ahead, a cluster of bright blue flowers caught her eye. Blue would go nice with yellow. Luna snorted and tossed her head.

"What's the matter, pretty girl? Come here." She held her hand out, but the horse didn't come any closer. In fact, she began to back up. *Maybe the trail's too rocky.* Izzy inched closer to the blue flowers. When she bent over, an odd rattling came from nearby.

"Izzy, don't move."

She twitched slightly, startled by Elle's voice.

"Don't...move."

She did as she was told. A large, diamond-shaped, scale-covered head rose from the rocks a few feet in front of her. The snake's tongue darted in and out. From the size of the head, the body must've been huge. Her breathing became erratic, her chest rising and falling dramatically as the snake swayed back and forth.

"Stay calm," Elle whispered. "And don't move."

Sweat trickled down Izzy's back. Soon the rattling stopped, and the snake ducked lower. It was no longer visible but still too close.

Elle's quiet voice pierced through the veil of fear surrounding her. "Slowly, take a step back. Slow."

Izzy moved her foot backward. Concentrating on keeping her torso and head still, she took another small step back. Her pace was excruciating. She wanted to turn tail and run.

After another couple of steps, Elle gave her the all-clear. "Okay. Let's go."

Now a safe distance away, Elle turned furious eyes on her. "What were you doing? Are you crazy, reaching behind rocks without looking? If that snake bit you, you'd be dying right now!"

"I didn't know."

"This isn't Boston. You can't walk around without a care in the world."

"I know it's not Boston."

"You're not gonna last long out here if you're not more careful. I can't babysit you every minute of the day."

The comment stung, and Izzy lashed back. "I never asked you to babysit me. I'm more than capable of taking care of myself."

"Pphht."

"I am!"

Elle narrowed her eyes. "You were this close," she said, her thumb and forefinger barely touching, "to getting bit by one of the most venomous snakes in the country. So pardon me if I think you can't take care of yourself."

Tears stung Izzy's eyes, but she refused to let them fall. *I won't give her the satisfaction of making me cry.* "I just took a walk." She crossed her arms and tried to appear defiant. "I don't know how anyone survives out here."

Elle leaned closer. "A lot don't." With that, she turned heel.

Izzy had half a mind to take another walk but then thought better of it, so she hurried after Elle, who had settled back down on the blanket.

Neither said a word for a few minutes.

Finally, Izzy broke the silence. "I'm sorry. I didn't mean to be careless. I'm still getting used to this place."

Elle answered with a grunt.

"But you didn't have to yell at me like I'm a child."

Elle heaved a sigh. "You're right. I'm sorry. I've seen people die from snakebites, and it's not pretty."

A tremor of fear rippled along Izzy's spine. She managed to survive another close call. First the stagecoach incident and now this. And her survival was due to one person: Elle. "Thank you. For saving me. Again. Maybe you're right. I do need a babysitter." Izzy pulled her knees into her chest and stared out into the valley. Luna and the herd were long gone, having melted away into the hills. "I don't belong out here."

"You just need to be more careful. You're doing good for a bluebelly."

"What's a bluebelly?"

A wide grin split Elle's face. "A Yankee."

"You get that from Shorty?"

"Who else? The question is, who used to save you before I came along?"

The tension between them melted away like the herd. "I didn't get into trouble a lot...well, maybe I did. But it was a different kind of trouble. It wasn't snakes and men with guns. It was women's rights. Specifically, the right to vote. Which got me into big trouble with my father. He said I was an embarrassment."

"Was that the reason you were ordered to marry J.B.?"

"Yes." *That, and a kiss. And here I am yearning for another one.*

"I'm sorry," Elle said. "That must've been horrible. To be banished like that."

"I was devastated. And, I had every intention of telling this J.B. that I didn't want to marry him. Or anybody else. I don't ever want to get married."

A silence descended on them.

After a few moments Elle said, "Sun'll be going down soon. Let's head back."

Izzy rolled up the blanket and grabbed Jack's reins. She carefully tucked some of the flowers under the tie-downs on her saddle. A small bunch of more delicate blooms remained in her hands. "This place is breathtaking. How did you find it?"

"This is where I lived for a couple of months." Elle and Blaze trotted off.

A shocked Izzy hopped into the saddle. "Wait!" She set Jack to a canter to catch up. "This is where you lived?"

"Yeah."

Izzy glanced around the meadow. "Where?"

Elle pointed to a large cottonwood tree about fifty yards away. "There." She steered Blaze toward the tree and slid from the saddle.

A stack of rocks lay nearby, the remnants of a possible wall, but other than that, no evidence of a dwelling was visible. "I don't see a house," Izzy said.

"It burned down." Elle removed her hat, and she sank down to her haunches.

Izzy knelt next to her.

Two makeshift crosses had been jammed into the ground, side by side. Elle brushed away some leaves to reveal a flat rock. Scratched into the rock was the word *Barstow*.

A lump formed in Izzy's throat. "What happened?"

"Some bad shit." Elle didn't elaborate.

Izzy's heart broke for ten-year-old Elle. She wanted to know the full story but didn't press her. *Maybe she'll tell me someday.* Izzy laid her flowers on the flat rock. A wayward strand of hair blew into Elle's face, and Izzy tucked it behind her ear.

Elle turned sad eyes toward her, and she cupped a hand around Elle's face. "I'm sorry."

They remained like that for a moment before Elle stood. "We should go."

* * *

Elle kept to herself on the ride back. Those few intimate moments with Izzy confused and confounded her. Visiting her parents' grave didn't help her mood either, but it was the interactions with Izzy that had the most effect. When Izzy caressed her cheek with such tenderness, Elle yearned for more. The urge to pull Izzy into her arms was so strong it took all her strength to stop it from happening. *I need to be more careful.* Maybe a visit to Miriam tonight would quell this sudden thirst for physical contact.

The sun had begun its slow descent behind the mountains when they arrived home.

When Izzy dismounted, Elle made no move to join her.

"Aren't you coming in?" Izzy asked.

"No. I'll be back later."

Izzy's face registered disappointment. "I'll see you when you get back." She grabbed Jack's halter and headed to the barn.

When she disappeared behind the house, Elle turned Blaze toward the heart of town.

Shortly after she arrived at the saloon, Raven joined her at the bar. "Howdy."

Elle grunted a greeting and gulped down her beer. She waved at Rob for a refill.

"You missed a nice fistfight between Jose Alturuz and Ben Gibbons. I put my money on Jose, so the drinks are on me."

Elle finished off the second beer and waved at Rob again.

"Whoa. Slow down." Raven studied her. "What's wrong?"

"Nothing," came out with more force than she intended.

Raven's brows headed north. "Trouble in paradise?"

"What?"

"Trouble with your girl?"

Elle was in no mood for Raven's teasing. "She's not my girl."

"If you say so."

"What's that supposed to mean?"

"Nothing." Raven fussed with her glass. "Just that, since we found Izzy, you kinda been extra happy and smiley and shit. But now you're miserable, so…" She shrugged. "I figured something might be wrong."

Elle had no retort, so she stewed. Raven knew her too well.

"What happens if there's no reward?" Raven asked.

The question came out of nowhere and caught Elle off guard. It was something that never entered her mind, because what man wouldn't want Isabella Collins in their bed and in their life? "Oh, there'll be a reward. And I'm sure it'll be a nice big one." Guilt nibbled at her, but she shook it off.

"Mm-hmm. And will we be collecting it?"

Elle was quick to reply. "Of course. That's the plan, right?"

"That *was* the plan."

"That *is* the plan." Frustrated by the conversation, Elle spun around and scanned the room. Miriam danced close with a sandy-haired soldier, and her eyes found Elle. In those eyes was an invitation, and Elle grabbed a bottle of whisky from behind the bar. "It's on her," she told Rob while nodding at Raven.

* * *

The sun had set hours ago, giving way to a full moon, and Izzy lay alone in bed. *It's the middle of the night and she's still not home.* The front door rattled, and Izzy froze. Her revolver sat on the stand next to the bed. Unsteady footsteps scraped across the floor outside the bedroom. Izzy held her breath as her hand hovered over the gun. Elle's shape appeared in the doorway, and she relaxed.

Elle stumbled toward the bed and collapsed onto it. She stripped down to her undergarments and lay down. The odor of whisky and smoke hung on her like an oversized garment. And another smell clung to her, one Izzy had encountered before. It had permeated the saloon on her first day in Loma, wafting from the women who plied their trade at Rose's.

Elle had been with a woman.

A strange emotion erupted within her. It wasn't disgust or revulsion, nor condemnation or judgment. It was none of those. It was something new.

It was jealousy.

CHAPTER TWELVE

"Let me see your alphabet," Izzy said.

Matsu handed over a piece of paper with her name written across the top and all twenty-six letters following in a neat column.

"Perfect. You're doing so well. Soon you'll be writing your story."

Matsu smiled and dipped her head.

They sat on a blanket in the backyard, as they had every day since Izzy arrived. The first part of the morning, Matsu taught Izzy how to defend herself, and then Izzy took over with her lessons. Matsu was an eager pupil. So far, Izzy had learned that she hailed from central Japan and that her father had taught her to fight.

"Okay. I got us a book at the store. The selection left a lot to be desired, so we're stuck with *Chip, the Cave-Child*. I don't even think it's the whole book, because there's no back cover. And this isn't an ending page. And from what I can tell, it's not very good either. But, we'll take what we can get." Izzy didn't want to use any of Elle's books, because she might very well have to rip out pages and write on them. So a five-cent dime novel would have to do.

Izzy turned to the first page and, using her finger as a guide, began to read. She pointed out letters and groups of letters and sounded them out. Matsu wrote on her paper and mouthed the words. If Matsu spoke, the task would've been easier, but that didn't deter Izzy. And having no teaching experience was no deterrent either. Izzy taught on instinct.

After an hour, Izzy put the book down. "I guess we can call it a day."

* * *

While Izzy taught Matsu, Elle relaxed on the front porch sipping coffee. She was still flustered by her reactions to Izzy on their trip to the canyon the other day. While she sorted through her emotions, she tried to keep some distance between them. She stayed away during the daytime hours, and at night she immersed herself in a book. Izzy seemed to be a bit off also. Perhaps she was puzzled by Elle's behavior, or maybe it was something else. Of course, at night, everything was normal. Izzy still sought out Elle's body for comfort or warmth. Or something.

Raven trotted up. "Howdy." She tied up her horse and slid into a chair. "Where's Izzy?"

"Out back with Matsu. Why?"

"Thought about our discussion last week and stopped by the post office yesterday, since Tuesday is when Poulter usually gets US Marshal stuff."

Elle's heart skipped a beat. "And?"

"He had his stack of new posters sitting there, so I went through them. Nothing about Izzy. Yet. I'll keep checking. Course, we don't know what's been posted anywhere else. I was in Cimarron a few days ago. Nothing there either."

Elle kept her expression neutral. "I'm sure it'll be soon. J.B. probably needed some sort of picture of Izzy, so if he corresponded with her family, that would take weeks."

"True."

A wagon meandered down the street, and Elle did a double take.

"What in hell's fire is she doing all the way out here?" Raven asked.

Rose, who rarely left the vicinity of the saloon, yanked the reins of the horses and stepped down from her buggy. "Morning."

Elle nodded. "Morning." A bit of wariness settled in her gut. Something must be up.

Rose ambled onto the porch and, with a groan, settled into a chair.

"You okay?" Elle asked.

"My back's a bit sore. But I'll live."

"What brings you out here?"

"Can't a woman visit her family?"

Elle smirked. "You hate this part of town. It's too quiet for you."

Rose's eyes darted around. "It is dull."

"Uh-huh. That's why you send Tim or Arthur."

"Well, I have some sensitive business, and when they drink, their lips get loose."

Elle cocked a brow. "Sensitive business?"

"I've managed to come into a wagon full of guns."

"Managed?" Raven snickered.

Rose glowered. "Yes, managed. Seems the army can't keep track of their shipments."

"Army guns? That's a dangerous game," Elle said.

"I need you to take them down to Mosquero. I have a buyer. I don't trust anyone else."

"Okay. I'll round up Shorty and Willy."

"Willy's wife's sick. He's got baby duty," Rose said. "You'll take Mac."

"Mac?"

Izzy bumped open the door with her hip because her hands were filled with a cup and the coffeepot. "Mac what?" She looked expectantly at Elle, then Rose. "I brought you some coffee, Rose."

"You and the gang need to run some guns down to Mosquero for me," Rose said. At Izzy's widened eyes, Rose looked at Elle. "What?"

Elle didn't know what game Rose was playing, but she needed to tread lightly. With a delicate tone, she said, "Mac's trying to lay low right now."

"She can lay low after this job," Rose said. "We all pitch in around here. I'm sure she don't mind showing some gratitude, right, Mac?"

Izzy's jaw clenched, but other than that, she showed no emotion. "I can...ah...help with that." She nodded.

"Good," Rose said. "You'll pick the wagon up from Paul Sutton in Santa Rosa and drive it down to Mosquero. Now, where's my coffee?"

"Right here." Izzy handed her the cup.

Elle leaned against the porch post with crossed arms and stared at Rose's buggy as it disappeared up the street.

"What was that about?" Raven asked.

"She's testing Mac," Elle said.

"Maybe she's testing you," Raven muttered.

"Testing how?" Izzy asked.

Elle nibbled on her bottom lip. "I don't know. Maybe she's seeing if Mac can handle herself."

Izzy placed her hands on her hips. "I can handle myself."

Elle shot a frown in her direction.

"Why don't you come clean?" Raven asked. "Tell her the whole story."

Elle didn't know how to answer the question. Up until this point in her life, she had shared everything with Rose because she considered her family. But something about Izzy's situation begged for discretion. "I'm not ready to," she said with enough force so as to brook no argument.

* * *

Elle clucked at the two sorrels in front of her. Blaze and another horse were tethered to the back of the wagon and followed along. They neared Mosquero. The dusty town was not as big as Loma and not quite as dangerous. But when you ran stolen guns, everywhere was dangerous, which was why she'd sent Raven and Shorty out ahead to scout for possible trouble.

When they entered town, Elle pulled back on the reins. "Let's tie up the horses here." She nodded to the livery stable to their right.

"Why here?"

"In case we run into trouble. Best to keep them away from the wagon."

"Are we expecting trouble?"

Elle hopped from the wagon and untied Blaze and the other horse. Jack had stayed back home because Elle doubted his ability to make a quick getaway. "We always expect trouble."

"I don't know if I like the sound of that," Izzy mumbled.

Elle climbed back into the wagon and snapped the reins. A knot grew in her stomach. Some nervousness was expected when faced with a dangerous job, but today was more nerve-wracking because of Izzy. She was the great unknown. How would she react if things jumped the rails? Would she be a hindrance? Or a suitable ally?

"Every main street is just a bunch of dirt," Izzy observed.

"A far cry from back East, I imagine."

"Have you been here before?"

"Couple times. It's usually a sleepy town. Meaning, the sheriff's usually asleep at his desk. Saloon isn't as nice as Rose's, but the music's better."

"Not when I'm singing." Izzy's eyes sparkled as she gave Elle a wry smile.

Elle tried to look stern but ended up chuckling. "Okay. I'll give you that."

"Wow." She bumped shoulders with Elle. "First time you've smiled in days."

So Izzy *had* noticed. "What do you mean?"

"You heard me."

"I'm an outlaw. Outlaws don't smile."

"That's malarky. You've been smiling since I've known you. So maybe it's me. I'm a good influence on you."

Elle cast a sideways glance at Izzy, who beamed back at her. *That smile. That smile could brighten anyone's day, and God help me, I can't resist it.* The corner of her mouth lifted.

"That's two."

Shorty and Raven galloped up and interrupted the smile count.

"Bit dicey up ahead, boss," Raven said.

"Yeah, we got quite a boodle waiting on us," Shorty added.

Izzy whispered, "Did he say poodle?"

"Boodle," Elle replied. "How many, Shorty?"

"I reckon about twenty nasty-looking jackaroos, all packing iron."

Elle pulled the wagon to a stop. "Let's split up. You two go ahead. If they don't know you're with us, you'll be able to catch them by surprise if things go south."

With nods, they yanked their horses around and headed back.

"Can you translate that for me?" Izzy asked.

"We got twenty armed men up ahead."

"A boodle of jackaroos with guns. Got it."

Elle slapped the reins, and the wagon bounced along the street. Up ahead was their meeting spot, right in front of the aforementioned saloon, and yes, at least twenty rough-and-tumble cowboys and banditos milled around. *Twenty against four. I don't like these odds.* Raven and Shorty leaned against the railing in front of a clothes shop. To an outsider, they appeared bored and uninterested, but they'd be ready to join any fight at a moment's notice. When she pulled to a stop, a man with an eye patch and a thin mustache held up a hand.

"You from Loma?" he asked.

Elle nodded as she slid down from her seat. "You Pedro Flores?"

"Sí." He spat some chew into the dirt at his feet.

"You got the money?" Elle asked.

He maintained eye contact. "Georgie, bring me the money."

A man with a massive belly and bushy beard approached with a burlap sack. "What's a fine filly like you doing prancing around in pants?" He reached out a filthy hand to touch her hair, and she slapped it away. He howled. "I like feisty women."

Elle seethed. She wanted to put him down right there, but she held her temper in check. Opening the bag, she flipped through the stack of bills. Everything seemed in order.

"We need to check the merchandise," Pedro said.

She pointed toward the wagon. "Go ahead."

A couple of Pedro's men joined him, and they peeked under the tied-down canvas cover.

One of the men whistled. "Damn. That's a lot of guns."

"Everything good?" Elle asked. The sooner they got out of here, the better.

Pedro walked back and stood in front of her, eyeing her up. "You Elle Barstow?"

Elle nodded.

"I hear you're a quick shot. Quickest around." When Elle refused to acknowledge her skill, Pedro jerked his head in the direction of the man standing next to him. "My cousin fancies himself a quick shot, right, Carlos?"

Carlos smiled, but his black eyes lacked humor. "Sí. Bet I could best her in a gunfight." His smile widened, showing off a mouthful of crooked yellow teeth.

Pedro hooted. "Well, let's see what you got Carlos. See if you can beat the fastest draw in New Mexico. How 'bout this? Winner keeps the guns and the money. Sound fair?"

"Sounds fair to me," Carlos said. "Ain't no chica can beat me!" His buddies pounded him on the back in agreement.

As the situation became more fraught, Raven and Shorty stared over at her. Raven gave her a slight nod and placed her hand on her gun. Shorty followed suit.

Elle set her lips in a straight line. Sometimes her reputation could be a help by instilling fear, but a lot of times it was a hindrance. Being the best at something meant others always yearned to knock you down or take you out. In this instance, she wasn't worried about losing, but it wouldn't end with the duel. These desperados would take the money and the guns, stepping over their fallen brother on the way out of town. Unless, that is, she and the gang put down a few of the men and made a run for it. The odds were not in their favor, but Elle had faced worse. Izzy was the wildcard, though. Could she react fast enough to make it to safety? Elle wanted to get out of town with limited or no bloodshed. On their part.

"Well?" Pedro asked. "You game? Or you chicken?"

"I'm game. Let's go."

Pedro grabbed the sack of cash. "Let's take this and set it down over here, bien?"

Izzy jumped from the wagon and grabbed Elle's arm. She whispered, "What's happening?"

Elle walked out of earshot a few yards away, Izzy close behind. "I have to duel this guy. Now listen—"

"Duel? What do you mean duel?"

"A duel. You've heard of duels."

"Nobody duels anymore."

"We do out here."

"That's barbaric. What if he kills you?"

Elle glanced back at her adversary. He yukked it up with his compadres. His holster was tied too far back on his thigh, which meant an extra half second or so to get the shot off. Plus, the whole lot of them smelled like they crawled out of a whisky barrel. "I'll be fine. After I shoot him, I'm gonna go after as many of the others as I can to cause a distraction. You run into the saloon and go out the back door. I'll meet you down at the livery stable where we tied up the horses."

"Do you want me to shoot some of them?"

Elle winced. "We got innocent people walking around. Maybe keep your gun holstered."

Izzy grumbled, "I can shoot a gun."

"Yeah. But it helps if you hit something."

"I can shoot in the air. Maybe the noise will scare them."

"With our luck, you'll end up winging someone's kid."

"Not if I shoot up."

"Izzy. Keep your pistol in your pants."

"But I can do it."

Has anyone tested my patience like this woman? Elle placed her hands on Izzy's shoulders. "Please. This is not an ideal situation for us. Just do as I say. Okay?"

Izzy tugged her hat lower, almost covering her eyes. "Fine. I'll meet you at the store."

"Good. Go stand on the porch of the saloon, and when all hell breaks loose, run inside. The back door is right in line with the front door and leads into an alley."

"How do you know there's a back door?"

"I've been in there before."

"Do you go to the second floor here too?"

"What?" Elle narrowed her eyes. "What kind of question is that?"

"I wanna know what you do up there."

"It's none of your business what I do up there."

"You makin' your funeral arrangements?" someone behind them yelled.

Elle stiffened. "Which one said that?"

Izzy leaned sideways to peer over Elle's shoulder. "The big one."

Elle gritted her teeth.

Izzy peeked around her again and with an earnest expression said, "I bet *I* could hit him."

Elle bit back a smile. Because an outlaw about to duel should not smile. And she had already chuckled, so she was in the red for the day. "Go stand over there and look mean. Can you look mean?"

Izzy made a snarly face but somehow managed to still be gorgeous.

It'd have to do. Elle sauntered back to the enemy. She pulled the revolver from her right holster and checked to make sure everything was in order. Satisfied, she slid it back. "Twenty or thirty paces?"

Pedro sought out the eager faces of his compadres. "I think thirty."

They all nodded. Some chuckled nervously. Carlos hooked his thumbs into his belt and smirked. He reeked of overconfidence.

"All right. Back-to-back," Pedro said. "I'll count off the paces."

"Don't kill her, Carlos," Georgie sneered. "Leave some life in her, 'cause I'd like to see what's under those pants."

"We all do," one of the other men shouted.

Georgie cackled before saying, "Yeah, but I git her first."

In her mind, Elle envisioned herself unloading some lead into Georgie's generous gut. *Yep, he's first after Carlos.* She got into position. Carlos's body odor was repugnant, and she was eager to start walking. She rested her hand on the revolver. Most times things went smoothly, her combatant walking the agreed-upon distance, but every once in a while an outlier tried to get the jump on her, and Carlos struck her as far from honorable, so she cocked the hammer on the pistol, holding it in position with her thumb. This would save a precious second or two.

"Listo? Ready?" Pedro asked. "Let's start walking. One, two, three…"

Elle took measured steps, her ears tuned to the man behind her, listening for any movement. *He'll probably turn on twenty.* Her fingers danced along the handle of her revolver. Adrenaline pumped through her veins as her heart pounded in her ears. When the count neared eighteen, her heart rate slowed. She was ready.

Sure enough, when Pedro said twenty, Izzy screamed, "Elle!"

Her whole body twisted quickly, her gun already pointed and firing, shooting Carlos in the right side of his chest. His gun fell to the ground. He stumbled backward and clutched at the red stain on his shirt.

The men surrounding the action reached down to their holsters. *Show time.* Elle took aim at Georgie and put a slug in his side before shooting Pedro in the leg. She took out another two of his men before the others returned fire. She emptied the chamber of the first gun and drew the second while diving behind the buckboard. The acrid smell of gunpowder hung in the air.

Raven and Shorty joined in the fun, and all hell broke loose.

Curious bystanders who'd been brave enough to watch now scattered in every direction like an army of ants leaving their tiny mound of dirt, providing cover for Elle to take off toward the saloon. She prayed Izzy had followed her instructions.

Gunshots rattled around. One struck the post near her head and the wood shattered into tiny fragments. She found the culprit sprinting after her, and a well-placed shot to the gut put him on the ground. She sprinted through the saloon, bouncing off tables and tipsy cowboys, and spilled out the back door into the muddy alley. She slipped and slid through the grime before righting herself. After passing a few buildings, she turned back toward the main street. Up ahead, Izzy sat astride her horse and held Blaze.

When Elle reached her, she hopped into the saddle and yanked the reins around. "Let's go."

They tore down the street, chasing townsfolk onto porches. Elle glanced behind them. A few of the men pursued on horseback, and they faced a race to safety and freedom. Shots continued to explode around them.

"Ooowww!" Izzy screamed. A red spot appeared on her shirt. She had been struck in the upper arm.

"Hold on."

Her face twisted and she moaned, but she stayed upright as they approached the outskirts of town.

Elle returned fire, striking the cowboy leading the pack, who tumbled from his horse. The man behind him tried to swerve away from his body, but his horse's hoof struck the downed man in the head, and the beast stumbled, throwing his rider forward and into the dirt. *One bullet, and two down. Pretty damn efficient.* They raced out of town and toward a large formation of rocks they'd passed earlier. "Pull over after we pass that big rock."

Izzy did as she was told, and they both dismounted. Elle grabbed her Winchester and dove onto the ground to steady her aim. The two remaining horsemen barreled toward them. Izzy groaned softly next to her. Elle shot the first man. The other, suddenly left alone, must not have liked his odds because he yanked his horse around and headed back to town. Elle had him in her sights but lowered the rifle. Shooting a man in the back was a cowardly act.

She turned her attention to Izzy. "Let me see." Taking her knife, she cut away the sleeve of her shirt.

"Hey! This is my best long-sleeved shirt."

"Now it's your best short-sleeved shirt." She inspected the wound and heaved a sigh. "The bullet just grazed you."

"Are you sure?" Izzy checked her arm. "It hurts like heck."

"I'm sure. You'll live." She grabbed the canteen from her saddle and squatted down next to Izzy. "Hold tight. This might sting." Not waiting for a reply, she poured water on the bloody spot.

"Ooowww," Izzy shrieked, and glared at her.

"Stiff upper lip, cowboy."

"Why do I get the feeling you're enjoying this?"

"I'm not enjoying it." With the cut-off sleeve, Elle fashioned a bandage around the area.

"I think you are."

Elle shook her head. "Nope."

"Will it scar?"

Elle nodded. "Yup."

Izzy scrunched her face up. "Great."

"Getting shot's part of being a cowboy. All cowboys get shot. So there. Now you can call yourself a cowboy."

"I don't think all cowboys get shot. You're making that up."

"No. We all get shot."

"How many times have you been shot?"

"A few."

"Prove it."

"You want me to show you my scars?"

Izzy narrowed her eyes. "Yes."

"Fine." She started to undo the buttons on her shirt.

Izzy gasped before grumbling, "Never mind. I believe you."

Elle rebuttoned. She took a deep breath and leaned against the rock. "Whew. That was exciting."

Izzy grimaced. "A little too exciting for me."

Elle's head sagged back. "Shit."

"What?"

"We lost the money *and* the guns. Rose ain't gonna be happy."

"Oh. I grabbed the money," Izzy said.

Elle snapped to attention. "What?"

"I got the money."

"You got the money?"

"I got the money."

"How?"

"It was sitting there, and when you all were doing your duel thing, I grabbed it."

Elle threw her head back and laughed.

"Who's a cowboy now?" Izzy crowed, the pain in her arm momentarily forgotten.

"You're a cowboy. Isabella Collins, cowboy!"

Izzy waved an index finger at Elle. "Don't tell Rose. I don't need her to think that I'm good at this stuff. One time running guns is one time too many for me."

The sound of pounding hooves set them both on edge.

"Are more coming?" Izzy asked.

Elle peeked over the rock. "No. It's Raven and Shorty." She waved at them.

Izzy's head sank low. "Thank God. I've been shot at enough for one day."

"Hey." Elle slid a finger under Izzy's chin and tilted her head up. "You did good."

"Thanks."

She stood and held a hand out. "Let's go."

Izzy grabbed it and her face twisted in pain.

"Matsu will stitch you up. She's good at this stuff."

* * *

After returning from Matsu's, Elle steered a woozy Izzy up the porch steps and through the front door.

"I feel pretty good," Izzy said with a slight slur.

"Probably the laudanum and whisky."

"I need a bath. Can I have a bath? Please? I feel dirty and dusty and...I want a bath."

Elle figured Iz had been traumatized enough today, and to refuse her a bath would be cruel. "Sure. I'll start heating up some water."

After filling the tub, she gave Izzy some privacy. But that didn't last long.

"I need help," Izzy called.

"What?"

"My arm's sore. I can't reach my back. Can you help?"

Washing a beautiful woman's back should never make her pause, but Izzy wasn't just any beautiful woman. She was her current housemate and future payday. Having to constantly remind herself about that was confounding.

"Are you coming?"

What could she say, no? "Yes."

A naked Izzy lounged in the tub, her body mostly hidden below the water, thank God. She handed Elle a cloth, who took it and knelt next to the tub. She dipped it into the warm water and rubbed Izzy's back. She avoided the bandage on her upper arm.

With a moan, Izzy said, "Oh, that feels so good."

The moan and the words jump-started Elle's libido. Her eyes wandered over the soft, pale skin of Izzy's back. *Flawless.* No scars, no marks of any kind. She tried to keep her focus there, but her eyes had a mind of their own. They caressed the swell of Izzy's breasts and dipped farther down. This was the first time Elle had seen Izzy's naked body, and an uncomfortable tug of passion settled in her gut. She yearned to wash the rest of Izzy and carry her to bed.

This will not do. She clamped down on her desire and handed the cloth back. "You can finish." She hustled from the room before Izzy caught the longing etched on her face. She plopped down on the sofa and opened a book. A nice boring book.

From the other room came an, "Uh-oh."

"What happened?" Elle asked.

"My legs won't work." A giggle followed. "You need to help me out of the tub."

"Oh, Jesus Christ," Elle mumbled. She took a deep breath before walking back into the bedroom.

"I'm too tired to get up," Izzy said. "Or. Probably the whisky has killed my legs." She giggled again.

Elle blew out a frustrated breath. Now besides washing a beautiful naked woman, she'd have to wrap her arms around one. Oh, well, no getting around it. "All right. You ready?"

Izzy nodded.

Elle slipped her arms under Izzy's and hauled her up. Izzy's breasts rested against her forearms, sending shivers racing through Elle's body. When she had her upright, she said, "Hold on to the edge of the tub and I'll grab the towel."

Izzy gripped the edges, and Elle wrapped the towel around her body.

Now that Izzy's body was mostly covered, Elle scooped her up and deposited her into the bed. "There you go." She made a move toward the door.

"Are you leaving?"

"Yes…why?"

"Isn't it bedtime?"

"I'll be back in a bit. Just wanted to…uh…finish the chapter I started." She left before Izzy protested anymore.

Half an hour later, Elle figured the coast was clear, so she headed back to the bedroom to find Izzy buried under the covers. She undressed quickly and slid in.

Almost immediately Izzy poked her head out. "Hi."

"I thought you were asleep."

"No. What are you doing?" Izzy's eyes were still glassy from the medicine and alcohol.

"I'm going to bed."

Izzy smiled. "I know that, silly. Are you tired? I'm not tired."

"I'm tired."

"Shoot. I'm not. Damn it." Izzy threw her good arm over her eyes and moaned. "I'm bored."

"Bored? It's time to go to sleep."

"I don't wanna sleep." She turned on her good side. "Tell me something about your childhood."

Elle had finally calmed her body down, and now this. All she wanted was some peace. Some nice, nonsexual peace. "Okay. Like when?"

Izzy waved a hand in the air. "I don't know. When you were six or something."

Elle made a face. "I don't remember too much when I was six."

"Oh, no. How can that be? Why don't you remember when you were six?"

Were those tears in her eyes? Elle almost laughed. No more laudanum for Izzy. It gave her a case of the dramatics. "Calm down. I do remember something. I got my own horse for the first time." Truth be told it was much earlier, but Izzy demanded a story so Elle would give her one.

Izzy's face turned serious. "What happened?"

Elle flipped onto her back and stared at the ceiling. "It was a gray horse with white stockings. Kinda like Jack, but smaller. I named him Smoke. He didn't have a saddle, but that didn't matter. My father placed me on his back and told me to hold on with my knees." She turned her head toward Izzy, whose mouth hung open. She was down for the count. So much for storytelling. Probably better anyway. Elle felt dog-tired and couldn't remember the rest of the tale.

She turned down the lamp on the bedside table and settled in. Within seconds, Izzy snuggled against her side. Her hand trailed across Elle's chest and rested on her breast.

Another long night lay ahead.

CHAPTER THIRTEEN

Izzy sipped her coffee as the sun inched up over the horizon. Elle was out back saddling Blaze and had informed her she'd be gone until the evening, so Izzy planned her day. First Matsu's lessons, then a trip to see Luna.

Elle poked her head in the back door. "I'm leaving now."

"I'm going to the canyon today," Izzy stated. "I wanna see Luna."

Elle stepped into the room. "No. I don't want you wandering off by yourself. It's not safe. You don't even know where you're going. Besides, you were shot a couple of days ago. You need to rest."

"My arm's better, and I know where I'm going."

"You've only been there once. The path is not well marked. It's too dangerous."

Izzy was transported back to Boston, and Elle became her father forbidding her to do something. She threw her shoulders back. "I'll be fine."

With lowered brows, Elle pointed a finger in her direction. "No. You stay here. Got it?"

After a pause, Izzy gave a slight nod, but not a full one. It was like crossing your fingers behind your back to negate a promise.

"I'll see you when I get back."

Izzy fumed. "I'm going," she said to the empty room. "And I'll be fine."

After spending an hour with Matsu, Izzy packed lunch for herself and a few apples and sugar cubes for Luna. She had a wild idea and threw Jack's brush into the bag. *Maybe Luna likes to be brushed.* After tying a blanket to the back of the saddle, she held her coat in her hand. The sun shone brightly, and the day was warm. *I don't need a coat.* The coat stayed on the porch. As she swung into the saddle, a joyful sigh escaped her lips. She looked forward to a nice, relaxing few hours alone.

As she galloped toward the mountains, a feeling of awe overcame her. The view still took her breath away and would never get old. So far life in Loma had been better than expected, save for the getting-shot part, of course. Her cowboy education was progressing. Here she was, riding a horse along a trail by herself. A feeling of pride took hold. If her father and mother could see her now, would they even recognize her? Her skin was sun-kissed, her body leaner, although not as muscular as Elle's, but it was a far cry from the soft curves of her Boston days. The thought of Elle brought a smile to her face.

"I don't know what it is about her, Jack."

He flicked an ear backward.

She had yet to sort through the myriad emotions from last week. *Emotions? Pfft. Emotion, singular.*

"Why was I jealous?"

Jack plodded along without answering.

Up ahead, two dirt paths converged. Izzy stared at the junction of the trail. Was this the turn? She put a finger to her lips. Yes. This had to be it. A tug on the reins sent Jack down the single-track trail to the left. "The canyon's up here, Jack. A few more minutes."

He shook his head and tugged at the bit.

Soon the meadow and all its color lay before her like a bright canvas painting. Izzy puffed her chest out and patted Jack's neck. "We did it." A nibbling of excitement shot through her. The herd had already arrived. Izzy slid from the saddle and spread the blanket over a soft, grassy spot.

"You stay here." After giving Jack an affectionate scratch under his chin, she edged closer to the wild horses. At first, she was disappointed because Luna didn't appear to be with them. But then a shrill neigh broke the silence, and the spotted mare trotted over to Izzy like she was greeting an old friend.

Izzy clapped her hands and laughed as Luna approached. The horse pushed her nose into Izzy's hand and chuffed. Izzy gave up the sugar cube hidden in her palm. "You like that, don't you?" Luna's lips flapped against Izzy's hand. "Hold on. I have more, but you can't eat them all at once." She produced an apple, and Luna gobbled it up.

"Will you follow me if I go back to my blanket?" She walked to her picnic spot, and Luna followed.

After an hour of reading and relaxing, she stood and stretched her arms over her head. "Luna, come over here." The horse trotted over and the sugar cube in Izzy's hand disappeared. "I think I'm spoiling you. How about a brushing?"

She slid the bristly brush along her back, and Luna's head dipped up and down while her tail swished side to side. "Somebody likes this." When finished, Luna looked like a new horse. All the mud on her legs had disappeared, and her mane and tail were knot-free. "You're even prettier now."

After eating a bacon sandwich, Izzy lay on the blanket and stared up at the sky. The day had shaped up to be exactly as she'd hoped. Peaceful and quiet. Of course, if Elle had accompanied her, it would've been even better.

Izzy closed her eyes. *Elle.* She was never far from Izzy's thoughts.

"Why does my body tingle when I'm around her?"

The horses nearby had nothing to say. "You're no help. Neither one of you."

The tingles grew stronger at night as they lay in bed together. Even certain times during the day, their eyes would meet and Izzy's breath would hitch as she fought to still the fluttering in her chest. A soft and rhythmic fluttering, like a butterfly beating its wings against her rib cage. And now, in addition to staring at Elle's lips and imagining how soft they would feel, Izzy would stare at Elle's hands and wonder how they'd feel on certain parts of her body. *Does Elle dream about touching me?*

The first day in the saloon played back in her head, specifically an image of Elle climbing the steps and one of Rose's girls following her.

She shot upright. *Is that why I'm jealous? Because her hands are touching somebody else?*

Izzy groaned. "That *is* why I'm jealous. I want her to touch me." She covered her face with her hands. "What's wrong with me?" First Catherine and now Elle—although these confusing feelings were stronger around Elle. Now Catherine seemed more like a young girl's crush. But Elle? Elle made Izzy *want* things. Crave things she didn't understand. Was her father right? Was she perverse and immoral?

"Ugh. What am I going to do?"

So far, besides a look here and there, real or imagined, Elle had made no improper moves. Until—or if—Elle ever showed her hand, Izzy would keep her feelings to herself. Maybe they would fade. But that didn't mean Izzy wouldn't still seek out Elle's arms at night. She would adamantly refuse to give that up regardless.

The afternoon sun began its journey down toward the mountains, so she packed up her blanket and book. She fed Luna the last sugar cube and hugged her. "Next time, pretty girl."

And hour later, Izzy pulled Jack to a stop and frowned. She didn't recognize anything. *Maybe I took a wrong turn.* "No worries. We'll take that other trail."

Another hour passed by, and still nothing was familiar. The sun dipped lower, and Izzy's pulse raced. Her belly grumbled from lack of food. "Let's backtrack." It sounded so easy, but a niggling of fear pricked at her brain. She finished another bacon sandwich as darkness crept across the landscape. A howl carried on the wind, and she shivered. Izzy was lost, and if a coyote didn't kill her, Elle would.

"I refuse to be helpless. What would Elle do?"

She'd build a fire, that's what she'd do. Izzy found a spot and dismounted. This was one of her first lessons on the trail to Loma Parda, and it needed to be done before the sun completely left the sky. She hunted for wood and kindling, and when she had a few armfuls, she fetched the matches from her saddlebag. Soon a tiny fire flickered, and Izzy grabbed her blanket. Her damn coat was on the back porch. *Lesson learned.*

She huddled in the warmth of the flames and prayed she'd make it through the night. Her rifle lay nearby, just in case. At least she'd had the forethought to shove the Winchester into the saddle holder. Her gun holster sat on the chest back at the house. Lesson two: Always wear your gun. She was even worse with the rifle than the revolver, but maybe the sound alone would scare off the beast who cried in the distance.

* * *

A dark house greeted Elle when she arrived home after sunset. Not a hint of a lamp burned. She hopped from the saddle and threw open the door. "Izzy?" She was met with silence. "Izzy?" She hustled through the house and onto the back porch. Jack was missing, and Izzy's coat lay on one of the chairs. "Jesus. I'm gonna kill her."

Elle grabbed Izzy's coat and an extra blanket, shoved some food into a sack, and hurried out the front door. Thankful for the light of the full moon, she set Blaze off at a gallop.

On the way to the canyon, Elle's mind went rogue, imagining every way Izzy could be hurt, or worse. Cougars. Wolves. Coyotes. Outlaws. Her belly twisted in fear. She wavered between worry and anger. *Is she okay? Why did she defy me and leave the house?* This was the way of things since Izzy had burst into her life, and Elle wasn't sure she liked it. She had enough to worry about, what with the threat of prison and possibly the gallows always lurking around every corner. Now she had a headstrong woman who drove her nuts and didn't listen. She was stubborn, willful... and stubborn, and bullheaded. She passed the time wracking her brain for more synonyms. Obstinate. Cantankerous. Pigheaded.

As the canyon neared, she steered Blaze toward higher ground. Maybe she could spot Izzy from there. Sure enough, off to the right, smoke curled slowly skyward. *Please let it be her.*

As she approached, she dismounted and dropped the reins. No sense barreling in. What if it wasn't Izzy? She crept forward, spotted Jack, and exhaled. A curled-up form huddled under a blanket near the fire. Elle could see her shivering. "Izzy."

A head popped up. "Elle?" Izzy tossed the blanket aside and fell into Elle's arms. "I knew you'd find me. I just knew it."

Elle squeezed her. All the worry from the last hour seeped away.

They stood in each other's arms for a few minutes, neither wanting to let go.

Finally, Elle dropped her arms and cupped Izzy's cheeks. "Are you okay?"

With a smile, Izzy said, "I am now."

"You're not hurt?"

"No. I'm cold. And hungry. But I'm not hurt."

Elle's shoulders sagged and her hands dropped back down to her sides. This woman would be the death of her. Not the marshals. Not the hangman. This. Woman.

"I built a fire, like you taught me."

"I see that. I also saw your coat on the back porch. And your gun in the bedroom."

"Yeah. I forgot those. But I had my rifle."

"'Cause you're so good with it?"

"I figured I'd at least act like I could shoot it."

"You know we have cougars in these hills."

"I may have heard one of those. Did you bring any food?"

Elle gave a low whistle, and Blaze trotted into view. "Of course I did."

They hunkered down by the fire and ate some dried meat and sipped whisky. After eating, Izzy still shivered.

Elle removed her hat and ran her fingers through her hair. "Come over here. We've gotta get you warm." She opened her arms and Izzy slid between her legs with her back against Elle's chest. Elle rubbed her hands up and down Izzy's arms because it was the quickest way to get her body temperature back up. At least, that's what Elle told herself. "We'll head home when you feel better."

Izzy snuggled closer. "Okay."

Elle sighed. She could think of worse ways to pass the time. Elle had stopped questioning how holding Izzy felt right somehow. And it didn't matter. This affection would end soon enough once J.B. took Izzy away, and Elle would go back to living alone. And being alone. *Why does that feel so depressing?*

"What happened to your parents?"

Elle stiffened.

Izzy pulled back and gazed at Elle. Even in the darkness, her eyes shone brightly. "Or is it too painful to talk about?"

"It was a long time ago." That horrible night sixteen years earlier was not something Elle talked about. Only Raven knew the whole story, but Elle quickly determined that there was probably no harm in telling Izzy. She'd sort out why she felt that way later. Much later. "Some vigilantes came to our house and hung my daddy and killed my momma."

Izzy's wide eyes held a look of horror. "Why?"

"They accused him of stealing guns and strung him up. My momma was…guilty of loving him. I would've been killed too, if they'd found me."

"You weren't there?"

"I was hiding. Witnessed the whole thing."

Izzy gasped. "That's horrible. Did he even do it? Steal the guns?"

"Oh yeah. He was a thief his whole life." She sighed. "It's a shame because that cabin in the canyon was the first time we'd settled down. He was always running from something, or someone. He wasn't a bad man, and he loved us. He was just…"

Elle didn't know how to finish the sentence. She had loved him back, despite his flaws.

"Where did you go afterward?"

"I went back the following day. The cabin was burned to the ground. Their bodies were left in the dirt. I dug a couple graves and buried them. After that, I didn't know where to go. Next day, a US Marshal showed up. He took me to the mission in Santa Fe and promised to find the killers."

"Did he find them?"

Elle sneered. "No. My daddy stole from the wrong man. And no marshal was gonna help. Hell, he was probably on their payroll. I found one of them, though. Made him pay."

Izzy's brows rose. "Was that the first man you killed?"

Elle nodded. "After running with Rose a few years, I spotted him. Frank Businsky was his name. Knew what I was gonna do the minute I laid eyes on him." She formed a fist. "I should've done more at the time. Maybe I couldn't have saved my father, but I could've helped my mother. I was scared and I froze."

"You were just a little girl. Like you said, they would've killed you too."

Elle stared at nothing as she relived the moment. "I felt helpless. I made a vow I'd never feel helpless again."

"I'm so sorry." Izzy threw her arms around her, and Elle welcomed the comfort that Izzy provided. They stayed melded together for a few moments.

When Elle's strength returned, she gently disengaged from Izzy's arms.

The fire crackled and sparks flew into the air. They sat in silence for a few moments until Izzy slipped her hand into Elle's. "How did your parents meet?"

On safer ground, Elle relaxed. "They met in Missouri. My daddy was a handsome man. A charmer. My momma said it was love at first sight. She came from a well-to-do family. Said she found him dashing and beautiful, and they ran away together." She chuckled at the memory of her momma telling her the tale of how they'd built a life together, a no-good outlaw and a high society young woman. "He may have drank too much and cursed too much, but she adored him. And in the end, she paid the price for loving him."

"So that's why you don't let anyone near that outlaw heart of yours," Izzy murmured. "You're afraid for them, not you."

"I suppose." Elle wasn't in the mood to analyze her "outlaw heart." "It's getting late."

Izzy kissed the back of Elle's hand.

The show of affection generated a mountain of movement inside Elle's chest. She jammed her hat back on her head and stood.

After kicking dirt on the fire, they mounted up.

A quietness settled upon them on the way home. Reliving that day sixteen years ago had left Elle shaken. She wrestled with an old friend—an old friend called guilt that had been her bedfellow for so long. Guilt for not helping her momma. Guilt for being a coward when her momma needed her the most. Guilt that she'd managed to bury for such a long time, and now it reared its ugly head.

Logic told her Izzy was right. A ten-year-old girl didn't stand a chance against a man with a black heart. No witnesses, he'd said. That meant he would've killed her also.

She trembled. Sleep would be hard to come by tonight, but having Izzy in her arms might bring her peace.

CHAPTER FOURTEEN

Elle groaned. Behind her in the tub, Miriam rubbed at the knots buried in her shoulders.

"You're still tight," Miriam said.

"Mm-hmm." Elle's head lolled side to side. She'd had no intention of dallying with Miriam today, but this morning Izzy had been wrapped around her, and again her wayward hand clutched Elle's breast. It had lit a fire in her belly. That want had stayed with her throughout the morning hours as Izzy bustled around the house, cleaning. It persisted as Izzy sat on the back porch with Matsu, patiently teaching her how to write. Finally, Elle's craving for release drove her from the house and into Miriam's arms.

"Things seemed different today," Miriam said.

"Oh?"

"Yeah. You seemed more…I dunno, more heated. More urgent." Miriam kissed the sensitive spot behind her ear. "Almost like you were having sex with someone else."

Shame washed over Elle. She was thankful that Miriam couldn't see the heat that rushed into her cheeks, because things indeed had been more passionate than usual. *Was I thinking of someone else while lying in the arms of Miriam? Yes.* And unfortunately, that someone was a fetching, beautiful, stubborn, Isabella Collins.

While kissing Miriam, it was Izzy's face that kept popping into Elle's mind. It was Izzy she stroked, Izzy's passionate moans that drove her crazy, Izzy's release that brought her as much or more pleasure than her own.

Her lack of a quick denial must've triggered something in Miriam. "You weren't, were you?" she asked.

"What?"

"Thinking of someone else?"

Elle had no choice but to say, "No, of course not."

Miriam gently turned Elle's face toward her. "Are you sure?"

Elle shot her a cocky smile. "Yes. I'm sure."

Miriam stared for a few extra seconds, then grinned. With a teasing tone, she said, "Good. Because I'm the only one who knows how to give you pleasure, Elle Barstow, and don't you forget it."

Elle tugged Miriam onto her lap. "Now how can I ever forget that." She nipped at her neck and reached a hand between their thighs, giving them both the friction they craved.

Between moans, Miriam said, "I know that woman is living with you. Mac? She better not find her way into your bed. Or your heart."

Elle's hand slowed before picking up speed. "Don't be silly." She winked and took a cue from Izzy. "Nobody will find their way into this outlaw's heart."

"Maybe not your heart. But maybe here." Miriam's hand joined Elle's between their thighs.

Elle's breath caught in her throat as Miriam caressed her center. She banished Izzy from her mind, but it was a short exile.

"She's beautiful," Miriam murmured.

Elle feigned innocence. "Who?"

Miriam's mouth was next to her ear. "You know who."

"Mac?"

"Uh-huh."

They both panted and gasped as their arousal peaked.

"Huh. I never noticed."

Miriam found some extra breath to push out a laugh. "Now I know you're lying. You always notice a beautiful woman."

Elle was close, so close. Somehow, this conversation increased her pleasure. "Okay, she's beautiful...but she's also stubborn...and, oh, oh yeah..." Another few seconds and she'd explode. "She's opinionated, she's, she's pigheaded—oh God oh—she doesn't listen, and..." An explosion of intense pleasure stole the words from her mouth. She threw her head back as the sensations rippled through her body. When spent, she collapsed into Miriam's arms. It took a minute to realize she hadn't returned the favor for Miriam, which was unlike her. She began stroking between Miriam's folds, but Miriam stayed her with a hand.

"It's fine." She tenderly kissed Elle's neck. "I have to get back downstairs." She rose from the tub, dried off, and began dressing.

Elle sank deeper into the tepid water. She'd never left Miriam hanging before. She didn't know what to say. The moment felt awkward.

Miriam opened the door and paused. Without turning, she said, "You better watch that outlaw heart of yours."

After getting dressed and regaining her equilibrium, Elle burst from the saloon and into the warm afternoon air. Something seemed off. She glanced up and down the street. The constant swirling dust was absent. No wagons rolled by. No cowboys hung out on porches smoking. It was quiet. Too quiet. Young Tom, the livery boy, walked by leading a tan quarter horse by a halter. "Tom, where is everyone?"

He pointed to the east side of town. "They're on Jerry Douger's farm. Playing baseball, I think."

Baseball? Elle fumed. *Izzy.*

She jogged the few blocks to Jerry's farm and stopped short at the sight in front of her. A big crowd of people surrounded a makeshift field. Hoots and hollering carried on the warm breeze. Izzy readied her arm to pitch. Raven and Shorty stood on opposite sides of the base paths.

Izzy tossed the ball and Harry Sullivan swung the bat, knocking the ball up the baseline. Joe Abbott picked up the ball and shoved Harry to the ground before he reached first base. Harry stood and slugged Joe in the chin. Shouts erupted from the crowd, and soon everyone got in on the action.

Izzy, probably trying to maintain some order, waved her arms in vain. Elle had seen some big dustups in Loma before, but this was probably the biggest. And there was no stopping anybody once they started pounding each other. If one could observe from a safe distance, it was amusing—as long as nobody drew a gun, of course.

Izzy managed to pick up the baseball and marched off the field. Her lips were moving, and her head bobbed up and down. When she spotted Elle, she headed straight for her. Elle was ready to berate her for not laying low, but when Izzy came upon her, she bit back her stinging rebuke.

Izzy pointed back at the melee. "Can you believe this?" Her eyes, full of fury, had taken on an emerald hue. "Why can't these people get along? Everything turns into a fight around here." Before Elle could open her mouth, Izzy poked a finger into her chest. "And don't you dare say anything about me laying low." The poking finger wagged in her face. "I'm not in the mood to hear it." And with that, she stormed away.

Elle's mouth dropped open. She had half a mind to give chase and impose her will on Izzy, because *nobody* talked to her that way. But this was Izzy. Who was damn cute when mad.

Across the way, the fight showed no signs of slowing down. Raven hung onto the back of some unknown combatant, and Shorty tussled with a couple of off-duty soldiers. No shots fired yet, so maybe it would all end with a few bruised faces and egos.

The image of Izzy poking her in the chest made a chuckle bubble up from her throat. A sudden need to be near her made Elle turn tail. "Mac, wait." When she caught up, she tugged on Izzy's arm. "Slow down. What's the rush?"

Izzy stopped. "What do you want?"

Elle tried not to smile. "What happened back there?"

"What happened? What do you think happened?" Izzy's brows drew together, and her top lip curled up.

Elle should've been annoyed at the condescending look, but she laughed instead. She found the whole situation comical, from Izzy's valiant effort to instill some civility into Loma to her combatant tone now.

Izzy was clearly not amused by Elle's amusement. "You think that was funny?"

The question only made Elle laugh harder.

A condescending tone replaced Izzy's condescending look. "*This* is what happened. We *tried* to have a baseball game. Only it *turned* into a baseball *brawl*." With a disgusted huff, she hurried off.

"Where you going?" Elle shouted.

"To load my damn bear."

Elle followed Izzy right up the steps to Rose's and through the swinging doors. A man grabbed Izzy as she passed by. He said something and leered. She twisted his hand and swept his feet out from underneath him. The poor cowpoke landed with a *thud* and an *oof*. The move screamed Matsu. Evidently, Izzy was an apt pupil.

Elle caught up in time to hear Izzy say, "I'm not interested." She made a beeline for the bar and banged her hand down. "Whisky."

Rob placed a glass in front of her and filled it to the brim.

Izzy's voice softened. "Thank you."

Elle snuck up next to her, and Rob filled a glass for her too.

Izzy drained hers in one gulp. She waved at Rob for a refill.

Elle leaned into her ear. "Maybe you should slow down, cowboy."

Izzy sneered and gulped down another glass full.

"Impressive leg sweep back there."

Izzy ignored her and waved at Rob again.

Elle changed tactics and shifted closer to Izzy until their shoulders brushed. "I'm sorry about your baseball game."

Maybe it was the third shot of whisky or maybe their intimate contact, but the tension in Izzy's body ebbed away. She made no effort to put any distance between them. "Thanks."

Before Elle could stop herself, she said, "I have to go to Santa Fe. Why don't you come with me?"

Izzy jerked her head around. "Really?" Her eyes, which had reverted to their hazel middle ground a second ago, turned a soft blue.

"Yes." Elle had no idea why she asked. Was it to boost Izzy's spirits? Or was something else at play? She had no idea, but she did know she felt a need. A need to...*what exactly?* Be near Izzy? Be somewhere away from Loma with her?

A fistfight broke out on the dance floor, and patrons shouted out bets.

Elle drained her glass. "Let's get out of here."

Izzy studied the brawlers. "Maybe we should bet on Fred."

Elle laughed. "I think this town is rubbing off on you. And not in a good way." She gently tugged her hand. "C'mon."

Once outside, Izzy pointed. "It's Willy."

Willy drove a small wagon with his wife and baby on the seat next to him. He tugged on the reins. "Afternoon, Mac, Elle. We heard about a baseball game. Came down to show Perlie here. She ain't never seen one."

Izzy shook her head. "Oh, Will. The game was over before it began. Joe and Harry got into a row, and of course, everybody joined in."

"Well, shoot. Maybe next time."

"Is this your wife and little girl?" Izzy asked.

"Heavens. Where are my manners? Iz—I mean Mac, this is my wife, Perlie, and this pint-sized spitfire is my baby girl, Hattie."

Perlie handed the baby to Willy and clamored down from the wagon seat. She patted down a wayward strand of brown hair before saying, "Miss Mac, I've heard all about you. It's nice to finally meet you." She embraced Izzy and whispered something in her ear.

Whatever she said brought a smile to Izzy's lips. "Hattie is adorable."

Perlie reached up to Willy. "Give her here." Willy handed Hattie to his wife and Perlie presented her to Izzy. "Miss Mac, meet Miss Hattie Pearson. We named her after my momma."

"How old is she?"

"Seven months."

Izzy shook Hattie's tiny hand and cooed, "Good afternoon, Miss Hattie." Izzy extended her arms. "May I?" Soon she had a bubbly seven-month-old bouncing in her arms. "Look at that radiant smile." Izzy glanced at Elle. "Do you want to hold her?"

Elle froze. She'd never held a baby before. "Oh, uh, I don't think I'm good with babies."

"Stop it. Hold the baby."

Elle frowned as Izzy thrust the baby into her hands. She held her up by the armpits, and Hattie kicked her legs and giggled.

"Don't drop her," Izzy teased.

She glared. "I won't."

"You're holding her like a sack of flour," Izzy said. "She won't bite."

"Well, she might," Willy joked.

"Hold her close to your chest." Izzy scoffed in Perlie's direction. "The quickest draw in New Mexico is afraid of an itty-bitty baby. Big bad outlaw Elle Barstow, bested by a seven-month-old."

Willy and Perlie hooted at Elle's expense.

Elle adjusted Hattie's position, and now the baby was pressed against her chest and, from the feel of it, drooling on her shoulder.

"Bounce her," Izzy demanded.

"When did you get so bossy?" But Elle did as she was told, and Hattie giggled some more. And drooled some more. Elle would make Izzy wash her shirt for all this humiliation. "Here. I don't wanna break her."

Perlie gathered Hattie into her arms, and Willy guffawed again. "Don't worry, boss, she won't break. She's tougher than you think."

They chatted for a while then said their goodbyes. Elle and Izzy fetched their horses from the stable and headed for home.

When they got back, Elle boiled water for coffee. "What did Perlie say to you when she hugged you?"

"That Willy told her my story and that my secret was safe with her."

"That's sweet. You were good with Hattie."

"I've had practice with my nieces."

It struck Elle how little she knew of Izzy's past life beyond the few tales she'd spun on the trail to Loma.

"You, on the other hand, were a disaster," Izzy said with a grin.

"I've never held a baby before."

"Really?"

Elle gave her a dumbfounded look. "When would I have held a baby? Oh, by the way, you're washing this shirt."

"Why?"

"It's filled with drool."

"Where?" Izzy inspected the damage. "Oh, that teensy spot?"

"It's a big spot."

Izzy inhaled. "You smell like soap."

"Are you sure it's not baby drool?"

"I'm sure. When did you bathe?"

Elle hesitated. "Um, at Rose's earlier."

The mood in the room chilled.

"I see." Izzy pressed her lips together.

Elle felt like she'd been caught doing something she shouldn't have done. She tried to read Izzy's eyes. Did their depths contain disappointment? Or an accusation?

With a dismissive tone, Izzy said, "I'm going out back to read." She grabbed a book and marched toward the back door.

Elle tried to make light of the situation. "Are you mad because I took a bath?"

Izzy paused but didn't turn around. In a quiet voice, she said, "No. I'm mad because of why you had to take a bath."

When the door closed, Elle threw her hands out. "What does that mean?" she grumbled. She tried to sort it out in her head. Did she know that Elle had sex with Miriam? And if she did, was she...*jealous*?

If Izzy only knew who Elle thought about during her time in Miriam's arms, would she be jealous then?

Elle found herself in bed alone. Izzy had yet to speak to her and had yet to come in from outside. She turned onto her side and punched the pillow. "Women," she muttered. She hoped Izzy thawed before they left for Santa Fe tomorrow.

Finally, Izzy crawled into bed.

Elle waited for her to speak. When she didn't, Elle forced the issue. "Are you all right?"

"Yes." The dismissive tone had disappeared.

"You haven't spoken to me in hours. Tell me what I did."

"Nothing."

Elle moved closer. "I did something. Why can't you just tell me?"

"It's nothing. Please, can we not talk about it?"

The moments that had passed between them the last couple of weeks were not figments of Elle's imagination. She sensed that now. Elle was witnessing Izzy's sexual awakening. Without thinking, she stroked Izzy's face. "What do you want, Iz?"

"I don't know."

At least she was honest.

Elle flipped onto her back and, with a sigh, pulled Izzy into her arms. If circumstances were different, if Izzy were any other woman, Elle would've tried to seduce her by now. What made the circumstances different? Because soon a reward poster would appear, and Izzy would be out of her life. But shouldn't that make the seduction more attractive? No strings. No attachments. Just pleasure. Hers and Izzy's, because Elle was sure Izzy had a passionate nature, and she ached to be the one to unlock it.

So, what held her back?

Miriam's parting words played in her head. *You better watch that outlaw heart of yours.*

CHAPTER FIFTEEN

Izzy nibbled on her thumbnail as she stared at the clothes on the bed.

"C'mon. Let's go," Elle called from outside.

Izzy ran to the back door and threw it open.

Elle sat astride Blaze. "You ready?" she asked.

"You said seven or eight days, right?"

Elle took a breath. "Yes."

"I don't know what to pack."

"Just pack a few things."

"My entire wardrobe is 'just a few things.'"

"Then pack it all. C'mon."

"All right. Give me a minute." Izzy rushed back inside and stuffed some clothes into a satchel. "I guess these will have to do," she muttered, not pleased with her choices. Clothes shopping in Loma was a limited affair. She hustled back outside. "Here I am."

"Finally," Elle said with an exhausted tone.

"Oh, stop. This is my first big trip, and I want it to be special." She checked to make sure the saddle on Jack was secure. "Unfortunately, I don't have special clothes for this special occasion." She shot a glance toward Elle, who stared back at her from under furrowed brows. "What's the matter?"

"You always take forever to get ready."

"I do not." She hauled herself into the saddle and picked up the reins. "And when do you ever take me anywhere?" She tried to imitate Elle's voice. "Lay low. Lay low! So your statement is ridiculous."

Elle made a face.

"Well, let's go," Izzy said. "What are you waiting for?"

Elle finally smiled and shook her head. "You are…"

Izzy loved that smile. She beamed at her. "I'm what?"

Elle opened her mouth, then closed it. With a shake of her head, she sent Blaze down the street.

Izzy squeezed her knees, and Jack followed her command. When she caught up, Izzy asked again, "I'm what, Elinor Barstow?"

"You are…something."

"Well, that's better than being nothing." Izzy was so happy to be going somewhere different. And the fact that she'd get to spend this time away with Elle made it even sweeter.

Once out of town, the trail became uneven, so they slowed to a walk.

"What's Santa Fe like?" Izzy asked.

"It's much nicer than Loma. Not as dusty. You can walk along and shop and not choke. Oh, and you probably won't get shot."

"Sounds like heaven."

"It has some nice shops. Dress shops, bakeries. This one bakery makes the most delicious strawberry tarts."

"I'll need to try one of those. Where will we stay?"

"I always stay at a hotel called La Fonda. Beds are comfortable. Food's good. There's dancing most nights."

"I love to dance."

Elle smiled at her. "Well, I guess we'll go dancing."

* * *

Two days later, they galloped into Santa Fe. Izzy gazed in awe at the buildings lining the street. "This is beautiful," she said. "Very Spanish looking." They trotted past a large single-story adobe building. "What's that?"

"The Palace of the Governors, built in the early sixteen hundreds."

Along the way, Elle pointed out the San Miguel Chapel and Mission where she'd spent time after the death of her parents.

A tall building with ornate spires dominated one block. "That's different architecture. Almost Gothic. Is it a church?" Izzy asked.

"Yes, the Loretto Chapel. They started building it in 1873."

Santa Fe had a rich history like Boston, and Izzy was impressed. Something caught her eye, and she pulled to a stop in front of a store. "I like that," she said, pointing to a blue cotton dress with white trim. It wasn't fancy, but pretty enough. *I'd love to wear a dress to dinner tonight.*

When they arrived at the La Fonda, a stable boy approached and took their horses to the barn around the back of the hotel. After checking in, they headed to the second floor.

Their room had one generous-sized bed, a chest of drawers, and an ornate bright blue washstand. A chamber pot sat nearby also. The linens on the bed smelled fresh.

"They have a bath and outhouse behind the hotel also," Elle said. "Tomorrow we can bathe. Unless you want one tonight?"

"I'm too exhausted," Izzy said. They had bathed yesterday morning, so waiting until tomorrow was fine.

Elle agreed.

They undressed and sank their weary bodies onto the soft mattress.

"This is so comfortable." Izzy flipped onto her side and rested her head on her arm. "What are we doing tomorrow?"

Elle lay on her back and stretched. "I have to go to the bank for Rose. Shouldn't take that long, and then we can walk around. Tomorrow night we'll have dinner, and we can dance afterward."

Izzy smiled. "Sounds like a perfect day."

Elle extinguished the hurricane lamp on her bedside table and closed her eyes. Within minutes, her breathing became shallow and her face relaxed.

Izzy assumed her usual position, curled against Elle's side. So far, she was more than pleased with her first real trip away from Loma and looked forward to leaving her gun belt at home tomorrow. She absently stroked a hand across Elle's stomach and dreamed of dinner and dancing.

She flinched when Elle grabbed her wrist. "Did I wake you?"

"Yes," Elle replied softly.

"Sorry." Izzy tucked the offending hand under her head, embarrassed at her own boldness.

Elle drifted back to sleep, but she did so with a frown between her eyes.

Is she troubled? Without thinking, Izzy made a move to smooth it out but quickly caught herself.

She pulled the covers up to her chin. *Why do I feel the need to keep touching her?*

The next morning, Elle left early to go to the bank and Izzy busied herself by taking a walk. When she came back to the room, Elle had returned. A brown package wrapped in twine lay on the bed.

"I got you something," Elle said.

"A gift? You got me a gift?" Izzy untied the string. "Oh! The dress."

"I guessed at your size."

Izzy held up to her body. "It's perfect." She jumped into Elle's arms. "Thank you. I'll wear it tonight."

Dinner was still hours away, so they walked around town, visiting shops and sampling a multitude of sweet treats. Elle imparted to Izzy all her knowledge of Santa Fe, from the Pueblo Indians to the Spanish expeditions to the history of the Santa Fe trail.

It was a wonderful afternoon, and Izzy was ecstatic to spend it with Elle.

Late in the afternoon, they headed back to the room to bathe and get ready for dinner.

Izzy put her new dress on. Wearing trousers all these weeks was different and comfortable, but occasionally she had yearned to wear a dress. And this was a golden opportunity. Izzy spun around. "Well?"

Elle smiled. "It looks great." Elle cut a fine figure in black trousers and a white shirt with a black vest. Her hair hung in waves and landed softly on her shoulders. She held out her arm, and Izzy linked hers through it.

They headed down to the already crowded dining area in the hotel. A band, consisting of a piano, fiddle, banjo, and a harmonica, played an up-tempo tune to the delight of the dancers twirling around the shiny oak floor.

They sat down at a table for two, and Izzy clapped along to the song.

After a hearty meal of beef tamales and rice, they enjoyed an after-dinner brandy. Izzy's father loved brandy but never offered any to her or her mother. Drinking brandy and smoking cigars were most certainly a man thing. Women drank claret or wine, or so she'd been told. "I've never had brandy. It looks like whisky but tastes sweeter."

"That's because it's made from fruit and not grain."

"I like it. A lot." Izzy held up her half-full glass and swirled the amber liquid around. "You know, this is almost the exact color of your eyes."

Elle smiled. With her elbow on the table, she placed her chin in her hand. "I didn't know that."

Izzy felt carefree and happy, no doubt from the alcohol. The brandy tasted especially delicious, and she took another sip. "Well, now you know. Your eyes are the color of brandy...or whisky. Whichever you prefer." Izzy giggled.

"I guess there are worse things than having whisky eyes."

"Oh, I'm sure." Izzy sipped from her glass before holding it up again. "It has flecks of gold, like the gold around your pupils."

"When did you become so fascinated by my eyes?"

Izzy raised her brows. "Right away. I noticed them the first day we met. They're an unusual color. Warm. Rich and deep." She widened her eyes to make a point. "Like brandy."

"Or whisky."

Izzy giggled again. "Yes. If you prefer whisky, then whisky."

"Whisky's more my style."

People crowded the dance floor and Izzy itched to join them. A man stood with the band and called out to the dancers, telling them what to do. "I think they're dancing a quadrille," she said.

Elle leaned forward and her whisky eyes twinkled. "I don't know what they call it, but it's fun. Let's go." She grabbed Izzy's hand, and they found some space on the floor.

Izzy laughed and had the time of her life. Sometimes Elle danced close to her, and sometimes she was across the way. Sometimes Izzy made the correct moves, and sometimes she didn't. But it was a rowdy good time. If she became winded, she returned to the table and sipped her brandy. Between the alcohol, the dance, and Elle's closeness, her body thrummed with excitement, and an unknown longing took hold deep inside her. She couldn't name it, having never felt this way before. Her body craved something…closeness, a touch, attention. And in her heart, she knew Elle was the one to satisfy it.

After dancing and drinking for a couple of hours, they made their way up to the room. The effect of the brandy relaxed Izzy, yet she remained in control. The only change in Elle was a wolfish look in her eyes, a look that excited Izzy, and she had no idea why. An aura had surrounded them all day and into the night. An aura of electricity and danger—not the scary kind of danger, an exciting kind.

Elle opened their door and waved her arm. "Madam." After they entered the room, Elle shut the door and leaned against it.

Izzy twirled in place. "What a great night. I don't want it to end."

"It doesn't have to." Elle pulled her into her arms, and they waltzed around the room. It seemed the most natural thing in the world to Izzy, to be in Elle's arms dancing. They kept perfect rhythm with the tune Izzy hummed, until they banged into the dresser.

After sharing a laugh, Izzy pretended to be indignant. "Kind sir, please take care."

With a rakish grin, Elle pulled her close, and their bodies pressed together. The dance slowed. She whispered into Izzy's ear, "I apologize, madam. I was so entranced by your beauty that I forgot my own strength."

Izzy's pulse became erratic. She was acutely aware of Elle's hips pressing into hers. The craving and need that had been with her all night became stronger. "Do you find me beautiful then, kind sir?" Her teasing tone masked her true intent.

"Yes. I find you very beautiful."

Izzy pulled back and gazed into Elle's eyes. Within their amber depths lay a seriousness and hunger that took Izzy's breath away. The dance stopped, and without thinking or analyzing, Izzy stroked Elle's cheek. She murmured, "I find you beautiful too."

Slowly, Elle bent her head, and Izzy stopped breathing. The kiss was soft and tasted of brandy. A surprising throb of desire exploded low in Izzy's belly. She pressed herself closer, but before the kiss deepened, Elle broke it off.

Elle rested her forehead against Izzy's. "I'm sorry. I don't know what came over me."

Izzy didn't want an apology. She wanted more kissing. Her body wanted an end to this puzzling aching and longing, and she knew Elle was the answer. Her lips found Elle's and demanded more. When Elle's tongue stroked hers, Izzy moaned. Inhibitions disappeared. Emboldened, she unbuttoned Elle's vest and then her shirt. She needed to possess Elle, to caress her skin, to run her hands along her rib cage, to kiss the column of her throat.

When all the buttons were undone, Elle grabbed her hands. "Iz. No. Wait."

The rejection stung, and tears sprung into her eyes. *She doesn't want this. She doesn't want me.* Izzy turned her face away to hide the hurt.

"Hey." Elle cupped her cheeks and forced eye contact. "What is it?"

A tear slid down Izzy's cheek. "You don't want me."

Elle shook her head. "That's not true. Not at all."

"Then...why?"

Elle brushed the tear away. "I want to make sure this is what *you* want."

"I do want it. I've never wanted anything this much." She grabbed Elle's hand and placed it on her wildly beating heart. Taking a measured breath, she spoke words that she never dreamed of saying to another woman. "I want you. Now kiss me, Elle Barstow."

It didn't take them long to undress and fall into bed. Elle's kisses were both heaven and hell—heaven because they were exquisite, and hell because Izzy wanted something more and it drove her crazy. Elle rolled Izzy so she lay on her back, and her hands wandered while her lips drove Izzy out of her mind. Elle kissed and sucked at her neck, nibbled on her collarbone, and when her lips reached her breasts, Izzy almost fainted from want. If this were an opera, Elle would be hitting all the high notes.

Elle's hand snaked across Izzy's belly and rested at the top of her legs. Izzy pushed it lower and groaned. Elle's hand soon found the source of the ache, and sparks radiated out to Izzy's limbs as Elle began to stroke her. The kisses continued, and Izzy was adrift in a sea of pleasure. The intensity built like a crescendo, and breathing became difficult. She resorted to panting between kisses as her hips urged Elle on. And then it happened—a burst of the purest pleasure exploded within her, and she cried out. It came in waves, and she couldn't breathe, couldn't think. All she could do was feel, and what a feeling it was.

* * *

Elle awoke the next morning with Izzy in her arms. They'd barely slept, because they'd been busy exploring each other's bodies all through the night. If they managed to drift off, soon someone's lips would be seeking, and hands would be searching, and their dance would start all over again. Izzy was passionate and eager to learn, and by the early morning hours, she played Elle's body like a finely tuned piano.

And now Elle was at a loss. A line had been crossed, and she wasn't sure they could go back. A small part of her wasn't sure she wanted to. At one point during the night, in the afterglow of satisfaction, Elle had surrendered a piece of herself to Izzy. Could she get it back? *I have to. It's too dangerous to feel this way about someone.* Her mother's face swam in front of her, and Elle's arms tightened around Izzy.

"Are you okay?" Izzy mumbled.

"I'm sorry, did I wake you?"

"I don't know. But I'm happy to be awake now." She picked her head up, and a mischievous glint sparkled in her eyes. She stared at Elle while her hand slipped down Elle's body.

Elle's breath caught in her throat. A smiling Izzy straddled her hips, and all thoughts of reining in her feelings rode off into the sunset.

* * *

They arrived home three days later. As soon as they closed the door, their lips came together and they tore at their clothing. Three *very* long days without this had been torture for them both.

Before they'd left Santa Fe, Elle had had a talk with herself. She preached self-control and demanded from herself that she keep away from Izzy. It was too dangerous for them to continue whatever was between them. So *stay away* became her mantra.

Foolishly, she expected it to be easy. Not touching or kissing Izzy would be no problem. Like a fool, she thought that once she'd had a taste of Izzy, she'd be satisfied. That the hunger, once satiated, would disappear.

The mantra lasted an hour outside Santa Fe. In a cruel twist, somehow the hunger had grown, and the heated glances from Izzy suggested she felt the same.

So, she preached self-control to Izzy. Told her having sex out in the open on the trail would leave them vulnerable, that they had to be careful on the way home.

They did manage to share some stolen kisses when they stopped to stretch their legs and held hands under the blanket at nighttime, thinking these trivial things could assuage some of their hunger. But like striking a match on a windy day, all it did was threaten fire.

And now that they were home, they wouldn't be denied.

Izzy pushed Elle's coat off her shoulders and nipped at her neck, sending waves of want crashing through Elle's body.

Before Elle had a chance to deepen the kiss, Izzy broke it off.

"Let's take a bath."

"Okay. I'll warm the water."

They pulled the tub to the middle of the bedroom and heated water on the stove. When the bath was ready, Izzy stripped down and crawled in. "This feels good. Hurry up and get in."

The sight of a naked Izzy caused a shiver of desire to course through Elle's veins. Thank God for Izzy's ridiculous curtains. "Let me tend to the horses." Izzy pouted in response, so Elle leaned down and captured her lips. "I'll be right back."

She hustled from the room and headed to the barn. She filled the trough with fresh water and threw some hay into their stalls. "Sleep well, boys."

When she came back inside, she tripped on her coat that lay in a heap on the ground. Izzy's passion made her smile, and she picked it up. A white paper stuck out from her inner pocket, and she pulled it out.

The likeness was uncanny, the reward substantial. Izzy's gorgeous face stared back at her.

Elle had ripped the poster down from the post office wall on the first day in Santa Fe and then, with everything that had happened since, had forgotten about it. A queasy feeling roiled her gut. *This is what you wanted. This was the plan.*

"Are you coming?" Izzy called.

"Yeah. I'll be right there." After a few moments of contemplation, she folded the paper into a small square and tucked it into the pages of *The Three Musketeers*.

I'll deal with it later. Not now. Not when her body needed release.

Needed Izzy.

CHAPTER SIXTEEN

Izzy explored all the scars on Elle's body. "What's this long one?" She slid a finger along Elle's back.

They had just finished having sex, and already Elle yearned for more. "That was from a bullwhip."

"A bullwhip? Who whipped you?"

"I was in the middle of a typical Loma brawl about four years ago, and somebody had a whip. And he caught me with it."

"Sounds painful." Izzy's lips began a slow, torturous trail down the scar, and Elle moaned. "Does it still hurt?" Izzy asked with a teasing tone.

"Hurt's not the word I'd use right now."

The front door opened and slammed shut. They both froze.

"Where is everyone?" Raven called out.

"Shit." Elle hopped from the bed and pulled on her pants. "I'll be right out," she called back.

Izzy dove under the covers.

When fully dressed, Elle opened the door and quickly shut it behind her. "Hey."

Raven replaced a book on the shelf and spun around. "Hey yourself." An odd expression crossed her face. "What are you doing?"

"I was…sleeping."

"It's the middle of the morning."

"Yeah. I was tired."

"Where's Izzy?"

"Uh. I think she went for a ride." Elle hated to lie.

Raven glanced at the bedroom door before saying, "I'm goin' fishing. Wanna come? Haven't seen you much this past week, ever since you got back from Santa Fe. You haven't even been to the saloon. Rose has been asking for you."

"I haven't been feeling too good. I'll stop by and see her tomorrow."

"Well, do you wanna go fishing?"

The idea of spending even a few hours away from Izzy was out of the question right now, even painful. "I'm gonna stay here if you don't mind. Next time, though."

"Sure." Raven walked to the front door and without turning around said, "Jack's out back."

"Oh."

"Maybe she took a walk." Raven didn't wait for a reply, and the door closed behind her.

Elle exhaled. "Shit." The suspicion in Raven's eyes was clear.

Izzy cracked open the bedroom door and poked her head out. "Is she gone?"

"Yes." Elle stared at the front door and tried to quell her uneasiness. She wasn't ready to share the change in her relationship with Izzy, but now their secret may be out.

Izzy walked into the room wrapped only in a blanket. She encircled Elle in her arms. "Are you okay?"

Elle returned the hug. "What are you doing out of bed?"

"I missed you. Can we go to the canyon today after Matsu's lessons?"

"Sure. Maybe you should get dressed. She'll be here soon."

With a gleam in her eye, Izzy grabbed her hand and led her back to the bedroom. "I think we have a few minutes."

* * *

Izzy lay on her stomach with an open book in front of her. The sun shone bright in the crystal-blue sky. A light breeze made the heat bearable. Luna grazed next to Blaze and Jack while the rest of the herd sought out the shade of the canyon wall. Such a perfect day, the kind of day that existed only in dreams.

Elle lay next to her in the same position, and every minute or so turned the page of her book. She'd removed her hat, and her hair hung loose, hiding her face from Izzy's eyes.

The past week had been the best of Izzy's life. Elle had revealed a whole new world to her, a world filled with passion and joy and incredible pleasure. She'd been admitted to a secret club with a membership of two.

When Izzy turned eighteen, she'd called herself a woman, but now…now she felt like a woman. She hungered for Elle's body. She hungered for the intense pleasure Elle brought her.

Izzy smiled to herself as her body jolted awake.

"I can feel you staring at me."

With a giggle, Izzy tucked Elle's hair behind her ear. Now she had a clear view. "I'm not staring."

"Yes, you are." Elle's eyes remained on the pages of her book. "The question is, why are you staring?"

"Why do you think?" Izzy scooted closer and nibbled on Elle's earlobe.

Elle's breathing hitched.

Izzy trailed light kisses down Elle's throat, and her hand slid under Elle's shirt. She caressed her back.

The book closed. Now she had Elle's attention.

With a boldness that would've shocked two weeks ago, Izzy pushed Elle onto her back, her lips capturing Elle's with a ferocious hunger. She undid the buttons of Elle's pants and slid her hand between her legs. She stroked through the wetness and drew circles around the very center of Elle's passion.

Elle labored to breathe, so she stopped kissing Izzy. Tiny moans turned into pleading words as Elle begged to be satisfied.

It was intoxicating for Izzy, knowing her touches and kisses drove Elle to such distraction. She felt powerful and in control.

Elle came hard, and she wrapped her arms around Izzy and squeezed. After the tremors stopped, Elle's body sagged and her arms fell back against the blanket.

Izzy brushed her lips across Elle's.

It took a moment for Elle to catch her breath, but when she did, she rolled on top of Izzy and kissed her deeply. With a ragged breath, she fumbled with the buttons on Izzy's shirt and ripped it open. Izzy whimpered with hunger and impatience. Elle's lips touched her everywhere, and when Elle pulled down her trousers, Izzy moaned. It didn't take long for Elle's tongue to bring her to an earth-shattering climax. Elle kissed her way back to Izzy's mouth, and Izzy thought that this feeling would never get old.

* * *

After their passion ebbed, Elle rested her head in Izzy's lap. Her body was languid. If she had to draw a gun right now, she'd be in trouble. She had no clue how they'd gotten to this point, how it seemed that every minute of every day they reached for each other with a hunger scary in its intensity.

Maybe it was simply Izzy's sexual awakening, and after a few weeks, their desire would diminish. The hunger that Elle was powerless to control would fade. Things would go back to some form of normal.

The reward loomed large. That was supposed to be the play—collect the reward and have a down payment for some land. *Why can't I pull that trigger?* The poster remained hidden in the book.

Izzy trailed a finger along her cheekbone and jaw. "What are you thinking?"

Elle did what she'd been doing for weeks now: pushed the thought of a reward far away. "I'm thinking that you've worn me out. And I need to eat to keep my strength up. What are you thinking?"

"I'm thinking…how perfect it is, right here, right now. And I don't want to leave. I want to stay forever in this moment."

Elle wanted to say, *You're perfect.* Instead, she said, "It is perfect."

"What do you think you'd be doing if you weren't an outlaw?"

Elle hummed before answering. "That's been a popular question lately. Maybe the universe is trying to tell me something."

"Who else asked?"

Elle checked herself because she almost said Miriam and she didn't want to spoil the moment. "Raven, for one."

"What's the answer?"

"I wanna own some land. Raise horses, maybe cattle."

"That would be a lot less dangerous."

"I don't know about that." Elle wrapped her arms around Izzy and drew her down for a quick kiss. "What if Mac steals my horses?"

Izzy grinned. "I think Mac would rather steal some kisses."

"I think I'd let her." They shared another kiss, this one a bit longer. Before things took a more heated turn, Elle broke it off. She touched Izzy's pouty lips. "What if you hadn't been banished? What would you have done with your life?"

"I told my father I wanted to study the law."

"And what did he say?"

A shadow fell across Izzy's face. "After he laughed, he told me in no uncertain terms that a woman can't be a lawyer because we're not intelligent enough. And we're too emotional."

"Hmm. I'm sure you loved to hear that."

"We got into a shouting match."

"Of course you did. I'd expect nothing less."

"I still want to do it," Izzy said. "Did I tell you that I borrowed a book from Mr. Berenson?"

"I don't think so. Although I did see a law book on the shelf."

Izzy gazed into the distance. "He was scared to death of me that day. Or I guess, scared to death of Mac. I may have to bully him into letting me apprentice with him."

"Sounds like a good idea to me. I may need some representation in the future."

"I don't know if you'll be able to afford me," Izzy teased.

Elle widened her eyes and pushed Izzy onto her back. "I'm sure we could work out some form of payment. Perhaps we could barter." She nipped Izzy's neck. "Like an exchange of goods." Elle's tongue tickled the pulse point at the base of Izzy's throat. "Or services."

Izzy licked her lips. "I like the services idea."

CHAPTER SEVENTEEN

After dropping off a wagon full of alcohol at the saloon, Elle and Raven rode out to Elle's house. She'd only been away for a couple of hours, yet still she ached for Izzy.

When they approached, Elle felt a pang of uneasiness. The front door was wide open, and one of the chairs was tipped over. "Izzy?" She slid from the saddle and hustled into the house.

The kitchen table had been upended. Elle's heart leaped into her throat. She ran out the back door and found Matsu lying motionless on the ground. "Matsu!"

Raven joined her, and they carefully turned her onto her back. Her face was bruised and bloodied. They gave the rest of her body a quick once-over and found no other obvious injuries. No cuts, no bullet wounds, no bloody stains.

Matsu's eyes fluttered open, and she moaned softly. She struggled to sit up, and finally managed to with help from Elle.

"What happened?" Raven asked.

Her eyes darted around. She grunted and her hands flailed about.

"Hey, take a breath," Elle said. "Get her some water," she said to Raven.

When Raven returned with a ladle, Elle held it to her mouth.

Raven squatted on the ground a few feet away. She brushed the grass. "These tracks are fresh. Like maybe half an hour."

When Matsu finished drinking, she wrote letters in the dirt. *Jed.*

The whole gang rode hard north toward Cimarron, a town as lawless as Loma Parda. Jed's father, John, held court there, so it was a good bet that's where he'd be. Elle prayed she guessed right. A half an hour was hard to make up, but she pushed Blaze as hard as she dared. The thought of Izzy in danger made it feel like a fist was wrapped tight around her heart and lungs. She struggled to breathe.

When they rolled into the town, it wasn't hard to find Jed. They must've lollygagged because they stood in front of the general store, tying up their horses. Poor Izzy's hands were bound in front of her. Jed removed his gun and holster and with a laugh handed it to the man standing next to him. "Won't be needing this. I'm sure she'll behave. Right?" He reached a hand toward Izzy's face, but she backed away.

Elle rode right into the middle of them, and they scattered. She hopped from the saddle with her gun already drawn and shoved it into Jed's chest. "Get your hands off her."

His mouth dropped open and he let go of Izzy, who ran behind Elle.

Elle tilted her chin up. "She's coming with me."

"Over my dead body," Jed snarled.

"Fine." Elle drew the hammer back on her gun and pointed it at Jed's heart.

Shorty laid a hand on Elle's arm. "Easy, girl." He motioned his head down the dusty street.

John Watkins and ten other men approached on horseback. He pulled his horse up and spit a wad of tobacco from his mouth. He had the same beady black eyes as Jed, only meaner, if that was possible. His clean-shaven face revealed a thick scar from the corner of his eye down to his mouth. "Elle. What brings you up here?"

"Your sorry excuse for a son."

"No argument there. He's the worst of the bunch."

Jed cursed his father under his breath.

John glowered at his offspring. "What'd you say, boy?"

Jed's eyes dropped to the ground. "Nothin'."

John smiled at Elle, but even that looked mean. "Kids today got no respect. I bet you respected your daddy. Did I ever tell you I knew him? Shame what happened."

As if the pain in her chest wasn't severe enough, another surge shot through it at the mention of her father. "What do you know about it?"

"I know a lot. Come have a drink with me someday and I'll tell you. Now. What's going on here?"

Jed pointed at Elle and Izzy. "She took my woman. Got her fair and square on the trail. And I want her back."

"She's not your woman, you son of a bitch," Elle said through gritted teeth.

John cleared his throat. His emotionless eyes shifted from one combatant to the other. "Looks like we got us a situation. My boy thinks this woman is his. And you think she's not. How do we solve this problem?"

Elle raised her gun again. "I put a bullet through his brain. That's how we solve it."

John chuckled. "Now, that hardly seems fair, seeing as how my boy is unarmed at the moment." A crowd started to gather, and he glanced around. "And from what I can tell, you are seriously outnumbered. So you can kill my boy, but I doubt you'll get very far after the fact."

No, the odds were not in her favor, but tell that to the rage that filled her heart at the thought of Izzy being touched by Jed Watkins.

Raven leaned next to her ear and whispered, "Say the word, and I'll shoot all these sons of bitches. We'll go down in a blaze of glory."

Shorty had her other ear and murmured, "If we all die, Izzy'll be left to fend for herself. Maybe we can talk our way out of this."

Sanity prevailed, and Elle lowered the gun. There were too many of them. She had no doubt she'd be able to take out a few before they got a shot off, but eventually a bullet would find her, and if that happened, Izzy was done for.

John smiled and rested his arm on the pommel of his saddle. "That's better. Now, I only see one way to solve this problem."

All eyes settled on John and murmurs circulated in the crowd. After a healthy pause, he revealed his solution. "A duel."

Raven nodded. "Now we're talking," she mumbled. She patted Elle on the back. "You've got this."

Izzy's eyes widened. "How can you say that?" she asked Raven. She grabbed Elle's arm.

"She's got this," Raven said.

Izzy's wild eyes sought out Elle. "No. Please don't do this."

"There's no other way," Elle said. It was actually a fortuitous turn of events. She had no doubt she'd best Jed in a duel.

Raven placed a hand on Izzy's shoulder. "Nobody can outdraw Elle. Nobody. And I've seen that scrawny asshole draw a gun. He doesn't stand a chance. Hell, you could probably beat him."

Elle checked the chambers of both guns and snapped them back into place.

Izzy remained unconvinced. "No. There has to be another way," she pleaded.

Elle thrust her guns into the holsters and undid the rope around Izzy's wrists. "This is the only way we'll get out of here alive." She gave Izzy's hands a squeeze. "Trust me. No two-bit outlaw is gonna outdraw me." She turned to John. "I accept."

The crowd roared its approval.

Perhaps knowing he was overmatched, Jed yelled, "I ain't agreeing to no duel."

John slid from his horse. "Shut up and be a man."

Jed clenched his fists and scowled. "Fine. Give me my damn gun."

John sauntered over and stood between them. "That ain't how this is gonna go down. No guns."

Both stared at him.

Jed squinted. "What are you talking about?"

"Where we from, boy?" John asked.

Jed's frown deepened. "What?"

"We're from Helena, Texas, that's where." He circled Elle and Jed and raised his voice, playing it up for the crowd. "And in Helena, we don't duel with guns."

"What the hell's he talking about?" Raven whispered.

When John finished his lap around the two duelers, he stopped. "We duel with knives."

Shit. Elle's heart skipped a beat. What was certain victory a moment ago became decidedly uncertain.

"Damnation," Shorty muttered.

"What is it? What's wrong?" Izzy asked.

Raven spat into the ground. "That's bullshit. This ain't Helena."

John glared. "We may not be in Helena, but Cimarron is my town. My town, my rules. You don't like it"—he pointed up the street—"ride on outta here. But the woman stays with my boy."

Izzy tugged on Elle's hand. "What's a Helena duel?" The whites of her eyes were like saucers, and worry lines tracked across her forehead.

How could Elle possibly describe the savagery of what would happen? Instead, she patted Izzy's hand, trying to exude more confidence than she felt. "It's fine." She even managed a cocky smile before turning back to John. "Okay. Let's go." She pulled Raven off to the side and undid her gun holster. "Promise me you'll get her out of here if anything happens."

"Nothing's gonna happen. You got this. Use that crazy fighting shit Matsu taught you. Try and put him on the ground."

"Raven. Promise."

"Okay. Yeah. I promise. Me and the boys will shoot the shit out of this place if you go down. But that's not gonna happen."

Elle appreciated Raven's bluster, but neither of them were fools. If it came to that, they'd all die. *I have to win.*

The crowd around them grew in size and raucous enthusiasm, creating a kind of carnival atmosphere. Money was collected as bets were placed on who would survive the carnage.

John whistled for silence. "Hear ye, hear ye," he shouted with some flair. "This is a duel to the death. Winner takes all. All being this lovely lady." He grabbed Izzy's hand and thrust it in the air, eliciting catcalls and hoots from the bystanders.

He motioned for Elle and Jed to come forward and held up two knives, each with an ivory handle and a shimmery, three-inch steel blade. And just in case anyone doubted their sharpness, he sliced through a rope hanging from his saddle—a clean, fast cut—and the crowd gasped. He handed a knife each to Elle and Jed. Next, he produced a long piece of rawhide. "Our duelists will have their left wrists tied together. Then it's a regular ol' knife fight. Last one standing wins."

He and his youngest son, Bobby, demonstrated. They clasped their left hands and pretended to stab at each other with their right hands.

Bobby woo-hooed and laughed, and the crowd cheered some more.

The circus atmosphere sickened Elle. She'd witnessed a Helena duel once. It had been a slow and torturous affair since the knives never struck deep enough to reach a major organ. A dueler would slowly bleed to death from the accumulated cuts, and onlookers loved it. Gun duels ended in seconds, but Helena duels gave them several minutes of gruesome entertainment. She studied the blade in her fist. The handle felt smooth and cool in her grasp. She twirled it with her fingers to familiarize herself with the heft and balance.

John and Bobby had finished their perverse dance and the crowd quieted. John focused his attention on Elle and Jed. "We ready?"

They both nodded.

He tied their wrists together. "On my word, we'll begin." He walked around, waving back the throng. "Now give 'em room." After the crowd backed away, he yanked out a wad of bills and held them up. "I'm betting fifty on my own flesh and blood." Cheers and jeers welled up from the crowd.

"This is barbaric," Izzy shouted, but her cry fell on deaf ears.

John walked back to Elle and Jed. "We're gonna spin you around a few times to get your blood pumping." Bobby came over to help. He grabbed Elle and John grabbed Jed, and they spun them round and round and round. When they stepped back, John yelled, "Go!"

Both fighters wobbled and almost tumbled to the ground.

Elle placed a hand in the dirt to steady herself. According to Jed's glassy eyes, he wasn't doing much better. Soon, the dizziness passed and both stood tall.

They moved in a slow circle at first.

Jed sneered. "I'm gonna enjoy guttin' you. And then I'm gonna enjoy Blondie over there."

Elle smirked. *Don't take the bait. Stay calm.* She needed her wits about her. Anger would only make her take risks. The rawhide bit into her wrist, but that was the least of her worries. Losing was not an option, not with Izzy's life on the line. She concentrated on the shiny steel blade in Jed's hand.

He made a short lunge.

Elle moved back to avoid the strike and slashed at his arm but missed. She began tugging on their bound hands, small yanks to try to pull him off-balance. She was taller and had longer arms, so she hoped to use that to her advantage.

Someone shouted, "Quit dancing. Let's go."

Elle suspected Jed itched to make the next move to impress his buddies and father. His knife glittered in the sunlight, and she stared at the weapon. She kept yanking until he became angry and lunged badly, offering Elle the opening she needed. She slashed at his right side, drawing first blood.

"Ow, damn it. Bitch," he growled.

A cheer rose from the crowd, and more money exchanged hands.

"C'mon, Elle," Shorty shouted.

Jed cursed and pulled hard on their bound hands, bringing Elle in close. He sliced her left arm above the elbow, leaving a deep gash.

"No," Izzy cried while the crowd cheered and crept closer.

Funnily enough, Elle felt no pain, felt nothing, in fact, except for the hot sensation of liquid running down her arm. Her blood dripped from Jed's blade, tarnishing it, dulling its shine.

He thrust again and she backed away just before it cozied up inside her rib cage, but he still landed a glancing blow. More blood seeped through her shirt. With a grunt, she whipped her own blade across his forearm, trying to do enough damage so he'd drop the knife. He howled, so she'd struck the mark, but the knife remained firmly in his grasp.

Their death waltz continued, each nicking the other until a steady stream of blood dripped from them both, soiling the dirt beneath their feet. To Elle's ears, the *splat splat splat* was louder than the crowd. The coppery scent filled her nostrils and sweat dribbled into her eyes, but she had no free hand to wipe it. She blinked it away as best she could instead.

Jed stabbed at her torso and missed, and she cut him again. It wasn't deep, but every wound mattered.

Both labored to breathe, and their movements slowed. They moved in a circle, sizing each other up. Time crept along, and the dripping blood sounded like a ticking clock.

"I'm coming for you," Jed said with a weak voice.

"C'mon." The only way to get the kill shot was if Elle put him on the ground. She needed him to make a move. "You don't look so good, Jed. Are you gonna let a woman best you?"

That was enough to egg him on, and he moved forward with a snarl. With her leg, Elle swept his feet out from under him, and he hit the ground hard. His momentum brought her down as well, but she managed to thrust her knife into his unprotected belly, and he screamed. She withdrew the blade, but before she stabbed again, he sank his knife into her back. It was her turn to howl as he twisted the blade. She gritted her teeth and drove the small bowie into his gut again and again and again.

His hand dropped off his knife and he flopped onto the ground, but the blade remained embedded in Elle's back. She lifted her head and locked eyes with him. His mouth opened but no words came out. Slowly the light left his hate-filled eyes, until he stared blankly at nothing.

"She killed Jed!" someone yelled.

Screams from the crowd became deafening. *Are they angry or cheering?* Elle winced. Pain radiated through every part of her body now that the adrenaline rush had ended. She felt weak and sick and struggled to get to her knees.

A gunshot rang out, and Elle's hands went to her belly. A new spot of blood spread across her white shirt. *Oh shit.* She dropped her knife and placed her hands on the wound to stanch the flow, but the crimson spot grew bigger. She bit her lip and closed her eyes. A blur of mayhem surrounded her—gunshots, shouts, screams, crying—but she couldn't focus. Unable to hold herself upright any longer, she pitched forward into the dirt. Was this the end? Was this how she would die? Bleeding out in the dirt on some unfamiliar street?

Someone hovered nearby, but the face was blurred. Raven's voice cut through the cacophony of sound. "Elle. Stay with me. We're gonna get you out of here."

"Izzy," was the last word that fell from her lips before the blackness took her.

* * *

When the bullet ripped through Elle's side, Izzy screamed and rushed toward her. "No!" In that instant, she finally understood the depth of her feelings for Elle. Gunshots rang above her head and fights broke out amongst the onlookers as they tried to collect their bets, but she paid them no mind. The only thing that mattered was Elle.

Mindful of the knife still embedded in her back, she and Raven gently turned Elle onto her side. Her eyes were shut, her lashes dark against the deathly pallor of her skin.

"Gotta stop the bleeding and get her to a doctor," Raven said.

Shorty took off his vest and placed it over the wound. It was soaked red in a matter of seconds.

Izzy's eyes landed on a buckboard parked in front of the hotel. A cowboy, unaffected by the chaos around him, leaned against it, casually smoking. She pointed. "Maybe he'll give us a ride."

Shorty nodded. "Good idea. Willy, help me." He gently hooked his hands underneath Elle's arms, and Willy picked up her legs. Raven held a revolver in each hand, pointing them at anyone who dared to come close. They navigated through the bedlam and stopped in front of the wagon.

Raven lowered the guns. "This your wagon?"

"Yeah."

"We need a doctor. Can you give us a ride?"

He took a drag on his cheroot and blew smoke in her direction. "I ain't helping you."

Izzy grabbed the gun from his holster and shoved it under his chin. "Take us to the damn doctor," Izzy growled. "Please."

His shaky hands rose in the air. "All right, all right. No need to get violent. Put her in the back. The doc's a few blocks up the road."

Izzy shoved his gun into her waistband and helped load Elle into the back of the wagon.

"Guess I forgot to say please," Raven murmured.

Izzy sat down in the back and gently placed Elle's head into her lap. "Let's go."

Raven rode next to the cowboy on the bench seat of the wagon. Blaze and Raven's horse were tethered to the back, and Willy and Shorty mounted up. Somehow, they managed to travel the few blocks without getting shot. With all the fights that had broken out, everybody was so otherwise occupied that nobody paid them any mind.

Izzy stroked Elle's face. Her eyes remained shut. "Please be okay," she whispered in Elle's ear. "Please." She placed a kiss on Elle's forehead, not caring a whit who might see. "Don't you dare leave me."

The wagon pulled to a stop in front of a small clapboard building. "Doc's in there," the cowboy said.

Raven hopped down and held the door open while the boys carefully carried Elle inside.

A thin man with round spectacles and a full head of white hair came rushing forward. "What's going on here?"

"We need some doctoring," Raven said.

He tugged on his vest before inspecting Elle's wounds. "Oh, my. Bring her back here." He led them to a room with a bed. On a side table were various medical instruments: a stethoscope, a bone saw, needles, bandages, various liquid-filled bottles, and an assortment of small knives.

At the sight of the knives, Izzy shuddered. She'd had enough of those today.

"She's in pretty bad shape," the doctor said.

Raven narrowed her eyes and placed a hand on her revolver. "That's why you need to fix her up."

Izzy and the gang waited in the front room of the doc's house. A steady stream of folks came to the door with various ailments from the earlier brawl, but each was met with a Winchester muzzle pointed at their chest. "Doc's busy," they were told.

Izzy twisted her hands as she waited. She stared at nothing. All she saw in her mind was blood. Elle's blood. Everywhere. *She's gotta make it. She's gotta make it.* Drawing a breath was impossible because of the pain in her chest born of an unrelenting fear. Fear of losing Elle, of losing everything they shared. *I can't lose her. I can't.*

The doctor entered with a bloody rag in his hands. "I did the best I could to stitch her up. Bullet went straight through, so that's good. Doesn't look like it hit any organs. She's alive, for now. Not sure if she'll make it."

"Can she travel?" Shorty asked.

"I wouldn't suggest it," the doctor said before leaving the room.

"We can't stay here, we ain't safe," Willy said.

Raven paced around the room. "Agreed. We'll have to risk moving her."

Izzy shot to her feet. "He said no!"

"We're all gonna be shot if we hang around this town much longer," Raven said. "I'll be back." She yanked on the front door and left.

Izzy grabbed Shorty's arm. "We can't move her, it may kill her. Please."

He patted her hand. "Look, she's above snakes for now, and ain't nobody tougher than Elle. She'll make it."

Izzy pointed back to the room where Elle lay fighting for her life. "She lost too much blood."

"We all have a better chance of living if we get the hell out of here," Willy said.

Izzy covered her face with her hands. There'd be no convincing them.

Raven commandeered another wagon, and the group made the slow, torturous journey back to Loma. Izzy tried her best to keep Elle from jostling around. She cradled her head and whispered words of encouragement. When Loma appeared on the horizon, she heaved a sigh of relief. At least they made it this far.

They headed straight to the doctor in town, a portly fellow named Elias Sturger.

Doc Sturger made Elle comfortable in one of the first-floor rooms, and Izzy pulled a chair close to the bed. She wasn't leaving.

Shorty and Willy headed out to get some sleep.

Raven stood by the window and lifted the edge of the curtain. "Ugh."

"What is it?" Izzy asked.

Rose's booming voice echoed through the house. "Where is she?" She burst into the room and hurried over to Elle's bed. "What the hell happened?"

"We got into a row in Cimarron," Raven said.

Rose waved a hand over Elle's body. "You call this a row?" Her eyes glinted with fury, and Raven cowered. "How could you let this happen to her?"

Raven's voice rose. "We were outnumbered."

"Why were you up there in the first place?" Rose yelled back.

Before Izzy came to Raven's defense, Elle stirred.

Everyone quieted.

Elle's eyes flitted open. "Quit yelling," she mumbled.

"Doc! She's awake," Raven said.

He rushed into the room and fussed over his patient. "She needs rest. Everyone needs to get out. Go on." He shooed them from the room.

Izzy didn't want to leave but had no choice. Begging to stay might pique Rose's curiosity. She'd try to sneak back after Rose and Raven left.

Once outside, Izzy walked in the opposite direction of Rose and Raven, who were still arguing. When they were far enough away, she rushed back inside. The doctor emerged from Elle's room.

"No more visitors," he said.

"I have to talk to her. I promise I won't stay long."

Elle's feeble voice called from the room, "It's fine, Doc."

He rubbed at the whiskers on his face and nodded. "All right. Just for a spell. She's not out of the woods."

"Thank you." Izzy hurried into Elle's room, shutting the door behind her. When she sat down, she placed a hand over Elle's. "How are you?"

Elle gave her a weak smile. "I think I've been better."

Izzy nibbled at her bottom lip. *She's so pale.* "You look good."

Elle rolled her eyes. "I doubt that."

"Shorty said you were above snakes. I have no idea what that means, but I hope it's a good thing."

"Means you're alive." Elle's eyes closed for a few seconds before opening again. "Were you hurt?"

Izzy shook her head.

"Was anyone hurt? Raven, Willy—"

"Nobody else was hurt. Just you." Izzy squeezed Elle's hand.

"Who shot me?"

"One of John's men. Who was then shot by somebody who lost their bet. It was a madhouse. Which was good because it gave us time to get you out of there."

Elle managed a slight nod. "Good. I'm so tired."

"Go to sleep. I'll stay here with you."

She mouthed *Okay*, and closed her eyes.

Izzy brushed a strand of hair from Elle's face and lightly cupped her cheek. "Sleep. I'll be here."

Elle's breathing shallowed out but remained steady. Izzy gathered courage from the thought that Elle was asleep and put her lips close to Elle's ear. "I'll always be here. I love you, and I'm not going anywhere. Do you hear me, Elle Barstow? I love you," she whispered.

CHAPTER EIGHTEEN

Elle sat up in bed and swung her feet onto the floor. With a slight groan, she stood. She was in her third week of recovery and feeling much better. Today she'd try to ride. Being cooped up in the house was getting old.

At first, it was fine. Izzy fussed over her, and a steady stream of visitors buoyed her spirits. They all marveled at her recovery, told her she was doing great, but they couldn't see the dark clouds gathering in her mind. Now they were fixing to burst at any moment.

She pulled on some clothes and then walked out to find Izzy with her head bent over a shirt that needed mending.

"Morning," Elle said.

Izzy smiled. "Morning. Sit. Let me get you some coffee."

"No. I can do it." Elle poured herself a cup and eased into a chair.

"Did I tell you that Amos and Fred got into a fistfight yesterday?" Izzy asked. With care, she drew the needle through the edges and tugged upward. "Over a slice of strawberry cake. Can you imagine?"

"Depends on the cake."

"It did look delicious. But still." Izzy shook her head. "I don't understand people out here. They never have civil discussions, just go straight to fisticuffs. Or worse." A spot of blood appeared on her thumb. "Ouch." She sucked it off.

"Want me to finish that?"

"No. You relax. I can manage."

"I'm tired of relaxing. I'm gonna go for a ride."

Izzy stopped stitching. "Are you ready for that?"

"Yes." Elle drained the coffee in one gulp.

"Okay. I'll saddle Blaze for you. Done." With a huge grin, she held the shirt up. "Not too bad. Not as good as you, but it'll do."

"I can saddle Blaze."

"No. You shouldn't be lifting a saddle right now. Not yet."

She grabbed Elle's cup and leaned down to kiss her. Elle offered up a cheek. After the kiss, Izzy pulled back, and hurt shone in her eyes. Hurt and confusion, a look that had become all too common these last weeks. But she never spoke of it. Neither of them did.

Izzy went out back, and Elle closed her eyes.

I love you.

Izzy had thought she was asleep, but Elle had heard it and now her world tilted upside down. Maybe she'd been naive thinking their physical relationship could be just physical and nothing more, something that would flame out over time. But now Izzy's heart was involved, and Elle had no clue how to handle it. Her gut told her to pull back emotionally and physically, and she always listened to her gut, so that's what she chose to do. Pull back. Keeping the physical distance proved easy, as Elle's injuries gave her the perfect excuse for not having sex. Keeping her emotions in check was another story, and trying to ignore Izzy's pain was damn near impossible. She ached to pull her into her arms and kiss away the hurt.

This was the right thing to do. It would keep them both safe, because no good could come from an outlaw loving someone or being loved. Izzy would always be a target, a way to get to

Elle, putting them both in danger. God knows what would have happened to her if Elle hadn't made it to Cimarron in time. She would have suffered unspeakable horrors at the hands of Jed Watkins. Elle shuddered.

It would be best for all if Izzy moved on, but to where? Not back to Boston. Izzy was adamant about that. *Do I want her to move on?* Elle chided herself. *Yes. It's the only way.* Would she miss the pleasure they brought each other? Their passionate kisses? Of course. Would she miss their quiet conversations as they lay entwined in each other's arms? Without a doubt. Would she miss waking up in the morning and reaching for Izzy? More than she cared to admit. But this was the only way.

She sighed. Life had been so much simpler when Elle only had to worry about herself.

Elle gingerly slid from her saddle and looped Blaze's reins around the fence post in front of the saloon. Surprisingly, the ride wasn't too painful. No way she could draw a gun with any kind of speed yet, but at least she could ride.

She pushed her way through the rowdy crowd and made her way back to Rose's office.

As she reached for the door, Raven burst through it and brushed past Elle.

"What's the matter?" Elle asked.

"Nothing." She hustled away from Elle without so much as a glance back.

Odd. She opened the office door.

Rose sat behind her desk, smoking her pipe. "There's my Ellie girl. How you feeling?"

Elle lowered herself into the chair in front of the desk. "Better. Almost back to normal. Probably need a few more weeks before I can get back to business as usual."

"Glad to hear it. You're the only one I trust with my affairs. My sons ain't the brightest candles in the church. Takes a woman to get things done the right way."

Elle brushed a piece of hay from her trousers. "I don't know, Rob's smart."

"He's soft. Tim's taken too many punches to the head. Arthur can't add numbers bigger than one."

Elle chuckled. "You're being a little hard on them."

"Eh, maybe." Rose leaned back in her chair and her eyes bored into Elle's. "You almost died."

"Almost. But I didn't."

"Not like you to put yourself into that kind of predicament."

Elle shifted in her seat. "The duel was…unexpected."

"What I mean to say is, it's not like you to put yourself in that kind of predicament over a woman. Or anybody, for that matter." Rose sent a puff of smoke skyward. "What's going on between you two? Ever since you got back from Santa Fe, you both seem…different."

Elle shifted again. This visit was supposed to be nothing more than a check-in, an exchange of pleasantries. "Nothing. Nothing's going on."

"I always know when you lie to me."

The intensity in Rose's eyes made Elle feel like a child caught stealing from the candy jar. An ominous feeling took hold. Her heart thudded in her chest.

"I know she ain't who you say she is." Rose reached into the desk drawer and withdrew a piece of paper. "Thing I don't get is, why'd you feel the need to lie about it?"

It was the same reward poster Elle had ripped from the wall in Santa Fe. The fold lines gave it away.

Rose waited patiently for Elle's answer. What could she say? *I didn't tell you because I wanted to keep Izzy away from you, and everybody else, to keep her safe. And failed miserably. Let's not forget that.* She rubbed her forehead. "I don't know," was the best she came up with.

Rose took another drag from her pipe. "You have feelings for this girl? 'Cause I know she has feelings for you."

Rose had Elle boxed in. Cornered. "I—"

"Feelings are dangerous in our business," Rose said. "They make you vulnerable. Your enemies will use 'em against you. Take it from someone who's lost four husbands."

Elle winced. Of course she knew that. She'd experienced it firsthand with her mother. Nothing Rose said was new or surprising. It was everything Elle had been telling herself for days now.

"You're not always gonna be there to rescue her. This time, you almost died. Next time, she might. And you know a woman who looks like that would meet an ugly end."

Picturing what unspeakable atrocities Izzy might experience from someone like Jed Watkins before he killed her caused a stab of pain near Elle's heart. Memories of her momma's death raced through her brain, her screams, her cries for help. Help Elle couldn't give.

Rose tapped the poster. "This is your solution."

"I...I can't..."

"If she marries J.B., no harm will come to her. She'll be safe."

"It's not right. I can't do that."

"He's a good man. I've had some dealings with him. Law-abiding. Kind. Powerful. Safest place in the world for her." Rose rapped her pipe on the desk and refilled the chamber. "She don't belong here."

"Maybe I'll take her away."

Rose's eyebrows disappeared into her hairline. "And go where? You're a wanted outlaw. Along with everyone else who lives here. Anywhere you go, you'll be looking over your shoulder. You're one US Marshal away from prison. Or worse."

"I'll quit outlawing. Been thinking about doing that anyway. I'll find a way to make an honest living. Maybe buy a ranch and raise horses. Soon I'll be forgotten."

A mirthless chuckle fell from Rose's lips. "You need to stay here. You're safe here. I keep you safe. I keep your secrets. Being an outlaw's in your blood. You were born to do it, just like your daddy." Her eyes narrowed. "And nobody forgets, Ellie girl. Those Pinkerton boys ever get a whiff of you and what you've done, they'll hunt you down no matter how long it takes."

Elle's muscles tensed. Was that a threat? Would Rose turn her in if she left?

Rose continued, "No, the only way that girl sees her next birthday is if she's safe on J.B.'s ranch."

Elle gave an emphatic, "No," and shook her head. "She doesn't wanna marry him."

"Most women don't wanna marry. But that's what we do."

Elle pitched forward in her chair. "I won't let that happen."

"If you care for this girl, you'll let her go. Let her be safe. Your little duel up there in Cimarron is still the talk of the county. A lot of people saw Mac, or Isabella, or whatever the hell she goes by now. Only a matter of time before someone comes snooping around, wanting to collect this." She again pointed to the poster on the desk.

Why did it feel like she was walking into a snowdrift? And it was getting deeper and deeper. "I can't."

"From what I'm told, it's the reason you brought her here in the first place."

Oh, Raven. "Things changed."

"'Cause you care." With pity in her eyes, Rose sighed. "You'll never be able to keep her safe."

Rose was right. Izzy had been stolen right from her own house. Her eyes welled.

"There's more men like Jed Watkins in the world than not. J.B.'s a good man."

Elle bit her lip to stop the tears from slipping out.

"You don't wanna bury her next to your momma, do you?"

At the mention of her momma, Elle's tears finally leaked out, and she took an angry swipe at them before burying her face in her hands. Everything Rose said was true. This was the best way to protect Izzy. Again, the thought of what Jed would've done to Izzy gutted her. Gutted her more than the thought of losing her to J.B. At least J.B. would take care of her, keep her safe. Perhaps someday Izzy could learn to care for him or even love him if he was as kind as Rose said. Better that Izzy loved him than an outlaw whose very being put her in harm's way.

Elle dropped her hands and her head sagged back. She gazed at the ceiling. "Okay."

"Good. I knew you'd do what's right for that girl."

Elle continued to stare upward. "I don't want the money."

"Suit yourself."

"When?"

"J.B.'s men are here now."

Elle snapped her eyes toward Rose. "You already sent for them?"

She raised her hands. "I did not. They came into town yesterday with some Fort Union boys, sniffing around, making inquiries." Rose shrugged. "Might as well get it over with now. No sense dragging it out. Is she at the house?"

Elle sagged in the chair and nodded. "She's gonna hate me."

"Probably be better if she does. She'll forget you quicker. Now, you wanna come? Or I can handle it for you."

She paused. Did she have the guts to face Izzy? It would be cowardly not to. And Elle was no coward. "I'll go."

Rose is right. Let her hate me. She'll be better off.

Elle pulled to a stop in front of the house. Rose trailed in her wagon, and three of J.B.'s men dismounted. Raven brought up the rear. Elle hadn't spoken to her, still feeling the sting of her betrayal.

Before she opened the door, Elle took a breath and tried to calm her pounding heart. Her breaking heart. *I have to do this. I have to. It's the only way to keep her safe.* The others waited for her to go in. After one last deep breath, she opened the door.

Izzy stood at the stove, and a radiant smile touched her lips when she saw Elle. Her tousled hair framed her face. "I'm making stew, so I hope you're hungry." Her smile waned when everyone else filed into the room. "What's all this?"

Elle removed her hat. She took a brief glance down at her white knuckles. "Uh, Iz. These are J.B. Jackson's men."

Izzy's face paled. She gaped for a few seconds. Confusion gave way to fear as her eyes darted around the room. "What... what are they doing here?"

Elle straightened her shoulders and tried to eliminate emotion from her voice. *Keep it together.* "They've come to take you to his ranch."

Izzy shook her head. "No. No. I'm not going." She focused on Elle. "Tell them I'm not going."

Elle's chest tightened. Her insides were breaking. Or maybe it was her heart shattering into a million pieces at what she was about to do. *Make her hate you.* "You're going." She reached into her pocket and pulled out the reward poster. "Otherwise, I won't be able to collect this." She handed it to Izzy.

Izzy's eyes filled with tears. "I don't understand. How could you do this?"

Raven cleared her throat before saying, "It was the plan all along."

Izzy glared at her. "Plan?"

"We knew they'd offer a reward for you," Raven said.

"We, or you?" Izzy demanded.

"It was my plan," Elle said.

Izzy whipped around and confronted Elle. "Your plan?"

Elle nodded.

"We'll wait outside," Rose said. Everyone shuffled out the door.

When they were alone, Izzy marched over to Elle and stood close. Her voice barely reached a whisper. "All along you were going to sell me off? To a man I didn't know and didn't want to marry?" Izzy huffed. Her voice remained low and angry. "And all of this was a lie?" Izzy waved her hand around the room. "Everything that happened between us was a lie?"

Elle had no answer. Her words stuck in her throat along with her heart.

"I trusted you, Elle Barstow."

"I guess that was your first mistake," Elle said. "Never trust an outlaw."

Pain flashed in Izzy's eyes before they turned a steely blue. "Oh, I know that now. Thanks for the lesson."

One of J.B.'s men opened the door. "Ma'am. We should get going."

"I'll be right there."

"Very good." He closed the door.

Izzy disappeared into the bedroom to pack and returned a few minutes later. She walked past Elle without a word. When her hand touched the doorknob, she said, "I hate you. I hope I never see you again." And then she left.

Elle stood frozen in place.

Mission accomplished. Izzy hated her.

Everything inside Elle went dark.

* * *

Slants of early morning sunlight crept across the floorboards. Sleep had been nonexistent. Elle's mind refused to let her rest. Betraying the one person who made your heart sing could do that to you. A cold, lonely bed could do that to you too.

Somehow, she found the strength to dress and boil some coffee. Taking her cup, she wandered to the back porch and collapsed onto the steps. All these years she'd kept her emotions in check, guarded her heart. How everything fell apart so spectacularly in a couple of months boggled her mind.

Matsu appeared in front of her.

Elle could barely get out of bed this morning, let alone be in any shape to spar. "Not today. I can't."

She took a seat next to Elle.

"Do you want some coffee?"

Matsu shook her head.

"Izzy's gone. And she won't be back."

Matsu frowned and spread her hands.

"She's headed to Albuquerque to marry J.B. Jackson."

Matsu headed inside and returned with a pencil and paper. She wrote, *Why.*

Because I sold her out. "'Cause she'll be safer there. She'll stay alive."

Matsu shook her head side to side. *She loved you.*

The words surprised Elle. Had she been Izzy's confidant? "Did she tell you that?"

Matsu pointed two fingers at her own eyes.

"Ah. You saw it." Elle sighed and rubbed at her face.

Matsu tapped Elle's chest, right near her heart and wrote, *You love her.*

"No, no. I don't. I can't. Love will get you killed." Elle closed her eyes and images of Izzy assaulted her. Her chest constricted. "I couldn't keep her safe. You don't know how it felt when Jed took her. When I lost her. You just…you don't know how it felt."

Matsu grabbed Elle's hand. Tears swam in her eyes.

Elle sucked in her breath. *She does know. Who did she love?*

Before she had a chance to ask, Shorty showed up at the back door. "Howdy."

Elle's emotional strength ebbed away. She didn't want to talk about this anymore. "Morning," she grumbled.

He laid a sack next to her.

"What's this?" Elle asked.

"The reward money. Rose gave some to Willy and me. We don't want it. Somehow don't feel right." He collapsed into a chair. "Somewhere along the line, I developed a soft spot for that bluebelly."

Me too. "Well, I don't want it either."

Shorty rolled a cigarette. "Want one?"

"No."

He struck a match. After taking a puff, he produced a flask. "How about this?"

"That I'll take." Elle filled her mouth, and the bitter hooch burned the back of her throat on the way down. She welcomed the pain. Deserved the pain. "Wretched-tasting as always. Thanks. Izzy said you must've brewed it in your dirty socks." A sad smile tugged at her lips.

"Hmm. That's not a bad idea," Shorty said.

Elle shot him a look and he grinned. He kidded, of course. Sometimes he was hard to read.

After taking another pull on his quirly, he said, "I git why you did it."

"You do?"

"Might've been a tad misguided, though."

"She wasn't safe out here."

"Says you. Maybe she deserved a choice. A chance to make her own decision."

Matsu pointed to Shorty in agreement.

The conversation had a two-against-one feel, and Elle's voice rose. "She couldn't shoot a gun. She couldn't defend herself."

His lips flapped with his exhaled breath. "True. But she *could* play some baseball." He took a drag and blew the smoke skyward.

CHAPTER NINETEEN

Izzy rested her forehead against the window. Her body swayed side to side as they rode over the rutted, uneven ground. She had the coach to herself, thank God. Her dark mood would not tolerate banalities such as small talk and chitter-chatter. She seethed, ached, and hated.

How could I have been so stupid, so naive to think she cared for me? I was a means to an end. A financial windfall.

She refused to cry. There'd be no tears like when her father betrayed her. She was tougher now. Hardened by this land. She'd survive. Somehow. Maybe a daring escape. Or a plea for her freedom. *I'll think of something.*

They'd passed through Santa Fe earlier. Santa Fe, where Izzy discovered happiness and passion. Now it was a painful reminder of how she'd been duped.

The coach slowed down and turned. A sign swung between two large posts: Jackson Ranch. The next chapter in her life was about to begin. They clopped along a wide dirt road for quite a while, passing pastures and open spaces with long grasses filled with cattle. The size of the homestead was impressive, but all Izzy saw was a big prison.

When they approached the house, Izzy peered out the window. It was a large single-story adobe structure with a shaded front porch and thick stone walls. Terra-cotta tiles covered the roof. Several other buildings surrounded the main house, one being a huge barn with its double doors thrown open. Ranch hands bustled around, and a woman carried a basket full of fruits toward the back of the house.

The coach pulled to a stop. A man opened the door and gave her a hand out. "Follow me, Miss Collins."

She didn't have much of a choice, so that's what she did. They walked in the front door. Izzy admired the Persian rugs on the floor and the artwork on the walls. They passed by a sitting room with a large couch and ornate side tables. She hadn't seen this kind of finery since leaving Boston. Mr. J.B. Jackson was a wealthy man indeed by the look of things. The man stopped and knocked on a heavy black door.

"Come in."

They stepped inside the room. An attractive man with a barrel chest and a white handlebar mustache rose up from behind a massive oak desk. His gray-streaked hair was thick and neatly trimmed, and he had an aura of virility about him despite his age. With a warm smile, he said, "Welcome to my humble home, Miss Collins. Or may I call you Isabella?"

"Isabella is fine," she said.

He nodded to his ranch hand. "Roy, thank you for safely escorting Isabella."

"You're welcome. Do you need anything else?"

"Nope. I think we're good. Oh! Ask Rosa to bring some sweetened tea and butter cakes. I'm sure Isabella could do with some refreshments."

With a smile, Roy nodded and left.

J.B. walked around his desk and pointed to a rose-colored Queen Anne couch that was against the wall. "Please, have a seat."

"Thank you, Mr. Jackson."

"Call me J.B. Everyone does. We're not big on formalities around here."

Izzy took stock of the room. The space had a very masculine feel and looked like an office suited to conduct whatever important business J.B. Jackson engaged in. The focal point was a large set of antlers mounted above the fireplace. Dark oak trim surrounded the doorway and windows. A bearskin rug sat in the middle of the floor. How sad that such a magnificent creature had lost its life at all, let alone for a decorative accessory. But that was the Wild West, where the strongest imposed their will on the weakest.

J.B. settled into an overstuffed leather chair next to the couch. "I trust your journey was uneventful?"

Before Izzy answered, two women entered, one carrying a pitcher of tea and glasses, and the other a basket filled with sweets. They placed everything on the small table in front of the sofa and left as quickly as they appeared.

"Thank you, ladies," J.B. said. "Isabella, please help yourself."

Izzy's mouth watered. The cakes looked warm and soft. "They smell delicious."

"Rosa, my housekeeper, is a marvelous cook. Go on. Try one."

Izzy took a napkin and picked up a cake still warm from the oven. She took a bite, and it melted on her tongue. Her eyes closed as the flavors burst in her mouth. Lemon. Vanilla. Sweet and rich. "This is scrumptious."

Underneath his thick brows, blue eyes twinkled. "I have to stop myself from eating them all at once."

They sipped tea and ate cakes, exchanging pleasantries about the weather and a host of other topics. Izzy found J.B. to be charming and intelligent. Not quite the ogre she imagined. Would he make a good husband? Yes. But she couldn't be happy here, not truly happy. She needed to make her own way, and she refused to answer to anyone. Her mood grew solemn.

J.B. must have sensed the change. "Are you all right?"

Izzy sighed and put her glass on the table. "You seem like a kind man. And I'm sure any woman would consider themselves lucky to call you husband. However..."

He leaned forward but didn't interrupt.

"However, I can't marry you."

She proceeded to tell him her story, starting in Boston and her father's valiant effort to find her a husband, and ending with her time spent in Loma Parda. She bared her soul and admitted to willingly leaving the scene of the crime, as it were, begging for rescue from a band of outlaws. Of course, she left out certain details about a certain someone.

When done, she collapsed against the back of the couch.

J.B., whose thoughtful expression never changed, cleared his throat. "You've had quite a rough go of it." He took a deep breath and expelled it. "I didn't realize you were so coerced into this arrangement."

She nodded. "It's been…very trying. All I want is to go to San Francisco, find Aunt Bea, and pray she'll take me in. From what I've learned about her, I think she has the same independent spirit I do."

"Let me think on this situation. Why don't you go wash up and rest a bit before dinner. We can talk more later."

"Rest sounds wonderful." And, she had to admit to herself with no small measure of surprise, a talk sounded promising.

Izzy woke from a nap feeling refreshed. The comfortable mattress was a far cry from the bumpy coach, and the room itself was lovely with its lace curtains and colorful bedspread. Any woman would be happy with all this, but she wasn't any woman.

Opening her satchel, she pulled out the dress that Elle had bought her in Santa Fe. Happy memories bubbled up but were soon replaced by her constant companion—pain. This was the only dress she owned, so she had no choice. Wearing trousers and a shirt would be disrespectful.

After a couple of wrong turns and with the help of Rosa, she found her way to the dining room. A large, rough-hewn table was ladened with plates of food—grilled steaks, roasted potatoes, carrots, onions, rice, beans—a feast for a king. And more food than two people could eat.

J.B. commanded one end of the table and invited her to sit next to him.

Izzy placed a napkin in her lap. "Will others be joining us?"

"No."

"This is a lot of food for two."

"It is." He winked. "Don't worry, it won't go to waste. Did you get some rest?"

"I did, thank you. I feel refreshed."

"Good." He waved a hand over the array of food. "Please help yourself."

Izzy felt awkward just diving in. In Loma, sure, it was every man or woman for themselves, but this was more like Boston, and back in Boston, her father was always served first.

Maybe J.B. read her mind, or was incredibly intuitive, because he grabbed his fork and stabbed a steak. "Follow my lead." He proceeded to load his plate with meat and potatoes and carrots, taking a little bit of everything. When his plate could hold no more, he sat down and began eating.

Everything smelled so good. Izzy's belly rumbled loud enough for all to hear. Heat crept into her cheeks.

J.B. chuckled. "Go on. Sounds like you're hungry."

She smiled. "I'm very hungry. And this all looks delicious."

Throughout their meal, J.B. talked about life on the ranch. He made Izzy laugh multiple times. He was a kind person. What a fine husband he would make for someone, but not for her. She could never be intimate with him. She could never feel passion for him, never hunger for him like she hungered for Elle. Elle made her want things. Made her feel things. Made her want to do things. Things that would make any woman blush. And despite Elle's betrayal, Izzy still yearned for her soft lips, yearned for them to whisper across her abdomen, to gently tug on an engorged nipple, to suck on the beating pulse at the base of Izzy's neck. She still ached to feel that exquisite explosion of pure pleasure when Elle's tongue stroked her very core. But what Izzy still craved most was touching and caressing Elle, kissing every inch of her body, hearing her soft moans of desire, hearing her beg for Izzy to continue kissing and stroking until she felt the same pleasure.

No, J.B. would make an excellent friend, and nothing more. He was like a comfortable sweater, warm and worn and true. But friendship was not what he wanted, nor what he had paid for. So despite the lively conversation and laughter, a dark cloud of uncertainty about her future still hovered in her mind.

Rosa and another woman cleaned away the plates and uneaten food.

"Would you like some tea or coffee?" J.B. asked.

Izzy patted her distended belly. "I don't think I could fit anything else in."

"You have to have room for dessert. We have chocolate cake."

Oh, my. Chocolate cake? One can't say no to that. "Well, maybe I have a little room left."

He smiled then pulled a pipe from his vest pocket and filled it with tobacco. The aroma of sweet smoke filled the air. It wasn't unpleasant, but it carried a reminder of life in Loma, which of course was accompanied by a stab of pain. Rose and her pipe. Rose and Elle. Izzy sighed. *How long will this last?*

J.B. puffed a few times on his pipe before setting it down. "I've done some thinking about our earlier conversation."

Izzy picked at a loose thread on the tablecloth.

J.B. continued, "I would never force a woman to marry me. I'm not built that way." His brows set in a straight line as though he was working through a complicated problem in his mind. "I have a proposition for you."

"Yes?"

"I'll take you to San Francisco, and along the way we can get to know each other. I'd like a chance to impress you and maybe change your opinion about marrying me. If by the time we get there you're still of the mind that you don't wanna marry, I'll let you go on your way."

Izzy hesitated. Was he trustworthy? The last person she trusted...well, that didn't work out so well. "That's a kind offer, but we've only just met. And pardon me for asking, but how do I know you'll do as you say?"

"That's a fair question, and indeed it would take some measure of trust on your part. But I give you my word. And my word is gold. Ask anyone."

Did she have a choice? She'd never make it to San Francisco by herself. Maybe had Elle still been in her life, they would have successfully made the journey together. At the thought of Elle, a sharp pain made her lip wobble. She commanded herself not to cry as she felt her eyes well up. Elle didn't want her. Elle had betrayed her. Elle was not worth her tears. She could only move forward now, and as she saw it, she had no other choice but to take a chance on J.B. Jackson and hope he was a man of his word. "All right, I accept your proposition."

"Good. I'll start making arrangements. I have some business to attend to tomorrow, so we'll probably leave in a few days."

Izzy was cautiously optimistic. He was a good man—she knew it in her bones—but a small sliver of trepidation about the journey remained.

What if Aunt Bea wasn't there?

CHAPTER TWENTY

Elle arrived at Rose's before noon. The saloon had been home for the last two weeks because being in her house was not an option. Izzy was everywhere. So she chose to be here, wallowing in self-loathing and guilt, drinking herself to death. Although death wasn't coming soon enough.

Rob poured her a shot of whisky. "How you doing?"

I don't sleep, and I can barely get out of bed in the morning. I feel like I no longer have a heart in my chest. I see Izzy everywhere. I feel her everywhere. I'm desperate to touch her and hold her and beg for forgiveness. "I'm fine."

When he walked away, Miriam tapped her on the shoulder. "I wanted to give you something." She glanced around and slid an envelope into Elle's hand. It was addressed to Belle MacPherson in care of Elle Barstow and had been mailed from San Francisco.

"Where did you get this?"

Miriam waited for Rob to pour a drink for a cowboy next to Elle. When he moved on, she whispered, "I found it in Rose's office yesterday."

"It came yesterday?"

She shook her head. "Mail came about two weeks ago."

"She's had this for two weeks?"

Rob stopped to fill Elle's empty glass, and Miriam pressed her lips together. "Mm-hmm."

Elle frowned. Why hadn't Rose given her the envelope? And who was this from? Izzy must've written to somebody and never told her. She tucked it into her vest pocket. Her mood darkened, though she couldn't quite discern if she was mad at Rose or at Izzy. *Probably both.*

"Do you wanna go upstairs?" Miriam discreetly stroked her arm. "It'll help you relax." She placed her mouth next to her ear. "I'll help you relax."

It'd been a while since Elle had enjoyed Miriam's body. In fact, the last time was before Santa Fe, which seemed like another lifetime ago. *Maybe this is what I need to banish Izzy from my thoughts.* "Hell, yeah."

"Room's open, go on up. I'll join you in a bit."

Elle waved at Rob and grabbed the bottle of whisky from his hand. "Put it on my tab."

When she closed the door, she sank onto the bed and stared at the floor. *This is good. I need this.* She guzzled straight from the bottle. *I want this.*

A few minutes later, Miriam slid into the room. "I hope you're gonna share that."

Elle handed her the whisky and Miriam took a healthy mouthful. After putting the bottle down on the bedside table, she knelt in front of Elle and undid the buttons on her shirt. Elle shucked it off and kissed her hard. *I want this.* Her lips slanted across Miriam's mouth, and her tongue plundered its depths. She tried to kiss away the pain of her own betrayal, kiss away the images of Izzy in her brain, but one image wouldn't leave—Izzy's face contorted in shock, pain, and hatred. *Go away!* She urged her body on, trying to will it into a state of arousal, but it refused to comply. Her body was as broken as her heart.

Miriam's hands moved to her pants and quickly slipped inside. Elle knew what they would find—nothing, no arousal. She stopped them and broke off the kiss.

Miriam sat back on her heels. Confusion clouded her features.

Heat rushed into Elle's face, and she turned away. "I can't."

"You can't what?"

"I can't do this."

Miriam joined her on the bed.

"Maybe we could...talk," Elle said.

"It's your hour. We can do what you want."

Elle was sure her dark mood was to blame and that she was reading way too much into it, but the comment stung. *I'm just another customer.*

Self-pity assaulted her. "You can go. I'm gonna stay for a bit."

At least she had her whisky for comfort.

Elle waved Rob over and tapped her finger on the weathered oak bar. "Give me 'nother one."

Rob placed his hands on his hips. "Maybe you've had enough."

"Pfft. I'm fine." She tapped again. "Pour."

He tsk-tsked but relented.

When she nodded, it felt like her head was going to fall off. "Thanks."

A young cowboy with bushy sideburns sidled up to the bar and gave her the once-over. "You Elle Barstow?"

She squinted and tried to focus. "Who's asking?"

"Harry Farland." He touched the brim of his hat.

"Where you from, Harry?"

"I hail from Oklahoma."

"Where 'bouts in Ok...la...homa?"

"Grew up around Stillwater. Don't call any place home now." Rob poured him a beer, and he took a sip. A bit of foam stuck to his mustache.

"What are you doin' here?"

He removed his hat and scratched his head. "Need to find some work. Checking here and Lincoln."

Elle toasted her glass in his direction. "You'll get yourself killed down in Lincoln." Her head pounded and she welcomed the pain. Pain took up a lot of space, which meant less room for Izzy.

Harry finished off his beer and signaled for another. "So, I got to talkin' to some boys, and they say you're the quickest draw around."

"They're right."

Harry chuckled. "Thought I might see for myself. If you're willin'. Trying to make a name for myself."

Elle was in no shape for a duel. Her side still hurt from Cimarron, and she was drunk as hell. But she couldn't think of a better way to go. Her misery would end, and a well-placed gunshot would be a quicker death than drinking. "When?"

"Sun's still up. How about right now?"

Rob leaned over the bar. "I don't think this is the time."

Harry smirked. "This your fella?"

Elle waved Rob off. "Nope. I ain't got no fella."

"What say you, then?"

Rob interjected again. "Can't you see she's in no shape for this right now?"

He gave a crooked grin. "She seems okay to me. Or maybe she's just scared. She looks a bit old and washed up."

Elle snatched the revolver from her holster and jammed it under Harry's chin. "You wanna say that again?"

At Rob's behest, Tim and Arthur inserted themselves into the situation, and Tim put her in a bear hug.

"You know the rules, Elle," Arthur said as he tried to pry the gun from her hands. "Get Raven," he yelled to Rob.

Raven hustled over and helped the men drag Elle from the bar.

She twisted in their grip, screaming profanities the whole way out.

When they deposited her in the street, Raven put a hand on her chest. "Calm down."

Elle slapped it away. "Don't tell me what to do. I got a date with Harry." She brushed past Raven and headed back to the saloon.

Suddenly, she was flat on her stomach and choking on dirt. Raven kneeled on her back. "You ain't going back in there."

It took all Elle's strength to flip her off. "Get away."

"No."

Elle stood and gave a two-handed shove to Raven's chest. "It's all your fault she's not here!"

Raven's mouth dropped open and she shoved her back. "That was the damn plan. Take her and get the reward." She pointed. "You're the one who changed it 'cause you didn't have the guts to go through with it, playing house with her these last few weeks."

"You're jealous because I liked her." Elle teetered and almost fell over.

"Look at you. You're a damn drunk. Go home and sleep it off." Raven stomped away.

Elle lurched after her. Grabbing Raven's arm, she twisted her around and slugged her in the face.

Raven stumbled backward and held a hand up to her eye. "Goddamn it." She came at Elle and punched back, connecting with her jaw.

The blow knocked Elle to her knees. She rubbed her face and glared at Raven. "You sold her out." She charged again, and her fist connected with Raven's nose.

Raven held her nose as blood seeped through her fingers. She pulled her hand away and growled, "You sold her out, not me." Then Raven punched her so hard lights exploded behind her eyes. Before Elle toppled to the ground, Raven's fist connected again, and this blow knocked her senseless.

Raven towered over her. "When the cards were down, you didn't have to go along with Rose, but you did. So don't blame me, blame yourself."

Elle wiped away the blood that dripped down her cheek. Raven had always packed a powerful punch. She blinked her eyes to clear her double vision. She didn't need to fight two Tims, two Arthurs, and two Ravens.

A gunshot rang out, and everyone froze.

Rose stood on the saloon porch with a Colt .45 raised to the sky. "That's enough. You're scaring away my customers. Both of you get out of here and cool down."

Elle had no more strength in her legs as she lay sprawled on her back, helpless in the dirt. Her face hurt and her heart hurt. She was bloodied and defeated and yearned to be put out of her misery.

A wagon pulled to a stop nearby. Arthur and Tim lifted Elle into the back of the buckboard. Matsu snapped the reins, and they jolted forward.

Elle's stomach roiled, and she heaved the contents over the side.

"Maybe you need to stop drinking," Raven yelled as the wagon trundled down the road.

Elle wiped an arm across her mouth. "Maybe you need to stay out of my life."

"I'll stay out of your damn life. I'm done with you!"

Elle curled into a ball and closed her eyes. "Good. I don't need you," she said softly. "I don't need anybody."

CHAPTER TWENTY-ONE

Two days later, Elle pulled Blaze to a stop in front of the saloon in Cimarron. If she feared for her life she would've never made the journey, but her current mental state made her immune to danger.

She found her mark and strode up to the bar. "Whisky, please." Her appearance caused a stir, and murmurs circulated around the room. If this was her last day on Earth, then so be it.

John Watkins turned, and the corner of his lip twitched. "You're taking your life in your hands, showing up here."

"Thought I'd take you up on that offer for a drink." The barkeep placed a shot of whisky in front of her, and she toasted John before downing it.

Since John didn't put a bullet in her head, the rest of the room grew bored and went back to their business.

He finished his drink and raised a hand. "Two more, Henry." Henry refilled Elle's glass and did the same for John.

"What happened to your face?" John asked.

"Got into a fight."

"Other guy look worse?"

Did Raven look worse? Elle didn't know because she hadn't seen her. "Don't remember."

"Ha. That good a night, huh?" He sipped his drink.

They drank in silence for a few moments. Finally, Elle said, "Sorry about Jed."

He stared at the bottles lining the back of the bar. "Boy was a bad seed. Besides, I got four more."

Elle almost laughed at the bad seed comment. Self-introspection must not run in their family, because John was worse than his cowardly son. "How did you know my father?"

"Ah. I figured you didn't come down here to exchange pleasantries." He finished his drink and motioned for another. "Let's see. Where does this tale start? I first met your daddy in Missouri. We'd both joined some bushwhackers and fought the abolitionists in Kansas. Neither of us liked it much. Barely escaped the massacre at Pottawatomie in 1856. After that, I headed to Texas. Not sure where your father took you and your momma." He swirled the liquid in his glass before continuing, "Years later, I met him again in Lincoln. He was rustling cattle and horses. Your momma wanted him to go straight, but he didn't take that seriously til you were about nine. And he tried to stay out of trouble, but outlawing was in his blood. So, he started selling army guns to the Mexicans. He would steal the shipments coming west from Kansas to Fort Sumner. Well, one day he lifted a shipment that was already stolen property. Stole it from the wrong man." He paused. "Or, should I say, the wrong woman."

It took a moment for the words to sink in. When they did, Elle's chest tightened, and she struggled to draw a breath. Only one woman in New Mexico Territory had the temerity to sell stolen US cavalry rifles. "Rose?"

John nodded. "Back then she was shacking up with Charlie Pettis. They were big into gunrunning. When she found out what your father did, she set about to make an example of him. Hired some boys to take care of it. I know, because she asked me. I was nursing a wound at the time, so I wasn't interested. Besides, I still had a soft spot for your pa."

Elle shook her head. "You're lying."

"Why would I lie?"

"Lots of reasons. One being you're trying to get me to turn on Rose. Two, I killed your boy, and it's some sort of emotional revenge."

"Believe me or don't believe me. Don't matter much to me."

She shook her head again. "Doesn't make sense. Why raise me like her own?"

John lowered his brows. "C'mon now, girl. Why do you think?" He leaned closer, and his foul breath made her nose wrinkle. "If she kept you close, you'd never suspect. Plus, she could keep an eye on you." It was his turn to toast his glass.

"Marshals blamed the Apache."

"Wasn't."

"I know. I was there."

He chuckled. "Rose had the marshals in her pocket. Same as she does today."

Elle squeezed her eyes shut and was transported back to that moment in time. "About fifteen of them showed up that night. None of them were Apache. They were all white men." The horrid scene played back in her head. "I recognized one of them a few years later."

"Let me guess. Frank Businsky?"

Another toast. "Good guess."

"Poor Frank. Shot dead in his bed. Couldn't even defend himself."

"Man like that didn't deserve an honorable death. Not after what he did to my momma."

He dipped his chin. "Can't blame a person for revenging the death of a loved one."

Elle wanted to ignore this new information. Pass it off as an old man trying to wound her. But deep down in her gut, she knew it was true. She finished her drink. "Am I walking out of here? Or will you be exacting your revenge on me?"

"It was a fair fight. I got no beef with you. Go on."

Elle nodded and walked out with her chin held high and a hand on her gun. Just in case.

* * *

Elle sat in the dark in Rose's private quarters above the bar. Buoyed by gulps of whisky from the bottle in her hand, she had murder on her mind. Her loaded revolver hung loosely in her other hand.

When the door opened, her heart rate shot up. Rose entered, holding a candle and humming some nameless tune.

Disgust roiled in Elle's gut. All these years, Rose had painted herself as Elle's savior, her pseudo mother. Her protector. And she was none of these things. She had taken everything from Elle. And now Rose's voice replayed in her mind: *"Keep your enemies close, I always say."* Keeping Elle close was Rose's plan from day one.

Rose lit a few oil lamps. The last one she lit threw light on Elle's face, and her hand flew to her chest. "Ellie girl! You scared me half to death." She took in the gun and whisky and stepped back. "You know the rule. No guns drawn in here."

Elle lifted the bottle to her lips, and the hot liquid hit the back of her throat. "You killed my daddy and momma."

The color drained from Rose's face. "Where'd you hear such a thing?"

"Doesn't matter."

Rose's hand moved toward her own gun.

Elle shook her head and said sharply, "I wouldn't. The minute you reach for it, I'll kill you."

Rose's eyes hardened. "Be careful. You'll never make it out of here alive if that gun goes off."

Elle smirked. "Who cares?" She studied the woman in front of her, a woman she had considered family and was now a stranger. "Why'd you do it? Why did you have him killed? Why not have one of your sheriffs arrest him?"

Rose sighed and raised her hands. "I'm gonna sit down. Don't shoot me." She slid her bulky frame into the chair opposite Elle. "I knew your daddy long before you all moved here. Long before you were born. He did a few odd jobs for me down in Texas. Couple times the take was light, and I suspected he might've been skimming some money for himself. But no matter. I let it go. Then he disappeared. I thought he got killed or was rottin' in jail somewhere. Mind if I smoke?"

Elle shrugged.

Rose grabbed her pipe from the desk and lit a match. After a few puffs, she said, "Years later, he shows up in Lincoln, with your momma and you. Claimed he was going straight. And for a while, he did. Kept himself clean. But he fell back into his old ways. Begged me for some work. I gave some and noticed the light purses again. Mentioned it to him and he lied, said it was all there. He left Lincoln the next day."

She paused again, and Elle shifted in her seat. She wanted the story over and her revenge complete. She waved her gun. "Go on."

"A few months later I had the opportunity to sell a large number of guns to my friend down in Mexico. Your daddy and his buddies intercepted the shipment. My Mexican friend was... well, let's just say he was angry. And my boys were angry because they lost their payday. Was a stain on my reputation. Your daddy had to be made an example of."

"So you had him killed."

"He had to pay for what he did."

"And what about my momma?"

"I did not tell them to kill your momma."

They sat in silence for a few moments.

Elle's fingers twitched over the gun in her hand. All she had to do was aim and fire, and two lives would be lost, because Elle would be shot dead before she made it to the front door. *Do it. Pull the trigger.* Her hand began to shake. She commanded her finger to squeeze, but it refused. *Coward.*

"You ain't gonna kill me. I know you too well."

Elle hated her. And hated herself because Rose was right. She didn't have the guts to do it. She didn't have it in her to avenge her parents' deaths. She bolted from her chair and stumbled from the room.

On the way out, she grabbed two more bottles of whisky from the bar and left. Rob called after her. "It's on the house," she yelled back. Swinging herself into the saddle, she squeezed with her knees and Blaze took off. She didn't know where she was going and didn't care.

She rode for hours, cursing herself, her life, her decisions. She cried and yearned for Izzy. She ached to hold her again and kiss her and tell her she loved her. And tell her how wrong she had been. Exhausted and disoriented, she fell from the saddle and hit her head. Blood seeped from her temple and into her eyes. She was weak and tired. Tonight, she'd die in the dark, and no one would care. Her eyelids drooped, so she closed them.

A coyote yipped in the distance before she passed out.

* * *

Something rubbed her head. Something soft and bristly at the same time. *What the hell?* Bright light pierced her eyelids, and she threw an arm over her eyes to shield them.

Pain throbbed in her temples.

She slowly opened her eyes and yelped. Something huge stood over her. She rolled away and forced herself to focus. It was a horse. And not just any horse. It was Izzy's Appaloosa. Luna came close again and nudged her. The bristly softness had been Luna's chin.

"What are you doing here, girl?" She struggled to her feet and took stock of her surroundings. "Where am I?"

The rest of the herd grazed nearby in the canyon. As the fog lifted from her brain, the events of the prior evening came rushing back. *Rose killed my mother and father.* The thought sickened her, and she fell to the ground and dry-heaved.

Luna pushed at her back with her nose.

"What do you want?" she asked with impatience. Luna meant Izzy, and Izzy meant heartache. She searched for Blaze and spotted him under a pine tree. With no strength to even whistle, she placed one foot in front of the other and swayed her way over to him. Her body tilted to one side, and she almost fell. She was in bad shape.

The *clop clop* of hooves followed. She turned as Luna approached. With a wave of her arms, Elle yelled, "Go!"

Luna tossed her head and fell back a couple of paces but didn't turn around.

Elle grumbled, "Stupid horse," and continued to walk away, but the horse kept pace.

When she neared Blaze, he nickered and ambled over. She tried to lift her leg into the stirrup, but her limb lacked the strength. "Okay. Let's go over here." She led him to a large rock and used that to climb into the saddle.

After walking for twenty minutes, Elle still had her shadow. She turned. "I don't know what you want." Images of Izzy and Luna washed over her—Izzy feeding the mare an apple, Izzy hugging Luna, Izzy laughing at Luna—and tears welled up in Elle's eyes. One by one they slipped down her cheeks in long rivulets. "She's not here. She's gone."

CHAPTER TWENTY-TWO

With a groan, Elle fluttered her eyelids and flipped over onto her back. Her head pounded and her body ached from sleeping on her stomach for God knows how many hours. At least she was in her own bed.

Another sunrise, which meant another day. Alone. No warm body to wake up to. No blond hair tickling her nose. The only thing she held on to during the nighttime hours now was Izzy's pillow, which still held her smell. *Maybe it's time to wash it.*

She squinted. The sun's position meant it was midmorning. She wracked her brain but had no memories from the previous night. Hell, the previous day. *Jesus. Did I black out?*

After inching across the mattress, she planted her feet on the ground. With great effort, she stood and trudged into the other room. Some old coffee festered in the pot, and she poured it into a cup. Her belly rumbled. Nothing appealed to her except her wretched days-old Arbuckles'.

She took a sip and her lip curled. Maybe she should spike it with some whisky. The pain in her temples begged to differ.

If she kept this up, she'd be dead in a week. The fastest draw in New Mexico felled by alcohol. She fingered the tender spot on her jaw. Yep. Still hurt. Raven could pack a punch. A mysterious crusty scab stuck to her temple.

Her eyes were drawn to a small brown stain on the tablecloth. *Damn it. Izzy loved this tablecloth.* Elle licked her finger and tried to wipe the stain away, but it stayed.

The front door opened, and Raven stood in the doorway.

They eyed each other in silence, neither having the courage to start the conversation, which wasn't surprising considering the events of a couple of nights ago.

Elle caved. "Morning." She was tired of feeling, tired of feelings. She wanted to be numb and not feel anything at all ever again.

"Morning." Raven, sporting a bruised cheek and black eye from their little donnybrook, wandered around the room. Her movements were stiff, her happy-go-lucky attitude subdued. After a few moments, she leaned against the desk and crossed her arms. "Whatcha doing?"

Banal small talk. *Okay.* "Nothing much. How about you?"

Raven inspected her fingernails. "Nothing. Passing by, thought I'd pop in."

Would they pretend nothing had happened between them? "Thanks for…popping in. Listen, about the other night—"

Raven raised a hand. "No. Let me go first. I stopped in to say I'm sorry."

"Me too. Things got out of control. *I* got out of control." Elle drained her cup and went for another. "Coffee? It's cold, and it's from yesterday, or maybe the day before."

Raven shook her head. "Sounds appealing, but I'll pass."

Elle shuffled back to the table and sank back into the chair.

"You were right," Raven said, with downcast eyes.

"About what?"

"About me wanting Izzy gone. I guess I was jealous." She paused, and Elle didn't press her. "For a long time, it was you and me against the world. Blood sisters." She raised her scarred hand. "Then Izzy came along, and I didn't matter to you anymore."

"That's not true."

"Well, that's how I felt. You're all I've got, and I was losing you. We stopped playing cards at the saloon. We stopped fishing in the river. I was replaced. By Izzy. And it hurt." Raven's eyes revealed the depth of her pain.

Everything she said rang true. Izzy had become the most important thing to Elle, and Raven had been pushed aside. She shouldn't have let that happen. "You're right. I'm sorry."

"I'm sorry too." Raven sighed. "I found the poster in the book, and I told myself, this was the plan. And if you weren't going to follow through with it, Rose would." She shook her head. "I shouldn't have done it. And just so you know, I never hated Izzy. I kinda liked her. But…I dunno." She threw her arms wide. "I'm sorry. I wish I could make it right."

Of course, Elle forgave her. They were sisters. "What's done is done. Let's put it behind us."

Raven's body relaxed and relief reflected in her face. She picked up a letter from the desk. "What's this?"

"Miriam gave it to me."

"It's addressed to Belle MacPherson. Mac."

"I know."

"Did you open it?"

"No. It's not addressed to me."

Raven made a face. "So? Open it."

Elle shook her head.

"I'll open it." Before Elle could voice her displeasure, Raven tore the envelope open and began to read.

Curiosity got the better of Elle. "What's it say?"

"It's from her aunt in San Francisco. Did you know she had an aunt in San Francisco?"

"No."

"It says that she got Izzy's letter. Did you know Izzy wrote to her?"

"If I didn't know she had an aunt, how would I know she wrote to her?"

"You don't know much, do you?"

Elle rolled her eyes. "What else does it say?"

"It says, 'You're welcome to come and live with us. Mary and I would be delighted to have you.' Who's Mary?"

"I don't know, give it to me." Elle snatched the letter from Raven and finished reading it. "Ugh. If I'd gotten this sooner, I could've taken her there. It would've been a better life for her." Her head sagged forward. "Instead, I sold her off to an old man."

"You didn't sell her off. Her family sold her off."

"I betrayed her."

"I did too. So we can both feel like shit." Raven peered out the back window. "Where'd you get the horse?"

"What horse?" Elle joined her. "Huh. I thought I dreamed that."

Luna's head hung over the fence of the corral while her jaw worked back and forth munching a mouthful of hay.

"Maybe you need to lay off the whisky," Raven mumbled.

"It's Izzy's horse."

"Izzy's horse?"

"Yeah." Elle was still drained, even after sleeping for hours. "It's too long of a story, and I'm too tired to tell it." She collapsed back onto the couch and hugged the throw pillow. Izzy's throw pillow. Izzy's horse. Izzy, Izzy, Izzy.

Raven ran a finger over the books in the bookcase and pulled out *The Three Musketeers*. "Rose wants to see you."

"Hell, no."

"She told me what happened."

"Good for her. It's now clear I was never her favorite. She just wanted to keep an eye on me."

Raven sighed. "I don't know about that. Anyways, I'm to bring you to her. So you better get cleaned up. You smell."

"I have no desire to ever lay eyes on her again."

"I think you're gonna wanna hear what she has to say."

"She'll probably kill me. Like she killed my parents."

"That's not gonna happen. C'mon."

Screw it. What did it matter if Rose shot her? Izzy was gone. *Because of me.* "Fine. I'll wash up."

The bar was subdued for once when Elle and Raven arrived. Maybe the heat had kept people at home. They made their way to Rose's office and stepped inside.

Rose sat behind her desk, smoking her pipe. She gave a tentative smile as the two women took the seats in front of her. "Hey, Ellie girl."

Elle cringed at the endearment, now tainted by Rose's betrayal. "Don't call me that."

A tinge of pain crossed Rose's face. "All right." She pushed a thick envelope across her desk. "I have something for you."

Elle eyed the envelope warily, half expecting it to blow up. "What is it? A stick of dynamite?"

"Open it."

She gave a half sneer and pulled the contents out. The first sheet of paper said *Title and Deed* across the top. "I don't understand." She flipped through page after page of legal jargon and her headache grew worse. "What is all this?"

"That's a deed to twenty thousand acres of land," Rose said.

"Why's my name on it?"

"Because it's yours now. I'm giving it to you. Do what you want with it."

Elle stared at the papers with her mouth hanging open. *Maybe I'm still asleep.* She shook her head to wake herself up.

"Look," Rose continued. "I can't undo what happened sixteen years ago, and I can't give you back what you lost. I'm not asking you to forgive me. This is my way of trying to make amends. I know you think I took you in to keep an eye on you, and maybe at first that's what it was, but eventually I developed a soft spot for both of you. Anyway, I figure you can have that ranch you've been dreaming about. There's enough room for a few homesteads, so if this one"—she nodded her head toward Raven—"wants to have a life near you, there's plenty of land."

A stunned Elle remained silent.

"Well? I just made you one of the richest women in this county and you got nothing to say?"

"I didn't ask for this." Elle slid the contents back into the envelope and pushed them toward Rose. "And I don't want it."

Raven gasped. "What are you doing? Do you know how much that's worth?"

"Yeah. And I'm sure it's got miles of strings attached to it."

Rose held up a hand. "No, it does not. I understand that you have no reason to trust me. But this is yours, free and clear. Part of it was your daddy's homestead, so it should be yours anyway. Get out of outlawing and make a life for yourself. You won't hear from me again. Unless you want to."

Raven stood and grabbed the envelope. "She'll take it." She yanked Elle from the chair. "Let's go."

"I don't want it!"

"Shut up." Raven dragged her from the office and out the door.

When they made it to the street, Elle wrenched herself free. "I told you. I don't want anything from her."

"Listen to me. This is your opportunity to build yourself a ranch house in the middle of twenty thousand acres and do whatever the hell you want. *Be* with whoever the hell you want." She took off down the street, and Elle, her mind now spinning with possibilities, had to hustle to keep up. Raven continued, "Shorty and I will work for you of course, provide security, do some cowboying. Not sure about Willy. Might be too far for him, but maybe he'll come too."

Elle focused on a certain thing that Raven had said. *Be with whoever you want.*

Raven smiled. "You thinkin' what I'm thinkin'?"

"Uh. I don't know. What are you thinking?"

"We need to go find your girl."

Elle scoffed. "She's married by now."

"She is not. I know that for a fact."

Elle narrowed her eyes. "How do you know that?"

"I know things, is all I'm gonna say."

"She hates me."

"So? I hate you sometimes too."

"You do not."

"I do," Raven said. "I did the other night after you gave me this shiner. I got over it. And she will too."

Elle pointed. "You deserved that shiner. What do I say to her?"

"I don't know. We'll think of something on the way."

Elle pondered. Then pondered some more. "I need to give her the letter, at the very least."

"It *is* the least you can do."

"And I need to apologize. She'll never forgive me, but I need to apologize."

Raven nodded. "Maybe best to lead with that."

Could she do this? Could she ride out to J.B. Jackson's ranch and stomach the vitriol that was sure to come from Izzy? Stubborn Izzy. Brave Izzy. Beloved Izzy.

"Well?" Raven asked.

Elle straightened. "Let's go find my girl."

* * *

"You lied to me." Elle glared. "You said Izzy wasn't married yet."

She and Raven sat under the Jackson Ranch sign.

"Are you sure I didn't say *maybe* she wasn't married?"

"You said you knew for a fact."

"Well, I might've stretched the truth a bit, but I got us here, didn't I?"

Elle's voice rose. "She could be married."

"So? You wanna apologize or not?"

"J.B. will shoot me before I even have a chance to."

"He will not." Raven yanked out her revolver and rolled the chamber. "I'm sure he's a reasonable man."

Now that she was so close to Izzy, Elle's stomach churned. *Will she accept my apology? Or will she throw me away like an old, threadbare blanket?* Luna tugged on her lead. The mare was a peace offering. "Do we have a plan?"

"You're the plan maker," Raven said.

"Well, if she's a married woman, the plan is out the window."

"I gotta plan. Shoot first and ask questions later."

"No."

"Ask questions first, then shoot."

"What is wrong with you?"

With a twinkle in her eye, Raven chuckled.

Elle gave a half-grin. "You're a pain in the ass." She sighed. "I guess we'll ride up and ask for Izzy."

"Maybe she'll be the one to shoot first and ask questions later. She won't hit anything though." Raven made a funny face.

Elle laughed and her mood lifted. "She was a bad shot, God love her." She glanced at the ground. "I love her."

"You broke your own code."

Elle nodded.

"I broke it too. Rob isn't a bad guy."

"You and Rob?"

"Yeah." Raven tilted her head sideways. "Love ain't that bad."

"Huh. I didn't see that coming. I knew he liked you, but you never paid him no mind. So we're both screwed."

"You're more screwed than me. At least mine don't hate me."

"True. Let's go."

Blaze set the pace with a leisurely canter. They passed pastures filled with cattle and orchards filled with apple trees.

"Have you figured out what you're gonna say to her?" Raven asked.

"No. I just hope she sees me. And that it's not too late."

"You sure you want this?"

"I do. I never wanted anything more in my life."

"And what if she tells you to hightail it back to Loma Parda?"

"I don't know. Not sure I can go back."

The main ranch appeared in front of them, and they slowed. A few cowhands milled about the barn but showed minimal interest in the two women.

Elle checked her revolver. If things took a bad turn, she'd go down fighting. After jamming the gun back into the holster, she pulled her rifle out and rested it on her thigh.

Raven did the same. "I just wanna say, if I'm gonna die in a hail of bullets, I'm glad it's with you."

Elle smiled. "Same. If I'm goin' out, I'm goin' out with you."

They galloped to the hacienda and pulled to a stop.

An older woman with graying hair swept the porch. She barely glanced at them. "¿Puedo ayudarle?"

Elle and Raven exchanged a look. The woman had to be on the other side of sixty. Maybe their display of firepower was a bit much. They both slid their rifles back into their saddle holsters.

Elle cleared her throat. "We're here to see Isabella Collins."

"No está aquí," the woman replied.

"What?" Raven asked.

The woman continued with her broom. "You deaf? She's not here."

Elle frowned. *Is this woman lying?*

Raven hopped from her horse and stuck her gun in the woman's face. "Where is she?"

The woman lifted a finger and nudged the revolver down. "Please do not point that at me. Where are your manners?"

An admonished Raven lowered her gun.

Elle dismounted and smiled. Sometimes honey worked better than vinegar. "Miss…?"

"Rosa."

"Miss Rosa. Are you sure Isabella Collins is not here?"

"Of course I'm sure. They went to San Francisco."

"They?" Raven asked.

"Yes, they. Maybe you should get your hearing checked. You're awful young to be deaf."

"I assume you mean J.B. and Isabella?" Elle asked.

"Sí."

"When did they leave?"

"About three weeks ago."

Elle threw her head back and groaned. San Francisco was at least a six-week journey, at most two months.

The woman leaned her broom against the porch railing. "Come." She waved them through the front door. "You look hungry. I made lunch. And oatmeal cookies."

"I love oatmeal cookies," Raven said.

An hour later, Raven and Elle crossed under the Jackson Ranch sign again, armed with vanilla cakes and oatmeal cookies.

They stopped on the main trail. To the left was Loma Parda, to the right, San Francisco.

"What now?" Raven asked.

Elle stared at the literal crossroads of her life. One path led back to her old life, one she didn't want anymore. The other led to the unknown. Easy decision. "I'm going to San Francisco."

"I'll go with you."

"No. It's gonna be a long trip. You need to stay. You got ties now."

Raven gave her a sheepish smile. "Rob said he wants to make an honest woman outta me."

Elle chortled. "That's a tall order. I hope he's up for it."

"I kinda hope so." Raven gazed into the distance. "Are you sure? I don't like you going all that way alone."

"I'll be fine. I'll stop in Albuquerque and get some supplies. Maybe hook up with a coach headed west. They're always needing extra hands. Hopefully I'll see you in a few months. Hopefully *we'll* see you in a few months. Ask Matsu to take care of my house and Jack."

An awkward silence followed. This would be the longest they'd ever been apart, and neither knew how to say goodbye.

"I love you, you know," Elle said.

"All right, don't get all sentimental on me."

"I won't. Take care, my friend. My sister." They clasped their scarred hands.

Raven bit her lip and moisture sprung into her eyes. "You too. You better make it back. We got a ranch to build."

"I will." Elle nodded one last time and tugged on the reins, leading Blaze to the right. Tears slipped from her eyes.

"I love you too, you damn chucklehead!" Raven shouted.

Elle laughed and gave one last wave.

CHAPTER TWENTY-THREE

The stagecoach pulled to a stop and Izzy glanced out the window. She fussed with the sash on her modest dress. A speck of dust clung to the hem, and she shook it off. They'd left the rest of J.B.'s crew at the Hotel Fortunato, then came straight to the address on Aunt Bea's envelope.

The door opened and the driver poked his head in. "We're here, Mr. Jackson."

"Thank you, Ted." He glanced across at Izzy. "Are you ready?"

Izzy nibbled on her bottom lip. "What if she's not here anymore?"

"There's only one way to find out." He left the coach and thrust his hand back in.

Izzy grasped it and stepped onto the street. A sign that read *Kearny Street Boardinghouse* hung from the post of the wooden front porch that was shaded by a large awning. The house itself was made of stone and rose three stories high. All the buildings along the street were of a similar height, and memories of

Boston flooded Izzy's brain. The front door was propped open, inviting guests to come in and allowing the cool breeze to flow through the building.

J.B. tucked Izzy's hand under his arm, and they strode into the foyer.

A plump woman with chestnut hair pulled back into a bun was bent over scrubbing at the baseboards. When she looked up, Izzy gasped. "Aunt Bea!"

Aunt Bea's mouth opened, then broke into a huge smile. "Izzy?" She dropped her brush and rushed into Izzy's outstretched arms. "My girl. We were wondering when you would show up."

Izzy pulled back but held on to her aunt's hands. "Then you got my letter?"

"Yes. We wrote you back right away."

Izzy drew her brows together. "I never got it."

Aunt Bea tilted her head to the side. "Not surprising. The post is never reliable. But you're here, and that's all that matters."

J.B. shuffled his feet and Izzy placed a hand on her chest. "Oh, my manners. Aunt Bea, this is J.B. Jackson. He's originally from Boston but moved out to New Mexico years ago."

Aunt Bea held out her hand and J.B. placed a kiss on the back of it. "I am happy to make your acquaintance, Miss MacPherson."

"J.B. was kind enough to escort me out here to find you."

"Well, it seems I owe you a debt of gratitude, Mr. Jackson."

"That's not necessary. I had business here in San Francisco and was happy to have Izzy's company for the long journey." His cheeks reddened. "We slept separately, of course."

Aunt Bea smiled. "I trust my first impression of people, Mr. Jackson, and it tells me you are an honorable man. Now come. I'm sure you need refreshments after your long journey."

Aunt Bea led them to the dining room, where a few people sat having lunch. The room was light and airy with open windows along the one outside wall. Blue and white gingham curtains fluttered in the breeze. "Here, let's sit at the big table. I need to hear all about your journey. Let me find Mary." She left and reappeared with another woman with reddish hair piled on top of her head. There was a touch of gray around her temples. "Izzy, do you remember Mary?"

"Of course I do." She hugged Mary, who had been her aunt's constant companion when she lived in Boston.

Mary held Izzy at arm's length. "Look at you, lass," she said with a hint of a brogue. "All grown up into a beautiful woman." She touched a lock of Izzy's hair. "And I love your hair this length."

Izzy was pleased because she liked keeping it shorter. "You don't think it's too short?"

"Not at all."

"Mary, let's set a table for four so we can catch up with my favorite niece," Aunt Bea said.

They sat down and enjoyed a lunch of roasted chicken and biscuits. Between bites, J.B. and Izzy shared their adventures on the trail from Albuquerque to San Francisco. After eating, Aunt Bea brought out the teacups and the conversation continued.

"Mr. Jackson, what made you leave Boston?" Aunt Bea asked.

J.B. sat back in his chair and rested his hands on his belly. "I guess it was just a lust for adventure. I find the trappings of cities too confining for my taste. Of course, my father was not happy with my choice. As the eldest, it was expected that I would take over the family business."

"And what was that business?" Mary asked.

"He was in cotton textiles, as was his father before him, and as was expected of me. But instead of learning the family business, I chose to spend most of my time with my grandparents on my mother's side. They had a large property in the countryside, which I found much more amenable."

"I used to love it when we took our trips outside the city," Izzy chimed in. "Remember, Aunt Bea? You, Mary, and I would wander through the open fields and forests. And you would point out all the different trees and flowers."

Aunt Bea nodded. "Those were happy times."

J.B. chuckled. "I'm sure I would have accompanied you on those trips. My grandmother was also a lover of nature. She was an intellectual and a strong-willed woman. And between you and me, she ran the household. And I think my grandfather didn't mind at all. He enjoyed their lively conversations about politics and world affairs. I loved them both."

Izzy rested an elbow on the table and put her chin in her hand. "I wish I could've met your grandmother. She sounds wonderful."

J.B.'s lip curled up at the corner and a hint of mischief danced in his eyes. "I must say, you do remind me of her."

After another hour of chatting, J.B. stood. "It's getting late. I should take my leave."

"It was lovely meeting you, Mr. Jackson," Mary said. "Do stop by again."

Izzy led J.B. to the front door. They both stopped before he opened it.

J.B. looked at her with his typical kindness. In fact, Izzy wasn't sure she'd seen anything but since she'd met him. Her hands twisted together as the silence grew. She wasn't sure how to say what needed to be said.

He cleared his throat. "I guess it's decision time for you." A tinge of sadness creased his face. "Although I have a sense of which way you're leaning."

A small, thankful sigh escaped Izzy's mouth. He was making it easy for her. Because that's the sort of man he was. Her voice trembled. "I want to thank you. Your thoughtfulness and generosity has been…refreshing, and something I've rarely seen since I've been out here." She took a deep breath. "But I can't marry you. It's not the life I want, even though you are a wonderful man. I need to follow my own path. And I know it'll be hard because I'm a woman, but I've got to try."

He reached out and took her hand. "I would've been honored to have you as my wife. But I understand. You have a wild spirit, Isabella Collins. No man should ever attempt to tame you."

A tear slipped down Izzy's face. "I don't know how you can be so understanding."

"Well, it seems you and I are cut from the same cloth. Both needing to find our own way despite pressures from family, or society in your case. I can respect that. Besides, my grandmother would turn over in her grave if I ever forced a woman to do anything against her will."

"But you paid for a bride, and you're leaving with nothing."

"Not nothing. I'm proud to call you a friend. If you're ever near Albuquerque, you make sure to stop in and say hello."

Izzy was overcome with gratitude, and she hugged him. She didn't care how inappropriate it was to do so, she just did it. When he released her, she wiped away the tears. "Thank you again. And I will stop by someday to say hello."

He placed his hat on his head and nodded before heading out the door.

With a pang of sadness, she waved from the porch as the stagecoach pulled away. She would miss him, but then her spirits lifted, and she raised her chin.

Another chapter in her life had ended, and a new one was just beginning.

CHAPTER TWENTY-FOUR

Izzy made the bed in room number four. She tucked the blanket and sheet under the mattress and fluffed the pillow. Working at her aunt's boardinghouse was challenging, but she didn't mind. In fact, it had been the perfect distraction this past month.

The day after J.B. left, Izzy had insisted Aunt Bea and Mary put her to work so she could earn her keep. Her mother used to say that idle hands were the devil's workshop, and her devil was a certain outlaw that needed to be forgotten. The days provided a measure of relief in the form of all the chores to be done to run the boardinghouse. Only in the overnight hours did her mind focus on Elle and what they'd had for such a brief time. The pain never left, so she tried to be angry instead of sad to keep the agony to a minimum. At first, the anger was easy, but then sadness started winning the day. She longed to be in Elle's arms again, to feel that happiness, to feel the passion they had shared.

Last night Elle had been in her dreams, and she awoke feeling lost and lonely and heartbroken. *Will I ever get over this? Will my heart ever heal?* After carrying the dirty linens downstairs, she headed into the kitchen to help her aunt cook the evening meal for the guests.

"I've made the broth for tonight's stew," Aunt Bea said. "Maybe you could prepare the flour for the bread." The Irish soda bread was a favorite of the guests and was made fresh every day.

"Yes," Izzy replied. She couldn't shake the melancholy that haunted her since she woke from the dream.

"Is everything okay?" Aunt Bea asked.

Izzy sighed. "I'm feeling a bit down today."

Aunt Bea gave her a sympathetic look. "I know what will help. A good cup of tea." She set about putting the kettle on. "Let's sit a spell. Tell me what's the matter."

Izzy smiled. Aunt Bea believed a cup of tea cured everything.

Mary walked in with a sack full of fresh vegetables, which she spread over the kitchen table. "I got some lovely tomatoes and squash today." Her reddish hair had escaped from her tidy bun. She took in the kettle and clucked. "Tea this early? What did I miss?"

Aunt Bea squeezed Izzy's hand. "Our girl's a bit misty-eyed this morning."

"Let's have a chat." Mary patted Izzy's back and placed three teacups on the table.

Less than a week after her arrival, Izzy had sensed that Bea and Mary's relationship was something…more. More than business partners, more than companions. They hid it well, but somehow Izzy just knew. So one evening she took a chance and poured her heart out. She talked about her life in Boston, her unwillingness to get married, her scandalous kiss, her banishment, and meeting Elinor Barstow. Elle became the topic of conversation from then on. And every time Izzy's mood dipped, they offered a sympathetic ear.

The kettle came to a boil and Mary poured water into their cups.

"What's got you down, lass?" she asked.

Izzy wrapped her hands around her teacup. "The usual. I had a dream last night. We were in the canyon, laughing." It was more than laughing, but Izzy kept that to herself. "And I could feel my love, and happiness. And after I woke up, all I felt was pain."

"One day you'll wake up and it won't hurt so much," Mary said. "But the pain's still fresh, and you have to get through it."

"It *will* get better," Aunt Bea said. "People who say time heals all wounds. Well…" She raised her cup. "They know what they're talking about."

Izzy nodded. Of course, they were right. "I wish I could have what you two have. You get to spend your days together and grow old together. And it's so beautiful." Tears welled up in Izzy's eyes and she brushed them away. *Pain will be my forever companion.*

"Maybe someday you *will* have what we have," Aunt Bea said.

Izzy hid her skepticism. After all, her aunt meant well and only wanted to lift her spirits. She tried to imagine loving someone else, but in her heart, there was only one person. Elle, her outlaw, her protector, her lover.

The bell on the front door jingled.

"I'll get it." Mary hustled from the room.

Her aunt squeezed her hand again. "You're strong. You'll get through this. I promise."

"I'm sure I will," Izzy said with false confidence. She didn't want to act like a sappy burden needing constant hand-holding. Eventually it would get exhausting for the two older women. *Stay busy. Pitch in and make yourself useful.* Maybe when she felt stronger, she'd see about an apprenticeship with a lawyer in town. "What's for dessert tonight? Shall I make a pudding? I can go to the store and get cream."

Mary poked her head into the kitchen. With a frown, she said, "Someone's here to see Izzy."

Izzy widened her eyes. "Me? Who is it?"

"You best see for yourself. In the front parlor."

"Um. Okay." *Who the heck is it?* She walked out of the kitchen and into the parlor. When the visitor turned around, she gasped.

She looked thinner, gaunt, with dark circles under her whisky eyes. A smell of leather and horse accompanied her, smells Izzy had always found oddly sensual.

"Hey, Iz."

* * *

Elle stood tall, hat in her hands. Her heart soared when Izzy appeared.

For a few seconds, Izzy's face registered shock. Then her expression turned guarded, and her eyes became wary. "What are you doing here?"

"I came to find you."

"Why?"

Elle ran a hand through her hair. She'd rehearsed this scene for the past seven weeks, but now the words abandoned her.

"Elle, why are you here?"

How could she lay bare her heart? It seemed like a monumental task. "I needed to see you."

"How did you even know where I was?"

"I crossed paths with J.B. on the way out here. We stopped for the night at the same spot. Got a chance to chat with him."

"What did you chat about?"

"You." Her mood had lifted considerably after that talk with J.B. Elle dug into her vest pocket and produced the letter. "I also have this."

"I can't believe you talked about me with J.B. You had no right." Izzy snatched the letter from her hands and inspected it. She locked eyes with Elle. "The postmark is from months ago." Her eyes narrowed. "How long did you have this? Did you hide this from me?"

"No, I didn't. Miriam found it in Rose's desk and gave it to me after you were gone."

Izzy's voice rose. "Well, I don't know why you're here. I thought you'd be spending your reward money."

Elle flinched. "Yeah. About that…"

Izzy crossed her arms and waited.

"I'm sorry."

"For what? For lying to me? For betraying me?"

"For everything. Look, I know you're mad—"

"Mad?" She took a step closer and sneered. "Mad doesn't even begin to describe what I feel. What you did to me that day was worse than what my father did. You were cruel and mean. You broke my heart, and I will never forgive you." Her voice shook and she pointed toward the door. "So why don't you hop back into your saddle and go back to Loma. Because you are not welcome here."

"Let me explain."

"No. Get out. Go back to New Mexico. I'm sure you can find someone else to kidnap." And with that she twirled around and fled the room.

"I didn't kidnap you." But Izzy had disappeared. "That didn't go so well," Elle mumbled. Her shoulders slumped and her body trembled from exhaustion. Getting right back into the saddle was about as appealing as Shorty's homemade brew. Before she could make up her mind what to do, the redheaded woman who greeted her a few minutes ago came back into the room, followed by another woman.

The redhead wrung her hands. "Are you Elle?"

"Yes. I am."

The other woman smiled and reached out a hand. Her chestnut hair was twisted into a knot at the back of her neck, and her green eyes crinkled at the corners. "I'm Izzy's Aunt Bea. And this is Mary."

"Pleased to meet you. Elle Barstow. I knew Izzy back in New Mexico."

"We know *all* about you, dear," Mary said.

Did Izzy tell them everything? Elle tried to be lighthearted. "That sounds ominous."

"Mm-hmm."

Both women scrutinized her.

Yep. They know everything.

"What are you doing here, dear?" Bea asked.

"I came to apologize to Iz."

"And how did that go?" Mary asked.

"Not too good."

"Well, you did break her heart."

"I did." The oddity of talking about her feelings with complete strangers was not lost on Elle. "But I'd like to make it right."

"Really?"

"Yes, ma'am. I'd do anything to make it right." She glanced down at her feet. "I love her. And I miss her. I made a huge mistake."

Izzy's aunt gave her the once-over. "You must be tired, riding all the way from New Mexico."

She kept her head down. "I am, ma'am."

"Bea will do."

Elle directed a weary gaze in her direction. "I am tired… Bea."

"We have a room if you'd like. Give you time to rest up for a few days. And maybe give you time to do other things." Bea's green eyes twinkled.

Other things? Like convincing Izzy to give me another chance? "I'll take you up on that offer."

"Very good. Mary, is room eight available?"

"I believe it is. Let's get you checked in." Mary walked behind the counter and opened a large book. With a wink, she asked, "How many days do you think?"

Elle smiled. Perhaps she had two allies. They both beamed back at her. Yes. One could never have too many allies when dealing with a very stubborn Isabella Collins. "I guess however long it takes. To do *other things*."

"Grand," Bea said. "It will be lovely to have you, dear."

* * *

Izzy tore upstairs and down the long corridor to her room. She slammed the door and threw herself upon the bed. "The nerve of her. Showing up here. How dare she?" She rolled over onto her back and hugged her pillow. Her heart still raced from the encounter. Never in a million years did she expect Elle to show up on her doorstep. At first, she thought she imagined her. But, no. There she stood, full of confidence and goddamn gorgeous. With those goddamn warm whisky eyes and those goddamn slim hips. Suddenly, the image of Elle's hips grinding into Izzy's center brought about an unwelcome shot of desire, a feeling so powerful it took her breath away. *Stop it. She's a liar. A Judas. An outlaw whose love of money drives her to do awful things. And she's killed people.* Then, another small inner voice said, *You've killed someone too.*

A knock on the door startled her. She quickly wiped her eyes. "Yes?"

"Izzy, may I come in?" Bea asked.

Izzy rose from the bed and opened the door. "I'll be right down to start baking the bread."

"Of course, dear. But I wanted to let you know that your friend is going to stay the night."

Izzy's heart leapt into her throat. "Excuse me? She's not my friend."

"She's exhausted," Bea said. "And I didn't see the harm in giving her a place to rest."

"She can sleep anywhere but here. She can sleep in a stable as far as I'm concerned."

"That wouldn't be comfortable."

"Why can't she get a room at the Fortunato?"

"She's already here. Poor thing needs to rest."

Izzy was flabbergasted. "Poor thing? *Poor thing?* She sold me off to collect a reward. She's no poor thing."

"I know, but I sense that she regrets her actions. It'll just be for a few days."

"Now it's a few days? What happened to staying the night?" Izzy glared at her aunt with her mouth hanging open. Was this happening?

"We put her in room eight."

"Room eight?" Izzy pointed to the room next door. "That's right here."

"Oh. So it is." Bea waved a hand. "Don't worry. You'll barely see each other." With a swish of her skirts, her aunt ambled back down the hallway.

Izzy remained frozen in place. This was happening. The woman who ripped her heart out would now be staying right next door. The woman who gave her unimaginable pleasure would be on the other side of the wall. The woman whose kisses drove her mad would be right here.

Okay, maybe stop thinking of the good times.

She swung around and slammed the door. Irish bread would have to wait.

CHAPTER TWENTY-FIVE

"Why didn't you tell me Luna was here?" Izzy demanded.

Elle placed her coffee cup into its saucer. She was in the middle of breakfast courtesy of Mary and Bea. Now well-rested, she felt like a new woman. A bit of her swagger had returned. "You weren't in the mood to converse yesterday."

With a harrumph, Izzy stormed off toward the kitchen.

The gentleman at a neighboring table showed keen interest in the goings-on. When she glared at him, he quickly lost himself in his *Chronicle*.

A minute later Izzy returned, still in a mood. "She's *my* horse. Why did you bring her?"

"Ah, because she's your horse?"

Izzy scowled and spun back to the kitchen.

The gentleman gawped again.

Elle widened her eyes. "Pfft. Women."

He raised his brows and nodded before returning to his newspaper.

Before she fell asleep last night, Elle made up her mind that she was not leaving without Izzy. No matter how many days it took to convince her they belonged together, Elle would wait. And if Izzy wanted to remain in San Francisco with her aunt, Elle would move here.

Bea brought out the coffeepot and refilled her cup.

"Bea, the railing around the porch is broken in spots," Elle said.

"Oh yes, we've been meaning to get that fixed."

Elle smiled broadly. "I'll do it." Might as well be useful.

"That would be lovely. Thank you."

* * *

Later that day, Izzy rolled the dough for the bread. She was about an hour behind on her chores because she had to spend some quality time with Luna this morning. The mare had remembered her, and a burst of happiness had bloomed inside her chest. Of course, the apples and sugar cubes didn't hurt.

Bea came bustling in with an armful of laundry. "Izzy, dear. Why don't you take a glass of lemonade out to your friend? She's been working in that hot sun for hours."

The mention of Elle raised Izzy's dander. "She's not my friend."

"I'm up to my ears in laundry, dear, and Mary is at the market. Consider it a favor."

"No. I don't want to."

Bea dipped her head and gave Izzy a disapproving look.

Izzy took a deep breath. "Fine."

Her aunt brightened. "Thank you."

"Grrrr." Izzy grabbed the pitcher of lemonade and a glass. Before pushing the front door open, she observed Elle through the window. She wore an untucked white shirt with the sleeves rolled up, displaying her sinewy forearms. If Izzy closed her eyes, she could feel their firmness. She used to love running her hands along them when Elle leaned over her in bed. The thought made Izzy's legs weak, and she almost toppled over. *No. I hate her for what she did to me.*

Izzy shoved the door open, and a startled Elle jumped. "My aunt wanted you to have a glass of lemonade." She filled the glass and placed it on the step. She wanted no chance of physical contact. Truth be told, she wasn't sure how she would react. Even an innocent brush of fingers might throw her into a sexual tizzy.

Elle picked up the lemonade. "Your aunt?"

"Yes."

"Not you?"

"Correct."

A cocky grin played upon Elle's lips. She wiped the sweat from her brow with the bottom of her shirt, giving Izzy a peek at more bare skin. "Well, thank your aunt for me." She toasted her glass and drank deeply.

Izzy meant to leave and not spend another minute in her company, but her feet felt like they were stuck in mud. "How is everyone?"

"They're good."

"Are you helping Matsu with her writing?"

"I haven't had a chance."

"You need to do that."

"I will. Oh, Hattie said her first word a few days before I left."

"What did she say?"

"I picked her up and she said 'boo,' or 'woo,' or…'coo,' or something."

"That's not a word. That's a gurgle."

With a tilt of her head, Elle said, "No. I think it was definitely a word."

"Are you sure she didn't say, 'Put me down before you drop me'?"

Elle laughed. "No. She didn't say that."

"And how's Jack?"

"He's good. I'm sure he misses you." And then, so softly Izzy had to strain to hear, she said, "We all miss you."

Izzy's resistance slipped, and the walls around her heart cracked. *No. She sold me off. Just like my family did.* "I have to get back to work."

She stomped back inside and attacked the bread dough, rolling it roughly with the pin. "Get a hold of yourself, Isabella Collins. She broke your heart once. Don't give her a chance to do it again," she mumbled under her breath.

* * *

Later that night, Elle dined with Izzy and the aunts. Bea invited her to dinner, and she accepted. Any chance to interact with Izzy meant a chance to convince her to come home to Loma. Of course, Izzy avoided all eye contact, but that was okay. A wild horse took time to break, and Izzy would too.

They sat around the small table in the kitchen enjoying a beef pie with roasted potatoes and fried squash. The aunts were wonderful cooks, and Elle relished the home-cooked meal after being on the trail for almost two months.

"So, Elle," Mary started. "Izzy told us you're an outlaw."

"Did she now?"

Izzy shot daggers in her direction. "I should turn you in."

Elle feigned shock. "Well, that's no way to treat a guest."

"I'm curious," Izzy said. "What did you spend the money on?"

Elle sipped some water before answering. "I didn't take the money. None of us did. Well, except for Rose."

"Rose. Such a peach."

"I returned the rest of it."

"When?"

"I stopped at J.B.'s ranch first. Rosa told me you and he went to San Francisco. So I left the money on his desk with a note saying I'd pay back the rest. Said the same when I met him on the trail."

"Was that your way of making yourself feel better?" Izzy asked. "If you gave the money back, somehow what you did wasn't so bad?"

"No, I—"

"I don't wanna talk about it." Izzy turned her attention to Mary. "This pot pie is delicious, thank you. Do we have any brandy?"

"No, dear. You know we don't have any."

"Maybe I'll pick some up tomorrow," Izzy said.

"I guess if you feel the need."

At the mention of brandy, Elle was transported back to Santa Fe. An image of Izzy in the throes of passion popped into her head, and a stab of desire shot through her. Was the mention of brandy on purpose, to prick Elle? If so, it worked.

Mary turned her attention to Elle. "Did you come all the way from New Mexico by yourself?"

"No. I hired on with some stagecoaches making the trip. To help provide security."

"How ironic." Izzy addressed Bea and Mary. "She usually robs stagecoaches. And kidnaps people."

"I didn't kidnap you," Elle said. "Besides, I'm giving it up."

Izzy's brows set in a straight line. "Giving what up?"

"Outlawing. I'm gonna build a ranch in the canyon."

"Our canyon?"

"Yeah." Elle toyed with the food on her plate. "But it won't be home unless you're with me."

An awkward silence descended over the table.

"That's not going to happen." Izzy stood. "If you'll excuse me, I have some work to do."

After Izzy left, Elle sighed.

Bea patted her hand. "Rome wasn't built in a day, dear. Now. We have butter cake for dessert."

* * *

The next morning, Izzy scoured the breakfast dishes. She was exhausted. Sleep had proven to be elusive the past two nights with Elle such a short distance away, lying in bed alone. She had fought the urge to go to her room and slip into her arms.

Elle's words at dinner the night before shocked her. Giving up outlawing and building a ranch? And wanting Izzy to join her? For an instant, Izzy's heart sang, but she silenced it. *She'll betray you again. She can't be trusted.*

Aunt Bea strode in, and Elle hovered close behind her. "We ran out of sugar. I need you and Elle to pick up a few bags at the store."

"There was a bag in the cupboard the other day."

"It's gone."

I must be seeing things. "Okay." Izzy removed her apron and dried her hands. "But I can go by myself."

"Nonsense," Bea said. "That's too many bags for one person to carry." She waved cash at her. "Here's some money. Now, go. I'll finish cleaning up."

Izzy grabbed the wad of bills and marched out the door, hoping to leave Elle in her dust. But alas, those long legs kept up with ease. "I know what you're doing, and it's not going to work."

"What am I doing?"

"Ingratiating yourself with my aunt in the hopes of getting to me."

"I think I'm just helping you carry some sugar."

"I don't think so." When Elle was physically near, anger was easy. When she was away, Izzy's resolve slipped, and longing for kisses and touches prevailed. Like last night in bed.

"Iz, can we talk?"

Izzy quickened her pace. "No."

"I'm sorry for what I did."

"So you've said."

"Can I at least try and explain?"

"No." The general store appeared, and Izzy darted through the door. Thank God for the crowd and the noise. After purchasing four bags of sugar, they headed home.

"I was serious last night," Elle said. "I'm building a ranch and I want you with me."

Izzy stopped. In a hushed voice, she said, "When I left Loma, or I should say, when you forced me to leave Loma, I cried every night. Your betrayal broke my heart. So go back to New Mexico and leave me alone. I have no interest in living with you or being anywhere near you."

Elle flinched, and Izzy puffed out her chest. *That hurt. Good.*

"I wish you'd let me explain."

A small part of Izzy was curious and wanted to hear Elle's explanation, but the bigger part that was furious with her held sway. "I don't want to hear it."

* * *

A sound startled Elle awake. She froze and wrapped her fist around the knife under her pillow. Her pulse raced. Someone crept across the room. She cursed herself for having her back to the door. *I'm getting soft.* When that someone leaned over the bed, Elle rolled over and dragged them onto the mattress, pressing the knife against their throat. "Izzy?" She quickly pulled the knife back.

Izzy scooted away and placed her feet on the ground before checking her throat for blood.

"Are you cut?" Elle asked.

"No."

Elle took a few deep breaths to calm her pounding heart. Izzy's face was hidden in the shadows, and Elle waited for her to speak.

After a few moments of silence, Izzy murmured, "Why did you do it?"

Finally, a chance to plead her case. Elle positioned herself with her back against the wall and rested an elbow on her knee. "I thought it was the only way to keep you safe."

Izzy didn't move. "By handing me off to a man I didn't want to marry?"

"When Jed took you, I...I'd never been so scared in my life. Thinking about what he was gonna do to you..." Even this far removed from that day, the horror of those moments still had the power to frighten her. "After getting shot, I was lying in the dirt, and I thought, *I'm gonna die.* And the last thing that went through my mind before I blacked out was that I failed you. Like I failed my mother." Elle ached to touch Izzy but didn't want to chase her away. "And then I heard you say you loved me, and it felt like a death sentence for you, because you'd become a target, a way to get to me. I convinced myself I had to let you go to keep you alive."

"You didn't ask me. You made the choice for me."

Elle sighed. "I know. I was wrong." Izzy remained silent, so Elle continued, "After you left, my life stopped. Nothing mattered anymore. I love you, and I'm sorry for all the pain I caused—"

"I don't wanna hear that you're sorry. I have to go."

Damn it. Alone once again, Elle rested her forehead in her hand. Was this nighttime visit a good sign? Or was it the end?

CHAPTER TWENTY-SIX

Izzy scrubbed the sheet across the washboard. Midmorning was laundry time. Her focus moved between the task at hand and the view in the corral. A few of the guests' horses milled about while Elle filled the water trough.

"Are you done with that one?" Aunt Bea asked.

"Yes." Izzy helped her aunt throw the sheet over the line. At least, she assumed she was helping. She kept getting distracted by Elle, who guided the horses over to the water.

"Izzy. It's not even."

She tugged down on her end.

Across the way, Elle laughed at one of the horses, who kept nudging her in the back. *I always loved her laugh.*

Aunt Bea clucked her tongue to get Izzy's attention. "Can you help me with this one?"

"Sorry. I don't know where my head's at."

"I think we all know where your head's at," Aunt Bea teased.

Izzy dipped her head. "I don't know what you mean," she mumbled.

"Mm-hmm. She's a fine-looking lass."

Izzy grunted, because she had nothing to say…out loud. In her head, she had plenty to say. *Yes. She's beautiful. Ever since she arrived two weeks ago, all I do is think about her.* She chose to stay mum. *And stop kidding yourself, you never stopped thinking about her since leaving Loma Parda.*

"You know, I'm a firm believer in giving someone a second chance," Aunt Bea said as she threw another sheet over the line.

"She doesn't deserve a second chance."

"We all make mistakes. Every one of us. I know she regrets it. She rode hundreds of miles to tell you so. And she loves you. It's there in her face, and the way she looks at you."

"You think I should forgive her?"

"Yes."

Izzy's voice rose. "You think I should let someone who betrayed me, and lied to me, and sold me off, to just…come back into my life like nothing ever happened. What does that say about me?"

"It says that you're a forgiving person. And that you love her. Love trumps pride."

Izzy's eyes filled. "I can't do it. Despite that." She raced back inside before the tears had a chance to fall.

* * *

Elle brushed Blaze's coat until it turned glossy. They'd returned from a nice brisk ride. He needed to stay in shape, so every day after lunch they headed into the countryside. Once outside of town, Elle eased up on the reins and the big bay would stretch out his legs.

"You were flying today." Elle scratched his chin. "I know. We're both used to more action than this, right? Do you miss the mountains and wide-open spaces as much as I do?"

Luna's head hung over Blaze's stall, and Elle gave her a scratch too.

It had been a couple of weeks and still no thaw from Izzy. Elle began to have misgivings of ever convincing her to come home. Soon, she'd miss her window to leave because snow would blanket the mountains, which meant she'd have to stay until spring or take a more southerly route, making a long trip longer.

The barn door opened, and Izzy wandered in. She stopped short when she spotted Elle. "I didn't know you were in here." Izzy's tone sounded almost normal, not combative as it had been since Elle's arrival in San Francisco.

"We just got back from a ride," Elle said.

Izzy walked into Luna's stall and fed her an apple, then gave one to Blaze. Dark smudges were visible under her eyes.

"You look tired."

"I haven't been sleeping very well." Izzy rested her face against Luna's neck.

Something was different today. Izzy's movements were fluid and relaxed. Her arms hung loose by her side, and the angry lines that had been etched into her forehead for two weeks had disappeared. The hostility that had been palpable was missing also. Was it from lack of sleep? Or was this the beginning of the thaw Elle had been longing for? Her heart lifted. She'd rather believe the latter. "I haven't been sleeping either." She put the brush down and inched closer. The only thing separating their bodies was a few slats of wood. She took a chance with her next statement. "It's hard, knowing you're on the other side of the wall."

"Hmm."

Not quite the response Elle hoped for, but at least Izzy didn't lash out at her.

Izzy fed both horses a sugar cube.

Blaze munched it down and swished his tail in satisfaction.

"Blaze thanks you," Elle said, trying to coax a smile from Izzy, but so far, no luck. "You can ride her, you know." Elle stroked Luna's muzzle.

"I can?"

Is that a small smile? "Yeah. I rode her at times on the way out here. She was definitely somebody's horse."

Izzy gave Luna a hug. "I'll have to take her for a ride."

"I'll go with you, if you want."

Elle waited for a stinging retort. When one wasn't forthcoming, her heart lifted even more.

Izzy sighed. In a surprise move, she ran a finger over the scar next to Elle's eye. "This is new. What happened?"

"I got into a fight with Raven." She closed her eyes and nestled her cheek into Izzy's palm. *God, I've missed her touch.*

"What did you fight over?"

Elle discovered a measure of solace in the warmth of Izzy's palm. "You."

Izzy dropped her hand and stared at the ground. "I need to start dinner." She left without another word.

Elle sagged. So much for the thaw.

* * *

When Izzy burst through the front door, she almost collided with a man walking out. Touching Elle had her befuddled. "I'm sorry."

He tipped his hat. "No problem, ma'am." He ambled over toward the barn.

"Do we have a new guest?" Izzy asked Mary. "I can get the room ready."

"No. He asked after Elle."

The first thing that raced through Izzy's mind was *US Marshal*, and panic leapt into her chest. "And you told him she was here?"

"He said he knew her. That she rode out here with him from Albuquerque."

"What did he want?"

"I don't know."

Izzy peered out the window, but the man had disappeared into the barn. She prayed the man didn't lie. Elle getting arrested was the last thing she wanted, despite everything that had happened between them. She paced around the front room. On occasion, she'd stop and close her eyes. Her palm still tingled from their first physical contact in months.

Elle and the gentleman emerged from the barn and shook hands.

Izzy put a hand to her chest. Phew. Elle would never shake hands with a marshal. With the threat of an arrest gone, Izzy's curiosity was piqued. What did he want with Elle? Perhaps she'd find out soon enough, because Elle was on her way back to the house.

When she opened the door, Izzy pretended to be writing in the guest book. Elle passed by her without so much as a glance in her direction.

Izzy huffed.

Ten minutes later, Elle descended the stairs with all her gear.

"What's going on?" Izzy asked. "Who was that?"

"Tom Morrison. He's the one who hired me in Albuquerque. They need another hand for a freight haul up north. One of their cowboys got hurt this morning, so he offered me a job. I've already worked with them, so…"

Elle kept walking and Izzy hustled to keep up. She found it hard to wrap her head around what was happening. "You're leaving?"

"Yeah." When they entered the barn, Elle tossed Blaze's saddle onto his back.

"Right now?"

"It's just for two weeks. Pay's too good to pass up, and I need the money. I'll be back on the twentieth." When Blaze was ready she grasped his reins, but before she walked away, she paused in front of Izzy.

For a moment, neither spoke. Izzy's breath became choppy. She'd been telling Elle to leave since she arrived, and now the thought of her gone for two weeks was almost too much to bear.

Elle frowned before her eyes dipped to Izzy's lips.

The street noises faded, and all Izzy heard was the beating of her own heart. *She's going to kiss me. And God help me, I'm going to let her.*

Elle's lips captured hers with a soft kiss at first, but soon Elle demanded more, and Izzy relented. Part of her wanted to push Elle away, to say *how dare you*, but she grabbed Elle's shirt instead and pulled her close. To Izzy's disappointment and chagrin, the kiss ended soon after it began.

In an unsteady voice, Elle said, "I'll see you in two weeks."

She departed the barn, leaving Izzy feeling empty, unfulfilled, and more confused than ever.

CHAPTER TWENTY-SEVEN

Izzy brushed the dirt from the porch while keeping an eye on the street. *Where is she?*

Frustrated as to why she even cared, she wielded the broom like a weapon, sweeping harder and harder.

Aunt Bea stuck her head out the window. "Izzy, if you keep that up, we won't have any porch left."

"Sorry."

"Are you okay?"

"I'm fine."

"She's only three days late. I'm sure she'll be back soon."

"Oh. Is she late? I didn't even realize."

Aunt Bea gave Izzy look that said, *Sure, you didn't.*

Izzy brought the broom back inside. She needed to clear her head. "Do you mind if I go for a ride?"

"Not at all."

"I won't be long. We can go to the market when I get back." Izzy hustled upstairs to change. Since her arrival in San Francisco, she'd been back to wearing simple cotton dresses, but today she'd wear her trousers. As she pulled them on, she was overcome by a wave of homesickness. Not for Boston, but for Loma Parda. *I miss that damn, dusty town.* And with the longing for Loma came the longing for Elle and the memory of that last kiss—and the way her heart and body reacted to it, like the betrayal had never happened. She'd gone to bed that night and imagined Elle's hands touching and stroking her. It was a recipe for another sleepless night.

Luna nickered when Izzy entered the stable. "Hey, pretty girl. How about we go for a ride?" She grabbed a spare saddle and bridle. "It's been a while. Hopefully I remember how to do this." When Izzy finished, she led Luna from the stall and out the door. "Here we go." Once in the saddle, her instincts took over and they trotted down the street. It felt wonderful to ride again. And Elle was right; Luna was smooth and responsive.

Once outside of town, Izzy lengthened the reins and Luna shot forward. She removed her hat, and the wind whipped through her hair. She had forgotten how exciting it was to be one with a horse charging across open land.

After an exhilarating ride, Izzy steered Luna back to town at a leisurely pace.

Once Luna was freed from her saddle, Izzy brushed her. "We'll have to do that again soon, right, girl?" Maybe with Elle. Maybe. "If I can let go of my anger. What do you think? Can I forgive her?" Izzy rested her forehead against Luna's muzzle. These last weeks without Elle had been trying, and Izzy's resistance slipped further away. Was her aunt right? Was her pride getting in the way of happiness? Was it time to put things in the past and love again?

* * *

Elle was happy to be back in San Francisco, albeit three days late, but that was fine. The job had been uneventful. No gun battles, no fistfights, no bloodshed, which was a far cry from a lot of her jobs in the past. Making an honest living wasn't so bad.

"This ought to cover it," Tom said. "Some extra in there for the delay." He shoved a wad of bills into Elle's hand.

"Thanks." She held up a small leather satchel. "I think I'm happier to have this back."

"Yeah. Don't know how it got mixed up with all the luggage on the way from Albuquerque."

"I thought it was gone forever. Let me know if you have any other jobs. I'd be happy to help."

Tom nodded. "We've got a few wagons headed back to Santa Fe next week, if you're interested in going."

"I'll let you know. Thanks." She climbed into the saddle and directed Blaze toward the boardinghouse. Her eagerness to see Izzy drove her to set a blistering pace. Every waking hour she'd replayed the kiss over and over in her mind. A kiss that Izzy returned. A kiss that held such promise. *Does she obsess about it too?*

When the boardinghouse came into view, her heart beat a wild rhythm inside her chest. She hopped down before Blaze had a chance to skid to a stop. First order of business was to take care of her horse, then she'd seek out Izzy. After removing his tack and brushing him down, she turned both him and Luna out to the corral. The troughs were already filled with water and hay, so she jogged to the back door and burst through it.

Mary was in the kitchen stirring a pot on the stove. Her hand flew to her face upon Elle's abrupt entrance. "My goodness! You gave me a fright, lass."

"I'm sorry." Elle removed her hat. "I just got back."

"Well, it's nice to have you back. Things have been a bit morose around here without you."

Mary winked, and Elle took it as a good sign. *Maybe Izzy missed me.* She poked her head into the dining room.

"She's at the market." Mary smiled.

"Oh." Elle worried at her bottom lip.

"Her and Bea had some errands to do, so it may be a while."

"Darn. I guess I'll take a bath. I've got two weeks of riding to wash away." She headed to the bathhouse. It took some time to heat the water and fill the tub, but once it was ready, she stripped down and, with a groan, eased into the water. Nothing was better than a hot bath after being on the trail. *Well. One thing's better.* She smiled to herself and closed her eyes. *Time for a nap.*

"You were supposed to be back three days ago!"

A startled Elle slipped below the surface and swallowed a mouthful of water. "Iz," she sputtered.

Izzy's hair was pulled back with a bandana, and a few loose tendrils curled around her face. Somehow, she looked even more captivating than before. Elle wanted to drag her off to bed and ravish her.

"Why were you late?" Izzy demanded, with her hands on her hips.

Elle cocked a brow. "Were you worried about me?"

"I…I just expected you back Wednesday, that's all."

"An axle broke on one of the wagons, and then a wheel broke on another one. It's sweet of you to worry."

"I didn't say I was worried." With a side-eyed glance, Izzy took in a very naked Elle, and her cheeks flushed.

"You wanna join me? The water's still warm." Elle grinned.

A deeper hue tinged Izzy's cheeks. "No. I have to peel the potatoes for dinner." She turned to go.

"It's good to see you, Iz. I missed you."

Izzy paused before leaving the bathhouse. "You may have been missed."

Elle's chest swelled with happiness, and she whistled a happy tune as she finished bathing.

* * *

That night, the dinner chatter flowed around Izzy, and she barely participated. Her eyes never left Elle, who entertained her aunt and Mary with tales of her adventures from the past two and a half weeks. Her face glowed as she spoke, and when she waved her arms around for emphasis, the scent of lavender soap filled Izzy's nostrils. It made her want to kiss Elle's neck and nip the sensitive spot near her collarbone.

Aunt Bea was right—she still loved Elle. And hated her. Was that even possible? Maybe she hated what she did more than hated *her*. Was it time to let her back into her heart?

Her aunt's voice pulled her back to the conversation at the table. "Izzy, you've been awfully quiet tonight."

"I'm sorry. I'm just…tired, I guess."

"I have something for you." Elle placed a leather satchel on the table next to Izzy.

"What is it?"

"Open it."

Izzy pulled out the sheets of paper inside. She picked up the first page and stared at the words. Her breath caught in her throat, and her eyes met Elle's.

"It's her story."

Aunt Bea touched the back of her hand. "What is it, dear? Can you share, or is it personal?"

Elle gave her a small smile and an encouraging nod.

She glanced back down at the paper and shook her head. "It's not personal." She gathered herself and began to read:

"My name is Matsu Yosh…Yoshiharu. I was born in Kyoto Japan in 1841 and taught the ways of the sama…samurai by my father, Komori Yoshiharu, descendant of the great samurai Horio Yoshiharu."

Izzy's eyes filled with tears. She bit her lip to keep them from spilling out. A partial sob tore from her throat and the kitchen walls closed in around her. "Excuse me." She rushed from the room and up the stairs. Safe in her bedroom, she sat on the bed and let the tears flow. Sadness engulfed her. *I miss everybody.* She missed her lessons with Matsu, she missed Shorty and his colorful lingo, she missed Raven's sarcastic wit, she missed sweet Willy. But most of all she missed Elle, missed being with her, kissing her, holding her.

After no more tears fell, Izzy lay on the bed and devoured Matsu's story. Her words were limited, and mistakes were made in grammar and syntax, but it was easy enough to understand. Each page contained a short retelling of a turning point in her life.

The story began when Matsu was six years old. She'd built her own version of a naginata, only instead of a curved metal knife attached to the end of a staff, she carved a piece of wood herself and fashioned the tip into the shape of a knife. When her father was giving fighting instructions to Matsu's older brother, Takeshi, and some of the other boys from the village, a young Matsu would insert herself into the lessons, wielding her homemade naginata. Finally, her father gave in, and she was allowed to train. When she was of age, she became an Onna-Bugeisha, a female samurai.

Izzy smiled. That's why Matsu trained Elle with a staff. It was a weapon she was intimately familiar with. Izzy couldn't imagine what hell she would've caught from her own father if she'd demanded to join her brother's fencing lessons. One thing was certain—he would have never relented like Matsu's father.

After becoming an Onna-Bugeisha, Matsu met another woman samurai named Hikaru Takeno. They fell in love and had a secret relationship for years.

Izzy's hands shook as the story took a dark turn.

Hikaru was killed in the battle of Azui in 1868, where many samurai fell or were imprisoned afterward by Emperor Meiji. As Matsu stood guard over Hikaru's battered, lifeless body, she was attacked by three warriors of the emperor. A severe blow to the head knocked her senseless and she was left for dead. Nearby villagers sympathetic to the shogunate had rescued her and nursed her back to health, but she'd lost the ability to speak.

Izzy turned to the last page, and on it Matsu wrote of how, after losing Hikaru, her homeland held nothing but painful memories, so she accompanied a family friend to San Francisco. Shortly after arriving, the friend fell ill and died, leaving Matsu to fend for herself.

Missing was the time between surviving on her own and meeting Elle. Izzy wanted to know more and yearned to help Matsu complete her story. She closed her eyes and rested the papers on her chest, marveling at how her star pupil managed to convey her heartbreak and the feelings of profound loss despite her limited vocabulary. More than that, the memoir highlighted similarities in their love of women in difficult times, as well as a stark contrast: Matsu had watched her lover die. Izzy's own lover was downstairs, begging for forgiveness.

Footsteps echoed down the hallway and stopped outside her door.

"Iz, are you all right?"

Speak of the devil I love. She wanted to yank the door off the hinges but didn't. No good would come from facing Elle while all these emotions swirled inside. She needed some time to sort through things. "I'm fine. Thank you."

"Okay. Good night."

Izzy rolled over and faced the wall that separated her from Elle. The ache to be near her grew and grew until it was impossible to contain.

* * *

Elle stared at the ceiling with her fingers linked behind her head. The rush of being near Izzy kept her awake. She toyed with the idea of barging into Izzy's room and kissing her senseless. With a sigh, she turned over. *Maybe tomorrow I'll get to spend some time with her.*

An hour later, the door creaked open, and Izzy's silhouette cast a shadow into the room. *Am I dreaming?* "Iz?"

Izzy approached the bed.

"Are you okay?" Elle asked.

"I can't sleep."

"Neither can I." Elle pulled back the sheet and held her breath.

Izzy slipped into the bed and lay on her side, facing Elle. "I'm tired of not sleeping."

"Me too."

"What do we do about it?"

Without thinking, Elle pulled Izzy into her arms and held her close. "We do this." At first Izzy stiffened, but slowly the tension left her body and she melted into Elle.

"Why can't I hate you?" Izzy mumbled.

"Because you love me." Elle stroked Izzy's back and buried her face in her hair. She inhaled the scent of her, the scent that clung to Elle's pillows back home and drove her mad. "And I love you."

Izzy sighed. "I do love you. So much."

"Iz, I'm so sorry for what—"

Izzy placed a finger against Elle's lips. "No more sorrys. Let's start afresh. Put the past behind us. Can we do that?"

Elle smiled. "We can do that." She kissed her tenderly on the lips.

"I wanna go home to Loma."

"When?"

"Now? I miss it."

"We can leave next week, if you want," Elle said. "Catch on with a wagon train heading to Santa Fe. If we don't leave then, we may have to wait until spring. The mountains will be impassable during the winter."

"Let's go. I'll talk to Aunt Bea and Mary tomorrow."

For the first time in months, Elle's soul found peace. She had no idea what the future held, or what challenges lay ahead, but as long as Izzy was by her side, they'd face them together.

"When we get back, will I be Mac? Or Izzy?"

The question brought a smile to Elle's lips. Yes. Her Izzy was back, and God, she'd missed her. "You can be whoever you want."

"I liked being Mac. Maybe I'll stick with Mac. You said you were giving up outlawing...was that true?"

"Yes."

"I can't imagine Rose letting you do that."

"Rose is out of the picture." She pushed a lock of hair away from Izzy's cheek.

Izzy pulled back. "What happened?"

"Those guns my father stole? Turns out they were hers, so she had him killed."

Izzy's eyes grew wide. "How did you find that out?"

"Had a drink with John Watkins."

"And you believed him?"

Elle nodded. "I confronted Rose. She confessed."

"I'm so sorry. That must've been painful."

"It hurt. One good thing came out of it, though. Remember when I said I was going to build a ranch in the canyon?"

"Yes."

"Rose gave me the deed to that land. Guess to assuage her guilty conscience."

"So it really is your canyon?"

"Our canyon. Our ranch."

A mischievous look crossed Izzy's face, and she brought her lips close to Elle's. "Are you planning on making an honest woman of me?" Izzy laid her hand on the top of Elle's thighs.

A fire lit deep in Elle's belly, and only Izzy could extinguish it. "I think you're supposed to make an honest woman of *me*." She pushed Izzy onto her back and kissed her neck, tiny whisper kisses meant to titillate.

Izzy moaned. "How about you make an honest woman of me right now, then I'll make you an honest woman in, oh, about ten minutes."

Elle chuckled. "I can do that." Her lips captured Izzy's while her hand wandered under her nightshirt. When her fingers brushed across Izzy's nipples, she had the urge to taste them.

Izzy moaned again. "It might be more like five minutes."

EPILOGUE

Two Months Later

Elle waited patiently for Izzy to get ready. They'd been back a week and had yet to go uptown. Today was the day.

"I'll be out in a minute," Izzy called from the bedroom.

Matsu pulled out a pocket watch and pointed to the time.

Elle raised her hand and tilted her head. "I know. You can't rush her."

Matsu snapped it shut and playfully huffed.

Izzy bustled into the room "Can't rush who?"

Elle's reply died in her throat as she gazed at Izzy. *Does she get more beautiful every damn day?* "Never mind. You ready?"

"Yes. Question is, are you ready?"

Was Elle ready to see Rose? Avoiding her would prove impossible because this house was still home for now. Might as well get it over with. "I'm ready."

The three of them moseyed down the street. Izzy had insisted on walking, saying she was eager to immerse herself in the town. Elle had no complaints, because walking meant she could be close to the woman she loved.

Quite a few people shouted out, "Hey, Mac."

"I guess I'm still Mac," Izzy said with a grin.

Elle ached to hold her hand and show off their love for all to see. Maybe someday. At least they had free rein inside their house. And in the bed. She grinned. They spent a lot of their time in bed.

"What are you smiling at?" Izzy asked.

"I'll tell you later." She leaned closer. "Or better yet, I'll show you later."

Izzy's cheeks turned a hot pink, and Elle's mind raced ahead to tonight. The thought of Izzy naked in her arms made heat rush into her own cheeks. She had half a mind to turn around and head back to their bedroom.

Izzy pointed. "There's Mr. Berenson. I need to talk to him. Mr. Berenson!"

He spotted Izzy and his face paled.

Elle snickered. "He's still scared to death of you."

He came closer and tipped his hat. "Good day, Elle, Matsu... Miss Mac."

"Mr. Berenson." Izzy placed a hand on her revolver. "I'd like a favor."

He swallowed and dabbed his forehead with a handkerchief. His eyes focused on her gun.

"Oh, I'm not going to shoot you. Today."

Elle bit back a laugh. Seemed Mac still had a reputation, and she enjoyed watching Izzy toy with the flustered lawyer.

"How can I help?" he asked.

"I'd like to apprentice with you. How about I stop by tomorrow for a chat?"

"Yes, ma'am. Stop by tomorrow."

"And don't be loaded for bear. I need you clear-eyed."

His mouth hung open for a second before he snapped it shut. "Of course."

"Wonderful. I'll see you then."

He high-stepped it away as fast as his stocky legs could carry him.

"You're awful," Elle said.

"I can't help it if he's afraid of me. And I don't want him drunk. I need to learn."

They passed the general store and had to dance out of the way of a pack of unruly children running, laughing, and carrying on.

Elle shook her head. "Where did all these kids come from?"

"Better get used to it," Izzy said. "Now that Willy and Perlie are going to have another, you'll be up to your ears in kids."

Elle lifted her lip. "Ugh."

The saloon came into view, and a knot twisted in Elle's gut. *Why am I tense?*

A big smile lit up Matsu's face, and she ran across the street to help Margaret Stenson with some packages.

"Did you see that?" Izzy said. "I've never seen her smile like that."

"Me neither."

Margaret returned Matsu's smile, and the two strolled away together.

"Doesn't she live with Mrs. Stenson?" Izzy asked.

"Yes, she does."

"Do you think they're…" Izzy lowered her brows.

"Maybe."

Tim stood with his arms crossed, guarding the front door. "Afternoon, ladies. Good to have you back."

"Afternoon," Elle said. Had it really been five months since she stepped foot in here? Her last visit was a hazy memory that had haunted her all these months. How would Rose receive her?

"Are you sure you want to do this?" Izzy asked.

"Now or never." Elle took a deep breath, and they pushed open the doors together.

Once inside, it was like she'd never left. Nothing had changed. Same tables, same bar, same patrons. Her knot disappeared. There was something to be said for being in old, familiar places.

"Howdy, Elle, Mac," Fred called out.

Clyde pounded Elle on the back. "'Bout time you got home."

Arthur still couldn't carry a tune, another thing that would never change. His off-key voice reverberated around the room and made them both wince.

"Oh, hell, no," Izzy said. She pointed toward Arthur. "I can't, I just can't. I need to fix that."

Elle waved her away and headed for the bar.

A cheer rose to the rafters as Izzy settled in behind the piano.

Raven slid a shot glass full of whisky toward her. "I knew you couldn't stay away." She imitated Elle's voice. "I ain't going there."

"I didn't say that. And I don't talk like that."

"You did, and you do. Let me refresh your memory. First day back I asked when you were coming down for a drink, and you said, 'I'm never setting foot in that place again.' How long did that last, Rob?"

He smiled. "About a week."

Elle tossed back the shot and wiped her mouth. "I guess old habits die hard. Since you're working here now, why don't you make yourself useful and pour me another?"

Raven tipped the bottle over her glass. "All right. Don't get bossy."

Elle had no idea if she still had a tab, so she dug into her pocket and put some change on the bar.

A hand touched her shoulder, and Elle stiffened.

"Your money isn't good here. Put it away and enjoy yourself." Rose patted her on the back and moved on.

Elle cocked a brow and stared after her. She waited for the surge of hatred and anger, but all she felt was…nothing. Maybe all the love in her heart for Izzy chased the bad stuff away. She'd never forget, but perhaps there was room to forgive.

"Ready for another?" Rob asked.

"Sure." She pushed her glass toward him.

"After we get married, I'm expecting the same consideration," Raven said to Rob. "Free drinks."

"You already get free drinks."

"Well, I want them freer."

He answered with a long, hard kiss, and Elle laughed. It was good to be back and to see Raven happy. The kiss continued, and she gave them some privacy. She spun around and scanned the faces in the room. Almost all were familiar. One face was missing, though. Apparently, Miriam had found herself a man. According to Raven, their courtship lasted a week, and then he swept her off to Oregon. *I'm glad she got out.*

Shorty sidled up to Elle. "Been talkin' to the boys, and we think it's high time we got another baseball game goin'."

She made a face. "I don't know. You'll have to ask Izzy. She wasn't too happy with the last one."

"We're gonna do better this time. I'll go talk to her."

"Good luck." She toasted him, but her glass was empty. "When you're done there, Rob, hit me with another."

* * *

"Where shall we build the ranch?" Izzy asked. She stood in the canyon with Elle's arm draped around her shoulders. Snow fluttered from the sky, lightly coating the grasses and boulders of the meadow.

Elle pointed to the large cottonwood tree. "Over there. To the right of the tree."

She nestled closer. "That's a perfect spot."

Elle gave her a warm, lingering kiss. They'd spent the last hour tumbling around on the blanket and were getting ready to head back to Loma.

"Are you sure you wanna do this?" Elle nodded toward Luna, who waited patiently at the end of the lead in Izzy's hand. Blaze and Jack were tethered nearby.

"That's funny. I just asked you the same question yesterday."

"Yes, you did."

"I do wanna do this." She kissed Luna's velvety nose. "She deserves to be free. She's home, and I'm home. It's like a perfect ending to a book, don't you think?"

"It is a perfect ending."

Izzy led Luna toward the herd grazing nearby. The stallion whinnied as she approached. After removing the rope from her neck, Izzy gave her a pat on her rump. "Go on, girl." A tear trickled down her face. She might not see Luna until the spring because the herd moved during the winter months. *What if something happens to her? What if she gets hurt, or worse? I'll never know.* Another tear escaped.

Luna trotted toward the big horse, and they touched noses.

Elle slipped her arms around Izzy from behind. "I love you."

Izzy touched her cheek. "I love you, too. Let's go home."

They walked hand in hand back to the blanket and packed up before climbing onto their saddles.

After one last glance at Luna, Izzy followed Elle out of the canyon. The path was wide enough to ride side by side. Izzy sniffled. She certainly never expected to care this much for a horse.

"Are you okay?"

"I'm sad. I'm gonna miss her." She rubbed Jack's neck. "I love Jack, but Luna was special. She chose me."

"She did. You had a bond."

Izzy wiped her eyes. "It's okay. I love you. And you love me. And that's plenty for one woman."

Elle placed her hand on Blaze's rump and looked behind them. "Hmm. Well, guess I'm not the only one who loves you."

"What do you mean?" Izzy turned, and her mouth fell open.

Luna trotted up the path.

Elle laughed. "I knew she'd follow you."

"How did you know?"

"Because the damn horse followed me home. How do you think I ended up with her?"

"But…she belongs out here." Izzy waved her hand around.

"Iz, she belongs to you. And you belong to her."

Luna caught up and nuzzled Izzy's leg.

Izzy's sad tears turned happy. "You know, she's ruining my perfect ending."

"Well, my love, I guess you'll have to write another ending."

More Titles from Bella Books

Hunter's Revenge – Gerri Hill
978-1-64247-447-3 | 276 pgs | paperback: $18.95 | eBook: $9.99
Tori Hunter is back! Don't miss this final chapter in the acclaimed Tori Hunter series.

Integrity – E. J. Noyes
978-1-64247-465-7 | 228 pgs | paperback: $19.95 | eBook: $9.99
It was supposed to be an ordinary workday...

The Order – TJ O'Shea
978-1-64247-378-0 | 396 pgs | paperback: $19.95 | eBook: $9.99
For two women the battle between new love and old loyalty may prove more dangerous than the war they're trying to survive.

Under the Stars with You – Jaime Clevenger
978-1-64247-439-8 | 302 pgs | paperback: $19.95 | eBook: $9.99
Sometimes believing in love is the first step. And sometimes it's all about trusting the stars.

The Missing Piece – Kat Jackson
978-1-64247-445-9 | 250 pgs | paperback: $18.95 | eBook: $9.99
Renee's world collides with possibility and the past, setting off a tidal wave of changes she could have never predicted.

An Acquired Taste – Cheri Ritz
978-1-64247-462-6 | 206 pgs | paperback: $17.95 | eBook: $9.99
Can Elle and Ashley stand the heat in the *Celebrity Cook Off* kitchen?